REALITY CHECKPOINT

When a grave is uncovered on the Fens, DI Sydney Household, with the help of forensic pathologist Veronica Sleaford, identifies the body as that of Edward De Beer, a Cambridge student who went missing in the early 1970s. The lamp-post on Parker's Piece, 'Reality Checkpoint', is the traditional marker between 'town' and 'gown', but De Beer seemed to have been caught between the two worlds. With the CID occupied in trying to catch the 'Cambridge Panther', who is terrorising young women and holding them hostage, is there any chance of discovering what happened to De Beer thirty years ago?

REALITY CHECKPOINT

REALITY
CHECKPOINT

by

Peter Turnbull

Magna Large Print Books
Long Preston, North Yorkshire,
BD23 4ND, England.

British Library Cataloguing in Publication Data.

Turnbull, Peter
Reality checkpoint.

A catalogue record of this book is
available from the British Library

ISBN   0-7505-2454-5

First published in Great Britain 2004 by Allison & Busby Ltd.

Copyright © 2004 by Peter Turnbull

Cover illustration © Old Tin Dog

The right of Peter Turnbull to be identified as the author of this work
has been asserted by him in accordance with the Copyright, Designs
and Patents Act, 1988

Published in Large Print 2005 by arrangement with
Allison & Busby Ltd.

Magna Large Print is an imprint of Library Magna Books Ltd.

Printed and bound in Great Britain by
T.J. (International) Ltd., Cornwall, PL28 8RW

1

The man loved the Fens. He was not a Fenman by birth nor even a man who lived in the Fens, but a man who had moved to this area of eastern England and who, whenever he could, walked out into the Fens. He loved the vast sky, the solitude, the clean, fresh air. The Fens, he had learned, were not to be trifled with. In the spring they could flood quickly and widely and in the winter they were swept by the biting east wind. But this was June, the water was low, the weather warm and windless. Just the kind of day for a man to get out by himself and clear the tubes, by walking across the fields from Bottisham to Waterbeach. Bottisham had a certain significance for the man, because thirty years earlier, and newly arrived in Cambridge, he had been in the bus station at Drummer Street when an elderly man had approached him, doffed his hat and with sincere deference had asked, 'Where be the bus to Bottisham, young master?' It had been as if transported back into the nineteenth century. That very same day he had found out why, of all the cities in England, the City of Cambridge has a railway station situated a considerable distance from the centre: because the university, the powerful, land-owning lobby that it was, would not allow it to be built any nearer. It was on that day that the man first knew the nature of his adoptive city.

Leaving the hamlet of Bottisham behind him the man strode out across the baked-dry fields to the larger and more compact village of Waterbeach some four miles distant. The sky was blue, the trees a rich green, the meadows a lighter, more pastel shade of green, the songbirds sang, a hawk hovered and then fell and a man walked. A man who enjoyed the route which he had done many times, once even as part of a longer midnight walk across the Fens with friends, a full moon, a cloudless, starry sky, and a compass. On this day, it was just the Bottisham to Waterbeach section, four miles, an hour and a half at an easy pace because he was no longer a young man, not old, but by no means the youth he had been, who once could have run the distance at a steady pace. Now the thought of running was anathema. Why cover the distance as fast as possible when each step could be savoured, each second might bring a view of nature at work, in all its diverse wonder, as with the hawk that had just fallen upon a vole or a field mouse? The man paused and leaned upon his stick. He didn't need a stout walking stick, but felt incomplete somehow without one, as if wanting something to do with his hands, and the thing had its uses, beating back tall grass that he might want to walk through to announce his presence to any slumbering adder so that it might wriggle out of his way, or testing the depth of new formed pools of water which appeared in the fields on wet days in the autumn, when the weather was beginning to make the walk a little more challenging. He took off his straw hat and wiped his brow. He replaced the hat, screwing it slightly to make the rim grip his head, pausing in his stride so as to glance about him, the broad sweep of this landscape, the distant skyline, the huge sky that can make a man feel very small, very insignificant. He swung his knapsack off his shoulder and plunged his hand inside, groping for the bottle of mineral water he carried. He retrieved it and unscrewed the top, breaking the seal of the blue cap and the clear plastic bottle. He drank deeply.

In later years he was to think how all that was subsequently to happen happened because of his keen eyesight and his preference for walking off the path. He knew suddenly, but without any sense of alarm, that the stone which caught his eye as he glanced down, briefly, to avoid the glare of the sun, wasn't in fact a stone at all. It was a dark grey colour, had a grainy texture and, from what he could observe, a slightly rounded surface. It was clearly a bone, but that in itself wasn't alarming; in the spring these fields are inundated with water when the drainage system of the Fens can't cope and animals – and occasionally human beings – are drowned.

The man knelt down and began to scrape away the soil from the bone using his walking stick which he held in two hands like a man paddling a canoe. Using the metal tip of the walking stick to good effect, he scraped away sufficient of the hard baked soil to reveal that the bone he had found was that of a human skull. He sat back on the grass and pondered his find, pondering the life of the person whose skull it was. Male or female, he thought, drinking again from the bottle of mineral water, young or old when you died? And when did you die? Not recently, that was certain, and hence the man's leisurely attitude. This could very well be the skeleton of a Roman soldier, or a man who died fighting the Romans, or the victim of crime or accidental death in any century from then until now. It was probably a find which would prove of more interest to the archaeologist than the police officer. He drained the bottle of drinking water and left it standing beside the partially exposed skull, weighted down with some of the recently turned soil to ensure it remained standing upright in the event of a summer zephyr and then pondered his location. Being marginally still nearer Bottisham than Waterbeach, he retraced his steps to the hamlet, found a phone box and dialled 999. He was a man of conservative inclination, he cared not for mobile phones nor for the recently introduced additional emergency number of 112. So he walked to Bottisham and phoned 999 from a phone box of the new square European style. He, of course, lived in a conservation area which still boasted traditional red phone boxes. He had moved house for that very reason. Having made the call, he sat beside the phone box on the grass verge and waited for the police to arrive. He anticipated a moderate wait, having emphasised to the sharp-voiced female officer who had answered his call that he had discovered what may be a skeleton, not a body, and added that really all he could say was that he had found what appeared to be a human skull, not even being able to say if anything was attached to it.

His wait lasted fifteen minutes. He saw the patrol car approaching, watched as it shimmered through a heat haze when about a hundred feet away from him. He raised his walking stick and stood as the patrol car neared him, slowing to a halt.

'Mr Whittaker?' The constable was young, keen, fresh faced.

'Tis I,' Whittaker smiled.

'A skeleton, you think?'

'A skull really, as I said on the phone. But human.'

'Would you care to show me please, sir?'

'Just you?' Whittaker smiled. 'Not the whole circus as you see on television?'

'Just me for the time being, sir.' The constable, white shirt, blue trousers, black shoes, locked the patrol car. 'Since you said skeleton, and not a body, then the first step is to verify your find. That's my job. Reckon I can tell a human skull from a sheep's skull. Would you care to show me?'

Whittaker led the constable back over the fields, walking in a silence which at first was a little tense. After half an hour's easy walking, however, the two men seemed to relax in each other's company. Although no words were exchanged, both Whittaker and the youthful constable sensed an easing of the atmosphere between them, walking side by side, very occasionally actually touching shoulders, accidentally so, but they did not put a physical distance between them despite the generous space allowed by the fields. They passed through a gap in a hedgerow and Whittaker stopped.

11

'Here,' he said. 'Here I stop and keep a respectful distance.'

The constable scanned the field. 'Where is it?'

'By the bottle ... you see the plastic bottle sticking up there, just to the left of the path?'

'Quite a long way left, but yes.'

'Yes ... if I didn't care to walk off the path I probably, certainly in fact, certainly wouldn't have found it, but the bottle is close by the skull ... you'll see where I have scraped the soil away to reveal all I needed to reveal to see that it is a human skull.'

Without replying, the constable left Whittaker at the hedgerow and strode across the field towards the plastic bottle, then paused. Whittaker watched as the police officer knelt down and examined the skull, taking a penknife from his pocket to scrape away a little more of the soil, though Whittaker knew he had revealed sufficient for there to be no mistaking the nature of the bone fragment: skull, human. The constable stood and reached for the radio attached to his shirt collar, spoke briefly, listened, spoke again and then walked slowly back to where Whittaker stood, watching him, but equally curious as to the cause of the rustling in the hedgerow beside him. Life is taken, or lost, but nature is relentless.

'It is of course as you say, sir ... had to verify it.' The constable nodded as he approached Whittaker. 'The circus, as you describe it, will be arriving shortly.' He took a notebook from his pocket, and brushed a fly from his face. 'Can I take some details, please? Your name?'

'Whittaker, David.'

'Occupation?'

'Scientist.'

'At the university?'

'Heavens, no ... I couldn't cope with all that back-stabbing. I am employed at Guest & Walls, the fertiliser people.'

'Can't place your accent,' the constable smiled.

'Bristol area ... not as strong as it used to be.'

The constable smiled. 'Just an interest of mine. You found the skull? There's hardly anything to see.'

'It found me, in a sense,' David Whittaker shifted his knapsack from one shoulder to the other, 'or it was serendipity.'

'Serendipity?'

'I think it means the art of making useful discoveries. I don't like walking on the path ... just don't ... the paths in these fields get obliterated in the floods but when the water recedes and the land dries you can still make out the route of the path ... and walkers, and fellas walking home from the pub...'

'And poachers,' said with a smile.

'Yes, and the jolly poacher boys setting for a hare ... well the path gets re-established quite quickly, more or less the same ... but I don't like walking on the path. I follow the path by walking off it, parallel to it. I do this walk quite often, perhaps once a fortnight.'

'The route?'

'Bottisham to Waterbeach ... a gentle stroll across flat countryside, just what a fella needs. Well, I was thirsty ... stopped for a drink ... just happened to glance down after the sun caught my

13

eyes, when I raised my head to drink from the bottle ... saw the skull. Didn't know it was a skull, still less human, but knew it was bone. Been walking in the Fens ever since I came to work at Guest & Walls ... used to hillier country, you see ... astounded by the flatness of Cambridgeshire. Anyway, often see bones ... sheep skulls ... so I knew it was bone. Don't know what possessed me to dig away at it ... impulse, intuition ... but I did and you and I stand here. One foot to either side, stopped a minute earlier or a minute later, even fifteen seconds earlier or later and I wouldn't have noticed it and it would have continued to lay there until some other walker walked this way.' Whittaker brushed a persistent horsefly from his face. 'So it found me in a sense.'

'Or it worked its way further to the surface.' The constable tapped his notebook with his ballpoint. 'It could be a very ancient skull.'

'That occurred to me.'

'Can I have your address, please, Mr Whittaker?'

Whittaker gave an address in Coton, and watched with a certain satisfaction as the constable raised an impressed eyebrow. Coton was a monied village, property in Coton doesn't come cheap.

'Age?'

'Fifty-six.' Whittaker was puzzled as to the significance of his age, but gave the information anyway. Then he asked, 'Do you need me any-more?'

'I don't think so, thank you, sir ... anxious to continue your walk?'

14

'Anxious to get home, thank you very much. Won't enjoy the remainder of the walk, I'm not that insensitive. Well, I'll leave you to it.'

Whittaker turned and walked back to Bottisham. He had to find another route for his afternoon walk. He knew he would never pass that way again. At least, not willingly so.

'It's male.' Veronica Sleaford looked down at the skeleton. She stood. The heat inside the inflatable tent which had been placed over the exhumed grave stifled her. She found breathing difficult. 'Quite a young man when he died, but I can see no apparent injury ... completely skeletal ... he could have been in the ground for any length of time, the alternating wetness and baked dryness of these fields would have helped the decomposition of the flesh yet aided the preservation of the skeleton.'

'Really?' Sydney Household took his fascinated eyes from the skeleton and glanced at Sleaford.

'Oh yes, you see the dampness would have caused rapid decomposition of the tissue, yet the dry summer months would have preserved the skeleton. Bodies buried in wet clay – permanently wet clay – have been lost, completely lost, skeleton and all, in as little as twenty years, but bodies in dry, arid conditions have lasted for decades, centuries even, with the tissue not fully decayed.'

'Mummified?'

'Not quite the same, but you have the right image and of course, deep frozen bodies show no deterioration at all. Can't tell the time of death from the condition of the body, or in this case,

15

the condition of the skeleton. All I can say is that he is male and probably youthful when he died. A young adult.' Sleaford knelt again and took a small glass jar and a metal spatula from her black Gladstone-style medical bag and scraped up a small amount of soil which she tapped off the spatula into the jar. She screwed the top onto the jar and labelled it with a felt-tip pen. 'Doubt if a soil sample is of any use, not after it has been in the ground for this length of time: in this ground especially. I passed this way in the spring ... you must have seen it too ... every field was flooded.'

'Yes ... bad spring.' Sydney Household recalled the scene, similar to many previous years, but last spring had been bad for the whole of East Anglia, and the Fens had had it particularly bad. He recalled the extended news reports, the items about the consequences of global warming, the newscaster anchorman who had asked a frighteningly young looking meteorologist what could be done to prevent future flooding, to which the cheery toothpaste selling smile 'neath a glistening mop of blonde hair replied, 'Turn the clock back and stop the industrial revolution.' Then there had been the interview with the representative of the insurance company, dressed in wet weather clothing, clearly a company man to the core, assuring the viewers that his company, which he lost no opportunity in naming whenever he could, would meet all legitimate claims for flood damage to property in full, and adding that he was certain that all other insurance companies would do the same. He then gave the sting in the tail: it was doubtful his company would offer insurance cover for flood damage on properties in this area following this incident. Adding, again, that he felt other companies would pursue the same policy. Household's own home had escaped flood damage, per se, but the limit of the water could clearly be seen from his bedroom window. It was enough for him. In the summer when the floods were a bad memory, he had placed his home quietly on the market, not allowing a 'for sale' sign to be pitched in the front garden and, amid much protesting, he and his family moved house. It had meant disrupting his children's schooling, it meant his wife had to give up a long held job in which she had settled, but he was insistent. The new house was on safer ground, and insurance against flood damage was obtained, and with it much piece of mind. Yes, Sydney Household had seen these dry, sun baked meadows a few months ago.

'Well, that amount of water, each year, would have leeched any poisons that may have been associated with his death out of the soil, but I'll take the sample for form's sake.' She placed the small jar inside her bag. 'If you'll excuse me, I must get some air, and I have finished here. I'll be able to attend to the p.m. first thing in the morning.' She glanced at her watch, 'Five minutes to five now ... my assistant will be shutting up shop for the evening.'

'Of course.'

'And it's not a fresh corpse. Had it been a recent death then ... well, the procedures would have dictated a post-mortem be carried out as early as possible, but this is not an emergency. He may not be of interest to you, could be more than seventy years since his death. But I'll be able to tell you that tomorrow. Will you be observing for the police?'

'I would think so.' Sydney Household nodded with firmly fixed jaw. 'I'll have the body removed and taken to Addenbrookes, for your attention, then we'll start looking for evidence of the late twentieth century onwards.'

'Zip fasteners, plastic buttons...?'

'That sort of thing. Anything that dates the skeleton to within the last seventy years, as you say.'

With a nod of her head Veronica Sleaford left the confines of the tent and walked, carrying her bag, across the field, past groups of police officers, male and female in white shirts or blouses, who stood in groups chatting quietly and softly. One officer, a black man, Afro-Caribbean, and she, had brief eye contact with each other. He inclined his head deferentially to her, and she smiled almost imperceptibly at him. Black and black. Veronica Sleaford and the black officer, whom she had seen before, had a mutuality of experience which allowed them a brief communication as equals. She walked on across the meadows, enjoying the flight of a heron low overhead, such a graceful motion she thought, regal almost. She brushed through the gap in the hedgerow where just an hour earlier David Whittaker had waited whilst he watched the young constable examine his find and then talk into his radio clearly confirming that the remains reported did indeed appear to be a human skull.

At the road she walked up to the mortuary van and upon her approach the driver folded up his copy of the *Cambridge Evening News*, wound down and leaned his head out of the window, beaming his approval as she approached. 'I think you can carry on now,' she said warmly. 'It's a complete skeleton, just to forewarn you.'

'Appreciated, miss.' The driver was middle-aged, well set, a slightly ruddy complexion.

Veronica Sleaford turned and walked back to her car. It was, she recalled, that selfsame driver who had wounded her feelings when she overheard him referring to her as 'a clever old girl'. She was then in her early thirties and her feelings remained wounded until she overheard a university porter marvelling at the undergraduates' ability to organise themselves for their rag day as 'clever old boys'. It was clearly she, then new to Cambridge, who did not appreciate the under culture of the city, their idiom, the near feudal attitude. She climbed gracefully into her car, placing her bag, like an honoured passenger, on the front seat beside her and drove home, grateful for an early finish.

The skeleton had been lifted gingerly into the body bag which lay on the stretcher, by four pale-faced constables, chosen for the task by Sydney Household because of their youth and therefore implicit inexperience. The body bag, of durable heavy duty black plastic, then having been zipped up fully to conceal its contents and carried back to the mortuary van under the gaze of a group of curious villagers, the search of the grave began.

The decayed, rusted zip fastener which was discovered a few inches beneath where the skeleton had lain, proved a surprising source of disappointment for Sydney Household. He had not expected to feel such a reaction. The zip fastener meant the skeleton was less than seventy years old and instantly made the find a police matter. It was not the prospect of work to be done that had disappointed Household, in fact quite the reverse, he relished the task. It was, he decided, that it meant old scars had to be opened, upon identity of the deceased; relatives, probably still alive, would have to be informed. It was the dreadful well of emotion that would have to be plumbed that caused Sydney Household disappointment. Each item found in the grave was placed in a self-sealing cellophane sachet and labelled – place, date of find, and description of the contents of the bag. Zip fastener, with 'Levi' logo, shirt buttons, white plastic; a watch, blue face; remnants of leather shoes, all were photographed by the S.O.C.O. as they were found, placed in production bags, labelled, and the bags placed on a plastic high-sided tray. The constables continued to dig, not just down into the ground, but also outwards from the shallow grave, and did so painstakingly, tirelessly, uncomplainingly, until the sergeant approached Household. 'I think that's it, sir.'

'You think so?' Household, taller than the sergeant, smiled as he replied.

'Yes, sir, with respect, nothing else has been found for an hour now, and the boys are getting into some very solid old soil.'

'Very well.' Household looked at the hole in the meadow, and thought the sergeant correct; any further digging would prove futile, a waste of effort and manpower and for no result at all. 'Better fill it in though ... we can always re-excavate if we have to.'

'Very well, sir.' The sergeant turned and with a forced grin told the tired, sweating constables to put the soil back where they had found it.

Veronica Sleaford turned the key in the front door of her home, and as she did so, she glanced behind her; the river, Jesus Green beyond, on which people, young in the main, did summery things, walked in pairs, lay together in pairs, sat in groups, dressed in bright coloured lightweight summer clothing, the scene marred only by a derelict sitting on the bandstand doubtless asking any and all who passed within earshot if they could spare any change. She pushed the door open as the lock turned with the key and entered the hallway of her home to the welcome sound of the clock which ticked loudly and chimed the Westminster chimes even more loudly. So loudly did the piece chime that the people who lived in the adjacent house had contrived to meet her as she was leaving her home one morning and said it was a very nice sound they heard through the wall but they would rather hear their own clock and wondered if she would kindly remove it from the dividing wall? Veronica Sleaford had mumbled an apology and returned inside the house, switched the chime to 'off' and later that day had remounted the clock on an inside wall, well away from her neighbours' earshot and had been rewarded by smiles each and every time she and her neighbours subsequently saw each other.

''Lo, Mum,' was the other warm and welcoming sound which greeted her.

''Lo.' Veronica Sleaford placed her black bag on the seat beside the phone, picked up the mail and walked down the hallway beside the stairs, down a short flight of steps, all covered with a brown hessian rug, to the kitchen, which was equipped in a country style with a large table and six matching chairs in untreated pine and a Welsh dresser with many mugs hanging from hooks, and plates balanced nearly upright on their rims along the shelves. There was an Aga with a blue front, a noticeboard in white cork with pine edging, onto which items of importance were fixed with pins, some red, some yellow, and a tall fridge-freezer. A window looked out onto a small rear garden, consisting of a modest lawn, where stood a bird table, and a pond with frogs and newts, and a garden shed, the latter liberally coated with creosote. Sojourner stood at the table kneading dough; she beamed at her mother as Veronica Sleaford entered. 'Busy, I see.'

'Making bread.'

'Mmm ... I remember the time well.' She switched on the electric kettle and dropped two teabags into a china teapot.

'Bread-making?'

'No ... that long, lovely summer between first and second year sixth form. Tea?'

'Love some. Well, I'm making the most of it ... as you keep telling me, Mummy, "the real world

22

loometh large".'

'Indeed it does. Where's the newspaper?'

'Front room.'

'In pieces, doubtless.'

'No ... actually I managed to keep it more or less intact today.'

'More or less...' Veronica Sleaford smiled as the electric kettle began to bubble and vibrate prior to switching itself off. 'Getting better.'

'Onwards and upwards...'

Veronica Sleaford placed a mug of hot tea beside her daughter and carried a mug of tea for her own consumption back up the flight of stairs to the hallway, and continued up to the first floor of her house, to her bedroom. She carefully took off her suit and hung it up on a coat hanger which she then hung on the wall. All other clothing she undid and removed as quickly as possible, as if removing the day, the pathology lab at Addenbrookes Hospital, the meadow near Bottisham, the skeleton of a young male of the human species, the stifling heat of the tent and Household's coldness and distance. She wound herself into a full length, dark blue bathrobe and, walking on raised heels as she often did in such circumstances, went from her bedroom to the bathroom, turned on the hot water tap and sat naked, enjoying the steam playing around her flesh as she sipped the cooling tea. When it came to baths, she was an unashamed sybarite and enjoyed the pre-bath steam as much as the bath itself. It was her way of relaxing at the end of a hard day. For an hour at the end of each working day she retired to the bathroom, shutting herself away from the world, and sat in steam so thick she couldn't see her hand if stretched at arm's length. Only when the steam had begun to clear and condense and water the plants on the windowsill did she slide into the deep bath she had drawn, and did so without causing a ripple on the surface of the water, and therein soaked and soaped herself. The bath when she came home had become an important part of her day, a phase, a period which separated her working day from her free time, her time at home in her own space. 'The real world loometh large...' As she lay back in the warm, soapy water, the words came unbidden to her mind, followed equally unbidden by her daughter's words ... 'Making the most of it' ... and with the words came a chill down her spine, a chill whose edge was not at all softened by the warmth of the water in which she sat, nor by the warmth of the liquid she sipped, because it occurred to her that this was the last summer her daughter would be at home. In twelve month's time Sojourner would be packing a cabin trunk prior to going to university, and thereafter she would visit two or three times a year and probably, without intending to, would annoyingly refer to university as 'home'. 'The real world loometh large' for her also; her warnings to her daughter had also been a warning to herself. This lovely, huge terraced house on Chesterton Road, overlooking the gentle Cam and the pleasance of Jesus Green, would one day soon be very empty. Very empty indeed. The chill which had run down her spine was replaced by a hollowness in her stomach and a tightening of her scalp. She too had something to make the most of.

She left the bathroom loosely draped in the robe, returned to her bedroom and rubbed and patted herself dry. She flung the robe across the double bed and dressed in jeans and t-shirt and trainers. She went downstairs as the clock chimed six-thirty and walked into the living room of the house, the front elevated ground floor of the property, and searched for the *Guardian*. She had to concede that Sojourner had kept the newspaper a little more together than usual. The main part of the newspaper was separated sheet by sheet and liberally strewn across one of the sofas and on the floor and on the coffee table. *Guardian 2* and *3* were however relatively intact, *G2* being found atop the piano and *G3*, unread, lying discarded and disowned on one of the chairs. Veronica Sleaford gathered up the news sheets, put them in order, settled back onto the sofa with her feet on the coffee table and began to read, feeling herself winding down as she did so, and also as she did so, thinking of mother and daughter things to do in this, their suddenly-come last summer.

Margaret Neston lay naked, face down, on the recliner by the swimming pool enjoying the warmth of the sun on her back. She knew that he enjoyed seeing her naked and she liked to be naked. It was an arrangement that pleased them both, although by then she thought that it was probably the only arrangement that did. The promises he had made had not been fully forthcoming. In fact, she thought that they had been largely reneged on, but it was still better than being back at home and back at work. For the first two or three weeks after accepting his offer she had found it hugely preferable to returning home, but now she felt the whole thing was beginning to pale. The charming, successful older man had revealed one or two unpleasant aspects to his personality, and she hadn't even smelled the 'generous allowance' she had been promised. Nonetheless, on balance - and only on balance – her preference was to allow things to continue, for the time being.

Margaret became aware of him approaching her. She turned and levered herself half onto one side looking at him as he approached her. Tall, good-looking, she thought, wrapped in a blue bathrobe. 'Finished early today?' she commented.

He sat beside her and placed his hand on her raised shoulder to push her back down onto the recliner. 'Got to the end of a scene.' He took the bottle of sunflower oil which stood on the tiles next to the edge of the pool and poured a generous measure of the oil onto her, massaging it into her taut, pert bottom and thighs. 'It's a natural place for me to stop for the day.'

She moaned with pleasure. 'So long as nowt's wrong.' She felt him stiffen with anger. It had become the nature of their relationship that she had come to enjoy finding ways of annoying him.

'Nothing is wrong, thank you,' he replied icily, but yet in cultured tones. 'I have also got to go into Valetta ... need another inkjet and a few other things. We will eat at eight o'clock tonight.'

'Will we?'

'Yes we will.' He stood. 'And I mean eight, not

quarter to nine like last time.' He strode back towards the villa.

'Yes, master,' she said softly, when she knew he was out of earshot.

Detective Inspector Sydney Household looked out across Parker's Piece and marvelled how young men could find the energy and stamina to play soccer in that sort of heat. Even then in the early evening it was still warm, much too warm for him.

'Male?' Perigo asked. He was a tall, thin officer, with piercing eyes.

'Yes.' Household turned and looked towards Perigo, at his corner desk, postcards on the walls beside him. 'I said so.'

'Sorry, so you did. The post-mortem will be tomorrow, I assume?'

'Yes.' Household once again turned and looked out of the office window across Parker's Piece, the once gaudily decorated lamppost – 'Reality Checkpoint' – now repainted in green, standing at the intersection of the two paths which criss-crossed the twenty-two acres of the piece. The University Arms Hotel at the far right of the open area from his vantage point, the slow crawling rush hour traffic beneath his window, turning left at the traffic island to go down East Road, or straight ahead into Mill Road and working-class Cambridge, or right along Gonville Place. Most of the vehicles went either right or left, most of the cyclists and pedestrians went straight on. Sitting in traffic wasn't Sydney Household's favourite occupation. It was his custom and practice to wait until six p.m. before commencing his homeward journey. That was his rationalisation, that was at least what he told his colleagues, even though his shifts that week finished at two p.m. He turned back to Perigo. 'How are you progressing with the Panther enquiry?'

'Slowly, boss.' Perigo leaned back in his chair. 'The whole thing has come to a full stop ... no new leads since the last conference. It's getting to the stage where we are almost wishing for another one ... I say *almost...*'

'Yes,' Household growled. 'Dangerous thinking.' But he knew what Perigo meant, a new victim would mean more leads but it would also mean another young woman traumatised for life, or worse. Next time the Panther might kill. It was the nature of serial offending against the person; the frequency of the attacks increase, as does the severity and they continue offending until they are stopped in some way, or until they burn out, and whatever is driving them to act in the manner they are acting in, leaves them.

'I'm still convinced there are more victims.' Perigo picked up his pen and toyed with it.

'I remember you saying.'

'Three abductions in close succession, then a gap of nearly two years, then victim number four. Three victims in nine months, then nothing for two years, then last week victim number four.'

'Still nothing from her?'

'Nothing ... she's well traumatised ... has night terrors, wakes up screaming. She's a town girl though ... close to hand when she is ready to talk. The first three were students who went home to have their night terrors and none have returned to Cambridge, all transferred to other universities. Have to be interviewed at a distance ... one came from Aberdeen ... took Wiseman three days out of her week to go and see her – one day up, one day during which she chatted to her for an hour, then looked round the Granite City, travelled south the day after that – three days for an hour's chat and even then she couldn't go into depth with the girl because her mum was there. Penny got the impression that the Panther did things to her that she didn't want her mum to know about, but she would only be interviewed with her mum being present.'

'I see ... frustrating...'

'You can say that again. The only benefit of the last attack is that we are now as sure as we can be that the Panther belongs to the town ... the other three attacks taking place in term-time might have meant he was a student, like his victims, but attacking them when the university is down indicates that he's town not gown, though some students do elect to stay up during the summer, or have to. As I did, in fact,' Perigo smiled. 'Much to the family's chagrin. Rented a flat down there,' he tossed his head almost contemptuously towards Mill Road, 'eye opening ... I was still young then.'

'I can imagine.'

Perigo continued, 'I doubt a student or postgrad would be our man anyway, because he has access to a facility, a lock-up where he can keep them for days before releasing them. And it's somewhere quiet, somewhere remote out in the Fens ... no sound from the outside, no human sound ... just owls at night and songbirds during the day ... the only sound the victims hear is the Panther arriving by vehicle and turning the key in the lock. That's a local man. It speaks of local knowledge.'

'Certainly speaks of it,' Household leant back against the central heating radiators, at that moment switched off and pleasantly cool to the touch, 'but I wouldn't dismiss anything yet ... speaking for myself, of course.'

'The voice of experience and wisdom, versus the voice of youth and enthusiasm, is that what you're saying?'

'No...' Household sensed Perigo goading him. 'No, I am not saying that. I am just saying that I wouldn't close my eyes to any possibility unless it is proven impossible ... but then it's your inquiry.'

'Yes, and precious little staff to do it with.'

'That's something you'll get used to.'

There was a pause. Perigo looked over to his right to make sure the open office area in which he sat, and in which Household stood, was quiet and, unusually, empty, then he fixed Household with a steely eye and said, 'You don't like me heading the Panther investigation, do you?'

Household held the pause. 'You see,' he said at length, 'that's making another assumption. You may be right, but it's still an assumption.'

'I was advised I would meet hostility from the "old guard". I suppose they had people like you in mind when they said that.'

Footsteps were heard in the corridor. Perigo and Household continued to look at each other as David 'Dick' Tracy entered the office, canvas knapsack on his shoulder. 'Evening, gents,' he smiled jovially as he unslung his knapsack and went to his desk. He sat heavily, stretched and stroked his beard.

'Evening.' Perigo and Household responded in unison and as he spoke, Household pushed himself away from the wall. Never, he thought, was an entry more welcome.

'What delights await I on this shift?' Tracy glanced at Perigo and then at Household. 'Six till two ... six till finish ... six till finish whenever ... anything happening?'

'Body in a field out by Bottisham,' Household said as he walked past Tracy. 'Complete skeleton but it's not ancient, so it's one for us. We'll pick it up tomorrow.'

Sydney Household drove home. He took his time. It was not a journey he enjoyed. He left Cambridge on the Madingley Road and was soon in open country, picking up the A45 at Hardwick. It occurred to him, with no obvious trigger, that more than a few years ago, but insufficient years to be called many, a group of students from the 'Tech' as it used to be, had pushed a bed to Bedford as part of a fundraising Rag Week stunt. They had taken about 18 hours over the journey which, to Household, seemed about as pointless as the team of Scottish undergraduates who, in the 1930s, pushed an Austin 10 to the top of Ben Nevis. At St Neots he turned south on to the A1 until the next exit where he turned onto the A428, which continued through pleasant countryside, and the village of Great Barford and towards Bedford. It would, in other circumstances, have been a pleasant journey of about fifty miles, a good distance between work and home, a winding down period on the way home, courtesy of soothing Radio Three, or civilised Radio Four, and a good 'psyching up' period on the way to work. But only in other circumstances. For personal reasons he disliked the journey home, and enjoyed the journey to work. He drove into Bedford and to his house on the newly built estate.

On that day she was in a cold mood, she glanced at him only once as he entered the door and continued to prepare the evening meal. He took off his light summer coat and hung it in the hall wardrobe. He walked into the living room where his two children sat, it seemed, transfixed by the television and both ignored him: he thought it because of their mother's influence. It was his experience that coming home to the house when his wife was absent, he would enjoy a warm greeting from his children, but her very presence had an influence which was all-pervasive. At least 'his' chair had been allowed to remain vacant and he sat in it resignedly, thankfully, too tired to complain at the inanity of his children's choice of viewing.

The evening meal was eaten in stony silence in the front room, with the curtains open so that a passing pedestrian, glancing in, would see two parents and two teenage children eating a meal and may think them a successful, healthy, functional family. The pedestrian would not be able to experience the stress in the room, the heavy silence of people communicating by clearing throats or pointedly tapping their forks or knives against their plate, the sort of tension that would have, indeed had, made visitors throw up their meal and scream and run for the door, grabbing their coat on the way out, and bringing on a remark from Mrs Household of 'What was wrong with her?' or similar. People visited once, and once only, and the only contact with the outside world was with people who had to talk to the family, relatives, neighbours perhaps, but only in passing. Sydney Household was pleased that his children seemed to have friends, and to have made new friends in Bedford, but saddened that they didn't think that they could bring said friends home. But neither did he. It just wasn't the sort of house that he, and clearly his children too, would invite other people in to. And it was all because of the woman who sat nearest the door as if by doing so she controlled the egress and ingress, a self-appointed gatekeeper to the room, who, whenever one member of the family seemed as if to be about to speak, would clear her throat which was an established signal that they mustn't, who collected the plates with masculine movements, clattering them together; she and she alone could make noise.

'Settling in alright?' Sydney Household took the opportunity of his wife's absence to speak to his children and received an 'OK' and a 'Yeah, OK' in return. It was in fairness probably all he could expect from teenagers, but it was at least something. If there were problems at the sixth form college, he would have doubtless found out by then, for by then they had been nearly a year in their new home. Any further conversation was prevented by his wife's return with the dessert, and the remainder of the meal was taken in the same oppressive silence as had been the first course.

After the meal his children repaired to their respective personal space. Sydney and Joy Household sat in the living room, tolerating the strange music which came from their children's bedrooms. The high notes couldn't be heard but the bass rhythm, even though the volume was turned down, filled the house. His wife sat in her chair, silent, immovable. It was by then nine p.m. Sydney Household rose and put on his coat and walked out of his house into the peace of the evening. As he walked away from the house, the key in the lock was turned behind him. She would not lock him out, that he knew was certain, but the turning of the lock in the first place said much.

He found warmth and solace in the pub. He had a chat with a man whom he recognised as a regular, a man like himself who seemed to want both the human company that the pub offered, yet also 'space' to drink alone. It was only a brief chat with him at the bottom end of the bar, a long way from the young set who dominated the greater part of the floor area. The pub itself was too noisy for Household's taste, as in fact many pubs were; the world was changing, that was clear, and he wasn't changing with it. That was also clear.

He left the pub before the stampede and the crush which always happens when last orders are called, especially on Thursdays, which social observers have noted to have become the unofficial last day of the working week, with some businesses adopting a 'dress down Friday' for office workers, and because of the increase in self-certified sick notes handed in on Mondays to explain the absence the previous Friday. 'Throwing a sickie' was, Household believed, the expression used. The stampede and the crush were things he didn't need and, still working shifts which straddled weekends and public holidays, the concept of the last day of the working week had never been part of his experience. He had missed it, and didn't want the experience now. He enjoyed the police officers' lot of needing to remain a little detached, one step outside mainstream society; like the sheep dog guarding the flock. He strolled home, enjoying the summer's evening which had just a scent of rain in the air and that, he pondered, would be no bad thing. East Anglia had basked these weeks past, the soil was concrete hard ... just that morning he had watched as a skeleton had to be freed with pick-axes as much as with spades. A shower of rain would be more than welcome, and after it, the freshness, the scents released from the herbs. It was his favourite time: England, summer, after a shower of rain, preferably in a rural location. And the great enjoyment about rain in Bedford was that it didn't bring with it the fear of his property being inundated. They had got less for their money in Bedford. The house in March was a rambling early Victorian pile with a huge garden, a lovely place for his children to grow up and he didn't doubt that in later years they would re-visit the house, probably bringing their own children with them. It was, he had to concede, an interesting house with a warm atmosphere, a house with a history, very, very unlike the soulless, cramped new-built thing he and his protesting wife had recently moved to, but he believed he had to be pragmatic. His children didn't like the idea, and his wife, he thought, really rather relished the excuse it gave her to be tantrum throwing and cutting him dead by turns, while he further suspected that she really actually secretly agreed with him and looked forward to running a smaller, more efficient home. She also seemed to have jumped at the excuse for giving up her job, but being Joy – the much, he thought, much mis-named 'Joy' – protested endlessly at the prospect.

He turned into his driveway, the lights burning needlessly in all rooms, left on 'for Dad to turn off when he comes home from the pub'. He unlocked the door and stepped into the hall, relieved at least that the strange music no longer filled the house, closed and locked the door behind him and put the security chain on for good measure. He side-stepped the cardboard boxes in the hallway. He had forgotten just how long it takes to settle into a house, and they, not yet out of the early stage of living out of card-board boxes, still had the greater part of that particular journey in front of them. He toured the ground floor of the house, switched off lights and even the gas fire in the living room, doubtless switched on by his wife before she went to bed, despite the heat, for him to switch off. He went upstairs and undressed and washed and climbed into bed next to his wife. Her back was turned to him and remained turned from him throughout the night, as if an invisible sheet of steel had been erected between them, and which was erected many years ago, and which Sydney Household felt, looked set to remain erected.

Sydney and Joy, and their two teenagers, one of each, who might look so perfect a family to any pedestrian who happened to be walking past their modest house whilst they were in the front room eating a meal, who still sent Christmas cards from 'Sydney and Joy and the hatchlings', who smiled when out together upon meeting someone they knew, especially in recent weeks, being keen to make a good impression among their new neighbours. But the actuality of the Household's home life was hidden from view. The only compensation that he drew was that his years as a police officer had taught him that many households in middle England are of the same ilk. As are many in lower England and upper England likewise. He said 'goodnight' to his wife as he switched off the bedside light. He knew she wouldn't answer, and she didn't, but he said it anyway.

Shortly after ten p.m. the man drove out to the mess that is Bar Hill. He thought of it as a mess, a blister stuck onto Huntingdon Road, outside the city, a sprawl of modern housing, without grace or style or character. But it was bricks, it was mortar, it was somewhere sensible to put his money. He executed a perfect left into the estate, and perfect lefts and rights within the estate, and a perfect left into his drive and parked his gleaming red perfect car in his drive so that the distance from the front bumper to the garage door was the same as the distance from the rear bumper to the gate when closed. Perfect parking. He felt it incumbent to be perfect. His house had an immaculately manicured garden, and the building itself was, on the outside, Ideal Home perfect. But he never permitted visitors. It was just him alone within. No callers ever got beyond the porch door. The gas meter and the electricity meter were both outside under waterproof covers, so that they could be read without having to penetrate the interior. It was just how he wanted it. In the hall he shed his clothes and climbed into shorts, nothing else, no top, no footwear. He went to the kitchen where the blinds were drawn to shut out the world and where he put a Marks & Spencer instant meal in the small Baby Belling he kept atop the work surface. When it was cooked, he poured the food onto a metal plate and then ate it with his fingers, hurriedly, greedily, wolfing it. Then he crawled out of the kitchen on all fours, hands and feet on the ground, feral, across the bare floorboards of the big room and sat against the wall, crouching until his legs ached, and still he crouched, occasionally glancing out of the window at the moon and the low clouds which promised rain, but mainly he stared straight ahead at the plain plaster of the wall opposite, straining his ears for the least sound that meant the soldiers were coming.

Panther slips, Panther slides, hunts by night, dressed in black, blending neatly, blending smoothly, blending deadly.

The man liked being called the 'Panther' – not really original of the press, but good enough. Panthers hunt at night, sleek and dark, prowling cunningly, it was a name to live up to. He liked the blending, he liked the sense of power it gave him, only he knew who he was, only he, not her, nor her ... nor he, nor he, nor they ... no one knew who he was, among these people in this dark warm summer's night, for there was nothing to set him apart from them. He was just another pedestrian, another foot passenger, a man walking alone, casually dressed, not sauntering, but walking as though he had somewhere to go, because appearance is so important. The police are hunting him, the public are scared of him, suspicious of everybody they don't know, but his appearance didn't arouse suspicion, a black t-shirt, dark blue tracksuit bottoms, dark jogging shoes – not all black, the shoes had a dash of white and reflective heels, the jogging bottoms had a golden logo on the front just to the left and the t-shirt had a white logo near the top, and also to the left. He was clean cut, clean shaven, mid-thirties ... he looked 'alright' and police officers and public alike glanced at him once and their glances didn't become suspicious stares. And that was the secret. Blending, looking 'alright', looking 'normal'.

The Panther prowled round two sides of the market square from Kings Parade, past the entrance to Rose Crescent, down past the Italian restaurant and turned silently and stealthily into Petty Cury. He walked like the hunting animal he was, effortlessly, looking ahead, not from side to side, for he was the predator. The top predator of this ecosystem, this smug self-satisfied city. The Panther thought Cambridge, Cambs, to be smug and self-satisfied. In narrow Petty Cury he sud-

39

denly recalled 'Mr Snowy' the street performer entertaining children on Saturday mornings with his barrow full of rabbits and birds and mice. He exited Petty Cury and walked into Hobsons Street, fewer people, more traffic, like the Rolls Royce which swept imperiously past him. It was cars like that and the people who own them that made the man think that this city was smug and self-satisfied. He did not think the same of Cambridge, Gloucestershire, nor of Cambridge, Otley, West Yorkshire, nor of Cambridge, East Lothian, all of which places he had visited, over time, and found them down to earth and to his liking. He didn't know about Cambridge, Massachusetts ... he had yet to visit there. About Cambridge Massachusetts, he kept an open mind. He was passed in the street by two excited tourist types, youths, chatting excitedly in a foreign tongue – French, he thought. They ignored him as they walked by. Evidently they hadn't heard about the Cambridge Panther, or if they had, they were unimpressed. That suited the man admirably, suited him down to the ground. He didn't loiter around the bus station – the police kept a watchful eye on it, watching from the moon shadows in plain clothes, or prominently in uniform, watching them come in, watching them go out, the people on the buses, looking for he who looked a little odd, a little misfitting.

'This man can kill'.

So the *Cambridge Evening News* had quoted, so had the television regional news quoted. 'Whoever the Panther is, he must be caught'.

Could kill. The Panther smiled as he walked.

Has killed. That would be more accurate. Has killed. My, has he killed...

He walked away from Drummer Street Bus Station towards Parker's Piece, along Park Side, and in front of the police station, a new, modern-looking grey concrete building, slab-sided, and glass, plenty of glass. That was dangerous for him, walking so near, but the thrill, the edge, fascinated him, and it would reduce suspicion, because the Panther lurks in dark places and creeps, and pounces and he looks ... well, different ... he doesn't look normal, even allowing for a taste for dark clothing, and he doesn't stroll past the public entrance of the headquarters of the East Anglian Constabulary, walking on the pavement between the police station to his left and Britain's first circular post box on his right. And beyond that, across Parkside, the vast expanse of Parker's Piece, with the lights of 'Reality Checkpoint' shining in the centre.

The Panther crossed East Road and entered narrow Mill Road, the small, cultivated open area of Peter's Field to his left, beyond which, glued to the grey brick wall, had once been a poster, a huge poster which had amused him. 'Christianity' it had read, 'The religion that knows no bounds. Look into it'. And how pray, he had thought the moment he had read the poster, and had continued to think each and every time the poster had subsequently caught his eye, how can one possibly 'look into' something that has 'no bounds'? To look into something, one has to stand outside it. Surely?

He walked down Mill Road, a road of small

41

shops, of terraced houses nearly abutting the pavement. Further down, past the railway bridge, the houses did abut the pavement, but here, at the Parker's Piece end of the road, the houses had a little bit of garden between the door and the pavement – not much, about three paces would take a grown human from one to the other, but it was enough to stop people tapping on your front window, just for fun, as they walked home from the pub in the evening. Or from throwing dustbins through the front windows, which had happened to the houses beyond Great Eastern Road. Conveniently placed on the pavement, by the Refuse Dept, awaiting the arrival of the lorry into which their contents would be emptied, they had proved irresistible to a group of intoxicated football supporters who had thrown the bins through front room windows into people's houses. Contents and all. The Panther had been in Cambridge then. He had lived in a house nearby and recalled the anger of the people. Just a single incident of riotous behaviour, horrible to have your front room window smashed and a dustbin and other people's refuse on your carpet, but in the scheme of things, not a serious crime, not a crime like murder … not a crime like multiple murder. But the incident had a significance for the Panther because he had become infected, contaminated by other people's anger. He had often lain at home, looking at the moon if it was visible, and wondering if he had been angry all along and the leglessly drunk football fans had, by their action, somehow awoken something in him? Had they, he wondered, managed to awaken his Kraken?

Just before the railway bridge he crossed and walked down St Barnabas Road, and slid his hand into his pocket as he did so, groping for a set of car keys which he had wedged there with a handkerchief. The keys were on a ring with a Datsun fob which he had bought from a petrol filling station some years earlier, where he had been amused and touched by the young female who served him who, when he asked to buy a key ring, had said, with an apology of passing sincerity, 'We've only got Datsuns left.' He had smiled and said that 'a Datsun' would do nicely, wondering if a similar key ring with a 'Ferrari' fob really would do its job any better? He stopped walking as he came to his van: ye good olde Ford Transit. A black one, in his case. No other colour could, would do, not for him, but like the dash of white on his jogging shoes, when he had had his van re-sprayed, he had asked the garage to paint the offside rear door panel canary yellow. 'It makes the van distinctive,' he had explained, 'keeps them off my tail.' It was his theory, he explained to the bemused garage proprietor that because yellow is a colour that people avoid, then a yellow rear door would stop the following motorist from driving too close to his rear bumper. The yellow rear door, he hoped, would also divert suspicion. If the Panther drove, he wouldn't drive such a distinctive vehicle, so he hoped the thinking of the police would be. He was, though, keenly aware that the ploy was double-edged. He had had to make sure, as sure as he could be sure, that no one had seen the vehicle at the time of the abduction. Again, he took it to the edge, because he drove the vehicle around Cambridge, just to get it noticed, buying off suspicion, in anticipation of the day he had to transport a victim. So far it had worked. Four times it had worked. He started the van, let the engine idle for a few minutes. He felt reasonably pleased with himself ... the gap of two years between the third and the fourth victim, that was neat, sent the police searching for felons who had been in prison during these months ... and all the while he was on 'furlough', just resting, taking things easy. Used up a lot of valuable police time for no gain at all. They had bought it, the 'busies', the boys in blue, the *Evening News* said so, as did the television regional news programmes. He let a slow moving car go by then drove away, crawling behind the car. He turned right into Mill Road, over the railway bridge. He was re-locating the van. He did that, never let it remain in the same place for more than forty-eight hours. He drove to the end of Mill Road to charge the battery, turned around and drove back towards Cambridge city centre. Strange road, Mill Road, he thought, it doesn't really go anywhere, just peters out at the far end, as though it generated its own traffic along its length. He turned right into Romsey Town and found a gap by the kerb in narrow, dark Thoday Street. There he left the vehicle, knowing it would soon be needed.

He knew it would soon be needed because the urge was upon him. Again.

2

It was a short and a pleasant walk for Veronica
Sleaford from her house overlooking Jesus Green
to Drummer Street Bus Station and the number
2C to Addenbrookes Hospital, and especially
pleasant, as then, during the summer months.
She turned left outside her door and crossed the
road as soon as a gap in the morning traffic
afforded her the opportunity. She crossed the
footbridge which spanned the river at the weir
and the lock, and stepped on to Jesus Green. To
her right were the bowling green and the tennis
court, and beyond was the graceful line of grey
terraced housing which lined Park Drive. Nearer
at hand, a group of people in period costume
were dancing an ancient dance of slow movements without musical accompaniment on the
small, octagonal concrete platform which stood
next to the bowling green. It was unusual to
observe such activity midweek but then this was
high summer, the university was 'down' and a
little more free time was available than was the
case during full term. The dancers all appeared
to her to be in their thirties and forties, the men
in blue coat tails, the women in long gowns, and
they were dancing daintily for their own
amusement. That, thought Veronica Sleaford,
that is Cambridge and always will be Cambridge.
The line is drawn at criminality but eccentric

behaviour is positively encouraged. She turned to her left and savoured the stroll through the avenue of mature trees and joined Victoria Avenue at Jesus Ditch. On the left-hand side of Victoria Avenue, at the junction with Maids Causeway, was a stand of old trees which at first glance looked like a small copse, but upon careful observation it was clear that the trees formed a near perfect circle. They had been planted thus by some unknown, unsung person with an eye to the future. The trees, she thought, were probably one hundred and fifty years old, probably older.

Plant trees. She smiled. Yes ... plant trees, something that she and her daughter could do together before adulthood took Sojourner from her, leaving her fighting the dread of 'empty nest syndrome'.

She crossed the traffic intersection using the safety of the pelican crossing and walked up Emmanuel Road to the bus station. She joined the queue for the number 2C and waited, patiently. It was a short queue, at that time of the day most folk were coming into the city, few were leaving it. Two town women, middle-aged, overweight, stood ahead of her, one talking, the other listening. 'Poor old Joe's lost his missus,' she said, 'give him something else to worry about. He's a worrier him ... never known him not worrying over something ... always worried ... if there was nothing to worry about, he'd find something.' The second woman seemed to be standing there and not listening to a word. Veronica Sleaford glanced beyond the small bus station, tucked away in a cul-de-sac which she thought could only accommodate about ten vehicles at any one time, nosed in under the perspex canopy, back the way she had come to Emmanuel Road; people walking, a few students on cycles, enthusiastic, seeming content to remain 'up' when the rest of the university is 'down' for the summer. Mostly, though, it seemed to her that the pedestrians were adult employees walking to work. She took a deep breath. She enjoyed living in Cambridge. Enjoyed it very much indeed, and at the beginning of the new century – and with the bloodiest century in recorded history behind humanity – it was as if a new age was dawning, an age that she was going to be part of, an age which her daughter and those of her generation would shape.

The number 2C bus entered the bus station, and as it did so, Veronica Sleaford plunged her hand into her shoulder bag for her purse. It will be a hot day, she thought, not a day for working out of doors and the controlled chill of the pathology laboratory, a constant two degrees Celsius, was at that moment very inviting. Veronica Sleaford did not care for heat, preferring to keep warm in cold climates, rather than keeping cool in hot climates. Once, many years earlier, she had taken a package holiday to the Mediterranean during the summer months for no other reason than to see what all the fuss was about, to see what was the attraction of lying on a beach in the kind of heat that evaporated sun-block. She had returned to the UK none the wiser.

She sat near the front of the single-decker, near the driver. Somewhat annoyingly, the two town women sat immediately behind her despite there being many empty seats, and for the entire

47

journey out to the edge of the city and vast Addenbrookes Hospital, she was regaled and entertained by turns about 'Joe' and his 'worries', by the one woman who spoke, the other steadfastly remaining silent. She left the bus at the stop outside Addenbrookes which seemed to her to gleam and glow in the sun, the tall, concrete and glass building looked as it always did to her, very confident, very strong. If the building was human, she had often thought, it would be a young man.

She entered the hospital by the main entrance and took the lift down to the Department of Pathology. She pushed open the department's swinging doors in a gentle, non-aggressive manner. Faces turned and beamed at her as she entered. 'Morning,' she said, warmly.

'Morning, Dr Sleaford.' Only the man spoke. The woman let him speak for her.

'Morning Harry, morning Sue.' Veronica Sleaford walked past her two assistants and into her office. She found it small and cramped, but it was her space, and all she needed to write reports about post-mortems she had conducted. She unhooked her bag from her shoulder as Harry Hewis entered her office, knocking on the door as he did so, mug of steaming tea in hand.

'Just made a pot,' he explained, 'just poured the water into the teapot a second before you arrived. Can't start the day without one.'

'Certainly can't.' Veronica Sleaford clasped her hand round the mug, turning it to enable her to take hold of it by the handle. 'Anything come in during the night?'

'Not a thing, boss. No deaths in the hospital

48

overnight, explained or otherwise, no sudden mysterious fatalities in the community.' Harry Hewis smiled. He was a well-built man, and moved in a way which Veronica Sleaford's professional eye told her of great physical strength, yet his manner was always warm and calm and gentle.

'So there is just the skeleton?'

'Just the skeleton, boss.'

Harry Hewis turned and left Veronica Sleaford alone in her office. She sat at her desk and glanced at the photographs, one or two of Sojourner by herself, smiling a radiant smile, one of mother and daughter standing side by side against a backdrop of endless sand and clear blue sky. It was a photograph which had proved to be a source of some humour, 'Where was that taken?' being a common query, with the questioner expecting an answer such as Morocco or St Kitts or some similar exotic location. The answer always dumbfounded: 'Norfolk, actually ... and it was a lot colder than it looks.' Veronica leaned forward, cupping the mug of tea with both hands. The skeleton, she pondered, just the skeleton ... meaning only the skeleton ... but it wasn't going to be just the skeleton soon, not to some wretched next of kin whose waiting and wondering and anguish will soon be over, if the remains can be identified, and if said next of kin are still alive because that skeleton could have been buried for many decades. She didn't know when zip fasteners had been invented, or more appropriately, had come into common usage, but she believed that they were already widespread by the mid-1950s. The skeleton could then be up to fifty years old, and it was that of an adult. An adult who lost his life by some means unknown some fifty years ago is unlikely to have close next of kin. Possibly an elderly sibling, but no parents. Not after that length of time. She thought about the agony of a parent, two parents living out their lives, never knowing what had happened to their son who had disappeared. Their son who was their life, but to the police was never anything more than another 'mis per', a file opened, date and place last seen, and a recent photograph. What was that awful statistic? Hundreds of people are reported missing in the UK each year. Most are found, or return, or make some sort of contact with their family within forty-eight hours, but only most. A minority, but a significant minority, are never seen again, not alive at least. In some cases not even the remains are found. Or if they are, they are found many, many years later, as clearly in this case ... just the skeleton. Just.

There was a tap on her door, she turned to her left, Harry Hewis stood there, behind him the tall, thin faced Sydney Household.

'Detective Inspector Household, boss, here for the p.m.'

'Yes, thanks, Harry.' Veronica Sleaford stood. 'Let's get scrubbed and changed. I'll see you gentlemen in the laboratory.'

Veronica Sleaford went to the female changing rooms, stripped to her underwear and climbed into green disposable coveralls, and put a white paper hat on her head which was held in place by an elasticated rim. She walked to the pathology laboratory, down a silent corridor, illuminated by filament bulbs behind thick Perspex shades.

The pathology laboratory was a rectangular room, the floor was covered by a pale cream coloured industrial grade linoleum, thoroughly cleansed with strong smelling disinfectant. Six stainless steel tables stood in a row in the centre of the room taking up the greater part of the floor space. Each table had a lip round the edge to prevent blood spilling onto the floor and was supported by a single column beneath the mid-point of the table, which was hollow to allow for the escape and proper disposal of any such blood spilled. One side of the laboratory was given over to a bench, the receptacles for instruments, and cupboards in which materials were stored. Veronica Sleaford pushed open the door to the laboratory. Harry Hewis and Sydney Household had, she found, already arrived, having scrubbed and changed into similar baggy, lightweight green disposable coveralls, and with similar white hats upon their head. A mound covered by a white sheet occupied the furthest table.

'Here already?' Veronica Sleaford indicated the mound on the table.

'Yes, boss. I phoned the mortuary, asked them to bring it up just after I gave you the mug of tea. No other business, you see.'

'Good for you, Harry' She turned to Household. 'I hope you are impressed.'

'Oh, I am.' Household gave her one of his rare smiles. Sleaford didn't know Household well, but from what she did know, she did not think of him as a man ready to smile. 'Very impressed.' He nodded to the beaming Hewis.

51

'Well, shall we begin?' Veronica Sleaford took the sheet, and with noticeable reverence, folded it back from the skeleton and handed the neatly folded sheet to Hewis, who with equal reverence, placed it on the bench. Household walked to the side of the room and stood a respectable distance from the table. He was there to observe for the police in keeping with Home Office rules, but observing does not mean taking part, and his place was away from the table, looking on, to come closer only if invited by the forensic pathologist, should anything of import be discovered.

'Do we have any photographs?'

'None,' Hewis said.

'Well, that's the first thing to do, please Harry. All round the deceased, from every angle.'

Hewis took a 35mm Nikon with a flash attachment and slowly and methodically photographed the skeleton, which lay on its back on the table, and which the mortuary staff had cleansed of soil debris. The photographs taken, Hewis retreated and placed the camera on the side. As he did so, Veronica Sleaford advanced to the table, reaching for the stainless steel anglepoise arm which was attached to the ceiling above the table. On the end of the arm was a small microphone which she switched on. When the microphone was positioned midway above the table, and just above her head height, she began the post-mortem.

'The remains are human and completely skeletal.' Veronica Sleaford spoke in perfect Received Pronunciation for the benefit of the microphone, her commentary later to be transcribed by an audio typist. 'They are of the male sex.' She paused. 'The sex is determined by the width of the sacrum which, in this case, is noted to be narrow, indicating a male. Similarly, the greater sciatic notch in the innominate bone, also the pelvis, is noted here to be deep and narrow, further indicating a male. Turning to the skull the general appearance is rugged, not smooth as would be the case if the remains were female. The skull is larger than I would expect it to be if it were female and with well marked muscle ridges. The orbits are lower in the skull than they would be if the remains were female and the nasal aperture is higher and narrower, as is usual in the male skull. Yes,' she turned to Household, 'he is a he ... he was a he in life ... an adult male. Exactly how adult, we'll soon see.'

'Any cause of death – that you can determine, I mean?' Household asked and instantly regretted it. He knew better than to push the pace of a post-mortem. It smacked of unprofessionalism. In reply, Veronica Sleaford glanced at him and smiled with raised eyebrows. He felt her response more crushing than a verbal rebuke.

'The mandible seems fused to the skull,' Veronica Sleaford continued, 'can't be by rigor mortis, all the soft tissue has decomposed.' She forced the jaw open with her hands and it gave with a soft 'crack'. 'The sockets fused over time,' she said, 'it's probably been buried for some years. A lot longer than the time taken for the flesh and organs to decompose. You could be looking at a twenty year old death here.' She glanced at Household, briefly, and then returned her attention to the skeleton. She opened the mandible. 'A large and "U" shaped palate … again, indicating a male … and a five cusp lower first molar. Yes, definitely a male.' She paused. 'Now there are two purposes to this post-mortem, we have to establish cause of death and if we can find evidence in respect of his identity. Sorry to have to cause you to wait, Inspector, but I propose to address the latter first.' She smiled at Household. Household nodded and smiled back. 'Fortunately we have an intact skeleton and so determination of height should be straightfor-ward.' She turned to Hewis. 'Can we have a tape measure please, Harry?' Harry Hewis opened a drawer in the bench and produced a retractable metal tape measure which he handed to Veronica Sleaford, who took hold of it with a clear 'thank you'. She extended the tape measure along the length of the skeleton, 'Five feet two inches … but in life he would be taller than this, marginally so, because we have to allow for scalp tissue, heel tissue, especially heel tissue and shrinkage due to cartilage loss. Possibly five feet three inches … I am sorry, but I still think in Imperial terms.'

'So do I,' Household grunted.

'The report will give the figure in metric measurements as the law now dictates … but Imperial or metric, he was a short fella … quite finely boned, definitely male, but a small chest … he was no rugby player. If he did any sport at all, it would be as a coxswain in a rowing eight.'

'I can capture the image.' Household shifted his weight from one foot to the other. He thought 'small, weedy' but further thought better of voicing his image. It would seem dismissive and

54

cynical and wouldn't at all sit well with the high minded tone with which Dr Sleaford was clearly conducting the postmortem.

'About 163 cm,' Veronica Sleaford said. 'Possibly a little more, but certainly no less. Can't claim rapid mental calculation, as you probably noticed.'

'Yes...' Household grinned. 'I have a tape measure like that at home, Imperial one side, metric on the other.'

'Very useful. Now, we address the issue of age, which is really more useful in assisting the determination of his identity. There are two ages of course, the personal age and the age of the skeleton. If the age of the skeleton is in excess of seventy years, the police lose interest, understandably so ... but in this case a zip fastener was found in the immediate vicinity of the skeleton, I believe?'

'Yes, it was.'

'And ... well, I would like the second opinion of a forensic ondontologist, but the teeth appear to me to have had dental treatment of a type which indicates modern dentistry, comfortably post Second World War – he had a lot of fillings.'

'Well if it's post Second World War, it's of interest to us.'

'Very post, I'd say. I really would like the opinion of a forensic ondontoligist, but I would say 1960s, 1970s, 1980s. Going by the dentistry alone, the age of this skeleton is between 40 and 20 years ... not much older than forty years, and not much later than twenty years.'

'Definitely one for us then.'

'I would think so.' Veronica Sleaford drummed her fingers on the lip of the stainless steel table. Sydney Household, looking on, again noticed the smell of formaldehyde in the laboratory. The smell, always strong at first, seemed to disappear, then would become briefly noticeable, and then unnoticeable once more. Harry Hewis stood silently, appearing keen to be of assistance. The two men waited for Veronica Sleaford to resume the post-mortem.

'Well,' she said, 'we turn now to the personal age of the skeleton.' She scanned the bones, as if, thought Household, reading them with a practised eye. 'There is no hard and fast rule, skeletons mature at different rates depending on the climate, sex and nutrition, females mature earlier than males. The skeletons of well-nourished persons mature faster than those of malnourished persons. The epiphyseal union in the major centres appears to be complete ... except those of the sternal clavicle and the head of the humerus, all others, the head of the femur, the greater tronchanter, the distal tibia, the acromial clavicle ... all have a completed epiphyseal union ... except those two areas which are often late in forming a union, anything up to 28 years of age in the case of the sternal clavicle.' She turned to Sydney Household. 'The overall impression is of a young man who had achieved his full stature. He wouldn't get any taller ... stopped growing in plain English. But his skeleton was not quite fully matured. He was probably twenty years old, plus or minus a couple of years. A young man, learning how to drink and anxious to lose his virginity, that

56

sort of age group.'

'I see.'

'That's only an impression, I can try and narrow it down. I do not place much faith in skull suturing, too many variables, in fact sutures will place a skeleton in its decade of life only, if one is being safe, and one would want to be completely safe.'

'Oh, one would,' Household added. He hoped he didn't sound sarcastic, it wasn't meant as a sarcastic remark.

'The best thing I could do is to remove a tooth ... it can be sliced in half horizontally, examined under a microscope by an ondontologist, it will give a personal age of the skeleton plus or minus twelve months. The problem is that it might hamper identification ... I'll leave the incisors, they will be needed in case of photo imposition ... any dental work will be needed to match with dental records, but I don't think that will be an issue in this case.'

'Oh?' Household was genuinely surprised. 'It's been very useful in the past.'

'With recently deceased persons?'

'Well, yes...'

'Assumed so. Dentists are legally obliged to retain all their records and patients charts for eleven years. After that period of time has elapsed they can be disposed of.'

'I see, didn't know that.'

'Yes. And if, as I suspect, this skeleton is at least twenty years old, and as much as forty, then it's highly unlikely that his dental records have been retained. I don't think dental records will be of use for that reason. I'll take one of the rear molars, but a healthy one, just on the off chance that his dentist was a magpie ... and with one tooth missing, dental records can still determine his identity. Your dental records are as individual as your fingerprints and DNA. I'll do that at the very end of the p.m.' Again she drummed her fingers on the table. 'Now,' she mused, more to herself than to the two attendant males, 'now we turn to the racial group of the deceased.'

Sydney Household once again shifted his weight from one foot to the other. Veronica Sleaford was, he had found, a very thorough woman, fully professional in her approach, painstakingly paying attention to detail. All very good, Household thought, all very good, but it did mean that the post-mortems she conducted were long, drawn-out and time consuming. The depressed fracture of the skull, which he could clearly see from where he stood, was clearly the cause of death but the good doctor was evidently not going to be hurried.

'This is not so clear cut as determining sex or age at death. The racial differences are not so neatly defined and have been complicated by racial mixing. Looking at the skull, I note it to be fairly shallow about the forehead and also narrow. It indicates a European: Negroid skulls are taller, Mongoloid skulls are broader. But only indicates, tall and broad skulls are not by any means unknown in the three European races of Nordic, Alpine and Mediterranean. The teeth are European or Negroid ... the Mongoloid races have shovel shaped incisors, as do a small number of

American Negroes. I can say he is not of Mongoloid race, not Chinese or Japanese or Far Eastern in origin.' She turned to Household. 'The field narrows ... determination of race has to be done by elimination, rather than positive identification and even then, I will only commit myself to a likely racial group, as would any pathologist worth their salt.'

'I see.'

'But, by eliminating Mongoloid, we are left with either European or Negroid and of the two, the skull strongly suggests European. But we must not rush our fences.'

'Clearly no danger of that,' Sydney Household thought. He was very tempted to say it, but erred on the side of diplomacy. Say what you think, but think before you say it, was a useful piece of advice he had once been given.

'The long bones seem to be short in relation to overall body length, again indicating a European person, the Negroid long bones are noticeably longer, especially in the legs. If you have ever watched sports such as athletics or basketball, you might have noticed how long the legs of the black athletes are in comparison to the legs of white athletes, or think of those long-legged black models who grace the catwalks. This gentleman, in life, did not have long legs, nor did he have long arms. No out and out clear-cut determination of his race, but I will say highly likely to be European. So, male, young adult, possibly European, lost his life between twenty and forty years of age ... oh yes, and he was of short stature and delicate build. Now we come to the cause of death. That

59

is quite simple. His skull was smashed. See?'

'Yes.' Household was both surprised and relieved that the search for the cause of death was clearly not going to be as painstaking as the search for clues as to his identity. 'It's fairly obvious, even from here.'

'There appears to be no other trauma to the skeleton. I will test for poisons, of course ... heavy poisons like cyanide, arsenic and so on will still be present even after this length of time. Heavens, even a lock of Napoleon Bonaparte's hair recently tested positive for arsenic.'

'Did it?'

'Yes, on Elba, he was convinced that the British were trying to kill him by slow poisoning ... which they were, though not deliberately. His villa was decorated with green paint and the Victorians used arsenic to dye things green, even icing on cakes, and the green paint was giving off arsenic fumes which he was inhaling. Explains why he always felt better after going for a walk outside.'

'Interesting.'

'The point of course is that heavy poisons will still be able to be traced if they are present and contributed or caused the death of this young man. Highly unlikely, of course, that method of killing someone went out with the gas lamp.'

'It may not even be murder?'

'Point.' Veronica Sleaford nodded her head in Household's direction in the universal gesture of concession. 'It appears to be the work of another though. It's difficult to imagine this type of injury being sustained accidentally ... it's very much in the manner of being struck from behind with a heavy, narrow instrument. Not just once, but perhaps three times. Certainly not self-inflicted and so if it's not murder, it's not murder because of a legal technicality, something that could be plea-bargained down to manslaughter. But this wasn't sustained accidentally, nor was it self-inflicted.'

'What sort of force would be required to do that?'

'Well, the injuries are severe ... the skull has been penetrated through to the dura – right through the bone to the soft bit. Death would have been instantaneous, so some considerable force was applied. Fractured skulls have been sustained by walking into a hard object – really, just impacting something at walking pace – but this was a hard and sustained attack from behind, a repeated chopping motion ... chop, chop, chop. Somebody wanted him dead alright, well out of the way. So the answer to your question is, a lot of force. A considerable amount of force indeed.'

'Wouldn't be easy to plea-bargain that down to manslaughter,' Household mused, 'but we won't know until we unravel the story.'

'As in all cases.'

'Indeed, and it's rarely clear cut. In my years as a police officer, I have often had more sympathy for the perpetrator than the victim in cases of murder. Not in every case, of course, but not a few either. On occasion I have thought the victim got just what they deserved, but I've had to arrest and charge someone who's often never committed any form of crime before, for doing something I could easily have been driven to do if I was in their shoes, and watched them go down for life for it.'

'Yes, I know what you mean. There but for the grace of God...'

'As you say.'

'Well, that will be the conclusion of this post-mortem. Death due to severe head injury. The person was male, short and slightly built, possibly European, in his early twenties when he died, and he died between 20 and 40 years ago. Possibly in the summer months ... but there I tread on your toes ... here I enter your department.'

'Oh, tread and enter all you like.'

Veronica Sleaford smiled. She appreciated Sydney Household's attitude of all help gratefully received. Other police officers she had met had jealously guarded their area of responsibility and closed their minds to good advice and what she had believed were beneficial observations. Household was clearly different, and she liked him for that, even if he was distant towards her.

'Well, it has just occurred to me, not a lot of clothing was found in the grave, just a zip fastener, and a few buttons and decayed soles of shoes.'

'That's correct.'

'Well it occurred to me that one reason for there not being a lot of clothing in the grave was because he wasn't wearing much when he died. High summer in the Fens ... lightweight shoes, jeans and a shirt. If he had been killed in the winter there would possibly be traces of clothing, heavier footwear, buttons or wooden toggles from winter coats, that sort of thing.'

'Yes,' Household nodded and smiled, 'that's a fair observation.'

'I'll test for poisons, just for form's sake, but I don't expect to find any trace of same.' Veronica Sleaford looked down at the skeleton. 'Early deaths, especially murder victims ... there's a poignancy here...'

'I know what you mean.'

'What potential he might have had. Was he fated to meet the end he met? Would he have gone on to do great things in life? Who knows?'

'Who indeed?'

'Well, I'll fax my report to you as soon as it's been word processed. Ought to be with you tomorrow.'

Sydney Household drove back to Parkside, to the headquarters of the East Anglia Police. He parked his car at the rear of the building and entered by the 'staff only' entrance. He checked his pigeonhole and was relieved to find it empty, then he signed himself in at the book kept behind the enquiry desk, at that moment staffed by a very young-looking constable in a crisply starched white shirt, serge trousers and shiny black shoes, who snapped, 'Afternoon, sir', as Household entered his space.

'Afternoon.' Household wrote 'in' and '12.05' beside his name on the sheet. He was pleased to be back before Perigo's shift started at two p.m. The man, he thought, clearly had a chip on his shoulder about something, and like many people he also seemed to view Household as distant and aloof. Not unusual feedback, but something Household never felt himself to be. He took the stairs in nimble steps, scuffing his soles on each step, and walked down the CID corridor to the open plan office in which his desk stood. The only recognition of his seniority was to have a corner desk, with the thrusting young graduate entry Perigo occupying the desk in the adjacent corner. The only recognition of his age was that he should have the corner by the window, which was a mixed blessing, he had found. Yes, the window position, the view across Parker's Piece from his chair was his, but any CID officer with idle moments would come and stand at the window, towering over his desk, nudging, but not actually invading, his personal space. In other nicks, men of his designation had their own offices – but not in this nick. In this nick open plan was the name of the game, unless you happened to be a very senior officer.

He sat at his desk and glanced round the room. At that moment he was the sole occupant, other CID officers on the six till two turn were evidently out or at lunch. The desk tops were untidy, files and sheets of paper, a copy of the early edition of the *Cambridge Evening News* and a much creased and crumpled edition of that day's *Daily Mail* hung half on and half off Penny Wiseman's desk – clearly she had returned from Aberdeen after interviewing the 'Panther' victim. He felt Perigo should have made more progress on that case, but it was not his place to judge, he told himself, and then he smiled as a joke he had heard came to mind, 'Never judge a man until you have walked a mile in his shoes – then you'll know you were right about him all along, and you get to keep the shoes ...' He glanced at the wall to his right. The Police Mutual calendar and a few, a very few postcards; the boss allowed a little decoration on the wall. He had two cards only, both sent to him at his place of work by his brother, one from Australia showing Ayres Rock by night and the other showing the Manhattan skyline with the World Trade Centre's twin towers clearly visible. This last he kept, intending to take home and put in a frame. He thought that, somewhat sadly, postcards which showed the Twin Towers might become collectors' pieces. If not, the card would still be of interest to any grandchild that might one day delight him and enrich his life. He took the file on the discovered skeleton, by then just a file number – 206/6, the two hundred and sixth open case that month – and wrote a record of his witnessing the post-mortem, and Dr Sleaford's verbal feedback. He then left the office, walked further along the CID corridor and knocked on the boss's door.

'Come.' The reply was prompt, if a little curt. Household pushed open the varnished plywood door.

'Ah ... Sydney,' Atkins smiled and folded that day's edition of the *Daily Telegraph* neatly and placed it on the side of his desk. 'Come in and take a pew. One serial abductor on the loose is sufficient, a murder we don't need. Was it murder?'

'Looks like it, sir.' Household glanced round Atkins' office, taking it all in with his police officer's practised eye, in one sweep. The sheer neatness of it was always the over-riding impression, nothing seemed to be out of place, not the

65

glass-fronted bookcase within which the books were arranged according to the length of their spines, tallest on the edges of the shelf, the smallest ones in the centre or the photograph of Atkins' wife and children on his desk, angled so that, at that moment, Household could also see them from his vantage point in the upholstered office chair in which he sat. Atkins himself was tall and well-built, even for a police officer, approaching retirement but looking fitter and healthier than many men of his age. He alternated three suits, the blue, the grey and the brown. That day it was the grey, but he always wore the police officer's tie, blue, with candles burning at both ends. He wore an expression which Household had always found stern and uncompromising. Household shifted in his chair and relayed the post-mortem findings to the Chief Inspector.

'Just awaiting the age, then?'

'Yes, sir,' Household paused, 'and the results of the poison trace, but as Dr Sleaford said, that will almost certainly be negative.'

'Never known it at all in my career,' Atkins snorted. 'What is your next move?'

'Missing persons file I think, sir. There's a huge time window during which he could have been murdered, but we have been given a good idea of his appearance ... short, slight build, probably European in terms of race ... enough to go on if he was reported to us as a mis per. He could of course have been murdered in South Wales and his body buried in the Fens ... if I draw a blank in our mis per files, I'll look into the possibility of a facial reconstruction. The National Missing

Persons Helpline is unlikely to be able to help us, only established in 1992, long after our boy would have been reported missing.'

'What did the owner of the land tell you?'

'Nothing yet, sir. He's still to be interviewed.'

Atkins raised an eyebrow as if to say, 'Really, why not?'

'Limited resources, boss. A lame excuse, but it happens to be the case.' Household, feeling growing exasperation, felt the urge to hold his hands up and say, 'There's one, and there's the other', or equally cynically, 'I've only two, one at the end of either arm', but he remained diplomatic. 'Dominic Perigo's been given all the bodies for the Panther inquiry ... I would like to have some assistance on this one, sir.'

'Difficult to see who I can spare, Sydney. I appreciate your problem, but the Panther has to be caught, he's active now, terrorising the city ... in a few weeks time all the students will be back, more young, female flesh for him.'

'He hasn't killed, sir, and I am dealing with a murder here.'

'He hasn't killed yet, Sydney. He hasn't killed yet, that we know of, but all the indications are that his violence is escalating, the last victim was badly knocked about. Learned advice is that his next victim, and we have to assume that there will be a next victim, will probably be his first murder. Yours is a one off...'

'That we know of.' Household echoed Atkins.

'Accepted. But it is anything up to forty years old. The perpetrator could very easily be deceased by now. If they are not, and are as old as the victim, they are going to be in their sixties, hardly a threat to the community.'

Household bit his tongue. The oldest known murderer in recent British history was ninety years old. People never stop being a threat to the community. He managed to remain silent.

'What else are you working on?'

'Burglaries in Romsey Town, sir, and thefts from motor vehicles.'

'Hardly high pressure police work is it, Sydney?'

'What are you implying, sir? That I am not up to the job?' Household flushed with anger.

'I wouldn't put it as strongly as that, Sydney, but you are getting on now, as I am. In fact, we are both the same age ... time to let the young thrusters get on with it.'

'Young thrusters ... like Perigo?'

'Yes ... like Perigo, graduate entrant, he's nearly twenty years your junior.'

'And my rank!'

'The inference is that he has energy which you, and I, no longer have ... that's why he has the Panther inquiry, not you, that's why he has the bodies to help him, not you.'

'He should have had a result by now.'

'Would you have had a result?' Atkins snarled the question. 'You think you would have had a result? Not a lot to go on ... four deeply traumatised young women, not easy to obtain information from such people. I will not discuss my officer's performance with their peers, but I will say I like Perigo, he's bright, he's single-minded, and he's serious-minded, all useful qualities for a police officer.'

'He's not a team player ... he doesn't go for a beer with the crew.'

'Enough!' Atkins stared at Household. 'I told you, this conversation is wandering into uncomfortable areas. I will not discuss my staff with their peers. Perigo doesn't have to go for a drink with the crew if he doesn't want to, if he wants to be a private person he can be. He's got the Panther inquiry, and the bodies ... you can crack on with your body in the bog by yourself. Thank you for appraising me about the p.m. result.' He picked up his newspaper and began to read it.

Household, having left Atkins' office, and closing the door behind him just gently enough to avoid being accused of slamming it, ate alone in the canteen, after which he went to the basement of the building. It suited him to be alone. Atkins' attitude stung him. Atkins' words rang in his ears. Spending an hour or two sifting through dusty files would suit his mood.

He took the lift to the second level basement and exited at 'Productions'. He nodded to the slightly overweight and balding constable who sat at the duty desk. The man, thought Household, had, like himself, been taken out of front line duties and had become the keeper of the void, down here for eight hours a day, little human company, and no natural light. Probably better than school crossing duty, though. There could, in Household's view, be little more demeaning for a police officer than to be set the task of escorting children across the road at the entrance to the school gates.

'Can I help you, sir?' The constable had a warm and pleasant attitude. When he smiled, gold-capped fillings flashed. He had a strong East Anglian accent. Household couldn't place it, it wasn't Cambridge though, probably more out towards the coast.

'Mis per files, prior to computerisation?'

'Dark ages, sir.' The constable stood.

'When were the files computerised?'

'That I can't tell you, sir ... about the 1980s I think, that's about the earliest date I've seen on a computer printout. The collator is the man to ask about that. If you'd follow me, sir?'

The constable, who revealed that he had a stiff leg when he walked, which belied the reason why he had been consigned to the void, escorted Household down a long, narrow walkway, at either side of which lesser aisles ran off at ninety degrees and were lined with metal shelving, on which were production bags, all labelled with specific case numbers. Many productions are kept even after a case has gone to trial and a conviction obtained, because of the possibility of an appeal. Only when the sentence has been served is the 'production' or 'productions' in question destroyed, or returned to any rightful owner, unless they have some relevance to any other inquiry or unless they have sufficient interest to be worthy of becoming an exhibit in the 'Black Museum' which every police headquarters keeps. The constable stopped at the entrance to one aisle, the shelves on either side of which contained not 'productions' in cellophane bags, but files, many evidently very old.

'How far do you want to go back, sir?'

'Up to forty years, no earlier than twenty years.'

'Well, twenty years and you're nudging the time when files were being computerised for the first time. Forty years, well, then you're into the days of the Cambridgeshire Constabulary. These are the "mis per" files, not many really, going back seventy years, after which they are destroyed, the mis per presumed by then to be no longer with us. As you know, sir, not many files, but each represents a mystery, each represents a family in daily, permanent anguish.' The constable patted the shelf. 'They start at this end.' He took a file and opened it, 'Sara Bullwood, reported missing January 1985 ... nice looking girl by this photograph, and still missing. As they all are, otherwise the files would not be on this shelf ... and that looks like the answer to your question, sir, this is clearly a mis per file opened before computerisation. So the mis pers were computerised some time after this date. The oldest go back to the nineteen thirties.'

'Well I don't want to go back that far,' Household advised the constable. His warmth was proving a very efficient antidote to Atkins' offhand unpleasantness.

'Leave you to it then, sir,' the constable smiled. 'I'll be at my desk if you need to ask anything.'

'Appreciated, thanks.' The file on Sara Bullwood intrigued him and he removed it from the shelf as an indulgence, a curiosity to satisfy before beginning his own research. She had, after all, achieved the distinction in her disappearance, and by this time, in excess of fifteen years later, her death, of being the last reported 'mis per' whose details had not been entered onto the computerised record system. In life she had been a thin-faced girl of only thirteen years when she was reported missing. She seemed to have a sweet tempered smile, though was probably very self conscious of the metal brace she had to wear on her upper teeth. The file detailed interviews with the parents, both rapidly eliminated as suspects, details of house to house inquiries and searches of houses occupied by single men who lived alone, all clearly without 'a result' in police speak. Local fields had been swept by lines of police and civilian volunteers, woodland had been searched, known sex offenders taken in for questioning, all to no avail. The search and the inquiry was wound down and eventually shelved. All that could be done to find the missing schoolgirl had been done. The only thing then was to wait until her body was found, if ever. That left her parents, grandparents, and any siblings in a state of perpetual anguish, not knowing what had happened to 'our' Sara. Especially difficult, Household always thought, on cold nights in the winter when the east wind slices across the Fens. The thought that Sara must be out there somewhere, in that weather ... and as the years went by, the realisation that they would never see their daughter/sister again sunk in, and later there must have been acceptance of that dreadful fact.

And all these files from January 1985, back to the pre-war days, all told the same story, all of families left in a state of terrible mental torture, of not knowing. Household always felt that must be the worst, the not knowing. He knew he would find it difficult to carry on if anything happened to either of his children, but their disappearance, he thought, would be worse somehow than the certainty of their early death. Especially as the days melted into weeks ... and the certainty of their death had to be accepted. Even then there was still the awfulness of not knowing what had happened to them. Had they been murdered? Had they died by some misadventure and by some ill luck or fate their body hidden from view? Was their death, as the haunting song has it, 'quick and clean, or slow and obscene?' The tortured relatives would never know unless the body was found, and even then, the full story might never properly unfold. He glanced at the address, Romsey Road in Romsey Town. Solid folk, Household thought, what the sociologists would call 'working class'. Romsey Town was still a solidly working class area despite attempts at gentrification by trendy leftie university types who buy in the town, rather than in the fashionable areas of Chesterton, or Cherry Hinton, or popular villages south of the city. He put the file back in its place on the shelf and began to take the files off the shelves one by one. There were, he counted, fifty-three to look at, fifty-three people who disappeared in the Cambridge area from the mid 1980s back to the 1930s who were still missing and by now had to be presumed dead. Others who had been reported missing in that time had been found alive, or their corpses had been discovered, or they had contacted their families to say they were alive and well but wouldn't be returning, having started a new life, caused by some dreadful family rift, or by disapproval of a fiancée or a fiancé, or by shame for some deed committed. People disappear for a variety of reasons, and between 1935 and 1985 fifty-three persons disappeared in the Cambridge area and were never seen again. About one per year.

The name of the person whose body was found in the meadows near Bottisham was, Household thought, likely to be Edward De Beer. He didn't know when the person in question had lost his life, or had been reported missing, because the two are not necessarily the same, as the current 'Panther' case was showing. Girls abducted, kept against their will, and then released approximately one month, or in one case, six weeks later. He did, though, know the sex and likely physical appearance of the deceased. Crucially, perhaps most crucial of all, he knew his approximate age and likely racial group. Further he only had to go back as far as the 1950s, when zip fasteners began to replace buttons in jeans and trousers. And of the open missing persons files from the 1950s to the mid 1980s, only Edward De Beer's file seemed to be a match, and a very strong match indeed. Household didn't allow his mind to close. There was a long way to go before the remains were identified as those of Edward De Beer, they could equally be those of a luckless person murdered outside the area so that consequently the relevant missing persons file would be held at a 'foreign' police station. It was though, a promising lead, a definite line of inquiry to be followed. Household leaned on the shelves and read the file.

Edward De Beer, by the photograph provided by his family, had had a serious looking countenance. He looked to be intelligent, a domed forehead, a neatly trimmed beard, a university scarf wrapped round his neck and draped over his shoulder, a white pullover and an ex-military greatcoat completed the image. His height was given as 5'4" in those pre-metric days, which accorded within reason with Dr Sleaford's measurement of the corpse. He was 22 years of age when he died and a student at Cambridge Tech, as it was then known. Now the institution is much expanded and has the loftier title of Anglia Polytechnic University. Edward De Beer had an address which caused Household to smile because of its coincidence. Edward De Beer's last address was on Warkworth Terrace. The view from Edward De Beer's window, if he had had a front room, would have been the side of Sydney Household's place of work. The exact date of Edward De Beer's disappearance was not known, but the alarm appeared to have been sparked when the owner of the house did not get her rent on the day it was due, waited for a few days, and when nearly a week had elapsed, and she being certain that Edward De Beer had not skipped off without paying his rent because his clothing and books and sundry possessions were still in his room, contacted his college to ask if they knew where Edward was. The college replied that they had been concerned by his disappearance, he hadn't signed in, he hadn't attended tutorials and none of his peers knew of his whereabouts. By the time the landlady had contacted the college, more out of concern for her unpaid rent than Edward De Beer's welfare, the college had already alerted his parents, who had by then notified the police of his disappearance. By then he could have been missing for up to five days. The last time he had signed in was the Friday, in the afternoon. There had been no known reason for his disappearance. He was described by his tutor as a 'struggling but not a problem student'. He had disappeared in the last week of the Easter term in his final year. Into thin air, it seemed. His home address was in Norwich. Household didn't know the city of Norwich, though 'Norwich Bitter' was by far and away his favourite ale, so De Beer's family address of Railway Cottages meant little to him. Household thanked the constable, signed out and went back up to his desk in the CID room. By the time he returned, Dominic Perigo had arrived for the 2-10 shift. The two men exchanged cold and perfunctory pleasantries as Household walked across the floor from the doorway to his desk. He sat at his desk and wrote up the result of his visit to productions, and the reason for his belief that the deceased was, in all likelihood, one Edward De Beer of Norwich, 22 years old when he died.

Veronica Sleaford knew little about psychology, but she thought Sojourner's room healthy. It was full, all space utilised, there was an order in the 'busy' feeling of the room, the posters on the wall, the poems which clearly moved her and which she had written in her own neat, full and well-rounded handwriting, and on a shelf was her collection of mugs with amusing prints. Veronica particularly liked the mug which had a print showing a building labelled 'Acme School for the Gifted', with a man pushing a door marked 'Pull'. She glanced out of Sojourner's bedroom window, across Chesterton Road to the cultivated and manicured expanse that was Jesus Green, the bandstand and the concrete square on which she had seen the dancers in period costume just that morning. Veronica Sleaford turned once again to the decorations on her daughter's wall; a new addition was a list of quotes. 'Where did you get these from?'

'Chat rooms.'

'Oh, I do wish you'd be careful with those, you know I don't like you going in them.'

'I find my own level, Mummy,' Sojourner Sleaford looked up from the book she was reading. 'Some are pretty weird, but I only go into the ones I like the look of.'

'Weird.' Veronica Sleaford smiled at her daughter, who at seventeen was long of limb, slender, mild of manner and still had not lost that childish sparkle in her eyes. Veronica Sleaford was very, very proud of her daughter. 'That's mild from what I have heard, extremely sick in the head is probably a better description. I understand that 60% of the net is pornographic.'

'Well 40% isn't, by definition. And it's that 40% that I use. What's pornographic about Cambridge Chats? I go in there, meet someone ... have a chat ... perhaps we meet up, but it won't interfere with my studies.'

'I am gratified to hear it.'

'How can I not be motivated to study, growing up in this city, with professional parents?'

'Have you thought about which university you want to apply to?' Veronica Sleaford sipped her tea. 'You'll have to make the choice after the summer vacation.'

'I know it won't be Cambridge. I have to leave home.'

Veronica Sleaford nodded. 'Fully understand that. I remember the thrill of leaving home to come to this university, my little room in New Hall, first time I had a room of my own, shared with your aunt Elizabeth when I was growing up. A three-bedroom house doesn't offer a lot of space for three children, and our brother Thomas had the little box room. Poor Tom – he was always complaining he was the eldest but he had the smallest room, and had to give way to girls – put his nose out of joint for the rest of his life. Black men are very traditional in their thinking, as you may be discovering. Few "new age" men are black.'

'There's a few at college like that.'

'So you are finding out?'

'Yes,' Sojourner smiled, 'but I am a "new age" woman and they soon learn that they won't get anywhere with me if they have conservative attitudes.'

'Good,' Veronica Sleaford smiled too. 'Always occupy the moral high ground wherever you go, and be seen to go there, and do that even if the moral high ground is the underdog.'

'Yes, Mummy.'

'So, university?'

'Durham.'

'You're decided?'

'Well, I have decided to apply, make it my first choice, got to get the grades, got to impress the interview panel, competition will be fierce.'

'Yes, it's a very popular university.'

'Second choice?'

'Newcastle, Manchester ... don't know yet.'

'The frozen north?'

'Why not? I have never been north of Cambridge in my life it's changed a lot since George Orwell wrote *The Road to Wigan Pier* and, personally speaking, I never believed that there are still mammoths in the Pennines, despite what some southerners would have you think.'

'Independent thinking, that's what I like.' Veronica Sleaford turned again to the latest wall decorations on her daughter's bedroom wall. 'So these gems all come from chat rooms?'

'Yes ... they're in people's profiles, click onto a name, check out where they live, how old they are, and read their favourite quote. Some are clearly homespun philosophy, others are quotes ... like the one at the bottom.'

'"If I can see the smoke from my neighbour's home",' Veronica Sleaford read aloud, '"I am too close", Daniel Boone. You like the idea of solitude? Don't know how healthy that is for a girl of your age.'

'I think it was the vision of space and woodland that is conjured by the quote that I like.'

Veronica Sleaford smiled inwardly. At just seventeen, her daughter had clearly mastered the language, more so than she had when that age.

'"Dance as if nobody is watching",' she said. 'I like that one.'

'That sounds a bit homespun, but I like it ... well, it wouldn't be up there if I didn't like it.'

'What is it saying, to you, I mean?'

'Well I think it's saying so long as your source of fun or amusement, or joy, harms no one ... then don't let what other people might think concern you, and what harm is done by dancing?'

'"Dance as if nobody is watching",' Veronica Sleaford re-read the quote. 'Yes, I like it too. In fact, I like it very much indeed.' She read other quotes, reading them not for herself but for what it was in them that appealed to her daughter, and for what it told her about her daughter. Some she found more cynical, 'Life is about getting up one more time than you are knocked down'; 'If you are going through hell, keep going', and were not of the state of mind she wanted her daughter to foster, but equally she was pleased that Sojourner was clearly shedding naivety. Other quotes had a common-sense and good advice quality: 'The toes you step on today might belong to the arse you've got to kiss tomorrow' ... well, the language was not to her liking, but there was no denying the implicit message – you never know when you are going to need a favour or from whom. Then she read aloud; 'He was born with a gift for laughter, and a sense that the world was mad.'

'Yes, I like that one too,' Sojourner said from behind *A Bond Maiden's Tale*, a gift from her mother, a reprinted autobiography of a female slave in the ante-bellum south of the United States. 'It reads like a quote from a man of words

80

but the author wasn't acknowledged. I don't know why I like it ... it reads beautifully, but there's something more.'

'Eccentricity,' Veronica Sleaford glanced out of the open window. 'I like eccentrics ... the English are very good at producing them and this city has more than its fair share. I confess I include myself in that category.'

'A cutter-upper of bodies. It is a strange way to earn a living,' Sojourner laughed.

'Yes ... you know, you and I must do something ... I mean we must do something together before you go away.'

'Well OK, Mummy, but I don't want to go to the cottage.'

'I know better than to try and drag a teenager to the country ... but something. We won't be mother and daughter for much longer.'

'Mummy, we'll always be mother and daughter ... you've let me have a lot of independence when I was growing up, this is no time to get possessive.' She stood and embraced her mother. 'We can do things together. Tomorrow is Saturday, let's go for a walk. Would you like that? That walk we used to do, out through Grantchester Meadows ... we can do that tomorrow.'

'Yes.' Veronica Sleaford returned her daughter's embrace. She felt close to tears but restrained her emotions. 'Yes, I think I'd like that very much. The weather's holding. It will be a good day for it.'

It was a slow drive home for Sydney Household, at his election. At three p.m. the traffic was light. He drove at a steady pace, enjoying it, glancing occasionally at the flat fields at either side of the road, but more, he drove slowly so as to extend the journey time. He did not want to go home, he did not want to reach his house. For him, his only source of space was to drive to and from work. He knew that what awaited him was a feisty, nay, icy reception from his wife, distance from his teenagers, and tension after the evening meal coming from his wife which would drive him out to the pub, in further search of space. That was exactly what happened.

The Panther slunk and slithered through quiet Romsey Town, creeping silently in the jogging shoes, dressed in dark clothing, panther-black, with eyes that were used to seeing in the dark. He glanced up at the rooftops, silhouetted against the summer sky, his vision hampered by the lights, too many really, streetlights and the lights from houses because it still lacked midnight and many folk were still up, watching the end of a late film, or preparing for bed. The Panther walked, conserving his strength and energy but was ready to break into a harmless looking jog if he heard someone approach. Tonight he was on edge, alert, more alert than normal, because he was not merely going to Thoday Street to move his van, because tonight he was going to pounce. Over the last few days the urge had grown, getting stronger by the hour, even the women at work had seemed like potential victims. Had to be careful there, had to be very careful, women are like that, have an intuition that men don't possess, have an insight, they can see things, a look in the eye that a man wouldn't notice ... these things the Panther told himself, and told himself repeatedly throughout the previous week. Now it was Friday night, as the weekend approaches, people may be less diligent, more relaxed. He turned into narrow Thoday Street and saw his van ahead of him, gleaming, highly polished in the spill of the street lamp and with the distinctive yellow square painted on the offside door. The yellow square was a chance he decided to continue to take ... that and keeping the vehicle clean and polished. He continued to hope that such a distinctive vehicle would not attract suspicion. He approached the vehicle, walked once round it, checking the tyres and for any sign of a break-in. Tyres fine, vehicle secure. The Panther unlocked the door and sat behind the steering wheel. He felt potent. He was in hunting mood, hungry ... thirsty even, stronger than hunger ... he thirsted for a victim. There would be one, this night there would be one ... if not, tomorrow night or even quiet-after-the-weekend-dull-Monday night. But something told him that tonight he would have a victim. He turned the key and started the engine. He let it idle for a few moments, then engaged first gear and drove slowly away. That, he reasoned, was the other key thing, no hurried movements, no screeching tyres or protesting engine, nothing to make the lieges prick up their ears and take notice of something out of the ordinary. Just a motor vehicle starting up and being driven calmly away, a sound heard and forgotten. The Panther drove back onto Mill Road, away from the city centre. At the bottom of Mill Road he turned right into

Perne Road, driving all the while a calm thirty miles per hour, not wanting to attract attention and, at the same time, scanning for prey. At the traffic roundabout at the end of Perne Road he hesitated, glanced in his rear view mirror ... the lights of the next car behind him were still someway off, no need to hurry ... left down into Cherry Hinton, right up towards Hills Road, or straight on? All quiet, all dark ... probably too many people still about in Cherry Hinton. He glanced again in the rear view mirror ... the car behind was getting closer, so he drove forwards to avoid giving the impression that he was loitering. He drove straight on after the roundabout, the car behind, he saw with some relief, seemed to be upon a pressing errand and turned to the left and was driven hurriedly away. The Panther drove down suburban Mowbray Road, right into Queen Edith's Way, across Hills Road and into leafy, straight as a die, very aptly-named, he thought, Long Road. Leaving the towering Addenbrookes Hospital behind him, lights burning bright, he continued a slow progress and then he saw his prey.

She was a young looking woman, dark hair, loud yellow jacket, jeans, heels, she walked with her head down as if troubled, he thought, doing the right thing by walking towards the oncoming traffic, but the heels were a mistake ... can't run in heels. She had walked past Sedly Taylor Road, there were houses on either side, she could be going to any one of those, she could at that moment be a matter of a few seconds' walking time from safety. Equally ... equally, she could still have a long walk ahead of her. The Panther drove beyond her without altering his speed. She didn't glance at him as he passed, enabling him to look at her. She did indeed seem pre-occupied, hands thrust deep into the pockets of her bright coloured jacket, walking with angry steps, in the manner of a woman who had just fallen out with her partner and felt she was the aggrieved party ... whatever, importantly for the Panther, she seemed to him to be so preoccupied that she was taking little notice of the world around her. He drove on, continually checking for her in his side and rear-view mirror. She continued walking, head down, hard, short, furious footfall. The Panther turned right into Rutherford Road, turning the vehicle so that it was parked facing outwards towards Long Road.

His heart beat faster.

His palms sweated.

He pulled on his gloves and reached for the metal bar he kept on the passenger seat. He slowly and silently got out of the vehicle. His plan was simple: walk up behind her, knock her over the head once, perhaps twice, so long as no cars were coming, move the body into a temporary place of concealment, some person's front garden, a bus shelter never used after the last bus had gone, then return for the van, hurriedly pick her up and carry her into the rear of the van and drive away. He'd done it four times previously, and four times it had gone like clockwork.

He walked to the edge of Rutherford Road and slid into the shadows. A car passed, an owl hooted, something in the shrubs rustled. The woman's ill-tempered sounding footfall came into his earshot, giving no impression of slowing to turn into a gateway, but rather as if choosing a measured pace in anticipation of a long walk home.

Closer.

Closer.

Click, click, click...

She approached the corner, the Panther gripped the cosh, she stepped into Rutherford Road... The Panther's heart thumped, she wasn't going straight on after all. She turned into where he was lying in wait, ready to follow her. She saw him, she stopped, she gasped, she held brief eye contact, she was about to scream, the cosh was moving before the Panther knew what he was doing, crashing down on her forehead, she buckled at the knees, he held her and swung her round and laid her in the shadows. He too stepped back into the shadows and stood over her body. Another car passed, without slowing. The Panther glanced at the occupants who seemed to be in jovial conversation with each other. Clearly they had seen nothing of the attack. He glanced round him, houses in all directions, large, prestigious suburban homes, a few lights showing in upstairs rooms but there seemed no reaction from within any house to his attack, to the taking of his prey. It had, after all, been carried out in near total silence. He walked back to the van, started it and drove it slowly forward until it was opposite where the woman lay. He got out, opened the rear door, walked to where his prey lay motionless but moaning softly. He glanced up and down Long Road; no cars were approaching, so he knelt and picked up his victim and carried her into the van, closing the rear doors firmly but quietly. He returned to the scene of the attack, picked up the woman's handbag and carried it back to the van. In the van he turned on the headlights; the scene of the attack seemed neat, with nothing out of place, no sign of a struggle ... nothing to say that it was here, at this very spot, that the woman had been spirited away. From start to finish, it had all taken less than sixty seconds. Just as the Panther liked it. He held the woman's handbag, wiping it with an oily rag and then placed it on the passenger seat.

The Panther drove slowly and sedately back into Cambridge; it was still busy, still a few vehicles on the road, not in the dead hours when any motor vehicle might look suspicious, especially vans, which the police were on the lookout for. He turned into Mill Road and followed it to the roundabout at Parker's Piece, where he glanced wryly at the police station just ahead and a little to his right. He drove down East Road with the new buildings of Anglia Polytechnic University to his right, older terraced buildings to his left. A few people walked the pavements, mostly in pairs, one or two lonely looking individuals, a group of rowdy, drunken youths. The Panther negotiated the roundabout of the junction of Newmarket Road and drove over the bridge. At the far end of the bridge he slowed and turned sharp left and parked the van beneath the bridge, older housing behind him, a medium-rise block of flats to his right, mostly in darkness, again one or two had lights burning. It was, he thought, too risky to do what he had planned, all it needed was one person whom he couldn't see, but who could see him from behind curtains in a darkened room. Someone who couldn't sleep on a warm June night. The more he thought, the more he realised that making this turn into this cul-de-sac by the river was a bad move. He glanced in the rear of the van. The young woman, his prey, lay still, but she could come to at any time. He didn't want to get out of the van and risk being seen, but he knew he had to assume he was being watched, and he therefore had to give some reason for turning into the road which led nowhere but the river. He put on the baseball cap with the peak low and to the front and got out of the van. He walked to the block of flats and pretended to press the button at the controlled entry system. Then he waited until he had counted to one hundred. Then he walked back to the van, started it, turned it round and rejoined Elizabeth Way.

Slipping, slipping, slipping. He tried to calm himself but he felt he had slipped up; trying to get rid of the handbag in the river was a sign of panic. Hopefully, anyone watching would have thought he was calling on a friend in the flats and, unable to get an answer from the controlled entry, had returned to his vehicle and driven away. Not enough there to seem suspicious. He hoped.

He joined Milton Road and followed it out of the city, past the Science Park on his left and the sewage works on his right. He drove round the roundabout and joined the A10, out through Milton towards Landbeach. Shortly after leaving Milton he turned off the road onto a rough track, a 'road unadopted' where stood a bungalow. It was of 1920s design, rounded bay windows, a wooden porch, wooden railings round a veranda over which the roof extended, a rambling garden. The man turned the van into a driveway at the side of the bungalow where he halted the vehicle. He switched off the engine and leaned back in the seat. Behind him the woman let out a low groan. He turned and saw her put her hands to her forehead, to where he had struck her with the iron bar. No permanent damage, he thought, that was good. She had startled him and he had struck her harder than he had intended. He wound the window down and listened. All seemed silent ... another owl hooted, he heard the high-pitched squeaks of the bats. It was too dark to see them, although he pictured them, small, darting, flitting creatures. Importantly, there was no human sound. The nearest house was a few hundred yards away, beyond the stand of trees. No lights shone from that house, but he continued to listen. He knew that there was a strong tradition of poaching in Cambridgeshire and knew it was not unknown for poachers to come quite near the house, setting for hares in the wood. Eventually the Panther left the vehicle, walked to the rear, opened the door and pulled the semi-conscious young woman out and into his arms. He carried her to the back door of the bungalow, and holding her in his arms, he fumbled for the house key with his free hand. He unlocked the door and carried the woman to one of the back rooms of the house and laid her down upon the floor. She was groaning still, but louder, longer, coming from unconsciousness to semi-consciousness. He carefully removed her clothing and chained her wrists behind her, then threaded the chain to a bolt in the skirting board and affixed it with a third small padlock. He placed a homemade gag in her mouth and covered her with an unzipped sleeping bag. He went back to the van and collected her handbag ... he would have to bury it. That had been a close call. Had he been seen stopping the van and walking from it to the river, at the side of the boatyard, and throwing the bag into the river, that would have been very suspicious and how many vans are there in Cambridgeshire with a large yellow square painted on the rear door? Not many. Not many at all.

The Panther returned to the house and placed the handbag on top of the pile of clothing he had taken from the woman. Then he stripped and slid under the sleeping bag beside her, holding her protectively in his arms. Always, the previous women had stiffened as he did that, but she was semi-conscious, and seemed relaxed.

He liked that. It was often many, many days before they relaxed, but this woman, because she wasn't fully conscious, relaxed immediately. Women never relaxed immediately with him, some never at all, but she did and he felt a flood of appreciation, of gratitude.

He would ensure that she did not suffer when she died.

3

'He was our first born.' The man stood with the aid of a stout wooden walking stick and a spring-loaded seat in an upright chair.

'Can I help?' Household asked.

'No ... I want to do it, my doctor tells me to take every opportunity to move, no matter how little it is, all helps to stop the joints from stiffening.'

The man walked with slow but steady steps to the mantelpiece and took a framed photograph from amid a line of similarly framed photographs of young looking persons, two males and two females, and handed it to Household. 'That's Edward.' He turned and retraced his steps and sat thankfully, it seemed to Household, in the orthopaedic chair.

'Thank you, sir.' Household studied the photograph, pleasingly it showed Edward De Beer's teeth. That was the first thing he looked for, the teeth, and in this photograph Edward De Beer was grinning, open lips, teeth not quite clenched, a warm look in his eyes. That was the second thing Household looked for, the eyes, this photograph was full frontal, the eyes were clear as crystal. This photograph could be super-imposed on the photograph of the skull of the skeleton found in the meadows. If the eye orbits and teeth aligned it would be sufficient to prove identity without the costly and time consuming need to rebuild the face in clay on a cast of the skull. The man in the photograph appeared to be in his early twenties, he had a neatly trimmed beard and moustache, neatly kept dark hair, all as in the photograph in the police file. He looked to be healthy and happy. Household asked if he could keep the photograph.

'Yes, if it will help you. And if you'll return it, I don't have many of young Edward. Killed his mother.'

'I'm sorry?' Household looked round the man's house. It was, he thought, in a word, cluttered, but neat and tidy and clean, and smelling only slightly musty. With age, Household noted, a person's home assumes a musty smell. The window behind the elderly man looked out onto a small garden with rich foliage and flowers in full bloom. But the house and garden could not be tended by the frail Mr De Beer. He clearly had help with both.

'Girl Mary, my wife ... she pined for young Edward, as any mother would, as any parent would. I pined as well, it would be better if he had been killed in an accident, or even murdered. See, that would have given us a body to bury, we could have said goodbye to him, had a gravestone to visit. But the not knowing ... there one day, full of life, talking about his future, then the letters, the postcards stopped coming, the phone calls as well. He was a bit lazy, we always appreciated something written but he would sometimes just pick up the phone in passing, and chat for the two minutes or so that his money allowed. It was them we first noticed stop arriving ... then no written word ... phoned his digs, his landlady said he wasn't at home but his things were in his room and she wanted her rent. All she was worried about was her rent, our son was missing and all she wanted was her money. It was then that we knew something was wrong. Like I told you, one way or the other Edward would contact us three or four times a week, even if it was just a phone call. Then the college phoned us. It was then we went to the police.'

'Suddenly all contact stopped?'

'Aye ... suddenly. You know I think Girl Mary felt something. Strange things happen in life ... the clock that stops when its owner dies, you've heard of that?'

'Known it, in fact.' Household smiled and raised an eyebrow.

'I have too ... and known that something was going to happen and it did happen, things like that that you can't explain.'

'What did ... sorry? "Girl Mary" that was your lady wife, you say?'

'Yes, she was Girl Mary and I was Boy Tom. Folk don't seem to talk like that in these parts no more ... the old ways are dying. I am not too happy about dying with them. Knew after a while that young Edward was dead, but Girl Mary, she just pined into an early plot. Even three more children ... we had four children ... even the other three couldn't keep her with us ... and even when young Sara got wed and had children ... well then there was a little bit of spark in Girl Mary then ... a little bit of her old self, but it didn't last long.

She and young Edward were close, seemed to know what each one was thinking. Then one evening Girl Mary, she was sitting in the chair you're sitting in now, she suddenly sat up and her hand went here...' Thomas De Beer put his hand on his chest, 'and she said "Someone's just walked over my grave" and she went up to her bed. We never heard nothing from Edward after that ... we had a phone call a couple of days before that, but nothing afterwards.'

'Do you remember what time of day that happened?'

'Daytime ... but it took the phone call from his college to really tell us that something was amiss. We waited for him to call, or for a letter from him ... then the college called ... he was a student at Cambridge you see.'

'So I believe.'

'April of the year ... first flowers were up ... birds were nest building ... it was daytime when Girl Mary had her funny turn. Well, you see, if something really important happens ... an incident that marks your life, you seem to remember details about the day ... little things ... you go over them in your mind, and I remember it was a fine spring day. And if Girl Mary was right, if she had her turn at the moment young Edward died, then ... well, it meant he died in the daytime, whether he was inside or outside. When he died it was about three o'clock in the afternoon. I was working then, a signalman on the railway, a quiet line ... suited me ... on the Cromer line from Norwich Thorpe Station.'

'I understand you reported him missing?'

94

'Aye … it was a few days after the Girl Mary had had her turn perhaps a week … but it was the day we received the phone call from the College. I went to the police station in Norwich – Girl Mary wouldn't come with me – gave the details … policeman took details and a photograph I had. Asked me to notify them if he turned up, and that was it. I must have looked a bit down-hearted but he explained that they can't search for adults, they'll search for children, especially young children, but they can't search for adults. He suggested I travel to Cambridge and report him missing there as well. He said it made more sense to report him missing at Cambridge, being as that was where he was living. So I travelled to Cambridge the next day and reported him missing at the police station there and gave them another photograph of him in that long coat he used to wear … a soldier's coat … bit daft I thought … who wants to be a soldier? But that's how they dressed. So I travelled to Cambridge the next day. British Rail let me have a day's compassionate … then went to his lodgings. He had a room in a big house round the corner from the police station … funny place, Cambridge, in Norwich the railway station is in the centre of the city but in Cambridge it's well outside it, a bus ride in … but young Eddie's lodgings were just a stone's throw from the police station. Swings and roundabouts, I expect you could say. Girl Mary was always saying that. That's Girl Mary.' Thomas De Beer nodded to a photograph hung on the wall above the mantelpiece. It was a black and white photograph of a strong, yet feminine-faced young woman. 'We were still to be wed when that was taken.' Thomas De Beer glanced longingly at the photograph. He wore brown cavalry twill trousers, a white shirt, and a blue cardigan. He was clean shaven, save for a silver pencil line moustache, neatly trimmed, and equally neatly trimmed silver hair. He had, thought Household, a very passable head of hair for one so old, and he was reminded that 'age' is a concept, some people age slowly – the lucky ones. Others, less lucky, age quickly. Still others, the really unlucky ones, don't get to age at all, the ones like 'young' Edward De Beer.

'Did you come by train?'

The question surprised Household. 'No ... drove ...'

'Ah ... liked that line, Norwich to Cambridge ... mind you, by car is a bit more direct. How long did it take you? About an hour?'

'About.'

'Loved working on the railway, like being part of a family ... aye...'

'Do you know much about Edward's time at the Tech?'

The old man looked at Household. There was disapproval in the look. 'At Cambridge,' he said, 'Edward was at Cambridge ... that's what we used to say in this family. "Our son is at Cambridge".'

'But he wasn't at the university?'

'No ... but he was still at Cambridge. Girl Mary was particularly fond of telling folk that her son was "at Cambridge". They could assume what they liked.'

Household had the sudden feeling that the De Beer family was not, or had not, been a particularly healthy unit. A family of secrets. He repeated his question.

'I don't. He didn't bring any friends home ... he didn't talk much, not to me or Girl Mary anyway, he may have said something to his brother, but we knew nothing of his mates. He came home each summer, took a job, a summer job, went back in the October.'

'I see. Easy life they had, grants and summer jobs. These days, students have to take out loans to pay for their tuition fees and living expenses. In those days they got a grant. Didn't have to pay it back, even if they failed the course.'

'Aye ... I had to make a contribution to Edward's grant, but some of them got full grants ... the ones whose parents were on low income or on the dole.'

'I know,' Household smiled. He was of the same vintage as Edward De Beer, deceased, but he thought better of telling the old man. I am alive, your son is not. It had once been Sydney Household's experience to learn of the death at the age of eighteen of one of his friends from primary school days. He and the other boy had first met when by mistake they wore each other's coats home. They became friends, taking the family dogs for walks in the woods beyond the suburbs where they lived. They were sent to different secondary schools and drifted apart. The friend died in a car smash aged eighteen years. Occasionally Sydney Household would pass his late friend's mother in the street, and she

97

would stare at him with undisguised hatred, that he should be alive and her son should not be ... even years later. The last time Sydney Household and his late friend's mother had passed each other had been when Household had been in his mid-thirties, and the look of hatred in the mother's eyes had not at all diminished, even then. It was with that experience in mind that he thought better about telling Mr De Beer he was of the same vintage as his son.

'Aye ...' the man sighed.

'You cleared out his room at his lodgings?'

'Yes, everything ... and we paid the money grabber what she wanted. I mean, we were worried sick about our son and all she wanted was money ... big fat woman with a piercing voice ... imagine Edward having to live there with her. There were a few other students in the house, coming and going, not one seemed to be interested in Edward, all a bit awkward looking.'

'Awkward?'

'Well, didn't seem to want to look at us ... looked a bit embarrassed to be honest ... just those we saw, but I think quite a few lived there. It was a huge house, didn't look so big from the outside, but once in the door ... big, well kept ... a strong smell of polish, like going into a hotel, that sort of smell. I liked that about it, that was welcoming, but the landlady ... and those other students, anything but ... one we passed at the door, he went out just as we had pressed the doorbell. He seemed to know who we were, me and Girl Mary ... he looked away from us and down to the carpet, tall, young fella, spectacles. As he passed us the landlady came up the stairs – she and her family lived in the basement and all the other rooms were let to students. Then when we were clearing his room we saw two others ... both quite short ... one very stockily built, in an army jacket ... the other less well built ... both looked like the first one did, the one at the door ... embarrassed, didn't want to talk to us, me and Girl Mary ... didn't offer to help carry our Edward's stuff for us, even though we were struggling, just didn't want anything to do with us.'

Household said nothing, but he thought it a strange reaction. They were, he presumed, at least on friendly terms with the missing Edward De Beer, if not friends ... young people in the same house. He had not attended university, but his brother, when he had come home from Swansea, had spoken long and loud about his mates in the shared house in which he lived. Nothing especially significant about the reaction of the young men in that house to Edward De Beer's parents removing his possessions, but it still seemed something he would not dismiss either. 'What did you do with Edward's possessions?' Household asked.

'Kept them.'

'Did you?'

'Yes, Girl Mary put her foot down about that. She never gave up hope that Edward would return. He'd want his things, she said, Edward would want his things ... so they stayed in his room. They're there now.'

'Are they?' Household's voice had an unintentional note of alertness. 'Is it possible for me to have a look at them?'

'Aye...' The man stood with some evident difficulty, then gasped and clutched his lumbar region.

'Please ... I can find his room myself, with your permission.'

'If you could.' The old man sank back into the upright chair with a sigh of relief. 'Lumbago,' he said by means of explanation, 'and general wear and tear. Still, not bad for eighty-two.'

'Very good, I'd say.' Household was genuinely impressed. He had seen older looking men who were only in their sixties, but then, as he had thought just a minute or two ago, age is just a concept.

'Well I carry on regardless, like my father used to say, "carry on" he'd say, "carry on regardless" but he'd been in the trenches you see, lost his arm at Ypres and he lived a long life too ... on the railway, a porter at Eccles station, little whistle stop but it had to have a porter. Dad worked for the Great Eastern before the war, so they found him a job when he came back a hero ... but he always said, "while there's a breath in your body, keep going". Edward's room ... top of the stairs, door on the left.'

Edward De Beer's room revealed itself to be small and cramped, with a two foot square window which overlooked the rear garden of the small house and to the gardens of the houses beyond and a 'roofscape' which must, thought Household, have changed little in the last one hundred years. He turned his attention to the contents of the room, the bed was not made up, the mattress folded, but in all other respects the room seemed to be a time capsule of the early 1970's, the poster of Bob Dylan on the wall, the vinyl records in a cardboard box which clearly once contained cans of Campbell's soup, the footwear – male knee length boots with solid 'Cuban' heels, softer ankle length 'desert boots' in suede with rubber soles – a 'kaftan' on a coat hanger which hung on a picture rail which ran round the room, denim jeans and a denim jacket were found rolled up neatly in a drawer. Household recognised the items of clothing ... his brother had worn similar when he had returned from Swansea, sporting a straggly beard and saying things like 'cool' and 'far out', describing things as 'heavy' if he didn't like them and telling Sydney Household over a beer in the Old Swan one evening that he thought he himself was too 'laid back' to follow Sydney into the police force. In a moment of indulgence, of personal curiosity rather than professional investigation, Sydney Household glanced through Edward De Beer's record collection. He smiled as he looked at them, here they were, the music of his era ... The Beatles, the universal *Abbey Road* LP, the Rolling Stones, Bob Dylan ... quite a few Dylan's, Household noticed ...Cat Stevens, Steeleye Span, Simon and Garfunkel LPs, The Incredible String Band... Heavens, he thought, it's all here and probably now quite valuable, a young man's music, played on a Dansette or Pye record player, 33, 45 or 78 rpm ... soon vinyl was to give way to cassette, and cassette to CD and some very sophisticated music centres indeed. He continued to look at the LPs ... Gordon Lightfoot ... oh my ... all the old songs flooded back into his mind ...

'If you could read my mind, what a tale my thoughts would tell' ... a Tom Paxton double LP ... 'My lady's a wild flying dove...' At least he and his generation listened to music, this, he thought, this could be called music, not the 'noise' his children listen to and make him and his wife endure. Al Stewart too ... De Beer had had taste. Household then turned his attention to the papers in Edward De Beer's room, always, he thought, a promising source of information.

Edward De Beer was a struggling under-graduate. That was the impression Sydney Household got by glancing through his work, C's in the main, one or two B's, certainly no B+. His essays seemed short, though Household would have been the first to concede that he was no tutor, but in comparison to the essays his brother wrote and which he was allowed to read, De Beer's work seemed dire indeed ... essays of just two sides of paper ... essays where the angry comments of the tutor were almost as long as the essay itself. He replaced the ring binder containing the essays, thumbed those containing his notes. He had clearly been a Geography student... 'Human Geography', 'Climatology', 'Physical Geography', 'Econ. Geography', were written on the spines of the ring binders. Household then saw that one had 'Eng Lit.' written on the spine. He opened it and saw that clearly, whatever Edward De Beer wasn't in Geography, he was in English literature, for here, in the same handwriting as the geography essays, were long essays about *King Lear* and *Julius Caesar*, about Chaucer and Bacon which had received B+ and

A's and glowing remarks from his tutor. De Beer had clearly being doing what Household understood to be called a 'joint degree', in his case, Geography and English. In one subject he had atrophied, in its twin, he had thrived. He put the folder down and picked up a third folder which seemed to contain poetry, not great poetry, but De Beer's own ... angst-ridden in places, clumsy to read to Household's untrained eye, but one had a note on the bottom, in the hand of another, which read simply, Mick Wales, 42 Collier Road. Household noted the name and address in his notebook.

The two men stood side by side at the balcony of the Members' terrace outside the House of Commons. Neither had spoken for a full sixty seconds. The sun glanced off the Thames, which was full, very full at that moment. They watched a Thames dredger punch its way against the current, just clearing the arch of Westminster Bridge. In other circumstances, either of the men might have commented on the narrowness of the barge's clearance of the masonry, but on that occasion they both had another pressing issue on their mind.

'This could be awkward,' the man spoke softly, 'this could cost us the election.'

The other man, the man who had brought the news, glanced at the first man. 'It could cost us twenty years in gaol. Do you want to go down for life, in maximum security at your age, after the comfortable life you've led?'

'Rather not.' The first man returned the look.

'Doesn't fit in with the plans I have made.'

'We'll keep quiet. I can't see how we can be linked.'

The second man turned and faced the Gothic beauty of the Houses of Parliament, which glinted in the sunlight. 'It's still only hearsay, it's still just hearsay. Don't breathe a word, not a word to anyone.'

The Panther made a start on the shallow grave. It would be the first he had dug. The first in a very long time, anyway. The soil was hard, the spade had little effect. He laid the spade down and went to the garage at the side of the bungalow for the pick. He wielded the pick with expert ease and the soil gave to it in large, solid chunks. It was a morning's work, but by lunchtime he had a grave. Not a hole in the ground, but a grave, with neat vertical sides and a flat bottom, just less than six feet long, and about three feet deep. Large enough to accommodate the girl. He cut some of the overgrown privet, hacking at it with shears, putting the long cuttings over the grave, and laying the smaller cuttings across the larger cuttings. The garden was a mess, the bungalow was ramshackle. Neither the pile of cuttings nor the spoil of soil seemed to look out of place. He saw a man whom he recognised approach. He put the shears down and mopped his brow and grinned.

'Hard work,' the man said.

'Getting there,' the Panther panted. 'But the weather ... hard work.'

'When will you be moving in?'

The Panther glanced at the bungalow. 'Not for a few weeks ... autumn. I really want to be in for Christmas. You think the garden's a mess, you should see inside the house. I'd invite you in for a cup of tea but...'

'No matter.' The man held up his hand. 'When you've settled in perhaps, but it's nice to see the bungalow being cared for again, and the garden. We knew old Jean ... like I said, we never knew she had a relative.'

The Panther slung the shears over his shoulder. 'She was always a private person. I never really knew her.'

'Well, I have to crack on.'

'Me too. I'll be packing up now, work to go to. Thanks for keeping an eye on the place for me, nothing inside to steal, but thanks, anyway.'

'Pleasure, Tom. We heard you arrive last night, late, but we knew it was you. Will you be here again tonight?'

'I plan to be. So if you see lights between ten and midnight, it's me.'

Tom. So that was his name. The woman lay on the bed in the sleeping bag, listening. The gag in her mouth prevented her from speaking, from enunciating, but it didn't prevent her from making a sound, and she fancied quite a loud sound. She could hear the man called Tom, whom she guessed to be her abductor. His voice was the nearer. He was asked when he was 'moving in'. The other voice seemed further away but was nonetheless quite distinct. If she could hear them, they could hear her, but she remained quiet and for some reason quite still. Intuition told her to remain silent, her life and the life of the man speaking to 'Tom' might, she thought, be placed in danger if she made a sound. She lay in the sleeping bag, her hands fastened behind her back with metal ... a length of chain, a pair of handcuffs, something like that; she was naked, her clothes had been removed, not just from her but also from her sight. The room was spartan, threadbare, bare floorboards, a window of wired and frosted glass, a dusty smell ... a lock up.

Her heart sank, then hope rose.

The Cambridge Panther. She had been abducted by the Cambridge Panther. She was his fourth, or was it his fifth victim, the crack on the head as she turned into her street, just a few yards from her parents' front door and safety. Though she didn't see the man who attacked her, not clearly, it was too dark and she felt consciousness leaving her, it was like being swamped by a huge black wave. Then she awoke, her head hurt badly, dreadfully, she was naked inside the sleeping bag, gagged and restrained. Outside she heard the sounds of someone gardening, cutting shrubs, digging a hole. It was then that hope rose in her because the Cambridge Panther didn't kill his victims. He kept them against their will for weeks at a time, and whatever he did to them was so awful that they were traumatised and unable to give clear and coherent accounts of their ordeal, but they had been allowed to live. That, she told herself, that was the main thing. She tried to calm herself by controlled breathing through her nose and through her mouth because the gag was not airtight, in fact it felt like a ball, one of those balls she had when she was a child, hard plastic, but hollow and full of holes, all the benefits of a gag but none of the disadvantages. She could breathe easily through it, but could not speak or scream for help, all she could do was make a near grunting sound. She lay there looking at items in the room, trying to memorise details, knowing that they would be of interest to the police, possibly even vital. She listened for sounds but heard only rural sounds, birdsong in the main, and silence ... a silence so long and profound that it could almost be heard. She knew then what was meant by the 'sound' of silence. No motor vehicles, no distant traffic ... she was deep in the countryside. The only sound beside the birdsong was the steady sound of shears clipping foliage. The sound told her something, the regular rhythmic clip, clip, clip ... it was the sound made by a man who is calm and in control. He had abducted her, had her restrained against her will, had stolen her clothing. If caught, he would be sentenced to life imprisonment and would probably have to spend his sentence, which might *mean* life, in the vulnerable prisoners' unit, because men like him fall outside the criminal code of ethics. Yet he was calm, she thought, as calm as calm could be. That she found both frightening and reassuring in equal measure. She wouldn't be injured or even killed because the man, the Panther, was in a state of anxiety or panic, but equally his calmness, his matter-of-factness, the implicit assumption by his gardening was that the man was insane. Totally insane. If he wasn't insane he was utterly amoral. He saw nothing wrong with his action. This man clearly was not going to be open to reason. She decided that her best hope lay in complete submission and co-operation. Whatever he wanted he could have. Whatever, whatever he wanted. She had been told that in such situations, if there were no hope of escape, no hope of imminent rescue, the only hope for survival lay in submission. She also thought, not a little ruefully, that she had also been advised against walking alone at night, and that even a short journey can be as dangerous as a long walk home. And her journey that night had been very short indeed. From the top of Queen Edith's Way to Rutherford Road. Twenty minutes. She had done the walk before many times, and on a warm summer's night, excellent visibility, what could go wrong?

What indeed?

She tried to calculate the time. It was daylight, fully so. She had slept or been concussed, or both, until well after daybreak. Blue sky was visible through the frosted glass, she felt hungry, not powerfully so, but looking forward to lunch hungry ... a round of beef sandwiches, a single fried fish in batter, would be appreciated at that moment, though she also doubted that the gnawing fear she felt in her stomach would permit her to eat.

Just lie still, she told herself, just lie at peace if you can, see what he does, see what he wants ... let him make the first move ... little else you can do, she said. You are not going very far without clothing and with your wrists fastened like this. She smelled the sleeping bag, it wasn't clean ... it had a stale smell, a musk about it, a man's musk ... and behind the man's musk was the faint trace of scent ... the last victim had been in here as well ... and his musk and her scent in the same place ... she wasn't surprised but the dread was strong and deeply felt ... there was little doubt in her mind what had happened in that sleeping bag, and little doubt in her mind what her abductor planned to happen again in that sleeping bag. It was the inexpensive sort with a zip down the side and round the foot – not the sort of down-filled bag used by hikers and mountaineers, but the sort that families buy for their camping holiday in the summer on camping sites. The sort that can be unzipped to allow two people to share it.

It was then that she heard the voices. The instinct was to make what sound she could but she checked it, or her intuition checked it. Something told her that sound, any sound from her, could be fatal. She listened to the short and amiable conversation and then lay there as the silence was broken only by the steady clip, clip, clip of the shears.

Presently that sound ceased and moments later she heard the man enter the building. She heard him put the shears down clumsily, but not angrily, they clattered against a wall and other tools, but his footfall was calm and unhurried. She heard him approach the door and he opened it without unlocking it. He stood in the doorway. Tall, lean, muscular, clean shaven, short hair. In a suit he would appear to be a salesman perhaps, she thought, or a bank manager. She stared at him. So this was the Cambridge Panther. In his hand, his left hand, he held a crossbow, black, powerful looking, threatening, deadly.

'How are you?' His voice was matter of fact, as if enquiring about a friend he had not seen for a while, but only a short while, not long enough to say 'Well, well, so good to see you' or long enough to say 'How are you keeping?', but 'How are you?' as if the time since they last saw each other could be most conveniently measured in days, and that there was nothing particularly special between them. He might, she thought, he might as well be greeting a colleague who had returned to work after a bout of influenza.

'Thank you for not trying to make a sound.' He crossed the floor towards her. 'I thought you might have been awake by now. If you had made a sound Richard would have heard you and I would have had to kill him. With this.' He held up the crossbow. 'He didn't know I had it ... no one does ... but it was at my feet. I can draw it and put a bolt in it in a matter of seconds. Richard wouldn't have seen me doing it because of the privet. Then I would have shot him in his chest. He would be dead, instantly. That would have been awkward because he lives in the next house, about two hundred metres away, but he is a neighbour and has proved a friend. No one would have seen me kill him – there really is no one else for miles around – but I would have had to dispose of the corpse. It would have been time consuming, but you didn't make a sound so I thank you for that.'

She listened intently, trying to identify an accent but she was unable to do so; he didn't speak with RP either. There was, she thought, perhaps just a trace of working-class Cambridge, but faint, and long lost, if it was there at all. He took the gag from her mouth and she saw that it was indeed as she had thought, a child's ball, hollow, with many holes in the hard plastic surface. Red, too, just like one of hers had been.

She exercised her jaws, and gasped; she shook her head, she had not realised just how uncomfortable a gag could be.

'It will have to go back in,' he said, 'but for now, it can remain out ... if you remain silent. Understand?'

She nodded.

'Well,' he smiled, 'you may speak. I want you to relax and feel at home. I am here to care for you. It is my purpose in life to protect you. How is your head?' He laid his fingers gently on her forehead.

'Sore.'

'I am so sorry I had to hit you ... so hard too.' He smiled again. 'I must be losing my touch. Are you hungry?'

She nodded.

'I have a pie for us. I was out at dawn, with the bow.' He nodded to the weapon. 'I took a hare, skinned it, butchered it, took the good meat, simmered it ... vegetables, some stock ... the rest of the animal I took back to the wood, the offal, the bones, the hide ... nature will deal with it in her own way as nature does. I used to be very good with a crossbow ... still am ... I want you to eat because I won't be back again for a while. I may come back tonight, it all depends. I work, you see. I am employed ... odd hours and no

111

guaranteed finishing time so it could be nearly twenty-four hours before I get back. I will go and get our meal ready now.' He stood. She could tell by the way he stood that he was lithe and muscular. 'Richard won't be leaving his house again today, so there's no one to hear you if you do scream out, but if you do, I will put the gag back in until it's time for you to eat.' His smile was warm. In another context, she thought, it could even be described as kindly, even fatherly, but then, just then, she could only shudder. His smile might be warm but his eyes were arctic blue, and looking into them was like looking into two endless tunnels, into two bottomless pits.

Sydney Household descended the narrow staircase in Thomas De Beer's cottage. He entered the living room as a train hummed by, the sound having a soothing quality it seemed to Household, as it filled the small cottage. Thomas De Beer glanced at the clock on the wall. 'She's on her way to Great Yarmouth,' he said.

'Really?' Household replied, for want of something to say.

'Yes, really. I get a copy of the timetable each time they are renewed, each spring and autumn. After a while I get to the point that I can glance at the clock and tell where the outbounds are going. Handy Norwich being a terminus, it means that all the outbounds leave on time. Well, mostly. The arrivals can be a bit ragged, time wise.'

'I can imagine. Do you mind...?' Household indicated a chair.

'No, please sit down, keep my old brain alert,

see, observing the timetable ... a lot of old railwaymen do it.'

It did indeed seem to Household a healthy interest in the local railway station. He was reminded of the news story of some years previous, about a middle-aged couple who spent their days in the attic of their house where they had built a model railway with a replica of their local station, and each day they worked the model railway according to the timetable of the station. So that if the London express departed at 10.00 a.m. from the 'real' station, then an express would depart the model station at precisely the same instant, and if a local 'sprinter' departed at 11.35 hours then a model 'sprinter' would depart the model station, also at 11.35 hours. It was their marriage, and when the railway workers went on strike for six weeks the couple went up to their attic and sat looking at each other for eight hours a day until the strike was over and their model railway could be operated again. That was also their marriage. In comparison, Thomas De Beer's restrained interest in the working of the railway just beyond his front door seemed, to Household, to be very healthy indeed. The man, though elderly, was still in touch with the real world despite the secrets his family had fostered. More than anything, that made his information very credible indeed.

'Find anything?' the man asked.

'Probably ...' Household paused. 'We may like to return.'

'We?'

'Well, the police ... not necessarily me in person

... but I found a note which referred to a person called Mick Wales. Do you know who that might be?'

'I don't.' Thomas De Beer shook his head as if genuinely searching the driest and dustiest recesses of his memory. 'Mick Wales, you say ... I can't recall Edward mentioning anyone of that name. Ernest might know, but not me.'

'Ernest?'

'My other boy. Of the two of them, Ernest was the brains. Yes, he went to Cardiff University, Ernest did. He and Edward were quite close as brothers when they were students, not so close when they were lads, but close when they were students. Had their own set of friends each when they were growing up, but when they were at college and university, they always knocked about together ... bought a car together and shared it. Ernest might know about, what did you say his name was? Wales? Ernest might know.'

'Where can I contact Ernest?'

A train rumbled past the window.

'That's come from Liverpool Street,' the old man smiled. 'Right on time. Be quiet now for a while ... scheduled services will be, anyway ... might hear some shunting in the yard opposite. But there won't be another scheduled train for half an hour now.'

'Ernest?'

'Oh, yes, sorry ... Ernest ... not so far, Thetford. On your way home in fact, not far off your journey at least, less they've moved Thetford since I was last there.' Thomas De Beer smiled at his own joke. Household was pleased for the old man. He had lost a son, had been widowed, Household had called on him unannounced, and had raised a dreadful ghost, yet the man clearly had 'moved on' from his tragedies and was able to smile, albeit briefly, at his own joke. Even though it had probably taken him the best part of thirty years to achieve it, he had at least moved on.

'Do you have the address?' Household allowed warmth to enter his voice in recognition of Thomas De Beer's humour.

'Aye, I do.' The man paused, then said, '132 Short Drove Way, Thetford, Norfolk.' Reciting the address from memory, as if the only way he could recall it was by reciting it by rote.

Household wrote the address down in his notebook. 'Do you have other photographs of Edward? I will have to ask if I may keep them for a while. I will, of course, return them.'

'Aye ... if you would. I have a number of photographs of Edward growing up, as a young lad. I expect you'd want one of him about the time yon disappeared?' Thomas De Beer stood, again with the aid of the sprung seat of the chair.

'That would be useful, thank you.'

Thomas De Beer turned and then knelt with some clear effort and discomfort at a sideboard and opened the door.

'Can I help?' Household asked as De Beer gasped with pain.

'No ... thanks ... I want to do this. My old body is racked with pain ... rheumatics, arthritis ... not as bad as some I've seen in the senior citizens' lunch club, some are in a dreadful way, but, like I said, my doctor tells me to move all I can, stop my joints from stiffening, even if it means a little pain ... a little pain, he says, it's actually a lot of pain, but it means I am alive.' He got hold of an old cardboard shoebox and retreated from the sideboard clutching it to his chest. He stood with some obvious difficulty and, thought Household, some courage and fortitude. He walked over to where Household sat and handed him the box. He turned and sat in his chair with no little relief that the exercise was over. 'Did well, though,' he said.

'You did very well.' Household took the cover off the shoe-box.

'No, I mean in life. When I was a nipper I remember adults saying "you don't know what pain is until you're past forty." I didn't really start getting rheumatics and a touch of arthritis until I was into my sixties.'

'Not bad.'

'You past forty yet?'

'Yes, but no pain yet.'

'Maybe it was an easier life I had. I was on the footplate of the last of the steamies ... then into the cab of the diesels ... well sheltered from the elements. Those old boys who worked the land hereabouts, out in all weathers ... they got old quickly.'

'Aye,' Household replied absentmindedly as he sifted through the photographs in the shoebox. He became absorbed by them, they were really what he had hoped to find in Edward De Beer's bedroom, photographs not just of De Beer, but also in groups, as one of a pair. 'This...' he held up a photograph showing a full-faced image of a young man, 'this I presume is Edward. Can you tell me about the photograph?' Household asked looking at the photographs and also checking the reverse for any commentary. Some did, others didn't, but he was particularly interested in a photograph which showed Edward De Beer and a group of other young people, on the reverse of which he had written, 'The Warkworth Terrace Crew'.

'These are the people he lived with?' Household held up the photograph for De Beer.

'Think so ... Ernest will likely know.'

Household looked at the photograph again. Edward De Beer seemed to stand out from the group but not in a positive way, thought Household, more of a negative way. He looked ill-fitting, out of place for no reason that Household could really identify, but there was an overall impression that Edward De Beer didn't really belong with or to, the Warkworth Terrace Crew, whoever they were. 'Mr De Beer,' he said, 'you remember a few moments ago, before I went upstairs?'

'Aye.'

'And you said that the people you saw in the house looked a bit uncomfortable at your presence?'

'Aye?'

'Well, can you look at this photograph here, showing Edward and some other young people, on the reverse he calls them the "Warkworth Terrace Crew". A long time ago now, but do you perhaps recognise them as being the people in the house that day?' He handed the photograph to Thomas De Beer.

'Well, I'm an old man,' De Beer's hand shook

as he held the photograph, 'and it's been a long time.'

'But you still have a keen eye and a sharp mind, Mr De Beer. It's difficult I know, but if you could try.' Household spoke softly.

'Even though it may still not be our Eddie?' The old man glanced up at Household. He paused, then added, 'I suppose you wouldn't be here at all if you didn't think there was at least half a chance of it being Edward?'

'I have been a police officer for a long time, sir, and I have learned to listen to my inner voice, my intuition...'

'Girl Mary used to call it "her waters" ... that what you mean?'

'Yes, in my waters. I feel certain that we have discovered the remains of your son.'

'The remains...' Thomas De Beer echoed the words. 'They don't seem to add up to Edward De Beer, that little lad that laughed and cried and pinched apples from my neighbour's tree ... the remains...'

Household felt awkward. It was all too easy to slip into police speak and it was never right or proper unless one was with other officers. 'I'm sorry, there just didn't seem to be any other way of putting it.'

'No matter. There isn't a clever way of putting it. Mind, it's not really our Eddie is it? I mean our Eddie's ... he's up there.' The old man pointed a saggy-skinned, liver-spotted finger upwards. 'I believe that anyway. Just his bones ... well, let's see.' He looked at the photograph of the Wark-worth Terrace Crew, a colour print showing a group of young men and women, all casually dressed, calm and relaxed in a woodland, round a small fire. The photograph was clearly candid, none of the people in the picture was looking at the camera, rather they seemed to be watching one of the group light the fire. 'Well, the thing that struck me was that there were no women in the house when we went to collect Eddie's things. The house seemed to be only male tenants ... mind you, in fairness we only saw a couple and then there was Eddie ... but the impression was that it was an all male household with the old bat of a landlady in the basement flat. Ernie will put you right about that, he visited our Eddie once or twice.'

'That should be interesting.'

'Well, the old boy there ... I think he could be the one who was going out as we were going in ... the one we passed on the threshold.'

'He looked uneasy, I think you said?'

'I remember that day well, like it was yesterday ... what parent wouldn't? Yes, that was him alright and yes, he didn't look happy to see us. And that one lighting the fire, he was the other one we saw, seemed happy to be going into his room as we got up the stairway ... so these must have been the young mates that our Eddie was living with when he disappeared. Our Eddie's there ... in the photograph.' Thomas De Beer handed it back to Household.

Household took the photograph and looked at it. Edward De Beer was there but, by his body language, seemed to be a hanger-on. The others tended to be more bunched up it seemed to

Household, more of a group, more accepting of each other, more needing each other, and De Beer, smaller, more finely made, was there, but on the edge, even a little beyond the edge. The dress too seemed different; all were casually dressed but seemed to look self-respecting in their dress; they were neat, clean-cut, looked as though they had money but cared not to spend it. Edward De Beer on the other hand wore a grey greatcoat, ex-army it seemed, and his trousers seemed inexpensive and threadbare. In contrast to the others, De Beer looked as though he had no money in the first place. Household placed the photograph on one side on the top of the full-faced photograph of Edward De Beer. He continued to delve. Few of the photographs seemed to be of other people. They were either of De Beer alone, or of places of interest to the tourist in the city of Cambridge, shots of the ancient college buildings in the main. A strange fascination, it seemed to Household, for a student at the Tech. It was as if a longing lay behind the lens. Only one other photograph interested him; it was a close up of a thin faced, bearded young man with straggly hair. On the reverse it read 'Mick Wales'. Household pondered the photograph. Here, in this one snapshot, here was a glow of companionship, of acceptance, for a close-up like this implies friendship between photographed and photographer, especially since Mick Wales was smiling and had clear warmth in his eyes. The photograph of De Beer and the Warkworth Terrace Crew showed De Beer to be a satellite of the group, in

Household's view, and the remaining photographs of the university buildings had the echoes of the loneliness of a person who holidays alone and takes photographs so as to take his long suffering relatives and acquaintance's and neighbours on holiday with him when he returns. Not so with the photograph of Mick Wales. Here was a mate taking a photograph of a mate, not posed either, an impulsive photograph driven by warmth of feeling and received with warmth of feeling. Household felt that he would like to talk to Mick Wales, if he could be traced. He would, after all, now be a man in his middle years, and could be living anywhere in the world, if he was still alive. But it was worth the long shot. He placed the photograph of Mick Wales back in the shoebox and replaced the lid. 'I'd like to borrow these two photographs, if I may?'

'You'll return them?'

'Of course.'

'Then, yes ... if it helps you find out what happened to our Eddie ... my lad Edward.'

'I think they will, Mr De Beer, I think they will.'

The woman raised her glass to her lips and sipped the white wine delicately. 'You have always struck me as troubled,' she said.

William Aughty raised his eyebrows and placed his knife and fork down. 'I didn't know it showed.'

'Oh, it shows.'

'As a psychologist, you'd notice such things.'

'Well,' she smiled. 'I am not a psychologist until I qualify – I haven't even graduated yet, and that's only the beginning. But I saw a troubled

121

man when I saw you.'

'Well, you are right.' William Aughty picked up his knife and fork. 'I can't tell you what it is, but I did something once ... and the remarkable thing is that for many years I forgot that I had done it, yet it is enormous ... then ten years ago I started to recall it ... bit by bit ... all out of sequence at first and initially I thought I was remembering a dream. Then, over a period of about a week, I was able to put all the bits in the correct sequence and realised it wasn't a dream. It's been plaguing me ever since, each day.'

The woman ran her fingers up and down her wine glass. 'You've just given a perfect description of a "recovered memory".'

'I have?'

'You have ... the suppression of traumatic events is a coping mechanism, but they won't be suppressed for ever and emerge eventually ... it's common amongst survivors of disasters or soldiers who have been involved in combat. But today you seemed more agitated ... you were just not interested in me...'

'I'm sorry ... but you're right, I am a bit agitated. I had some news today ... there has been a development about "it".'

'I'm sorry.' She reached across the table and took his hand. 'We can go back to the flat again, if you like, after the meal.'

'No,' Aughty shook his head. 'I have to return home. When the House is sitting, I can stay overnight without my wife becoming suspicious, but during the summer recess, I have no excuse not to return home ... and being unfaithful is bothering me. I just don't like who I am anymore.'

The woman paused, then asked, 'Does that mean you are going to let me go?'

'Wasn't planning on it. Why, what would you do if I did?'

She shrugged. 'Find another wealthy, middle-aged professional man who would take me for his mistress, pay the rent on my flat and take me out for a meal three times a week.' She smiled at him. 'A man like you, William. I would not work in a pub or a shop like many of the other girls ... they work up to thirty hours a week in what is supposed to be a part-time job, they are always exhausted and have little time to study. I am attractive enough to be able to avoid having to do that, and there's no shortage of professional middle-aged men in London.'

'And you're also ruthless enough. You would do well in politics.'

An observer sitting at a neighbouring table in the restaurant might see them for what they were, a more charitable, more naïve observer might take them for father and daughter.

Margaret Neston wrapped the sarong about her and strolled out of the villa to where the man lay on a reclining chair by the swimming pool. 'What's that weird smell?' she asked as she approached to within earshot of the man.

'Scent,' the man replied sniffily. 'It would take a girl from Liverpool...'

'Birkenhead.'

'Whatever ... it would take somebody from up there not to know the difference between a smell

and a scent. It's from Africa, from the Sahara ...
pockets of desert air waft across the Mediterranean if the wind is from the south.'

'Oh, look, I'm due some money, I've run out ...
and the deal...'

'Later, later.'

'When later?'

'Just later. I've just finished work, my head is
spinning ... later ... later ... later...'

The woman lay on the bed listening to the
Panther. His movements seemed slow, deliberate, very feline, but also very manly. The pans she
heard being placed on the cooker were placed
calmly and deliberately, the cutting she heard
being done on the work surface was also
methodical, purposeful, not at all like the noise
her mother made in the kitchen, clattering,
banging, dropping cutlery and, not uncom-
monly, plates. The woman thought about her
mother for the first time since her abduction; her
mother who had an anxiety state and was kept
almost calm by taking large quantities of pills on
a daily basis. The least thing could set her off ...
the slightest interruption in routine would make
her run round the house talking incessantly,
putting upon the patience of her long-suffering
husband, who had taken her for better or worse
and, the young woman thought, had clearly taken
her for worse. What sort of state her mother must
now be in she dared not contemplate. She tugged
at the chain which held her wrist to the ring in
the skirting board. It was a futile gesture. The
chain was lightweight and the padlocks small, but

too strong for her to break. The Panther came into the room, dressed in black, just like a panther. It was the first time she had noticed that, that he wore black training shoes, black jeans, a black t-shirt, black hair above a thin predator's face. He glanced at her as he crossed the room. 'Not too uncomfortable?'

She shook her head.

'It's not the Ritz.' He opened up a folding table and placed chairs against it. 'I do like making my guests as comfortable as possible. I hope to get a bed soon, but for now it has to be the sleeping bag on the floor.'

'S'ok,' the woman managed to say. She had once read that if abductees can strike a rapport with their abductor, their chances of survival increase, their treatment is less brutal. 'It's summer, I won't get cold.'

'But it must be uncomfortable for you.'

'It's alright, really.'

'You are very polite.' He smiled a warm smile beneath cold eyes. 'I'll try and find something to put underneath you, a blanket or something...'

'Thank you, the floor is a bit hard.'

'I hope you are hungry.'

'A bit,' she said.

'Meaning a lot? When did you last eat?'

'About six p.m. yesterday ... then it was just a snack.'

'You must be starving, it's midday now. I have to be at work soon.' He left the room and returned with plates and knives and forks. He walked back out of the room and returned with a pie in a dish which he held with oven mittens. He placed the pie on the table and pierced the crust with a knife. Steam rose from it. 'A hot pie on a hot day ... perhaps it's not appropriate, but I enjoy cooking. Come on, let's get you up here.' He walked over to where the young woman lay and, taking a key ring from his pocket, undid the padlock which fastened the chain to the wall. He pulled an extra length of chain, which the woman hadn't noticed, through the ring bolt and then re-fastened the lock. He smiled. 'Should allow you enough room,' he said warmly. With another key he unfastened the chain which held her wrists behind her back and then reattached the padlock, fastening one wrist only. 'That'll keep you in the room, but allow you plenty of movement, allow you to stretch your legs. The chain isn't too tight?'

'No.' The woman rubbed her wrists. 'Really ...'

'I can let it out one more link, I think ... but it's not compressing you, the blood is flowing. I think that's OK. Come on, up to the table. I always eat with my guests. Don't worry about not having any clothes. I know what a woman's body looks like.' He unzipped the sleeping bag and stood and turned his back on her, walking once again out of the room.

Not wanting to stand naked before him, the woman shuffled out of the sleeping bag and crossed the room on tiptoe and sat at the table before he returned.

'Sorry, it's only Adam's wine,' the Panther said as he placed a jug of water on the table. He held two tumblers in the other hand, which he also placed on the table. He poured the water. The woman grabbed her tumbler and drank deeply.

'You're thirsty ... I am sorry, I didn't realise.'

The woman smiled. 'S'OK ... really.'

'Well, I'll leave you plenty to drink. I know from my own experience what a terrible thing thirst is.'

'Really?'

'Yes.' The Panther spooned a generous portion of the pie onto the woman's plate. 'Overseas once ... a long time ago ... so long ago it feels like a different lifetime ... please start.'

The woman picked up her knife and fork. The pie did indeed smell good, very appetising indeed. It had a pleasant texture, not runny as she had feared, like meat in water covered with pastry, but solid. It had been thickened and contained vegetables and had been flavoured with herbs. She ate gingerly, it was still hot, but she knew it was nourishing. 'This is good.' She smiled at her captor. 'You have a definite skill.'

'You think so?' He returned the smile. 'Thank you.'

'Oh yes...' Keep him talking, keep him talking.

'I am pleased you like it ... really.' He began to eat his own meal. 'Is there anything I can get you ... books to read, a magazine? Enough natural light gets in here even though I board the windows up.'

'You'll board the windows?'

'Yes, from the outside. I have told my neighbour that I am scared of the village lads throwing stones at them, but really it's to keep the sound in. They are lined with foam on the inside you see, but the light gets in round the edges ... there's enough light to read. I checked and made holes in the boards. So, magazines?'

'Yes, please.'

'Any particular ones?'

The young woman shook her head. 'No ... just women's fashion magazines.'

'I'll see what I can do. You can call me Harry.'

'Harry? That's your real name?'

'No,' the Panther smiled. 'It's the name I use. Dare say I'll find out your real name soon enough, when you are reported missing.'

'My parents will have reported me already.'

'Probably, but the police won't take a missing person report about an adult until the person has been missing for twenty-four hours. I know how the police work, and you are not my first guest. I know when I captured them, and I know when they are reported missing ... it's in the *Evening News*, you see. I'm a bit of a celebrity now.'

'Why do you do this?' The woman found her confidence growing. She was clearly at extreme risk but on a minute by minute basis she felt safe. 'I mean, you are a good looking man ... you must have success with women?'

He smiled a thin smile. 'Don't try to charm me.'

'I wasn't.'

'Yes, you were. Mind you, I'd do the same if I were you, so I can't blame you.'

The woman fell silent and ate. Not only was she hungry, but she knew she would need all her strength.

'Why?' the Panther pondered. 'No logical reason, I don't abuse my guests ... I don't violate them, I look after them.'

'Oh...'

'Yes. I didn't hit you too hard, I hope?'

'It's a bit sore but getting better.'

'The soreness will pass. I've had head injuries too.'

'Have you?'

'Yes. That was another country too. And by another country I could mean Scotland or Australia, or anywhere in between, so don't ask where. But why do I do this? It's a good question … actually I know why I do it, it's a need to have someone to look after.'

The woman felt a hollowness in the pit of her stomach.

There was a period of silence in which the man and woman ate, captor and captive, eating together. She was naked and chained to the wall, yet she realised that in his mind she was a wife, a daughter, the person he provided for, the person he sheltered … and they were sitting down eating a meal together. If he can't find someone to be dependent upon him, he can steal someone and force her into a state of dependency. She began to toy with her food as she realised just what a dangerous man he was. It wasn't what he might do to her that made him dangerous. In fact, the likelihood was she would be released with or without physical harm in a few weeks' time, but it was his mind … he was insane … those bottomless pit eyes … an animal would instinctively fear him. She had read that too, somewhere, that psychopaths can't keep animals as pets, or if they do, it's something you don't make a relationship with, like a tank full of tropical fish, but it's not a dog, a cat, a horse, where bonds develop and

129

emotion is expressed; the dog's wagging tail, the cat's purring, the horse's delighted whinny ... nothing of that sort is the psychopath's experience. He couldn't get any nearer humans, especially human women with their honed and natural intuitiveness, than he could get near cats or dogs or horses. So he stole one, a human female, a daughter figure, she thought, hence the absence of sex, so far at least ... a little girl to care for ... to feed and keep warm, someone to come home to, someone who depended upon him for survival. He was her provider, as nature intended him to be, her provider and her protector.

The remainder of the meal was eaten in silence during which she sensed him deeply appreciating her presence. Just by being there, she was giving him something, answering his needs.

'Finished?' he asked warmly as she placed her knife and fork on the plate.

'Yes, thanks ... Harry.' She forced a smile.

'Good. It will have to do you until I get back. Drink some water, you'll need to fill yourself full of the stuff. You can't drink with a gag in your mouth ... go on, do as you're told.'

She drank deeply while he cleared the table and washed up. Later he placed her back in the sleeping bag with her hands fastened behind her back, the gag in her mouth and a chemical toilet next to the sleeping bag. Then he kissed her, very gently on the forehead, and told her that she was his 'good little girl'. He left the room and she lay in the sleeping bag, on her side, as one by one the boards were placed over the windows, plunging her into a gloom penetrated by only a few shafts of light, which illuminated the dust in the air that entered the room via the edges of the boards and, as 'Harry' the Panther had promised, by small holes drilled in the boards themselves.

Later, as evening fell, it became dark. Very dark indeed.

Sydney Household thanked Thomas De Beer for his time and bade the elderly man to remain seated whilst he saw himself out of the terraced cottage. He closed the front door behind him and glanced in front of him, the railway lines at the same level as the path on which he stood, branching immediately upon leaving the railway station, the lines nearest to him going south and west, to Cambridge, to London, the furthermost lines reaching away from him, leading eventually to Great Yarmouth, Cromer, Lowestoft. Beyond the permanent way was the roofline of Norwich, a blend of new build and Victorian, plentifully interspersed with foliage. He turned left and walked back along the pathway, along the row of terraces, all of similar design, with a central doorway, with rooms either side, a small front garden which one cottager had given over to a garage for his car, another to a shed and a small lawn or a well tended vegetable patch. At Hardy Street he climbed the steps up to the main road, turned left and followed the road down to the traffic lights at the road junction. He crossed the road and turned right, following the banks of the gentle Wensom to the bridge, where he turned left into the city centre. He had not before been in the city of Norwich. He particularly enjoyed the ancient street pattern which had clearly been allowed to survive. The skyline of the city he found to be tolerably free of brutal, angular high-rise blocks, while the magnificent cathedral, with its complete cloisters still remaining, clearly dominated the centre. Walking near the cathedral he was intrigued by a road called 'Tombland', with 'Tombland Abbey' nearby, and amused to see that 'the Law Courts' and 'the Puppet Theatre' shared the same arm on a street signpost: the names he thought had a certain degree of inter-changeability. He ate a substantial steak and kidney pie in a pub, washed down with a soda water and lime and then strolled up Elmhill, so quintessentially Medieval England, a cobbled road lined with pale yellow, half-timbered thatched cottages forming a continuous terrace. He felt his visit to Norwich had been successful, both professionally and personally. He had learned more about Edward De Beer, and he had discovered the charms of a delightful city. He collected his car from where he had parked it in an unrestricted parking area near the inner ring road and drove out of the city, across the green fields of lush East Anglia to Thetford. In Thetford he obtained clear and perfect directions from a man whom Household recognised as a plain-clothes police officer, and who clearly also recognised him, causing amusement to both, though neither commented. Moments later, halted his car outside the De Beer household, number 132, Short Drove Way. There was, he thought, the off-chance that Ernest De Beer would be at home, even though it was by then early afternoon. The house looked to belong to a man of prosperity – the well-tended front garden, the neatly painted house with hanging flower baskets by the front door. Worryingly, the driveway was empty. No car meant the possibility that no one was at home and he would be obliged to make a return visit. He got out of his car, locked the door and walked up the concrete flagstones which formed the drive, to the front door, and pressed the doorbell. The sound echoed loudly in what seemed to be a long hallway and, he guessed, given the volume of the echo, with no softening features like a carpet.

'I would ordinarily say you were lucky to catch me at home.' Ernest De Beer revealed himself to be a short, balding man, smartly but casually dressed, white slacks, open-toed sandals, grey socks, a yellow long-sleeved casual shirt, clean-shaven save for a pencil line moustache similar to his father's. Household knew his age to be 47 and thought he could pass for ten years younger than that. Life, and his genes, had been good to him. He looked not just slender but fit, and his face was absent of worry lines; though balding, what hair remained above his ears and round the back of his head was a strong, healthy black; not a trace of grey. 'Still would say it in fact, the luck is yours, not mine.' De Beer paused. 'The company downsized and I got downsized with it. A sort of semi-precious metal handshake, but no pension to speak of ... my wife teaches and that doesn't pay a great deal. So what is there for me now, at my age? Not a lot, I can tell you.'

Household read the room. It was neat, well ordered, a sense of quality pervaded, the french windows looked out onto a large and well manicured back garden.

'Oh, it looks desirable,' De Beer seemed to read Household's thoughts, 'but not a lot of it is paid for. We won't be going on holiday again for a while, if at all. So, Edward?'

'Your father has phoned you?'

'Yes,' again De Beer read Household's mind, 'from his neighbour's house.'

'Ah ... I don't recall seeing a phone in his house.'

'You didn't,' De Beer smiled.

'Well, yes, Edward. I have to tell you that positive identification has still to be made, but we think that your brother's remains have been discovered.'

'Yes, so Dad said ... he's unbelievable for his age, his mind is still as sharp as a tack ...'

'So I found. But even if the remains do not turn out to be those of your brother, making inquiries about a missing person is never a waste of time.'

'No, and the family appreciates it, I can assure you. So what can I tell you?'

'Well,' Household relaxed on the settee, 'I suppose anything and everything is the answer to that question. We are still trying to build a picture of your brother's lifestyle. Do you know who the Warkworth Terrace Crew might be?'

'The people Edward lived with. Like all the students at the Tech, as it was in those days, he had a succession of bedsits, then he moved into a room in a large house in Warkworth Terrace and seemed to take to it quite well. It was quite pricey, his weekly rent was over the odds, but it was spacious, warm and dry, which was something, and he had a cooked breakfast each morning.'

'Really?'

'Oh, yes, luxury indeed for a Tech student. Most of them stumbled out of bed and made a cup of coffee, if they had breakfast at all, but Eddie went downstairs in a lovely house that smelled like a hotel, you know, the smell of wood polish, carpets on the stairs and in the hallway.'

'You visited him at university?'

'Yes, as siblings do.'

'I see.'

'So Eddie started each day with a bottomless teapot, a full English breakfast, toast and marmalade ... all very civilised. He seemed to lap it up. What he did like about it was that all the other lodgers were at the university. So he sat down to breakfast with university students, people who really were at Cambridge.'

'I detect a note of resentment in your voice, Mr De Beer.'

'I am a bit confused about what to think. Edward ... well, things were difficult for him at home because our mother had told all her neighbours and friends and relatives that Edward was "at Cambridge", leaving them to assume that he was at the illustrious university, whereas in reality, he was at the humble Tech. Now it's called Anglia Polytechnic University.'

'I know. APU for short.'

'Yes, one of the new universities, but at least it doesn't do "Golf Management". One of my children looked up their website. Very impressive, Law, Earth Sciences and guaranteed accom-

135

modation in APU property for all first year students. When Eddie went there he had to walk the streets looking for accommodation. He was given a list of addresses and off he went, door to door. He told me once of a group of mates who could not get accommodation, so they borrowed tents and camping stoves from the hiking club and set up camp on a small lawn in the Tech grounds. The place has come a long way in thirty short years.'

'Seems so.'

'But Eddie seemed to feel obliged to carry off the pretence and held himself with a certain swagger when he was in Norwich. Living with a group of university students seemed to appeal to him. I only visited on a couple of occasions but I got the impression that he was trying to ingratiate himself with the university students he was living with ... living is the wrong term.'

'Lodging in the same house as?' Household suggested.

'Better put, yes. I think there was a certain degree of social interaction, but he wasn't fully integrated, he would never be allowed to be.'

'Do you recall the names of the people at the boarding house?'

'I don't. He talked warmly about a man whom he mentioned by his Christian name only, 'Jim'.' Ernest De Beer shrugged. 'That won't help you much.'

'"Jim",' Household repeated, but he wrote the name in his notebook nonetheless. In the hallway, which had indeed proved to be carpetless, the De Beer's preferring varnished floorboards, a clock chimed two p.m.

'That's paid for,' De Beer smiled. 'The clock. It's one of the few things that is.'

Household returned the smile. 'I have a photograph here, your father has loaned it to us.' He took the photograph from his pocket and stood and walked across to where De Beer sat in a cavernous armchair and handed it to him. He returned to his seat on the settee. 'As you see, on the reverse is written 'The Warkworth Terrace Crew'.'

'Yes, that's Eddie's handwriting. It's quite strange, like reaching out and touching him ... it feels strange ... but, yes, that's Eddie at the edge of the group, looking in.'

'Do you recognise any of the others?'

'I don't ... the tall bloke there, he might have been there when I visited. I think that must be him, the same bloke, I mean. "Jim" I largely suspect is the one who took the photograph. I seem to recall Eddie mentioning Jim had an interest in photography and also because I can't see any of the others bothering enough about "Eddie from the Tech" to give him a print of a photograph.'

'Do you know the story behind the photograph?'

'No ... you mean where it was taken?'

'Yes.'

'I'm sorry, I see only what you see, a group of young adults lighting a fire in the woods, it looks like ... in the country, anyway.'

'OK.'

De Beer stood and crossed the floor and

handed the photograph back to Household. 'You will return that to us?'

'Yes, of course.'

'It's one of the ones of Eddie we can't replace ... haven't got the negative you see.'

'I will personally see it's returned. We will copy it and I will post the original back to your father.'

'Thank you.'

Household put the photograph into his jacket pocket.

'I suppose...' De Beer hesitated. 'I suppose you now know what is relevant and what is not?'

Household remained silent. Something was clearly going to be offered. The clock in the hall ticked, the interior of the house smelled strongly of air freshener.

'Well, he was my brother, and I want to do all I can to help find out what happened to him. Do the remains show signs of violence?'

'Yes ... the skull is fractured.'

'Badly?'

'Sufficient to have been the cause of death in the opinion of our forensic pathologist.'

'So he was murdered?'

'It's too early to tell, but that is the indication, yes.'

De Beer fell silent. He looked around the room. Then he said, 'He was a social climber.'

'Edward?'

'Yes. We come from a humble background, well, you have met Dad and the little house by the railway that we grew up in, nothing to be ashamed of, nothing at all. But when I visited Eddie at Cambridge I saw something in my brother that I didn't want to see. You see, I went to Cardiff University – three years of delirious happiness, despite the rain.'

'The rain?'

'Yes, you've never known rain until you have lived in south Wales. You can actually feel the weight of it on your head and shoulders ... quite an experience for an East Anglian. We had got used to the icy cast wind but we didn't get rain like they do in south Wales. But anyway, I mixed with the people on my course, went to the pubs with them and the university bars, watched plays at the Sherman Theatre and films at Chapter One and Chapter Two in Canton, and when Eddie visited me in Cardiff, he came out with us, the mates from my course.'

'Yes?'

'Well, the striking thing about visiting Eddie was that we never went for a beer with his friends from the Tech. We went into the city for a drink, or drove out in his car to a pub he knew in the country, but we didn't mix with anyone from the Tech. He also said something once. We were walking across Parker's Piece, which is across the road from the end of Warkworth Terrace, and he showed me "Reality Checkpoint" and said that the good thing about Warkworth Terrace was that it was on the right side of the lamp-post.' De Beer held eye contact with Household. 'I didn't like him for that ... I didn't know he thought like that.'

'Did he explain what he meant?'

'You must know what he meant, you are a Cambridge-based police officer. In fact, if I know Cambridge, doesn't your police station overlook

Parker's Piece?'

'It's on Parkside, yes.'

'So you know what he meant?'

'Just tell me what he said, please, for form's sake, so we are very clear.'

'Well ... Parker's Piece in Cambridge, twenty-two acres of mown grass, used for football and hockey games in the winter, cricket in the summer ... it's a vast area of green in the middle of a city, but yet it's not a park as such, like Regent's Park in London, and what that land wouldn't be worth if you could obtain planning permission to build on it ... you'd pay central London building land prices for it.'

'I imagine you would.'

'Well, the Parker's Piece is more or less square in shape and criss-crossed by two footpaths, as you know, and the lamp-post, Reality Checkpoint, is situated where the paths cross so it is in the dead centre of Parker's Piece. On one side are the university colleges and the places the tourists visit, which Eddie called the 'gown' side of the Piece, and on the other side is what Eddie called the 'town' side. Rows and rows of small terraced housing, Co-op food shops, working class employers such as hospitals, the railway station and the marshalling yard, pubs with names like 'The Locomotive'. An entire town all in its own right, schools included. Those are the two realities that combine to make the city of Cambridge as represented in Parliament, and in the middle of the two, keeping them apart, is the buffer zone of Parker's Piece, which is why no one will ever be allowed to build on the Piece.'

'Because then the two realities would merge?'

'So Eddie said. He went on to explain that if you walk from "the town" to "the gown" and take the most direct route, you would have to walk across Parker's Piece from the East Road and swimming pool corner to the University Arms Hotel corner and within a few steps, as you past the lamp-post, you would move from one reality to another.'

'Hence "Reality Checkpoint"?'

'Yes ... Eddie said that as you walked past the lamp-post, it really was like walking through an invisible membrane. You passed from one reality into the other. So when he said he liked living in Warkworth Terrace because it was on the right side of the lamp-post, he meant the socially correct side. Warkworth Terrace itself is marginally on the "wrong" side of the lamp-post but what Eddie clearly meant was that the house he lived in with all those university types was, culturally speaking, on the "correct" side of the lamp-post. That evening we went into the town ... I think the pub was called "The Baron of Beef" and was full of students with very plummy accents, all university types. I felt out of my depth but Edward relished the atmosphere. But what I didn't like him for was that he was snubbing his mates at the Tech. As we sat there, there was a gleam in his eye and he looked at me as if to say "isn't this great", but really if we tried to talk to anybody in the pub they wouldn't want to talk to us. That evening I found out that my brother was a social climbing snob. To put it bluntly. I never visited him in Cambridge after that.'

'I see.' Household was beginning to get a clearer picture of Edward De Beer, and was not wholly liking what he found.

'I could easily see Edward becoming active in Conservative Party politics, and from an early age ... but ... well, he disappeared the following summer.' De Beer paused. 'I must say I know the police are thinly stretched but we would have appreciated some contact from the police over the last thirty years, just to let us know that Eddie's case hadn't been filed away and forgotten. Even if it had.'

'We would equally appreciate being able to do that, Mr De Beer. It is as you say, a matter of manpower.'

'Yes ...'

'Not enough hours in the day, not enough feet on the ground.'

'Yes, I'm sorry ... but there's a big hole in your life when a close relative disappears. It's the not knowing that eats away at you.'

'I can imagine, but may I please remind you that a positive identification has yet to be made. If it isn't...'

'It will be Eddie. I haven't known Dad's waters to be wrong yet.'

'Well, we will find out very soon.'

'You'll let us know?'

'Yes. The police usually have only one contact person with the family ... but in this case, I'll make a point of contacting both you and Mr De Beer the elder.'

'We would appreciate it, it would save one of us from telling the other the awful news.'

142

'Now, do you remember your brother ever mentioning a man called Mick Wales?'

'Yes,' De Beer raised his eyebrows, 'heavens, yes ... haven't heard that name for a while.'

'You know him?'

'Know of him. You see, my brother's passion was literature, and like many young people, he tried his hand at writing, poetry and short stories ... that sort of thing, and he mentioned Mick Wales once or twice as a fellow aficionado of literature.'

'Was he one of the Warkworth Terrace Crew, so called?'

'That I couldn't tell you, Mr Household, but what I can tell you is that that gentleman may be the one person you can still contact who knew my brother at Cambridge.'

'Now that is interesting...'

'What the police call a "lead"?' De Beer smiled.

'Probably. How do we contact him?'

'Well, that I don't know, what I can tell you is that over the years I have seen posters advertising the Fenland Poetry Festival which takes place in Cambridge organised by one Mick Wales.'

Household smiled. 'Has to be the same bloke.'

'That's what I thought.'

The realisation came to the woman like a flash of lightning. She lay in the sleeping bag, her hands held behind her with the thin chain, which in turn was attached to the wall, the ball gag in her mouth held in place by elastic. The man, the Panther, had left a matter of hours ago, outside it was now dark and not even the slightest glimmer of light found its way past the board which had been put up over the windows. She needed no confirmation that night had fallen but an owl gave it anyway, as did the high-pitched squeaking of bats. She knew it was going to be a long night. The pattern was the same as she had read in the press based on what they could glean from the previous victims. The abduction was the same, a blow to the head, the back of a van, the remote building which seemed to them to be a lock-up, that she was kept as a trophy, and cared for, food to eat, warmth, rudimentary toilet facilities ... but with her it was different. She knew now that the building wasn't a lock-up at all, nor a shed on a farm, it was a house or a bungalow that was being renovated, and she knew what he sounded like ... none of the other victims had heard his voice. But above all, she had seen him, she knew what he looked like ... she was being treated differently. It was then that the realisation flashed in her mind like a streak of lightning.

It was then that she realised the Panther intended to kill her.

4

Dominic Perigo sat back in his chair. In the chairs in front of him sat David 'Dick' Tracy and Penny Wiseman. Across the floor, by the window, writing up a case file was Sydney Household. Perigo knew that Household was listening and

Household knew that he knew.

'Thoughts?' Perigo asked.

'I think we have to assume it's the Panther, sir.' Penny Wiseman wore her blonde hair in a tight bun. She was short for a policewoman but perfectly proportioned. Plain clothed in a blue skirt and matching top, white blouse, and highly polished black 'sensible' shoes, and, with an air of gravitas, she was found to be very fetching by all who saw her.

'The timing was right,' Tracy added. He was tall, slender, neatly trimmed beard. He spoke with a soft Irish accent. 'He is establishing a pattern and within that pattern we would be expecting another abduction about now. The victim fits his victim profile, a highly respectable girl from a good family.'

'Yes...' Perigo murmured. 'This makes him pretty well unique. Many, if not all, serial offenders start with "low life" victims, working girls, teenage runaways...' Perigo stopped talking as klaxons blared from the fire station which stood next to the police station, and he remained silent as two appliances left the building and drove away down East Road. When the sound of the klaxons had reduced, he resumed speaking, 'but this fella goes for respectable girls. What do we know of the latest?'

'She is a nurse, sir.'

'A nurse?' Perigo raised his eyebrows. 'A respectable girl, as you say.'

'Yes, sir. Joyce Dance, twenty-four years old, still living with her parents, still...' Penny Wiseman consulted her notes. 'She was really – is

145

really – quite an independent woman. She had been backpacking in Australia on an extended holiday, back with her parents as a stopgap measure before she moved on to a new job and her own flat.'

'So not a dependant woman?'

'Not at all, sir ... parents were distraught when we saw them, they want us to do more than we are doing, but we're doing all we can.'

'Indeed.' Perigo paused. 'Do we know anything about the actual abduction?'

'Very little, sir. She left her friend's house to walk to her parents house which would have entailed her going up Long Road. The walk would have taken about thirty minutes ... dare say backpacking round Australia had given her a sense of invulnerability. Australia can be a very dangerous place ... it's not an easy ride, especially if you are a "Pom" ... the outback is a big place.'

'You've been there?' Perigo was genuinely interested.

'Twice,' Penny Wiseman smiled. 'We think we have fights in pubs in England, but nothing like the battles I witnessed in Australia in bars, and they let 'em fight as a form of entertainment. Here we'd break them up or call the police, there they let them fight and if it goes to the death, it goes to the death and nobody says anything. They'll even take the loser's body out and throw it off a bridge onto a motorway, or dump it out in the bush.'

Tracy glanced sideways at Wiseman.

Perigo gasped.

'Oh, I saw it happen.'

'Did you give information?'

'Nope. Even though I was a police officer ... when in Rome, I thought. I was staying with relatives who were regulars at that particular bar, if I had named names to the local police, it would have made things difficult for them ... I mean dangerously difficult.'

'Your point being?'

'My point being that if Joyce Dance had back-packed in Australia for an extended period, as she had, she would have taken that in her stride, and so a stroll up Long Road in civilised Cambridge on a summer's evening wouldn't have been a problem for her. That gives me some hope in this case.'

'Hope?'

'Well yes, sir. You see, all the other Panther's victims have been much less worldly-wise than Miss Dance. I mean that girl I visited in Aberdeen, she had never been away from home before, convent educated ... sheltered life is not the expression ... she is totally traumatised, can't remember any details at all, same as the others, sleeping bag, chained to the wall, chemical toilet in a building in the country ... but Miss Dance ought to have more about her than the other victims. If any of his victims is going to remember a significant detail, it's going to be her.'

'We can but hope. Nothing from the appeal for witnesses?'

'Nothing yet, sir.' Tracy spoke. 'But as you know, witnesses can sometimes be slow in coming forward.'

'Indeed, indeed.' Perigo paused. 'But unlike other missing persons, we must assume that she has been abducted and is still alive and being held against her will. We had better make a renewed appeal to all farmers to check their outbuildings and for people to report any remote building where they have noticed activity, especially on the night in question.'

Household, at his desk, head down, thought, 'Now you're thinking ... about time too.'

'I'll get onto that, sir.' Tracy sat forwards.

'OK,' Perigo scribbled on his pad, 'just a phone call to the Press Officer, really.'

'Yes, sir.' Tracy relaxed. 'Hugely important though.'

'I'll say, we really need the help of the media on this one and you'd better renew the appeal for witnesses.'

'I'd like to go back and see the Dances, sir.'

'It's an abduction, as you say, sir.' Tracy echoed Penny Wiseman's request. 'Vital to reassure the next of kin that we are not abandoning them ... nor the victim.'

'Yes ... yes...' Perigo nodded his assent, 'do that, do that. When do you want to go?'

'Well, today, sir,' Penny Wiseman said suddenly and strongly, 'this evening.'

'Both of you?'

'Yes, sir. We are their link officers,' Tracy added.

'Yes, very well ... that will be a good thing to do.'

Household fought against sarcasm entering his thinking but could not help but think 'yes, and anything else they suggest as well', 'the tail', he thought, 'the tail is wagging the dog. And that is a fast track graduate entrant'.

The two women walked arm in arm, both tall, both slender, through Grantchester Meadows. As they walked, they received an occasional scowl, usually from an elderly person, who in their thinking belonged to a different, earlier era, because prejudice will die a slow death in Britain, so the elder of the two women believed. On some occasions she believed that it wouldn't die at all, but it would be hounded to the extremes of British society, where it will survive, thrive even, like an evil looking and evil smelling plant which is allowed to live because nobody wants to go near it.

'Haven't done this for a long time,' Veronica Sleaford squeezed her daughter's arm, 'walking together.' She smiled, 'My job, your studies, and your age.'

'My age ... seventeen?'

'Forging ahead with your own life.'

Sojourner Sleaford twisted her baseball cap so that the peak was towards the sun. 'That's what you are frightened of is it, Mummy? I thought you'd be pleased for me.'

'I am, off to university. I am pleased for you, proud of you ... it'll be one of the last times that we do this walk.'

'Oh, Mummy...'

'No, it's true. We have to accept that.'

'Mummy, listen ... I promise that we'll do this walk again before I leave to go to university, if I get in.'

'Oh, you'll get in.'

'And each vacation, Christmas, Easter and summer, we'll do the walk at least once.'

'I'll hold you to that.'

The two women walked on in silence, the Cam to their left hidden in the meadow but its course delineated by rows of willow trees and its presence emphasised by the occasional punt which looked as if it was being propelled through the grass, a young man at the stern with the pole, a young woman reclining at the bow, facing backwards, looking up at the man, sometimes admiringly, lovingly. The two women were dressed differently, the younger woman wore jeans and a t-shirt, white with SMILE in large, bold, black letters at the front and a loud yellow baseball cap, on the front of which 'New York' was stitched on in silver material. The older of the two women wore a light summer dress and a wide brimmed straw hat with a blue ribbon round it. To an observer they were clearly mother and daughter, clearly very close to each other.

'Did you never want to get married again, Mummy?'

'Yes, but my standards were too high.'

'Ha ... and you are the one that told me that I may have to compromise.'

'Hypocrite, I know ... and the job too ... but that's medicine, highest divorce rate of any profession. So be warned.'

'Yes, but I can't go in expecting to get divorced, that's wholly the wrong attitude, surely?'

'Yes, it is, you're right ... and yes, I did and still do want to remarry, but time's getting on. I still can have children, just, but you run great risks at my age both to yourself and the child, so I will have to find a man who doesn't want children.'

'Another divorcee, plenty about.'

'Oh yes...' The two women moved into single file to allow two youths on gaily coloured mountain bikes to pass them going in the opposite direction. Arrogantly, thought Veronica Sleaford, neither youth acknowledged their gesture with a word of thanks, or even a nod of the head. 'But it's the old question of finding the right one,' she said when she and her daughter were once again walking side by side on the baked hard pathway. 'Here I am, telling you that I am worried about losing you to your life's great adventure and I find out that you are worried about me.'

'I would like to see you settled with somebody, Mummy. I would worry about you being all alone in the house ... that big house all to yourself, you'll lose yourself.'

'No, I won't. I like big houses.'

'I'm going to visit Daddy soon.'

'Alright ...when?'

'Don't know, but soon ... don't like London in the summer, especially hot summers like this one ... but certainly before the Christmas term starts. I have to keep in touch.'

'Of course ... he'll be scared of losing you to your adult life as much as I will.'

'I'll travel down when the weather breaks, at least there's green space in Cambridge, there isn't a lot of it in Whitechapel.'

And mother and daughter walked on, continuing to keep their arms linked, their steps perfectly synchronised, walking easily, tea and buttered scones in Grantchester village and a bus back into Cambridge.

An afternoon to remember with fondness.

151

Sydney Household made two phone calls. He had received a phone call from the Anglia Police's forensic laboratory at Warboys. It confirmed, as he had suspected, that the skeleton in the ground at Bottisham was indeed that of Edward De Beer. It was news that Household wanted to hear, it meant that the work done on De Beer's disappearance was going to be relevant, it meant that another fresh murder inquiry was going to be opened. He then phoned Ernest De Beer with the result of the photo matching and asked him to convey the news to his father. It was news Ernest did, and also did not, want to hear but on balance he said that both he and his father would rather know than be kept wondering. Ernest De Beer asked when the body could be released for burial, to which Sydney Household advised that the post-mortem having been completed, the body could be released there and then. Though 'body' was not really the word to describe fully skeletonised remains, he didn't comment nor correct Ernest De Beer. His lasting memory of his brother would be of him as a living, breathing young man. He didn't want to dislodge that image and replace it with that of a skeleton. Ernest De Beer then politely reminded Household about his promise to return the photographs that had been borrowed from his father.

'They've been copied,' Household said. 'I'll put the originals in the post today, first class.'

'Many thanks.' De Beer paused. 'I'll drive over and see Dad, he'll need a bit of company ... but at least we know. It's been a long thirty years.'

'Yes, I can imagine, Mr De Beer. We'll keep you fully informed, of course, and if anything occurs to you that you think would be of interest to us, you will of course contact us?'

'Yes, of course ... I have your number.'

'We are particularly interested in your brother's friends at the time ... any names that occur to you, even nicknames ... anything at all.'

'If I remember anything at all ... but there's really only Michael Wales.'

'Yes. I will be seeing him shortly, but your brother's associates will certainly hold the key to his murder.'

'You believe so?'

'Yes, stranger murder is very uncommon.'

'Stranger murder?'

'People who are murdered by total strangers.'

'I see.'

'Acquaintance murder is much more common.'

'Hence your interest in Eddie's mates?'

'Exactly.'

'Well, if I think of anything, or particularly anybody, I'll let you know without delay.'

'Thank you. Goodbye.' Household replaced the receiver. He glanced across at Perigo's vacant desk, having watched Perigo get up and walk out of the office, clearly leaving the building as if something had clicked in his mind, some task to perform. Household dialled the enquiry desk and asked if Mr Perigo was in the building.

'Just left, sir,' came the crisp, prompt reply.

'Where did he sign out to?'

'Just a moment, sir ... he has signed out as "enquiries, unlikely to be back today".'

153

'I see. Thanks.' Household glanced at his watch. It was by then nearly five p.m. He, on his shift, had put in three hours overtime. Perigo had come in at two p.m., and had gone already, leaving Tracy and Wiseman to do the work. The man was coming apart at the seams, it was something he would have to bring to Atkins' attention.

'It was Sam, really.' Mrs Dance sat in the deep armchair. She glanced out of the open french windows at her husband, savagely cutting the privet hedge. 'He always has done that.'

'Sam?' Penny Wiseman asked.

'No ... my husband. Whenever something has troubled him he has gone out and attacked the garden ... better than attacking us, I suppose, but our only daughter has been abducted, so he's picked up the shears... Anyway, Sam, yes.' The brown mongrel sat up at the mention of his name. 'Took him out this afternoon and he showed fear at the corner. Stopped in his tracks ... dogs sense things ... have you ever had that experience of going into a room and suddenly thinking, something's happened?'

'No ...' Penny Wiseman shook her head.

'I have,' David Tracy said, 'once. It was utterly unmistakable, so I know what you mean.'

'Well believe me, I know dogs, and they are many times more sensitive to atmosphere like that than we are, and since we have had Sam, six years now, it's the first time he's done that.'

'What happened?' Penny Wiseman sat forward, keenly interested.

'Well, when we take Sam for a walk, we walk on

the right-hand side of Rutherford Road and turn right towards Trumpington Road to the woods over Trumpington Road. This morning, after you had left us, on a whim I took Sam to the left, intending to walk towards Hills Road.'

'Retracing Joyce's route home?'

'Yes, but walking in the opposite direction, of course.'

'Of course.'

'Didn't want to wander too far ... it's a hot day ... dogs don't like heat, especially brown and black ones. We got to the end of the road and he stopped dead. Would not move forward. He's gone round that corner before, quite happily.'

'But today?'

'As I said, he wouldn't go past the corner ... stopped dead in his tracks ... growling.' Mrs Dance held herself erect, even when sitting, clearly no slouching in her chair for this lady; though her speech was forced as if she was heavily sedated. She showed little emotion. The only emotion that either officer could detect was an eagerness to be of whatever assistance she could to the police. Yet her mind must have been in turmoil, Penny Wiseman thought. She knew that hers would be if a daughter of hers had been abducted. The large bottle of pills beside Mrs Dance told their own tale.

'We'll go and have a look,' Tracy said. 'I wouldn't dismiss a dog's reaction ... there may be something there, some small trace. As we say in police work "every contact leaves a trace".'

'Really, is that what you say?'

'Well, it's what the scientists have been able to

tell us over the years.' Penny Wiseman smiled what she hoped was a reassuring smile. 'Rest assured, Mrs Dance, we are doing all we can to find your daughter.'

'But there really isn't much you can do, is there, if you don't know where she is? Is there?'

'There is little we can do, Mrs Dance, but little does not mean nothing. We are assuming that Joyce has been abducted by the Panther.'

'Yes?'

'There is good and bad in that. The bad we must confront that he is very efficient at what he does, he – or they, but we assume it's a man operating alone – he has a means of transporting his victims.'

'Well, you know that ... a van.'

'Yes, and a lock-up, we believe in the country.'

'Yes ... heavens, all this I knew before Joyce was abducted.'

'And we are looking at all lock-ups within a ten mile radius of Cambridge.'

'Ten miles?'

'We calculate it's within the radius of the city centre from what the other victims have told us.'

'And that's generous,' Tracy added. 'Could be within five miles, we don't want to draw the circle too close, but the more we extend it, the more ground there is to cover.'

'I can appreciate that.'

'The good news ... well, the thing to cling to, Mrs Dance, is that he hasn't murdered any of his victims, though he may have molested them.'

'So you said before ... he seems to want to care for them, to ensure their comfort and well-being

... he's very ill, I think.'

'It would appear so, definitely so, I would say, mad not bad ... a candidate for the secure hospital rather than prison.'

'But mad ... in a sense, that can be more dangerous than bad. Mad people are liable to do anything, anything at all, just as the whim takes them. It's of little consolation, frankly. This is killing my husband.' Mrs Dance glanced sideways, out into the garden. 'Look at the energy he's putting into the hedge cutting. You wouldn't think he has a pacemaker fitted, would you? The doctor told him to avoid stress, excitement, hard work and he's got all three, two of the three, anyway, and possibly excitement as well, this is a form of excitement, I suppose. Tell me, are you both in charge of this investigation?'

'No, we are your contact officers. The man in overall charge is a Mr Perigo.'

'Perigo,' Mrs Dance echoed the word. 'Foreign?'

'No,' Penny Wiseman smiled. 'A Cambridge man, by which I mean a man of the town, not the gown.'

'Ah ... my husband's a Cambridge man ... of the gown. He teaches classics.'

'I see ... well,' Penny Wiseman stood. Tracy followed her cue and did likewise. 'We had better go back and look at the corner. I go along with what Sergeant Tracy says, I too wouldn't dismiss your dog's reaction.'

'If you could see yourselves out?'

'Of course.'

Wiseman and Tracy left the Dance house, large and impressive to those of more modest incomes, like those of detective sergeants, ivy covered, just a number. It was neither small enough nor large enough to carry a name, a lush garden to the front and a lush and larger garden to the rear, a very modest car sitting on the gravel driveway. It was definitely the home of a classics tutor. They walked across the road to the corner with Long Road.

'Well, I don't feel anything,' Tracy smiled.

Penny Wiseman returned the smile. 'But it would make sense.' She looked at the location. 'I mean, the ground is too hard to leave any foot-prints on the verge or beneath the hedge, no tyre tracks on the road surface ... no indentation in the hedge itself, as if she had been pushed there, but look ... houses to the left and right ... but houses well back from the road, trees in the garden obscuring a view of this particular spot ... and across Long Road, what's that?'

'That's Long Road Plantation,' Tracy said, 'and cycle track ... a designated cycle track on the other side of Long Road.'

'So, in the absence of a passing cyclist, and not many of them about late at night, this corner can't be overlooked.'

'It can't, can it?' Tracy looked about him. 'Bang in the middle of Cambridge and for all the eyes upon us right now, we might as well be in the middle of the country. All the eyes, that is, except the occupants of the cars. But this is rush hour ... there would hardly be any cars on the road when she was abducted.'

'She must have thought she was safe home ... look at that, her front gate is just beyond stone throwing distance.'

158

'But isn't that the most dangerous time?' Tracy asked. 'When you think you're safe, think you've won...'

'Dare say, but she was doing everything right ... walking facing the oncoming traffic, even if this is a blind corner, who could have blamed her for walking round it when her home is just there, a few paces away?'

'Well, that's us for the day.' Tracey smiled at Wiseman. 'We have something to show for our overtime, the possible place of abduction. We'd better knock on those doors, just for the sake of completion.'

'Yes.'

'You take that one, I'll take this one. Bet you a tenner nobody saw anything.'

Tracy and Wiseman rendezvoused at the police vehicle fifteen minutes later. Tracy was first to arrive, he unlocked the door and wound down both the driver's and the passenger's window. He enjoyed the birdsong and the lush green of the midsummer foliage as he leaned upon the car waiting for Penny Wiseman. Being a police officer has its drawbacks and its rewards, but it was on days like this that he knew why he could not ever have been an office worker. He saw Penny Wiseman leave the house, he also saw that she looked pleased with herself.

'Pity you didn't say "see or hear",' she said as she approached him, 'otherwise you would be a tenner light just now. We've got even more to show for our overtime.'

Tracy stood, taking his weight off the car. 'What have you got?'

'Possible time of abduction. Lady in that house.' Wiseman nodded to the house she had visited. 'Elderly, not so old, mind's still there and so is her hearing. Tells me she has lived in that house for forty years. She can identify her neighbour's cars by their engine sound, by the time they come and go. She's learned to do that over the years. Even if the people in the street change their cars once every two or three years, she notices the change, she tells me...'

'And...?'

'And on the night in question, she heard an unknown vehicle, not previously heard by her, turn into this road from Long Road. It entered Rutherford Road as Channel Four News was starting, turned round in the road and then the driver switched the engine off. She heard the driver's door open and then shut. She presumed it was the driver's door because just the one door opened and shut.'

'Could have been a passenger getting out.'

'Don't think it was,' Penny Wiseman held eye contact with Tracy, 'because of something she said. Anyway, a second door then opened which she said had a hollower sound than the first door.'

'The rear door of a van?'

'That's what I thought. Moments passed, a few minutes she thinks, possibly about five, and the rear door still hadn't been closed.'

'Alright ... following you.'

'Then there is a sound, a dull thump ... but not very loud or violent and then, and only then, is the rear door closed with the louder, more echo-ing sound than the driver's door. A few seconds pass and the vehicle is started and drives away slowly, unhurriedly down Long Road.'

'That was the abduction?'

'I think it had to have been.'

'And she didn't come forward with that information?'

'Well, to be fair, we didn't do a house to house, only found out just now that that corner was the likely point of abduction, courtesy of a brown mongrel called Sam.'

'Fair point.'

'But I think it tells us a lot, something for us to tell Perigo tomorrow. If it was the Panther, and it seems likely, it means he cruises for his victims. He doesn't lie in wait for a likely victim to come along, he cruises, and he doesn't pre-select days in advance.'

'An opportunistic predator?'

'I would think so. He drove up Long Road, so he would have seen Joyce Dance walking along, also going up Long Road, so he turned the vehicle into the first road on the right, hoping to snatch her as she passed, but by coincidence she turned into the road, this road, because this is where her parents had their house.'

'Right into his arms,' Tracy sighed. 'Oh, boy...'

'So she was concussed and bundled into the back of the van. The door was shut and then the van started. That's one man.'

'It is, isn't it? If he had an accomplice the passenger door would also have opened and shut.'

'And the engine would start before the rear door closed. Well, possibly, but the sequence of sound, the bundle going in the back, the closing of the rear door, the opening of another door, the shutting of another door and then the starting of the engine, well, that has to be one man. Confirming he's a lone operator.' Penny Wiseman looked pleased with herself.

'It also means he's going to kill her.' Tracy watched colour drain from Wiseman's face. 'All the other victims reported a blow to the back of their head. He didn't expect her to turn into this road, he was going to step out behind her, check for cars, bang her over the head if all was clear, drag her back into the shadows. But she turned into the road, she must have come face to face with him. He has abducted her to kill her, to prevent her identifying him.'

'I rather wish you hadn't said that,' Wiseman said.

'So do I,' Tracy said. 'I mean, in a way...'

'We'd better tell Perigo, tell him immediately.'

'He's out.' Household noted the fear in Penny Wiseman's eyes. 'Why? You look agitated.' Penny Wiseman told Household about her and Tracy's fears.

'I see.' Household put his pen down. 'But I doubt if there's anything you can do. You'll have to record your fears and reasons for your fears in the case file ... it's on his desk, I can see it from here.'

'On his desk!' Tracy couldn't hide the surprise in his voice.

'Yes, should be in the filing cabinet and the filing cabinet kept locked at all times, Home Office regulations ... but anyway, apart from that, there's little you can do, I'm afraid.'

Penny Wiseman sat wearily in the chair in front of Household's desk. 'There isn't, is there? That poor girl.'

'Is there anything in the statements of the previous victims anything you might have missed?'

'Trying to think.' Tracy sat back against a vacant desk. He turned to Wiseman, 'We could go over them again, Mr Household is right, there might be something.'

'It'll be in the details,' Household said, 'and only in one of the statements ... it'll be a detail that one victim noted, if it's there at all.'

'Yes, thanks ... sorry to trouble you, sir, appreciate it's not your case. Do you know where Mr Perigo is?'

'I don't, I am sorry ... but he'll be back, could be back anytime, he's on the two till ten turn, as you know.'

'Yes.'

'Unlike you and unlike me,' Household shrugged, 'but that's police work. If you wanted to punch a timecard you shouldn't have joined, but I am sure that's been said to you before, and I'm sure you don't want to punch a timecard.'

'Certainly has and I certainly don't.' Tracy levered himself off the desk as Wiseman stood. 'Well, let's go over those statements. I'll dig them out, if you make the coffee.'

The Panther reversed the van up to the side of the bungalow. He got out, noisily slamming the door behind him. Inside the bungalow Joyce Dance started at the sound. She expected the man, the

Cambridge Panther, to come into the bungalow, to see if she was well, being the one he allegedly cared for, to ask her if she was hungry or thirsty, staring at her with those devouring eyes. She tried to keep calm, she had a plan, but she knew it would only work if she could remain calm. But he didn't come into the bungalow, instead she heard him moving about outside. He occasionally murmured, as if talking with someone, or to himself, most likely to himself, she thought, because the man was clearly deranged. He was dangerous. Dangerous, she thought, dangerous wasn't the word. If there was a word to describe something which was ten times more than dangerous then that word could be applied to him. She lay on her side, listening. The Panther showed no indication of coming into the house, content, it seemed, to address a job to be done on the outside of the house, calmly so far as she could tell, because whenever she heard him, he seemed to be moving slowly and methodically Eventually he seemed to stop working and began to take the shutters down from the windows. She shut her eyes against the glare of the sun as it streamed directly into the room. That, she thought, that was something to remember if she ever got out of this alive: she guessed the time to be mid afternoon, and at that time the sun shone directly into the room she was in at that time of the year. From that the police could work out the compass direction of the room in which she was being held in. That, she thought bitterly, would narrow it down to a few hundred buildings. She even tried to work it out herself ... mid afternoon, looking directly into the sun,

Cambridgeshire ... south west, she thought.

The Panther unlocked the door of the bungalow, placed what sounded like a can on the floor. He then went to the sink, in the small kitchen; she heard the sound of running water, and the tap seemed to run for a long time before it was turned off, as though something was being rinsed. The Panther then left the kitchen and dropped something metallic onto the can. Only then did he enter the room in which Joyce Dance lay.

'Did you sleep well?' he asked, as he removed the gag.

'Yes.' She smiled a warm but wholly artificial smile. *Did I sleep well!* The man is mad, as if I am a guest who wants to be here. 'I did. I didn't expect you back so early, Harry.'

He smiled. He seemed to respond to his name being spoken with affection.

'Yes ... I have a few things to do.'

'Really?' She tried to sound interested.

'Yes.' He sat down and picked black paint off his hands. 'I have painted the van.'

'The whole van?'

'No, just the back door. You see, I had a yellow square on the back, sort of out thinking the police, you see, thought they'd be looking for a plain looking van not one that is distinguished by something as "loud" as a yellow square on the back door. I put it there originally to keep the following vehicle off my rear bumper. Yellow, you see, is a colour you shy away from ... that was the thinking, then I left it on when I started collecting.'

'Collecting?'

'Yes.' He smiled, that same warm smile she had

165

seen before, yet beneath eyes that were at once glassy and bottomless. 'My girls ... girls like you, Joyce ... you've been reported missing, as you know, your photograph's in the paper, not as flattering as it could be ... you're much nicer looking in the flesh.'

'Thank you, Harry.'

'Harry' the Panther smiled again. 'No, I mean it, but then I only collect attractive girls.'

'Harry...' said with warmth. Got to keep this up, she thought, have to keep up this dialogue.

'But today I thought I was pushing it a bit ... yellow square on my van is just too distinctive, but it's not easy, the paint doesn't stick to the yellow ... the black paint. The van's black, as you know.'

'I didn't actually.'

'Well, it is ... anyway, I am painting the yellow square out. Trying to anyway. I've bought some spray paint as well. I reckon if I put enough on, then enough will stick to blot out the yellow... They say that people like me like to taunt and provoke the police.'

Joyce Dance leaned upon her elbows and pushed herself back into a sitting position. The sleeping bag fell away and exposed her breasts. As she had hoped it would ... all part of the plan, all part of the desperate gamble ... the desperate, desperate, oh, so desperate gamble that just might save her life. 'Men like you?' she asked. 'What is a man like you, Harry?'

'Psychopaths. Isn't that what they call us?' He peeled paint from his hands. She saw that it was coming away in small slivers, the largest about the length of a person's thumbnail. He laid the paint slivers on the table-top. 'That's who we are, psychopaths ... have to be ... have to be insane ... but you know the really interesting thing, Joyce?'

'No ... tell me, Harry.' She saw his eyes gaze admiringly at her breasts, a neat, firm 32A – small is beautiful. She had never had any complaints and many women had said 'I wish I had a figure like yours'. For the first time in her life she, normally so coy, was disporting herself.

'Well, the interesting thing is that it doesn't feel wrong, Joyce. It feels right, and not only does it feel right, but it feels good. It feels ... well, I enjoy it ... it's not just that it's so nice to have someone to come home to ... it's not just the sense of reward I get when I know I am caring and providing for someone ... it's not just the sense of honour I feel when I have a young woman, an attractive, desirable young woman in my custody, in my total and complete control, and yet I do not, as other men would, I do not despoil her ... I do not use her for my pleasure ... I feel proud of myself for that. What it is, Joyce, what it is, is the sense of power. I feel so powerful having you here.'

Honour, she thought, he has a sense of honour about this. But she smiled, still she exposed her breasts. Take me, Harry, she pleaded silently, take me, take me ... make me real in your mind, no matter how twisted and corrupt and con-taminated and perverted and downright evil your mind is. Take me and make me real to you ... not just a 'trophy'. I want to be real in your mind, Harry, you animal. I want to be real because I want to live. I want to live to say how sorry I am

167

to my mummy for stealing ten pence from her purse when I was little, and I want to live to tell my daddy I love him, just once before the first one of us dies. I want to live because I want to touch velvet again, I don't know why. I want to see a sunset and a sunrise. Please, Harry, take me so we can be one, take me so we can become an item in your mind ... then perhaps you'll let me live ... and if you do, I promise, I swear, I swear, I swear I will never complain about anything again. I live in the west amid peace and prosperity, I see now that each day is a gift. Please take me, Harry, as roughly and savagely as you like ... take me so that I can live.

But all the Panther saw was a naked, smiling young woman who was chained to the skirting board. 'You see, Joyce, I am not very successful in the pit.'

'The pit? Are you a miner?'

He smiled. 'No ... the "pit" is out there.' He inclined his head to the window. 'No, you see that's the "pit" out there ... the world, life ... the city of Cambridge and the countryside around it. The pit, the dump, the landfill site ... I don't get on too well there, I have no power there, no authority.' He stopped picking away at the paint on his hands. 'I just ... I can't fit in out there, in the "pit" ... not since I came back, but even before I went away. I ... well but here ... in this bungalow ... well, here I can find peace ... and here I have company that won't run away from me.' He smiled at her. 'What would you like for tea, Joyce?'

'Don't mind, Harry, really ... whatever you like.'

'OK,' he smiled, 'I'll see what I can find. But first I'll go and see if I can put some more paint on, should be nice and tacky now.' He stood and left the room.

She waited until he had left the bungalow, until she saw him walk past the window, raising his hand in greeting to someone, the elderly neighbour, she thought, but by the gesture, fully raised arm, it seemed that the neighbour was a long way away, far out of earshot. Then she wriggled out of the sleeping bag and crossed to the table, and lowered her head and licked as many of the slivers of paint as she could into her mouth, leaving some, but the greater number went into her mouth.

He didn't want her. That was plain. That he didn't want her and was letting her see him could only mean that she was never going to be able to say the things she wanted to say to her parents, never touch velvet again, nor see a sunset or a sunrise, or live, just being grateful to be alive in the western world, knowing only peace and prosperity.

There was, thought Household, something death-like about the property. It was neat, very neat, too neat really, as if it had an absence of human frailty. The front garden had been overlaid in concrete as if to smother all life. The curtains were closed in the downstairs rooms, but open in the front bedrooms, upstairs. The house colour too, black painted woodwork, contrasted with the red brick. Black gloss was not necessarily a depressing, or depressive colour in Household's opinion, he always thought it worked well on the front door of number ten Downing Street, for example, and even here it might, just might have worked, but on this particular house it seemed to add somehow to the overall lifelessness of the property.

Household turned and saw a woman walking along the pavement towards him. She was short, stocky and, he thought, her grey suit and heavy black shoes must be very uncomfortable for her in this heat. He knew she was going to speak to him.

'Can I help you?' She stood close to him, a little too close to be proper in respect of body language. Just a few centimetres closer, Household thought, and an observer might think they either liked or disliked each other very much indeed. Her bad breath told Household of rampant gum disease.

'I was just about to call on the gentleman who lives here.' He spoke softly, held eye contact and didn't give any ground.

'You looked a bit suspicious.' The woman's voice softened as she sensed she wasn't going to intimidate Household. 'We get a lot of burglaries in Bar Hill ... mind you, you don't look like a housebreaker, the ones they catch are always very young.'

'Oh, you are right to be suspicious,' Household continued to speak softly and to hold eye contact, 'and I am gratified to learn that I don't look like a housebreaker. But I am a friend of the gentleman who lives here.'

The woman made a menacing sound in her throat. 'He hasn't got any friends ... no one visits

... he goes to work, comes home, goes to work, comes home. We try to get some form of community spirit going here, but it's not easy. Anyway, we tried a street party in a cul-de-sac, a communal burning of Christmas trees on Twelfth Night with mulled wine and sausage rolls and carols ... things of that nature, but he hasn't attended anything ... never says hello if you pass him in the street. He might go to the shops on foot, that's when you pass him in the street, but if his car isn't there, he isn't at home. We don't even know what he does for a living, works odd hours though. Only know his name because his mail has been delivered to our house on a few occasions ... not all of it, just one letter addressed to a Mr D Perigo mixed up with ours. That's my house, next door to his. Mind you, it could be worse, we could have anti-social neighbours. So that's D Perigo ... he comes and goes and speaks to no one. Don't even know what the D is for ... Davie? Daniel?'

'Dominic,' said Household. 'His name is Dominic Perigo.'

'So, after ten years, we have found out his Christian name ... in such contrast to our other neighbours, moved in last summer and once they were settled in, had a cheese and wine party to introduce themselves to their new neighbours, Peggy and Frank, lovely couple ... but him...' she snarled towards Perigo's house. 'The children on the estate give him a wide berth, that's always significant. Shall I tell him you called? I dare say he'll reply if I speak to him?'

'No,' Household smiled. 'I was passing ... just

called in on the off-chance, on a whim really. I tend to do things on a whim.'

'I see.' The woman turned slightly and strode away to her home, she entered it and shut the front door behind her with a slam.

'Thank you, madam.' Household smiled to himself and walked to where he had parked the car. He extended the journey home by driving further away from Cambridge, rather than returning towards the town and driving to Bedford on the Madingley Road. He was in no hurry to reach home and he let the A10 carry him as far as Godmanchester, where, with some reluctance, he followed the signs for St Neots, and points south, to Bedford.

Arriving at his house, he parked his car in the drive and opened the front door. His welcome was a stony silence and an icy look from his wife. He took his jacket off and slung it over the banister rail. He walked into the kitchen and poured water into the kettle. It had been a long time since his wife had made him a cup of tea to welcome him home.

'You're late,' she said tetchily.

'Yes, I had to make a visit, and there was some paperwork to catch up on ... and quite frankly, I'd be home a lot earlier if you didn't live up to your name so well.'

And that comment lit the blue touch paper. He knew he shouldn't have said it. He knew the reaction it would cause from Joy Household and he wasn't surprised. There followed much screaming, much banging, much slamming about the house, the children upstairs pointedly and noisily throwing the bolts across their bedroom doors, locking themselves in. Household bore the tirade with a stoicism he had honed over the years, burrowing himself into a siege mentality. Dinner that night was delayed, much delayed, after which Joy stormed up to their bedroom and slammed the door behind her. Household washed up and then, as usual, went for a stroll, finding peace in the streets and as usual, in such circumstances, he fetched up in a pub.

Later that night, lying next to the unresponsive Joy Household, he questioned his moral right to regard Perigo's house as dead: is own household was hardly a fountain of emotional warmth and psychological wellbeing. And worse, much worse, there seemed to be no end in sight. Sleep came to him with some difficulty that night, with more difficulty than usual.

He loved to see her naked. He rested on his right elbow, on his side on the double futon mattress, gazing at her as she was bathed in moonlight, a soft, delicate pink form in a room of overwhelming blue, with the moon so large and bright, at its perigee, or its apogee, he could never remember which, but bright enough to illuminate the room so that the room appeared to be blue. The blue carpet, the blue wallpaper, the blue vase with dried reeds, the print of Vincent van Gogh's 'The Blue Nude' on the wall above the futon. She turned from the window and looked at him and smiled. She shrugged her shoulders. 'Sorry,' she said.

'It's OK.' He reclined, and lay on his back. 'It's probably insensitive of us.'

173

'It would be if we did make love. It's knowing that that girl is going to be killed, or is already dead.'

'Or what is worse, is that she is being murdered at this very moment ... we just don't know the instant.'

'After what we said to her parents, reassuring them that none of his victims had been murdered.' Penny Wiseman wiped her forehead. 'It's warm ... too warm. It's midnight and I am perspiring ... windows open, heat's off and I'm dripping.'

'Me too.' Tracy kicked off the duvet, he felt the sudden coolness envelope his body. 'But Sydney's right, you know, what can we do? He has her ... she's at his mercy somewhere. Unless we know where...'

'I know.' Penny Wiseman turned and looked up at the moon. 'Tell us what to do, and we'll do it. Isn't that the attitude? But I feel so frustrated ... so helpless, so angry. The moon at its perigee,' she said, 'high tides tonight.'

Tracy remained silent. Perigee, perigee, perigee, he repeated in his head, perigee is close ... apogee must therefore be...

'You know, I have the impression that if Sydney was in charge of this investigation, there'd be a bit more movement. Perigo he's...'

'He's floundering, if you ask me. Came with all promise ... fast track graduate entry ... full of promise and no delivery. Tell you something as well, Household would have been at the Dance's house and he would have visited all the other homes, he wouldn't have left that to the likes of thee and me.'

'I don't think he would have sent me on that fool's errand to Aberdeen. That poor girl wasn't ready to talk and if she was, the Grampian police would have interviewed her for us. She might even be more willing to talk to a police officer with a familiar accent. I come from the Fens, my accent would be associated by her with the kidnap. Dominic Perigo didn't think of that.'

'Good point.' Tracy too wiped sweat from his brow.

They had left the police station separately, as was their custom, and had rendezvoused in the market square, where they had a late lunch, or early dinner, they couldn't decide which, in the Italian restaurant. Then they walked arm in arm, not caring if they were seen by any of their colleagues, through the bustling city centre. They escaped down Jesus Lane, past the Friends Meeting House, and Jesus College to the Four Lamps roundabout and across Midsummer Common. They walked by the river, past a group of young 'dossers' who sat drinking super lager and tossing the empty cans contemptuously into the Cam. They were mainly males with a few heavily tattooed females, each with a sleeping bag tied up with string. They looked up at Wiseman and Tracy with suspicion, seeming to recognise, or sensing 'police', and Wiseman and Tracy in turn eyed them coldly. They would not dip into their pockets for twenty pence 'for a cup of tea'. At night the dossers would sleep by the river, Wiseman and Tracy knew well, and the next day would walk to the bus station which, for some reason, had a magnetic attraction, and with their

175

dogs for an added touch of sympathy, would hassle but not threaten any likely looking foot passenger for 'loose change'. Wiseman and Tracy walked on, enjoying the gathering evening, the swallows whirling and darting, catching insects which were carried on the high thermals, cyclists travelling in singles or pairs, or family groups going homewards; on the river there were oars ... single sculls, pairs, a four and a smooth and graceful eight, clearly a practised crew who moved as one with gentle timing from a slightly built female cox, leaving only ripples on the water. Still arm in arm they negotiated the stile at the footbridge and crossed the river into the expensive new build flats at Manhattan Drive, walked along Cutter Ferry Path to Elizabeth Way, then crossed Elizabeth Way into Chesterton and to Penny Wiseman's gently decorated house in Mulberry Close. They sat in the kitchen for a moment and, gazing at each other warmly, decided they would go 'straight up'. In the bedroom they embraced and kissed whilst laying on the futon, their sweat smeared bodies sliding against each other, until Wiseman pushed Tracy off and away from her. She rolled out of bed feeling his eyes upon her, knowing his eyes were both adoring and wondering at the same time. She stood at the side of the window overlooking the green space outside her house. She watched a cat she recognised as belonging to her neighbour prowl among the shadows of the trees, and an elderly woman wheel her cycle with plastic bags draped over the handlebars ... she looked up at the moon, so vast that evening, and said 'Sorry'.

It was futile. She knew it was futile but it gave her something to do while she waited to die. She touched everything she could, leaving her finger-prints on every surface which she knew would be wiped, but also on hidden surfaces, on the walls, on the underside of the table, anywhere, any-where at all so that if the police, by some means, could link her to this man in black, with his black van, and could link this bungalow to him, then her prints in the bungalow would link him to the murder. She would not be alive to see him con-victed but it gave her a last purpose in life. She sank back on the sleeping bag and looked at the moonlight stream through the cracks between the boards and the window ... how beautiful it seemed, and how real, more real somehow than if she didn't know she had only a little time to live. Fear left her suddenly. Very suddenly she was no longer afraid. She had read that when hope goes, fear goes with it. How true it is, she thought, how true ... but how unfair that I can't tell anybody. She thought that her life had been a good life, it had been short, but nothing to complain about, never known hunger, had loved, once, had had good sexual experiences, she had seen the Southern Cross. Once she had developed she was pleased to have been born female, she would not have wanted to be a man, especially since she was considered attractive to men and, she had discovered, to one or two women as well on occa-sions, and so now it was at an end. What might have been was going to be stolen from her. She was sorry for her parents, they would probably

177

never know what had happened to her. All she could hope was that the Panther's weird and misplaced sense of duty to his victims might not extend to her death, that he would not make such a good job of disposing of her that her body would never be found. If you had time and space, the easiest thing in the world is to make someone disappear, and he had both. She had read of such disposals, the actual murder is the easy part in a practical sense ... the difficulty comes in disposing of the body, that is where time and space are needed, all he had to do was make sure no blood ... no blood...

The thought came to her in a flash.

She looked for something to do it with. There were one or two items in the room, seen dimly in the moonlight. She needed something hard, something that wouldn't bend, and something that could be made sharp. She stood up, crawled as far as the length of chain would allow, scouring the floorboards for something, anything that would do the job because her mind was made up, she was set upon a determined course of action. She had always said she would do this, take her own life rather than have it taken. She had said that thinking of her grandmother's dreadful death from an internal growth that had seemed to eat the poor woman alive, from the inside, like a maggot inside an apple. If that happens to me, she had said, much rather a bottle of sleeping pills and a glass or two of wine, taken in a comfortable bed, just a week or two before the end comes anyway. She had never envisaged this, what young person would have? 'Twas indeed the stuff of nightmares. She touched something, cold, metal ... a nail. Ideal, she thought, ideal. She sat by the table. She didn't want to go back to the sleeping bag because the bag would soak it up and she wanted it spread about. She placed the nail beside her and began to pluck at her scalp hair, one strand at a time, and placed hairs in nooks and crannies, pushing them down between the cracks in the floorboards ... not too many, she thought. If she put her hair everywhere ... she moved to her right as far as she could, placing her scalp hair where she could. She then moved to her left beyond where the sleeping bag lay crumpled on the floor and, when at the furthest reach of the chain, she placed the nail point at the artery in her left wrist.

She hesitated ... she hesitated ... she tensed up for the act, then hesitated and relaxed. She tried again ... again she hesitated ... the nail stung against her flesh ... she gasped ... then eventually, tears running down her cheeks, she said, 'Sorry, Mummy ... sorry, Daddy' and pressed the nail home. Blood, warm blood, flooded out with each pump of her heart. She transferred the nail to the fingers of her left hand and placed it on the artery in her right wrist. She already felt her strength failing, she already felt faint ... again she apologised to her parents, and weeping uncontrollably, forced the metal into the blood stream. She dropped the nail and held both arms outstretched, letting the blood run from her body onto the floorboards. She moved her arms so that blood might find its way into the cracks between the floorboards. She fully expected the Panther

179

to scrub the blood from the floorboards but she knew that even a microscopic trace of her blood would be sufficient to prove she had been in this awful house.

Still blood dripped from her arteries ... again she muttered an apology to her parents, and a prayer. Never a particularly spiritual young woman, the concept of a Greater Being, of an afterlife, came to her and she didn't know what to say, nor really to whom to say it, but found herself apologising for all the things she had done and wished she hadn't done, and things she had said and she wished she had not said.

She felt cold ... very cold ... cold from the inside of her body, not the outside, but the chill came from within. She felt herself drifting into a dream-like state ... then she came to again ... and then the Panther was in front of her, kneeling, holding her wrists. She had not noticed him come, he had seemed to creep out of the gloom.

'You poor girl,' he said softly. 'I can't save you now, you have lost too much blood.'

She nodded gently.

He stroked her chin. 'I was going to kill you,' he said softly, gently, 'so there is nothing lost.'

'Thank you for telling me that,' she held eye contact with the man, 'I appreciate it.'

'Yes ... you took a gamble, but it paid off, you wanted to die on your terms ... I can understand that.'

'I want my parents to know what happened. I don't want to disappear. I am their only daughter, their only child ... I want them to have a grave to visit ... please.'

The Panther nodded. 'My sweet child … I promise, your body will be found. I was going to keep you here, in the ground, but I won't now.'

'Thank you … thank you.'

'Sleep now.' The Panther smiled and spoke gently. 'Sleep now.'

5

More than any evening that summer, or any evening in many a summer to come, and cold winter's evenings and wet spring evenings and blustery autumn evenings for that matter, Archie Good wanted his pint of strong Abbot Ale. And a few more pints after that one, but the first one was the one he needed most. He had walked to work that morning along the narrow lane which led from his cottage to Byres Farm. It was a beautiful summer's morning, with a mist at ground level, which was deepest in the hollows and ditches but which cleared rapidly as the sun rose. Archie Good walked out that particular morning when the haze started at his kneecaps and totally concealed his boots from view. He strode out of his cottage, leaving his wife still sleeping on the horsehair mattress they had shared since they were first married, his hobnails crunching the gravel outside his door, and then kicking on the tarmac of the lane. It was a journey he had done every working day for over twenty years. There was nothing which made that day's walk to work any different from any other morning's walk to work, yet it was that journey that made him want his Abbot Ale that evening.

Archie Good arrived at Byres Farm and in the farmhouse kitchen, whilst enjoying a steaming mug of tea, provided by the rosy cheeked wife of the farm owner, the farm manager gave out the jobs, and recorded the jobs on the job sheets. All in good humour, all on first name terms. Archie Good's job for that day had taken him back towards his cottage. He had retraced his steps of earlier that morning, before turning off into the field where hedging had to be done. By the time he left the farmhouse, the mist had completely cleared, and he walked, carrying the tools he needed, in shirt sleeves, corduroy trousers and a wide brimmed hat worn against the sun. He turned a corner in the lane and his heart thumped in his chest, he felt a chill shoot down his spine and he stopped walking, stopped suddenly, involuntarily ... some subconscious part of his brain telling his feet to stop moving as in a split second his brain registered what his eyes were seeing. It was the naked body of a young woman, lying on the grass verge, legs extended, arms raised up over her head, the palms laid one over the other, not dissimilar, he thought, to the posture of a diver, just before diving off the high board. Except she was lying flat, face up, on the grass verge. He approached the body cautiously, he knew she was dead, she just looked dead, that pallor ... the lack of movement could mean unconsciousness, but Archie Good was the son of a farm labourer, and a labourer himself. He

182

had worked from the day he was fifteen, not waiting to the end of term as others of his class, but walked home at the end of the school day on his fifteenth birthday and straight to the fields and helped with the harvest until two the following morning, anxious to prove he was a willing lad. As a countryman, he was closer and more used to death than were town dwellers who led sanitised, censored lives, he knew the terror of the animals in the slaughter house; town dwellers knew only cellophane wrapped meat on refrigerated shelves in the supermarket; he knew the woman was dead. Upon nearing the body he knelt beside her. As he did so, he heard the sound of a motor vehicle approaching from the direction of Six Mile Bottom. He clasped his meaty hand round the ankle as he heard the approaching vehicle slow, cautiously. The woman's body was cold and clay-like to the touch, 'clammy' being the only word the man knew that could describe the way a recently deceased body felt. He stood and turned. The vehicle was the postman delivering to the farm, as Archie Good knew he must be. He looked at the postman, a man in his thirties, who was wide-eyed and speechless. The postman then looked at Good.

'Can you go to the farm,' Good said, 'phone the police from there?'

'Got a mobile, mate.' The postman plunged his hand into the jacket which lay beside him on the driver's seat of the small red van. 'I can do it from here.'

'Aye...' Good murmured, 'reckon those things do have a use after all.'

David Tracy drove the unmarked police car slowly through the lanes of the west fens. Beside him Penny Wiseman sat in silence. It had been an unexpectedly early start to the morning shift. The coffee and tea making had been done, the papers had been read as the sun, still low in the sky, cast long shadows across Parker's Piece, the banter had taken place, the waking up, between Household and Tracy in the first instance, and then ten minutes later Penny Wiseman entered the room, smiling sheepishly and apologising for being late. Tracy made her a cup of coffee and put it down on her desk. Household watched him do it, looking for just the glimmer of a knowing smile from either of them towards each other, just a flicker of eye contact, and seeing neither, concluded that there was nothing between them, they were not an 'item'. Rather a pity he thought, both of a similar age, both single – they would make a good couple. They had, he concluded, perhaps other interests outside their working relationship. Whatever, it was little of his business. It was then, just then, before the shift's work was done, that the phone on Household's desk rang. It was so unusually early for a phone to ring in the CID room that all three officers exchanged rapid glances. There did, in fact, seem an urgency about it.

'Household.' Sydney Household let the phone ring twice before answering it. When he answered it he did so in a voice which was calm and yet authoritative: he was in control, no matter how urgent the call. He listened and scribbled notes on his notepad as he did so. Moments later he put the phone down gently after promising 'an officer will be attending', and looked at Wiseman and Tracy. 'One for you, I think.'

'What's that, sir?' Tracy was keen, alert.

'Well, your name isn't on it, might be un-connected to your fears of yesterday.' Household shrugged. 'The body of a young adult female has been found. The uniforms are there and requested CID presence. The police surgeon is on his way.'

Wiseman and Tracy looked at each other, and they said in total and spontaneous unison. 'Joyce Dance.' Tracy turned to Household. 'Alright, boss, we're on it.' He reached for his jacket.

'Out by Six Mile Bottom,' Household wrote on a fresh page of his notepad, 'this is the exact location.' He tore off the page of his pad and handed it to Tracy.

Less than thirty minutes later, David Tracy drove the car, at a careful speed, knowing that speed in this case was not of the essence, and approached the scene of activity. A marked police vehicle with a blue flashing light, blue and white police tape across the lane ... another vehicle, a car ... a civilian in brown trousers and a grey hat sitting on the green verge. A vast blue sky above, and about them, the flatness of the fens. David Tracy halted the car and he and Wiseman got out and walked to the blue and white tape. They lifted it and walked to where a heavy duty black plastic sheet had been draped over something on the verge.

'Morning, sir, ma'am.' The constable was tall, youthful, quite calm and in control, crisp white shirt and serge trousers, highly polished black shoes. 'We have a corpse, a young female,' he indicated the mound covered by the black plastic sheet. 'The police surgeon has just pronounced life extinct.'

'Yes ... at seven forty-eight.' The police surgeon turned upon hearing mention of his designation. 'You'll need the pathologist. There are suspicious circumstances.'

'Can we see?' Tracy stepped forward, Penny Wiseman followed him. The police surgeon peeled back the sheet, and first revealed the wrists with distinct puncture points at the arteries and then pulled the sheet back to reveal the face of Joyce Dance.

'Joyce ...' Wiseman gasped.

'You know her?'

'Know of her. Thank you, doctor.' Tracy stepped back as the police surgeon re-covered the corpse with the plastic sheet.

'Well, what makes it suspicious is obvious.' The police surgeon was a finely built man, he had alert eyes and a ready smile, he was, thought Tracy, still in his twenties. 'The wrists are injured at the artery, could be suicide, could be murder, it's one or the other, definitely not accidental. Naked. Out here ... that isn't a voluntary act, and the fact that she appears to have died of blood loss, yet there is no blood at all on the verge...'

'She bled to death somewhere else.'

'If she bled to death ... that's for the pathologist to determine, but the wounds to her wrists would have caused bleeding, profuse bleeding at that, so she has been moved, by A.N. Other.'

'A.N. Other,' Tracy repeated.

186

'So I haven't called the mortuary van. The forensic pathologist will have to have a look at the body in situ.'

'Of course.' Tracy turned to Wiseman, 'Can you...?'

Wiseman nodded and walked back to the car. She opened the door and reached in for the radio.

'Time of death, well...' the police surgeon breathed deeply, 'that's a massive time window, and I'll bet the pathologist won't be drawn on it but off the record, I'd say sometime in the last twelve hours ... possibly a little longer ... rigor is just beginning to establish itself.'

'Thanks,' Tracy smiled, 'Even an off the record opinion can be useful.'

'Well, I'll be on my way.' The police surgeon picked up his black Gladstone bag and walked back to his car.

'Who found her? The chap over there?' Tracy turned to the constable.

'Yes, sir. Gentleman by the name of Good, Archie Good.'

Penny Wiseman returned to Tracy's side. 'They're contacting the pathologist now.'

'Thanks.' Tracy smiled at her. 'Fella over there found her. Good, by name.' Tracy and Wiseman walked to where Archie Good sat on the verge. He stood as they approached him.

'Mr Good,' Tracy nodded. 'Can we ask you a few questions?'

'Aye...'

'You found the body, Mr Good?

'Yes ... she was dumped in the night from a motorcar.'

187

'So we believe.'

'Well, it's the only way she could have got there and it was before the dew formed.'

'How do you know?'

'I lifted her leg, I could tell she was dead. Her leg was a little stiff, but the grass under it was dry ... and the person or people who dropped her, put her there, didn't step onto the verge ... they would have left footprints. The grass is quite long, due for cutting, and the dew would have ... don't know the words, but it would have made the footprints obvious.'

'I see.' Tracy was impressed. 'That could be helpful.'

'Walked right past it on the way to work ... there was a mist covering the ground, I knew the road, just kept walking between the hedgerows ... I reckon I can walk this road blindfold ... but she was concealed by the mist. Got a job which took me back this way and there she was, the grass underneath her was dry, so that's how I knew she was put there in the night, and not after I had walked past this spot this morning, while I was having my tea at the farmhouse. Mrs Grundy, the farmer's wife, makes a cup of tea each morning, and a bacon roll too in the winter.'

'I see.' Tracy paused. 'Did you hear or see anything in the night which you think might be connected to this ... a car in the lane for example?'

'I didn't ... and girl Meg, she sleeps sounder than me, and there's only our little cottage between the farm and the road to Six Mile Bottom.'

Penny Wiseman suddenly felt inspired. 'Who

188

wanders about a night in these fields?' She spoke with a strong Fenland accent.

Archie Good glanced at her, then he smiled. 'You're no townie, girl...'

'I grew up in the Fens ... out by Wicken.'

'Wicken ... I haven't been there in years.'

Wicken being only about ten miles from Six Mile Bottom, gave David Tracy an unexpected insight into just how small Archie Good's world was. He probably knew every blade of grass within a mile of his cottage, he could tell one of his employers' cows from another, knew exactly when the wheat had to be harvested ... was the sort of man who would wander into the cornfield and come back to where his employer and the combine harvester crews were waiting and would say, 'Another hour yet, sir', and that at the dead of night, but anything beyond that mile and he was in a foreign land.

'Oh, it's still there.'

Tracy kept quiet. Wiseman was speaking Archie Good's language, she was making progress. He knew better than to interfere.

'Well, there'll be Old Bob.'

'Who he be?'

'He's the wide boy round these parts. He sets for hares and shoots rabbits ... nothing bigger ... the landowners, they don't mind Old Bob taking the rabbit, but they want the hare, they do.'

'Where be Old Bob?'

'You won't tell him it was I that told you, young mistress? I'll tell you for why ... he helps me and girl Meg with meat, gives us a rabbit, even a hare now and then ... farming don't pay, fresh meat

189

we don't get each day.'

'I won't say.'

'Nor you, young master?'

'I won't say a word,' Tracy smiled. 'Promise.'

'Well, Old Bob has a cottage, an old keeper's cottage.'

'A keeper's cottage?'

'Aye,' Archie Good smiled at the joke of a poacher living in a cottage that was built for a gamekeeper. 'End of the road. You'll turn right for Six Mile Bottom, instead turn left, Old Bob has the whole cottage ... first building you see on the right.'

'Thanks.'

'Well, I'll be getting on now, I've a hedge to see to.'

Sojourner Sleaford lay in bed, unable to sleep, the morning sun streaming through the window. Her bedroom overlooked Jesus Green and so she would indulge in the luxury of sleeping with her curtains open. She didn't particularly want to shut out the world, and no one could look into her room, so the curtains remained open, winter and summer, and being south-facing, the sunlight flooded into her room, a direct line from Old Hannah, 93 million miles away and ten minutes by travelling time. Her mother, for some reason, favoured a north-facing window, it offered purer light but no direct sunlight to caress you into wakefulness each morning, and her mother's room had a less pleasant view of the back garden and the walls and rooftops of CB4, between Chesterton Road and Victoria Road. She had heard the phone ring and being answered, she had heard her mother leave her bedroom, visit the bathroom and go back to her bedroom, leave the bedroom a few moments later. By her body movements, she seemed to be about a specific purpose, it was not hurried, but neither was it a normal waking and dressing, preparing for a day's work. It was also about an hour too early. Sojourner Sleaford rolled out of bed, curled herself into a housecoat, hooked her feet into a pair of slippers and went downstairs. She found her mother in the kitchen. 'You're up early, Mummy.'

'Well, I could say the same for you.'

'I was awake … I wake with the dawn … tends to be early in the summer.'

'So I have noticed in my forty-something years. Cup of tea?'

'Yes, please.' Sojourner Sleaford clambered onto a stool at the breakfast bar and curled her fingers round a mug, into which her mother poured a little milk and a lot of tea. 'Thank you,' she murmured, 'I couldn't get back to sleep.'

'Poor you,' said with a smile.

'Heard you getting up, just after the phone rang.'

'Yes, work to be done.'

'A gruesome dead body, all mangled and splattered, cut to pieces on the railway line? Passengers wishing to inspect the gore of our latest victim which is liberally spread beneath the first-class carriage, should enquire at the guard's van.'

'I think they are called conductors these days … and the days when passenger trains had guard's vans was even before my time.'

'Oldie but goldie.'

'Which is a better state than dying young as this particular "victim", as you put it, is reported to be, out by Six Mile Bottom.'

'Saw a woman in Petty Cury who could fit that description.'

'Sojourner!'

'Well, she could.' Sojourner Sleaford reached for the toast rack. 'Mind if I have the last piece of toast? Too late.'

'That's not the point ... I don't like you being judgmental about people's appearances.'

'Sorry, Mumsie.'

Veronica Sleaford leaned forward and kissed her daughter. 'Put the chain on the door behind me, or lock it with the mortice ... big house ... you're not safe alone with only the Yale holding the door shut. I won't lock you in on a matter of principle, but I want you to lock it behind me.'

'OK, Mummy,' said drearily, whilst buttering the toast.

Veronica Sleaford drove out to Six Mile Bottom. She had been given clear directions from the village which she followed carefully, and driving along a narrow thread of country lane with high verges, and hedges beyond the verges, in a landscape where the skyline, when glimpsed through a gap in the summer green hedgerow, was distant and flat, she saw a collection of vehicles ahead of her. She saw a police tape hung across the road, she saw a police vehicle with a flashing blue light on the roof, needlessly, she thought. She had noticed before how fond the police are of flashing lights on their vehicles, even in a situation like this;

a lovely July morning in a remote part of Cambridgeshire, where a felony may well have been committed, but any urgency is long past, even here, even here, if there is a flashing blue light to shine, let it shine. She said, as she slowed her car to a halt beside the hindmost vehicle, 'Shine on, soul brother, shine on.' She got out of her car and was met by Penny Wiseman. She smiled at the policewoman. 'Good morning, sergeant.'

'Morning, doctor.' Wiseman was smartly but sensibly dressed for the weather, a lemon coloured suit, brown sensible shoes, blonde hair in a bun, white blouse, shoulder bag. 'Sorry to drag you out so early. I am DS Wiseman.'

'There are worse places to be dragged out to, and this isn't early, I confess good country air is a pleasant change from the disinfectant and formaldehyde laden atmosphere of the pathology laboratory, which is doubtless where I will be later this a.m. What have you got for me?'

'Young adult female, ma'am.' Wiseman and Sleaford walked side by side along the lane, beyond where the mortuary van had parked and in which, calloused and hardened by their job, or out of plain lack of imagination and sensitivity, Sleaford could not decide, the driver and his mate sat with their feet on the dashboard, reading tabloid newspapers. At least, she observed, they had enough about them to purchase different tabloids, although the difference between the two newspapers would be minor.

'Here, ma'am,' Wiseman indicated with an outstretched hand and an open palm to the mound on the verge.

'Thanks.' Sleaford knelt by the mound and peeled back the plastic sheeting. 'Oh...' she groaned.

'Ma'am?'

'Nothing ... it's the young ones that reach me somehow, everything ahead of them, and she so pretty too. Heavens, I have a daughter not much younger than this ... should anything happen to her ... this girl's poor parents. Do you know who she is?' Sleaford opened her black bag.

'We believe so, ma'am, but she will still have to be formerly identified. That's to be done yet.'

'Of course.' Sleaford removed the sheeting, exposing the body in its entirety. 'Very pale,' she said as she took a battery powered handheld tape recorder from her bag. She rewound the tape and pressed the recorder button, allowing the leader tape to wind past the tape heads and then spoke into the machine. 'Subject is an apparently healthy northern European female, aged mid-twenties, believed to be but as yet unconfirmed...' Sleaford glanced up at Wiseman.

'Joyce Dance,' Wiseman said. 'In fact it is her, I recognise her from the photographs her family provided.'

'Joyce Dance.' Sleaford switched off the recording machine. 'She has been in the newspapers ... the latest victim of the Panther? That's the right name, isn't it? I seem to remember it because it's such a pleasant sounding name.'

'Yes, ma'am ... she was abducted a few days ago.'

Sleaford relaxed her posture and bowed her head. 'He's started killing ... it was inevitable. I

194

am not a forensic psychologist, but that progression happens ... people, serial killers, very rarely start out killing, they progress to it. A spontaneous assault leads on to premeditated assault, which leads to murder and one murder leads to the next.'

'So we understand, ma'am, but we are hoping he killed this victim because she saw him. We think we have identified the location where he abducted her. We believe he expected her to walk past the side road and that he planned to hit her from behind. All the other victims talk about being hit on the back of the head, but she lived in that street, she would have turned into it and come face to face with him.'

'I see. So you think if he bangs the next victim over the back of the head, he will let her live?'

'We hope so, ma'am.'

'Well, I hope you are right. But I have to tell you that he may have found a taste for killing ... a bit like an alcoholic – once he gets the taste, he doesn't stop until someone stops him.' Veronica Sleaford switched on the tape recorder. 'The body has been laid out in a pose which would imply a desire to increase its shock value.' She turned back to Wiseman. 'Have you got a photograph of this?'

'Of the body? Yes, ma'am.'

'From all angles, without any of the vehicles being in the photograph?'

'I don't know...' Wiseman looked suddenly awkward. She turned to the S.O.C.O. 'Have we?'

'No, ma'am.' The S.O.C.O. stiffened when spoken to. 'Not without the vehicles getting into the shot.'

'Well, I strongly suggest that you do that, sergeant.' Sleaford spoke calmly. 'It is my understanding that forensic psychology has moved on now and the term "organised" and "disorganised" serial killer' has been discredited and are no longer used, can't separate them so easily ... but I think a forensic psychologist would want to look at the way the body has been left. So, photographs from every angle, and from a distance as well. When I have finished ... clear the vehicles from the scene, by as much as about one hundred and fifty metres ... show the scene as the killer would have seen it before he left her here in that pose.'

'Very good, ma'am.'

'The victim,' Veronica Sleaford spoke into the tape recorder, 'has two distinct injuries, namely puncture points in both wrists above the artery, there are also abrasions to the left wrist which are of a type caused by a restraint, such as a length of chain or a thin rope. The body has been clearly laid out in a manner which seems intended to shock the person who discovers it. The arms are stretched out above the head, the legs are straight, feet together, the body is face up.' She felt the legs and tried to lift one at the foot. 'The body has a distinct "clammy" feel to the palm and rigor is not fully established, indicating that death occurred not more than twelve hours ago.' She stood and turned to Penny Wiseman. 'The twelve hours is a...' she opened her hands, widening the gap between them, 'is a generous time window. I know Mr Household of your police station, Mr Perigo also. I haven't had the pleasure of meeting you before, nor, do I think, the gentleman ... DS Wiseman, you said?'

'Yes, ma'am ... my colleague is DS Tracy.'

'Not Richard, I hope?'

Wiseman smiled. 'No, ma'am. David, but he has to endure "Dick" as a nickname.'

'As any policeman with that surname might. But my point is that both Mr Household and Mr Perigo will tell you that I won't be drawn on the time of death. Too many fictional police officers on television have fictional pathologists pinning down the time of death and so helping to solve the case, and we as a profession have allowed ourselves to be pushed into that role. It's as clear a case of life imitating art as ever I came across, and it's not really in our job description. We ascertain cause of death and only cause of death. Time of death is an issue which has been allowed to creep in at the side and is gaining a foothold.'

'I see, doctor.' Wiseman shielded her eyes from the glare of the still low sun. It was going to be another very hot day. 'You can't blame us for trying.'

'I can't and I don't, but I make the point. Well, that's all I can do here ... if you take the photographs, as I suggested. Have you had this man profiled?'

'No.' Wiseman was embarrassed by the answer she was obliged to give.

'No?' Veronica Sleaford raised her eyebrows. 'You surprise me.'

'It's Mr Perigo's case, really, ma'am. Dick and I are the foot soldiers.'

'Well, you seem to be doing too much for foot

soldiers, if it's his case. If he is the senior investigating officer, he should be here, or so I would have thought.'

'He's on the afternoon turn this month, ma'am.'

'Well, it's not my place to comment but I have known senior officers lead by good example, and being willing to attend a situation of great relevance when off duty is not unknown among officers whom I have grown to respect.'

'Yes, ma'am.'

'I would press for a profile of the Panther, so called, as soon as possible, were I you.'

'I'll mention it, ma'am.'

'But that's all I can do here. I'll move my car and have the mortuary van moved. I do strongly suggest you ask the Scene of Crime Officer to take photographs as I suggested, then we'll remove the body before the winged carnivores arrive.'

'The flies?' Wiseman glanced at the corpse. 'They're here already.'

'Not in anything like the numbers that are on their way here. A fly can detect a dead body from up to two miles away.'

'Really?'

'Yes, really. Let's move these vehicles so your snapper can snap.'

Tracy and Wiseman walked reluctantly but purposefully from the side of the road where they had parked their car to the front door of the Dances' house. Wiseman rang the bell. The door was opened after a short delay by Mr Dance. His face was ashen, lined with grief. He nodded at the two officers.

'Mr Dance...' Tracy began.

Dance held up his hand. 'It's alright, I know why you've come. You want me to identify Joyce's body ... as I have seen on television.'

'Yes. How did you...?'

'My wife and I could tell when we saw you drive up and get out of the car. We felt it, somehow.'

'I am sorry, sir.'

'Where was her body found?'

'Out near Six Mile Bottom, sir. At the side of a lane.'

'Oh...' The officers saw the man's stomach contract beneath his thin summer shirt as if he had been punched. 'Dumped like a sack of rubbish ... what's that term "fly tipping", as if she had been fly tipped.'

'Well, no, sir. Actually she appears to have been placed there, quite gently.'

'Oh, heavens ... in the night?'

'Yes, sir. Before the dew formed.'

'And it is Joyce?'

'I ... we think so, sir. From the photographs you have shown us of her and from what you have just told us ... even though, as you say, we can't offer it in evidence.'

'The identification will still have to be done?'

'I am afraid it will, sir.'

'I will do it. I don't think my wife will want the last view of her daughter to be in a metal drawer covered with a sheet. That's no way to remember your only daughter.'

'It's not exactly like that, sir.' Wiseman spoke.

'It's really quite different ... very sensitive.'

Half an hour later Mrs Dance, who still seemed to be heavily sedated, Mr Dance, Penny Wiseman and David Tracy sat in a small room in Addenbrookes Hospital. The room always reminded Tracy of a vestry in a church, he being quite familiar with it. Penny Wiseman, never having been in this particular room, though having performed this unpleasant duty before, glanced around as discreetly as she could, remembering at all times that not only must her focus be with the Dances at this dreadful hour, but be seen to be with them. Nonetheless, she noticed a dark, mildly patterned carpet which softened the room and deadened sound. She noticed solid polished benches with hard seats along three of the four walls, each wall being about fifteen feet long. One of the benches was smaller than the other two, to allow for the door through which they had entered the room. The door, like the benches, was of varnished and polished hardwood. The walls, except for one, were lined with wood panelling of a slightly, but only slightly, darker hue than the door and the benches. The fourth wall had a second door in the corner and for the remainder was covered with two heavy velvet curtains which, drawn shut, met in the middle of the wall.

The four people waited in silence, Tracy and Wiseman sitting apart on separate benches, the Dances sitting close together and clasping hands. There came a sound from behind the curtain, a metallic sound which seemed, to Wiseman, to have a quality of inadvertedness about it, as though no sound should have been made at all, for it was followed by no other sound at all for a full minute, it seemed, when the door beside the curtain opened, and a solemn faced nurse in her middle years and wearing a dark blue cape with red lining, entered the room, shutting the door rapidly but silently behind her. She looked at Tracy who nodded his assent. The nurse took hold of a cord which hung vertically beside the curtains and pulled it down in a hand-over-hand motion. The velvet curtains slid apart silently and revealed a large pane of glass, and beyond the pane of glass lay the body of Joyce Dance upon a stretcher. Her head had been tightly bound in a bandage leaving only her face visible. The blanket covering her body had been similarly neatly and tightly tucked beneath her. By some trick of light and shade, nothing but an unfathomable blackness lay beyond the body, giving the impression that Joyce Dance was sleeping her final sleep, at peace, floating in space.

Mrs Dance turned and buried her head in her husband's chest, and Mr Dance said, 'Yes. Yes, that is Joyce.'

Tracy smiled his thanks at the nurse who proceeded to shut the curtain. She then exited through the door by which she had entered. The Dances retired to the bench on which they had sat, Tracy and Wiseman also resumed their seats.

'Was she ... violated?' Mr Dance looked at Tracy, then at Wiseman.

'There is no indication of that, Mr Dance,' Wiseman said. 'But I am afraid that there will have to be a post-mortem.'

'Oh...' Mr Dance groaned, 'hasn't she suffered

enough? It isn't enough that she has lost her life when it had only just begun ... is it necessary to cut her open?' He pointed to the curtain. 'That you see, that was as you said it would be, which is why Mrs Dance attended, and that was a good last image of our daughter ... she was at peace ... and now you have ruined it by telling us that she is going to be put on a slab and carved open ... now we have that thought to live with.'

'I am afraid there is no other way, we don't know yet how she died. The law demands it.' Wiseman spoke as gently as she could.

'Yes,' Mrs Dance turned away from her husband and looked at Wiseman. 'Yes, I understand that and it can only help.' She stood. 'Protesting is useless, it has to be done ... and that image I will keep of Joyce, I will keep in my mind. It is not an unpleasant final image of her. Can you take us home now, please?'

'Perigo's sick?' Veronica Sleaford glanced up at Sydney Household. 'Makes me feel guilty.'

'Oh?' Household looked around the cramped office, a small desk with a computer on the left-hand side, a blotting pad in the centre, utterly anachronistic in the age of the microchip, in Household's view, but he was pleased to see it, it made the desk look complete somehow. Photographs on the wall showed a happy looking girl in various stages of growth, of her at the beach aged about ten or eleven, of her on horseback aged about fifteen, a full face close up of her about eighteen. They were photographs of Sojourner Sleaford of whom Household had heard when

202

attending previous post-mortems.

'Yes ... at the crime scene.' Sleaford shrugged, 'Well, perhaps not the crime scene, but the location where the body was found. I regretted that Mr Perigo had not deigned to attend as head of the investigation, and young Miss Wiseman excused him on the grounds that he wasn't on duty until two, but he was sick all along, and she wouldn't have known that.'

'No, he phoned in about an hour ago, nothing serious, he said – sounds like a summer cold or some mild food poisoning, something like that. So the boss asked me to represent the police at the p.m. Sergeants Wiseman and Tracy have returned home with the parents and will be staying with them for a while, then they want to go and quiz a potential witness, so that left me. Confess I protested but the boss pointed out my case was thirty years old, so a few hours delay in that investigation will hardly matter.'

'And you can't argue with that.' Sleaford stood.

'Certainly can't.'

'Any progress with that case? I read in the paper that he has been identified.'

'Yes ... a little ... getting to know his lifestyle and his friends, but it's going to be difficult to solve, any trail will be cold by now. We might have to content ourselves with having identified him.'

'And his family? They have some compensation now, I imagine? Shall we go?'

'Yes.' Household, being the nearest to the door, turned and walked out of the office. Sleaford followed him and they walked side by side towards the male and female changing rooms. 'They have said as much, his elderly father...'

'Still alive!'

'Yes ... very elderly as you can imagine, but his mind is all there. He said as much. They will have a grave to visit now.'

'A little compensation.' Sleaford stopped at the door to the female changing rooms. 'So, I'll see you in there.'

'Very good, doctor.' Household went into the male changing rooms where he selected a set of paper green disposable coveralls, removed his jacket and top clothing, and climbed into the coveralls. His shoes were replaced with white slippers which had elasticated lops and fastened round his ankles. He placed a white cap, also elasticated round the rim, on his head and walked to the pathology laboratory. When he arrived, Veronica Sleaford was already in attendance, as was Harry Hewis, who was at that moment making a thorough photographic record of the corpse which lay naked on the dissecting table, save for a starched white towel placed over the genitalia. Household walked to the far end of the pathology laboratory, to where Sleaford and Hewis and the corpse were.

Veronica Sleaford adjusted the microphone. 'The subject,' she began, 'is as noted earlier, a well nourished female, Northern European by racial grouping, and has been positively identified as Joyce Dance, aged 23. There are injuries to the wrists which appear to be puncture points and ...' she examined the left wrist closely with the aid of a powerful, pencil beam torch, 'the left puncture point has severed the artery' She

204

turned her attention to the right wrist. 'The puncture points have penetrated both arteries. Death was probably caused by blood loss. There may be contributory or complicating factors so at this stage, I can only say that death by massive blood loss was a probable cause. It's noted how clean the body is. No trace of blood is to be found upon the body despite the probable cause of death.' Sleaford turned to Household. 'That's something to draw to the attention of the interested police officers and the psychologist.'

'The psychologist?'

'Yes, I suggested that this man "Panther", be profiled. I was surprised to find Mr Perigo hasn't asked for it to be done.'

'So am I.' Household felt his scalp crawl with embarrassment.

'But the point is that whether these wounds are self-inflicted, or not, there would have been a lot of red stuff, about eight pints of it. Yet she has been scrubbed clean. Very interesting from your point of view, I would have thought.'

'Certainly is.'

'The puncturing of the arteries has a self-inflicted quality about it ... that is puzzling, but again that's for the psychologist. It is by no means impossible to murder somebody by puncturing their arteries, a hard, thin object like a small screwdriver or a bradawl would do very nicely, though these particular puncture points are very small calibre ... something about the size of a nail would have caused these wounds ... but to murder someone by slitting their wrists is ... well, unheard of. I have never come across it, nor have I even read about it.'

'Confess, neither have I,' Household replied.

'Have you, Harry?' Sleaford turned to her assistant. 'Ever come across murder by this means?'

Household instantly warmed to Sleaford for that, he thought, it was good man management to make someone feel included, especially someone of lowly status, but it was also polite and, he thought, a demonstration of proper respect. Harry Hewis evidently thought the same, as Household watched him flush with pleasure and pride at being asked and stammered to the effect that no, he hadn't ever come across anyone ever being murdered in that manner.

'You see, Mr Household, a slit throat, yes, that's not an uncommon method of murder ... nor is a stab to the chest or back ... but to puncture somebody's arteries, that speaks to me of self-infliction.'

'Puzzling,' Household said for want of something to say.

'Hugely so, I would have thought. She must have been in fear of her own life ... so why commit suicide? We may never know, but as I said, that's one for the psychologist.' She paused as she examined the wrist. 'There are abrasions to the left wrist indicating that some restraint was applied there ... the sort of abrasions I would expect to be caused by a chain or rope.' Veronica Sleaford took a scalpel and drew it from the breast bone down to the stomach where she divided the incision to right and left. 'I am performing a standard mid-line incision.' She spoke as she performed the operation, leaving a large cut on the anterior of the corpse which reminded Household of an inverted 'Y'. Sleaford peeled back the three folds of flesh created by the incision, exposing the organs of the late Joyce Dance. 'She had a small stomach,' Sleaford observed. 'It wouldn't have taken much food to make her feel full. Feels full now, let us see if we can identify her last meal.' Sleaford took the scalpel and made an incision across the stomach, she pulled her head back as the gases escaped with a 'hiss'. 'Digestion will continue for a little while after death, it's a chemical rather than mechanical action...' Sleaford addressed Household without looking at him. 'But we can nonetheless hazard a guess at the time gap between the last meal and time of death, and here I can identify what appears to be mince and potato ... a few vegetables ... it seems to be the remains of a meat pie.'

'A meat pie!'

'Yes ... come and look if you wish.'

'No thank you, I will take your word for it, Dr Sleaford, but it's strange as you say ... a meal associated with winter time. In this weather ... I couldn't face a meat pie in this heat.'

'This p.m. is flagging up more and more questions. Why would a young woman in fear of her life, or suicidal, want to eat? Her appetite must have been the first thing to go.'

'Good point,' Household conceded. He admired Dr Sleaford's ability to put herself into another's shoes ... there was a word for it ... 'empathy' ... yes, that was it. He admired Veronica Sleaford's power of empathy. He also doubted his ability to see the incongruity of a full stomach in a young woman who believed her death was imminent. He doubted his wish to eat if he thought his life was at an end.

'Narrows the field a little, though.' Sleaford stood upright, exercising her spine, 'Too much bending in this job. I mean, meat pie is a very British dish, particularly a very English dish. The Scots would have haggis and neaps, not a meat pie, but it means that the person who cooked this meal is not of the ethnic minority groups ... it isn't Afro Caribbean food, it isn't Asian food, nor Chinese ... and so on ... it's very basic British food.'

And that, thought Household, was yet another good point. 'Specifically English, as you say,' he said. 'I'll make that point to the investigating team.'

Again Sleaford took the scalpel and opened the venous artery 'Not one drop of blood ... death was caused by massive blood loss, as I first suspected. There will be extensive blood stains where she was murdered, or where she took her life.' Veronica Sleaford pondered the body. 'I wonder...'

'Sorry, doctor?'

'Well, that would normally conclude my examination. I have established the cause of death, the body can be handed to the relatives for burial but ... but ... but...'

'Something is bothering you, doctor?'

'Yes ... and I don't know what it is. The job is done but something calls me to this young woman, she is trying to tell us something.'

Veronica Sleaford turned to Household. 'That's possibly why she ate the meal. I would do the same. She was leaving you a present, if she was found before her body had decomposed the food may still be identifiable ... she must have known that. That may explain why she forced herself to eat even though she knew she was going to die ... courageous girl. She was doing what she could to take her murderer with her and if she left one present, she may well have left others. Where would you hide a present if you were her, Mr Household?'

'Any body cavity ... or in my scalp hair.'

'So would I. Well, women have one body cavity that men don't possess, so we'll start there.'

The vagina, the anus, the nostrils, contained nothing. Veronica Sleaford ran her fingers thoroughly through the scalp hair and was satisfied that nothing had been entwined in the lower layers of Joyce Dance's hair and concealed by the upper layers. 'That,' she said, 'that leaves only the mouth.' She took the head and jaw, one in each hand, and tried to force them open. 'Set firm ... can you let me have that please, Harry?' She pointed to a stainless steel length of metal which lay on the instrument trolley. Harry Hewis handed it to her and she forced it between the teeth of the corpse. 'Even in the twenty-first century, it's still down to leverage and brute strength,' she said as she pressed the metal bar down until the rigor broke with a loud 'crack'. She handed the length of metal back to Harry Hewis who placed it in a tray of disinfectant.

'Ah, now what have we here?' Veronica Sleaford

peered into the mouth of the cadaver, which, just a few hours previously, had been the living, breathing instrument of Joyce Dance with her entire adulthood ahead of her.

'You've found something, doctor?' Household asked involuntarily.

Veronica Sleaford paused, replying in her own time. She was the professional, she was in charge of the post-mortem. 'Yes ... I think so ... odd ... black ... I don't know how to describe them flecks, like bits of black plastic ... definitely not food and very definitely not natural secretion. Can I have a tray, please, Harry? Better make it a dry tray.'

Harry Hewis took a stainless steel tray from the shelf beneath the instrument trolley's surface and handed it to Sleaford, who muttered her thanks. She turned and took a pair of tweezers from the instrument trolley and began to extract small items from the mouth, too small for Household, from his vantage point, to make out what they were. He watched intently as Sleaford extracted about half a dozen such items from the mouth, and placed the items neatly on the dry tray.

'Think that's all.' She stood up and turned to Household. 'Come and see.'

Household strode silently forward and looked at the tray. He saw seven small, black objects, very thin, like small insects without legs, he thought. 'What are they?' They could only, he agreed; have been described as 'flecks'.

'Well, whatever they be,' Veronica Sleaford attempted a mock East Anglian accent, 'they be not natural, they be not.'

'Don't look like they be,' Household added and they both held eye contact and smiled.

'We'll bag and tag them, get them straight out to Warboys for you. My intuition is that they will be relevant. Joyce, leaving us a present.' Veronica Sleaford glanced at the body and laid a sensitive hand upon the arm and patted it softly. 'Good girl ... brave girl.' She looked again at Household. 'She ate so as to leave us something if her body was found in time.'

'In time?'

'Before decomposition. The food itself might be of interest so I will send a sample of that to Warboys too ... just for form's sake, but you never know, doing things for form's sake has provided gold dust before.'

'Certainly has,' Household smiled. 'Heavens, it certainly has.'

'Well, she died from massive blood loss as I first thought. I'll send tissue samples for analysis in case she was also poisoned ... never know. I get the impression that Miss Dance is only just beginning to give up her secrets. You might like to tell her parents what she did, they'll find out at the inquest anyway, but it would be politic to tell them ... your decision, of course.'

'I'll tell the investigating team of your findings, doctor.'

'Well, it's midday. The dead can bury their dead, but the living must eat. What are you doing for lunch?'

The question took Household by surprise. 'Well, I was going to go back into Cambridge ... the canteen at the station.'

'Why don't you have a change of scenery? Join me for lunch in our canteen. It's actually quite good.'

Household nodded and smiled. 'Yes ... alright, thank you. I think I'd like that. Canteen grub is canteen grub, but the change of scenery sounds interesting.'

'Good. See you in my office.'

The Panther looked at the room. He was pleased with what he saw. He had done well. It had taken some time, more than he thought it would have taken, but he had done it. That was the main thing. He settled into a crack in the doorway, resting his right elbow on his right knee, the left knee being at a lower angle, and more angled outwards. He placed the paintbrush in the old tin saucepan which contained soapy water. White spirit might be better to stop the paint solidifying in the bristles, enabling the brush to be used again, but warm soapy water would do the job.

He thought about the girl. She had been clever, quite clever ... but only quite. She had taken her life before he had taken it from her, spreading her blood as liberally about the room as she could, leaving a trace, a substantial trace, behind her. He knew that even microscopic splashes of blood can be analysed for their DNA profile ... a pinprick of blood was all it would take to link her to this room in this house and to give him some serious explaining to do. She must have known that. Attempting to clean it up would be time consuming, very time consuming indeed, and even then it could not all be washed away. It was, he had to concede, a brave attempt and, had he been in her shoes, then he thought he too might have done the same thing, but unfortunately for her, her actions were futile because he knew a little bit about forensic science as well. Importantly, he knew the futility of trying to sanitise a crime scene.

So he didn't try.

Instead he hosed the blood down while it was still a little fluid. It was congealing, but hadn't fully congealed, and the amount of water he used diluted it vastly. It all helped, not so much as to hinder the work of a forensic chemist – diluted or undiluted blood would make little difference to him or her – but rather the diluting of the blood on the floorboards and the walls made his next step much easier. When he had slept after returning from leaving the body at the side of a lane somewhere in deepest Cambridgeshire, laying her out, neatly, arms and legs fully outstretched – a shocking sight for someone – he had then eaten a leisurely breakfast and driven back towards Cambridge, to the DIY shop he used much, and where he was known, and purchased paint and paintbrushes. A gentle cream, he thought, for the walls and a pale blue for the floorboards. Yes, that, he thought, that would be a pleasant colour scheme. He returned to the bungalow and started work. The walls first, three of the four walls, the fourth wall which contained the door-frame seemed to him to be too far for the girl to contaminate it with her blood. It would, of course, have to be done for the sake of thoroughness, to cover the pinprick of the stuff his naked

213

eye couldn't see, but time pressing, he saved the fourth wall for later. It was a risk he felt he had to take. Then he painted the skirting board a strong, dark blue, where there was plenty of dried, diluted blood. That done, there remained only the floorboards, which he painted with the light blue paint, painted himself back to the open door, and when the painting had been completed, he knelt in the doorway surveying his work. Don't clean a crime scene, he said, don't ever clean a crime scene because you can't. Smother it instead, because you can: any amount of luminol sprayed in this room would not show any dried blood when viewed in ultra violet light, because the paint had covered it. He had been especially careful to paint as much as he could in the gaps between the floorboards to cover any blood which had dripped down there. The only possibility of blood being in the room was any microscopically small trace which was on the ceiling or the fourth wall. The ceiling and the wall would be jobs for tomorrow.

The first and most important task done, the Panther padded silently outside and in the garden in the growing heat of the day, he wiped every surface of every item which had been in the room in which he had kept the girl – Joyce Dance by name, so he had found out – because, he reasoned, any girl who was determined enough to leave her blood at the crime scene would also leave her fingerprints. The sleeping bag he rolled up and placed in his van to be taken to the dry cleaners. The girl's clothing was burnt on a bonfire, in the grounds of the bungalow, and he stood over the fire whilst it burned, during which he waved warmly to his elderly neighbour as the man ambled past on the lane. There was, he reasoned, nothing suspicious about a bonfire in the garden of a house which is being renovated. His elderly neighbour thought the same, for after he called out 'Good afternoon,' he added. 'A fire is a good friend'.

'Indeed,' the Panther replied. 'Indeed it is.'

After the fire had burned out, after the ashes had been buried, the Panther boiled water on the camping stove in the kitchen of the house and made a pot of tea. He sat on the veranda of the bungalow and thought how much he had enjoyed killing the girl; forcing her to take her own life was as good as killing her, it was odd how good it felt, again. And placing the body ... it was all very, very pleasant. A cuckoo sang in the woods beyond the overgrown garden. A blackbird was also singing, a cricket chirruped. Yes, it was good, as was the skill of avoiding detection ... power followed by cleverness. What could be better? He would do it again. Sweat ran down his forehead. He wiped it away.

Soon.

Very soon.

David Tracy left Penny Wiseman with the Dances in their quiet and very subdued household on Rutherford Road and drove back out to Six Mile Bottom, following Archie Good's directions to the old gamekeeper's cottage, now, ironically, the home of 'Old Bob', poacher by occupation. The cottage he found quite easily, and parked his car up on the verge, even then allowing little, but sufficient, space for another vehicle to pass. He switched off the engine, pocketed the ignition keys, but left the driver's window fully wound down, knowing that unless he did so, it would not be possible to breathe in the interior of the car when he returned to it. He walked up the overgrown pathway to the cottage which, on closer inspection, revealed itself to be near derelict, rotten window frames, windows layered with grime, decaying grey thatch on the roof with large areas of exposed roof beams. It was often the way of it, Tracy had found, working in the East Anglia force, he had had occasions to visit both urban and rural homes, and when folk, the media, pressure groups speak of 'poverty in our midst', they always seem to use photographs of inner city squalor, but for real poverty, you need to go into the country; even in the 21st century, the living conditions in many homes owed more to the nineteenth century than to the present day. He had once watched a documentary about life in the Soviet Union, which showed peasants in the Ukraine living as they had lived for hundreds of years, except there was a television perched on a stool, powered by a diesel generator which stood outside the house, and had exclaimed to himself, 'It's like that in the Fens'. He brushed a fly away from his face, glanced at the wide green expanse around him, the flat, distant landscape under a light blue canopy with just a wisp of white, as if knowing, fearing at least, that he was going to be inside a dank and airless place for an unknown period. He knocked on the door.

The reply came instantly. It sounded to David Tracy like a word previously unknown, to wit 'Haaasssa'. He decided what he had heard was Old Bob for 'who is it?'

'Police,' he said with a voice which was not a shout, but sufficiently loud to carry clearly inside the house.

He heard a loud groan and the movement of something wooden.

'You're not in any trouble, Bob,' Tracy called. 'Just want to ask you a question or two.'

'Said that the last time and I got six months in Bedford gaol. Do you know what it's like for a countryman to be locked in a cage for six months? No clean air, no wind ... no seasons changing.'

'I'm not after you, Bob.' Tracy brushed another fly away. 'I want your help ... you might be able to help me.'

There was a silence from within for some time before the reply.

'Help you?' The tone of his voice was clearly one of puzzlement. 'How can the likes of me help the likes of you, young master?'

'Just want to know if you saw or heard anything last night.'

'Bout the body?'

'Yes ... how do you know about that?'

'A little bird told me.'

And this being deepest Cambridgeshire, thought Tracy with a wry smile, and Old Bob being a poacher, then that reply was probably not so fanciful, not so fanciful at all. News travels very fast in the rural areas, so fast that urban dwellers are amazed at its speed, and in this instance, the

217

proximity of Old Bob's cottage to the scene of the crime, Archie Good's house and Byres Farm was such that in this case speedy travelling news didn't have very far to travel at all. 'OK. Well, yes, it's about that.'

'You don't want to come in?'

'No,' Tracy called, and murmured, 'Thank goodness.'

There was another pause, more shuffling was heard from within.

'You sure you're police?'

'Sure.'

'I got a 4.10 here...'

'It had better be licensed.'

'It is ... I use it to keep the rabbits down.'

'I bet you do ... you mean the rabbits that look a lot like hares and the starlings that look a lot like pheasants. Come on, Old Bob ... open the door, this is costing the taxpayer a hundred and fifty quid an hour ... not that you'd be bothered about that, the amount of taxes you pay, but the Chief Constable's got to show something for his budget.'

The next word spoken sounded like 'kermm', which David Tracy thought must mean 'Coming' and so he paused and waited.

The lock clicked loudly, a lock which, in Tracy's view, clearly needed lubricating, and a heavy bolt was drawn back with a solid 'clunk'. Tracy looked straight ahead, he was not particularly tall for a policeman, he had in his mind's eye an image of a 'poacher' which he fully expected 'Old Bob' to meet. When the door opened, there was nobody there, just a gap between the door and doorway, and a dark gloom between. In an instant he looked down, and for the first time saw Old Bob, who he saw suffered from cretinism, standing three-feet tall if he was an inch, much shorter than the shotgun he held upright in his right hand.

'Put the 4.10 away,' Tracy said. 'You won't need it. I'm not going to harm you.' He pondered the cruelty of sending a three-foot tall cretin to prison, even for a brief stretch. There were times when he believed the police could and should turn a blind eye. But perhaps it had been that Old Bob hadn't played the game, hadn't heeded the warnings, had persisted and had taken one pheasant too many and had given the police no alternative ... and the Bench too. Even if they were drawn from the squirearchy whose neighbours had lost game to Old Bob's 4.10, they must have been swayed by some dreadful statement of facts and previous convictions to send a man of Old Bob's stature to the slammer. David Tracy tried to conceal the surprised look which he knew must have flashed across his eyes as he absorbed Old Bob's appearance. The old man was small, very small, but not at all in proportion. His legs were very short proportionately to his chest, so much so that his hands seemed to be level with his kneecaps. His face had a handsome quality, Tracy thought, classically balanced, like the faces on the heads of statues created in ancient Greece and Rome, except it was about half the normal adult size, and thick with silver whiskers. Silver hair, in uneven clumps, as if self-cut, sprouted from his scalp.

'Bob,' Tracy remained standing, having

dismissed the idea of squatting on his haunches as being patronising to the old man whose life could not have been easy, 'that girl who was murdered, did you see or hear anything last night?'

Old Bob put the 4.10 out of sight behind him. 'What can I tell you?'

'Anything that you saw that wasn't right hereabouts, last night.'

'Aye ... I did.'

'You did?'

'Yes, saw that girl taken from a van.'

'You saw it!' Tracy gasped. 'Why didn't you report it?'

'Knew you'd come knocking.'

'What did you see?' Tracy felt for his notebook with one hand and his pen with the other.

'Black van in the lane.'

'Black?'

'Yes ... black as a black night ... good moon last night ... keep my house dark, see, train my eyes up for the night, but last night, no cloud and a large moon ... bright as day ... could see to the skyline.'

'How far away were you?'

Old Bob looked beyond Tracy, his eyes darted from side to side until they settled on an object. 'From here to yon oak.'

David Tracy turned. 'Yon oak' stood by itself, a proud looking, imposing tree. It was two fields distant, about four or five hundred yards. 'Close enough,' he said. 'And you saw the girl's body.'

'Taken from the back of the van, laid out on the ground, real careful, the old boy was careful with her ... gentle ... I thought she might be alive ...

saw she was dead when I got closer.'

'You went there!'

'Oh, yes ... Old Bob had to have a look see ... saw she was dead ... laid out like.'

David Tracy restrained his impatience. He was fast losing sympathy with Old Bob and thought that the common abuse of the word 'cretin' to mean 'fool' or 'half wit' could equally be applied in this case. The man was a cretin and a 'cretin'. 'You didn't touch anything?'

'No ... Old Bob was really careful, like that, young master.'

'Alright ... what time was this?'

'Two o'clock ... possibly just after.'

'Sure about the time?'

'Sure.'

'How can you be sure?'

'I looked at my watch.' Old Bob who wore a shirt, a pair of child's jeans and a pair of child's sports shoes, shut the door on Tracy and reopened it again and held out a watch on a chain. It was a gold hunter. Old Bob allowed Tracy to hold it but he kept a determined grip on the chunky gold chain. The watch was engraved with the words, 'To my dear husband, upon our anniversary, from his loving wife, Sophie'.

'You didn't set a snare for this, did you?' Tracy said coldly, pondering the grief that must have been caused by the loss of what was obviously obtained by theft.

Old Bob remained silent.

Tracy looked at the time given by the watch, 12.10. He checked it against the time given by his inexpensive quartz watch which, with only two moving parts, kept perfect time. By this it was just three minutes after midday. Tracy let the watch go, and Old Bob silently and swiftly pocketed it. Tracy noticed a gleam in the man's eyes. All and any sympathy he may have had for the man had by that time evaporated. 'Alright, about two a.m.'

'How many men?'

'One.'

'Can you describe him?'

'Tall, strong ... held that old girl like she was nothing more than a fishing rod ... but put her down gentle he did ... that takes more strength than dropping her like she was a sack of potatoes.'

'Fair point. What was he built like?'

'Slim ... strong and slim.'

'The van?'

'Black, like I said, nothing special about it, no writing on the side ... nothing like that ... no ... and I didn't see the numbers...'

'What sort of van?'

'Old Bob doesn't know... That like a police van, only black.'

'Like a Ford Transit?'

'If that's what they're called. Old Bob only knows how to take a pheasant or a hare.'

'And how to turn windows. Is that why you collected six months for poaching? Everybody knew you were the thief so they hammered you for what they could pin on you?'

Old Bob just smiled, glassy-eyed.

'I'm going to pull your record when I get back to the nick. What's your full name?'

'Old Bob. People just call Old Bob, "Old Bob".'

'I could do you for obstruction for that, would you like that? Then we could have a real rummage round your house.'

'Piggot.' Old Bob seemed disappointed.

'Better be right, Bob,' Tracy said. 'There's no more common name in East Anglia. If you're not telling the truth, I'll be coming back, with a search warrant, after I've seen what I've just seen.'

'The watch? Old Bob bought it from a stall in Thetford market twenty years back, and that's the old truth, so it be.'

'I'll check anyway.' Tracy wiped another bead of sweat from his brow.

'Hot enough?'

'Too hot.'

'Good old poaching weather. Dry, and the lack of rain brings 'em out, looking for water.'

'I'll take your word for it. Anything else you can tell me about the man?'

'Well, he was a stranger. He didn't know this area.'

'Really?' Tracy replied wearily. That the Panther was a stranger to these fields meant, he guessed, that the police could safely eliminate about six people from the enquiry.

'No. And I'll tell you for why. Drove from the direction of Six Mile Bottom, put the poor old girl on the old grass verge and then drove on ... but once past Byres Farm that lane stops, just comes to a dead end it does, from the end of the lane you get the old choice of three old fields, but the road stops. Knew he'd have to turn round, and he did, came back and drove on back to Six Mile Bottom. Slowly, not in a hurry, calm as old calm can be.'

The staff refectory at Addenbrookes Hospital was light and spacious and offered a pleasant view of the area to the south of Cambridge. Veronica Sleaford and Sydney Household sat opposite each other. They had found that they relaxed quite easily in each other's company. Household's gaze was drawn to a doctor in a white coat ploughing his way through a mound of chips. Nothing else was on his plate, just chips, and a large quantity of same.

'He's running a half marathon,' Sleaford followed Household's gaze, 'but yes, it is a strange meal for a medical person to eat, hardly a balanced diet, but that's the reason. I was talking to him just the other day and he explained that for a few days before the marathon all the runners eat nothing but starch.'

'I see. Explains why he looks so healthy on a diet of chips and chips. How are your cutlets?'

'Lovely. Delicious. How's your meal?'

'Equally so ... you eat better than we do.'

'It's disabling though ... makes you lazy ... you lose your culinary skills.'

'I can understand that. I haven't cooked a meal in a while.'

'You are married?'

'Yes.'

'Oh.' Sleaford looked and sounded disappointed. 'I thought you were a bachelor, I don't know why.'

'I think I do.' Household put his knife and fork down and sipped his mineral water. 'You mean I have that threadbare, hungry look of an ageing bachelor.'

'I wouldn't put it as strongly as that, but yes,' she smiled.

Household returned the smile. 'I might as well be a bachelor, things have not been going too well with us for a while now. It's been worse since we moved to Bedford ... we had a house in the fens, north of Peterborough ... we were very close to some flooding in the spring.'

'Oh, yes, dreadful ... those poor people ... their houses, four feet of water in some places.'

'Higher, I believe, the downstairs rooms were flooded, few houses have cellars in East Anglia because of the high water table, otherwise it would have been worse for them, much worse.'

'Horrible situation.'

'Anyway, because of the Grace of the Almighty and a slight incline in the landscape, we escaped the flooding but it was close enough for me. So I insisted that we sell up and we have recently moved to Bedford.'

'No flooding there.'

'Not on the same scale, but I confess that I can't help but check on the rivers each time it rains.'

'Which has not been for some time.' Veronica Sleaford glanced out of the window. 'Not quite a drought, but we could do with some rain.'

'Yes ... but anyway, that didn't go down too well on top of everything else. Frankly she couldn't put up a valid argument for staying, but it gave her an excuse to increase the cold shouldering intermixed with the occasional tantrum.'

'Well, I fully understand that ... it's no home to go home to.'

'You sound as though you have the same experience.'

'Had.' Veronica Sleaford, having finished her meal, placed her cutlery neatly on the plate. 'Divorced now. Can't recommend it too highly.'

'Divorce?'

'Yes. It's lovely. It's like a weight being lifted from your shoulders. Half the marriages in Britain fail these days, so there's plenty of company. A divorcee isn't a freak of nature, doesn't carry the stigma it used to.'

'Confess, I have been thinking along those lines.' Household too placed his knife and fork on his plate, and reached for his dessert of peaches and cream. 'The children are of an age now.'

'How many do you have?'

'Two – one of each. Still dependent but over 16 and have reached that stage where they hide away in their rooms, playing weird music. It allegedly helps them with their college work. You any children?'

Archie Good stood at the taproom bar of The Red Cross, the name of which was allegedly given in reference to the Crusades, though the pub, having had many, many rebuilds over the centuries, was to all intents and purposes a Victorian building, and to an observer would probably seem of modest and homely proportions. He caught the publican's eye and raised his empty glass.

'Sure, Archie, sure?'

Archie Good scattered some coins on the

polished oak bar as the publican pulled a pint of Abbott's ale into a pint mug.

'Pushing the boat out, Archie?' The publican placed the pint of beer down in front of Archie Good and picked the exact money out of the spread coins, leaving the change on the bar top. 'It'll have to be the last one anyway, I should have stopped serving an hour ago ... can't stick my neck or my licence out too far, but the boys were enjoying their game of dominoes. It's your head I'm thinking of Archie, that's your tenth this evening ... Abbot as well ... you've got a fair old walk home and you have to be up at ... well, in six hours.'

'It's the way she was lying there.' He gripped the pint glass in a meaty fist and gulped the beer, drinking like a soldier, large, full mouthfuls, pointedly avoiding holding the glass by the handle, again, soldier like. 'I walked past her ... she was hidden in the mist ... walked right past her. She was somebody's old daughter lying there ... been lying there all night ... and laid out.'

'Laid out?' The publican leaned on the counter, resting his weight on his folded muscular forearms.

'Not like a doctor would, not arms by the side or across the chest, but arms up, over the head ... as if she was stretching herself like kiddies are told to do at school.'

'Well, it'll stay with you, Archie. That's the way of it.'

'Reckon it be.' Archie Good swallowed the remainder of the beer in two mouthfuls, gathered his change, and turned and walked out of the pub, walking, thought the publican, as straight and as steady as a man who was a lifelong teetotaller. Beer seemed to have no effect on him, distressed as he may have been.

6

Household drove back to Cambridge, parked at the rear of Parkside Police Station, signed in, checked his pigeonhole, and went up to the CID rooms on the first floor. Penny Wiseman was at her desk writing up a file.

'Is that the file on the Dance girl?' Household smiled at her.

'Yes, sir, the identification was made by her parents. I've just got back.'

'You went back to the parents and DS Tracy has gone out to interview a possible witness?'

'Yes.'

'The boss asked me to represent the police at the postmortem, Mr Perigo has phoned in sick.'

'Oh...' Household thought Penny Wiseman's reaction seemed to be a strange mixture of relief and disappointment.

'Anyway, the cause of death was massive blood loss.'

'Blood loss? He bled her to death?'

'Well, that isn't known,' Household glanced out across Parker's Piece, people sunbathing, a group of young men kicking a ball, stripped to the waist, but football in this heat... Household

228

turned and sat at his desk. He told Penny Wiseman of the post-mortem findings.

'Flecks of black stuff in her mouth?'

'Yes. It was Dr Sleaford's impression that the lass was leaving us a present ... it was definitely not food stuff and would have been put into her mouth just before she died, otherwise it would have been swallowed.'

'But...' Penny Wiseman let the pen drop onto the continuation sheet, 'wait a minute...'

'Yes?' Household smiled, but not a smile of approval or pleasure, but of recognition that the implication had reached Wiseman. 'She knew she was going to die and imminently so.'

'Oh...' Wiseman's head sank forward. She rested it on her palm.

'The actual mechanics of death were two puncture points at the wrists, over the artery. They could easily have been self-inflicted.'

'Killing herself before he killed her?'

Household shrugged. 'We don't know, we'll only know what we can fairly assume and deduce from the available evidence, or what the Panther tells us when you nail him.'

'You have confidence in us,' Wiseman smiled. 'I wish I had the same.'

'I'll write up the PM findings when you have finished your recording. The pathologist made some comments which would be of interest to a psychologist. I assume Mr Perigo wants a profile to be done?'

'DS Tracy and I have been pressing for one, sir.'

'I see... Well, I can't comment on Mr Perigo's approach to the case, but if I were you, I'd go and

229

see him,' Household raised a finger in the direction of Chief Inspector Atkins' office. 'Do it on the q.t. ... informally ... the Chief Inspector is approachable, really.'

Penny Wiseman smiled. 'Thanks, sir. I think we will.'

Household, having written up the findings of the postmortem in the Joyce Dance file, left Parkside Police Station, turned left towards Mill Road and then stopped. He turned round and walked in the opposite direction, the length of the police station, to Warkworth Terrace, and turned down it and stood looking at the building where, thirty years ago, Edward De Beer had rented a room. The building was, like all those in the terrace, an imposing house, wide, angular bay windows, four, possibly five storeys high if the cellar was included. It was a very desirable residence in Household's opinion, if it was used as it had been clearly designed to be used, as a single family dwelling, but less so if the owner had to live in the cellar and let out rooms to undergraduates to make the building pay. But, whatever, here was the last residence of Edward De Beer. He had walked out of that doorway, once, for the last time, and some time later, his parents had walked in and cleared his possessions from the room he had rented. Which room was it? Household struggled to remember. First floor room ... he looked at the window. It would have offered a view of the side of the police station, and a little of Parker's Piece would also be visible. He looked left and right, waited for a young, female cyclist to pass him, smiling her thanks as she did so, then crossed the road and walked up the steps of the grey brick building and pressed the doorbell. He didn't know why he was doing it, thirty years had elapsed since Edward De Beer had lived there, and the ownership must have changed in that time. Even if it hadn't, even if the owner was the same, there was little possibility of her remembering an individual tenant of a third of a century previous. Nonetheless, he rang the bell.

The door was opened by a young woman in a cheesecloth shirt and a long cotton skirt, sandals on her feet. She wore her long black hair in a ponytail. She smiled a warm smile. 'Yes?' Household thought her teeth could sell toothpaste. 'Can I help you?'

'Police.'

'Oh.' The smile faded. 'Anything wrong?'

'Not that concerns you, or anybody in this house. Can I talk to the owner?'

'Daddy? Yes. Would you care to come in?'

'Thank you.'

Household stepped into the hallway. He thought it generously proportioned, wide hallway, wide stairway, high ceilings with elaborate plaster work.

'If you wait here. Who shall I say wants to speak to Daddy?'

'Detective Inspector Household.'

'Not far to come to get to this house, have you?' The young woman smiled.

'Not far. About the nearest visit I've made to the station. Couldn't get nearer in fact.'

'I'll tell Daddy.' She turned and stepped lightly

away, at the end of the corridor she turned to her right and descended a flight of stairs. 'Daddy' was clearly in the cellar.

Household waited. It was cool inside the house, the air smelled of furniture polish. The carpet was deep and welcoming. It was, Household had to agree, as Edward De Beer's father had described it when he had visited to assume possession of his son's chattels, 'like going into a small hotel'. A heavier footfall was heard coming up the stairs, a man turned into the corridor. He was short, stocky, had an aggressive manner. Household found it difficult in his mind to match the young woman who had opened the door, and this man as being father and daughter. Only the age gap seemed right; manner, disposition, attitude, build, all seemed a mismatch.

'Yes?' The man demanded.

Household smiled in an attempt to placate the man. 'There is nothing to worry about.'

'Oh...' The man visibly relaxed.

'In fact, I am not sure why I am here, and to be perfectly honest I pressed the doorbell on a whim.'

The man remained silent, although relaxed and less aggressive in his manner there was still suspicion in his eye.

'It's in connection with the body that was discovered near Bottisham recently ... you might have read the reports in the paper or seen the TV news?'

'Yes...' The man wasn't giving anything away.

'Well, the reason I am here is that he rented a room here when he was a student.'

'The one who disappeared?' The man relaxed completely. He might, thought Household, might have been up to something that would be of interest to the police, but when he learned of the reason for Household's visit, great tension clearly left him.

'You know the young man I am talking about?' Household pressed.

'I know of him. I was about fifteen when he disappeared. I remember it well.'

'Really...' Household became intrigued.

'Yes, really. I grew up in this house, I run it now. My mother still owns it but she's retired, she's in her eighties. I remember the student going missing ... I remember his parents coming to pick up his things ... my that's going back. So it was his body that was found out by Bottisham?'

'It was.'

'Well ... that's a turn-up for the books, alright. What can I tell you? Mum's the one to speak to, she's still got her mind ... doesn't move much, but her mind is all there. I remember how she didn't like asking his parents for the rent he owed, but she had a business to run.'

Household remained silent. He thought it unpardonably insensitive of the woman to ask for rent in such circumstances, but he wanted the man's co-operation.

'Where is your mother?'

'She lives out at Willingham. She has a bungalow there. She grew up in the village and has retired there. Mrs Telford is her name.'

'That sounds quite neat.'

'It is. I think Mum thinks that too ... she'll

likely die where she was born ... sort of completes the circle.'

'Could I have a look at Edward De Beer's room?'

'If you like, but thirty years on, there's nothing left of his or "him"... if you see what I mean.'

'Appreciate that,' Household smiled. 'It would help me get a feel for the man ... it's for my benefit really, it has no evidential value.'

'Yes, in that case, you've come at good time for it, we do bed and breakfast for tourists in the summer.' The man turned and walked up the stairs. 'This way. An American couple had this room for a few days, they left this morning. The Tourist Board asked if we could take another couple for a night ... just one night, they are on their way now.'

'Couldn't have timed it better then.' Household walked up the stairs behind the man.

The room Edward De Beer occupied was, Household found, like the entire house, of generous proportions with a bed against each wall, two easy chairs in front of a fireplace, a chest of drawers and a table in the window. 'Good accommodation for an undergraduate.'

'It is, especially for a Tech student as he was. I don't quite understand how he came to be here because Mum only let to university students, but he was here and got a full cooked breakfast each morning ... not many Tech students got that.'

'OK ... well, thank you for letting me see the room.' Household walked to the window and looked at the police station. It seemed odd to view it from that angle. He smiled as he saw

234

David Tracy enter the rear of the building. 'One of my colleagues returning,' he said, without looking at the man.

'The people in this room and the one above it watch you lot come and go.' The reply was warm and humorous.

Household turned. 'We'd better remember that. Could you let me have your mother's address? I'll have to talk to her.'

'Yes, but if you could telephone her to let her know when you'll be arriving. She has a bad heart and anything unexpected could be dangerous for her.'

'Certainly.'

'I'll phone her as well, let her know you've been here and why and that she can expect a visit. It'll give her time to think about him. What was his name?'

'De Beer. Edward De Beer.'

The Panther lay on the floor of his living room. Lying flat … lying flat … not moving, not making a sound … not daring to breath because the soldiers were here … prodding, poking … but they don't have dogs … they don't have dogs … there's a chance because they don't have dogs. It's hot, can hardly breathe, but can't open a window. The Panther lay there … feeling hungry … he hadn't eaten that day … food is to be rationed and he got less than a fighting man … he may not get any at all today. Later, when the soldiers had gone, he rolled onto one side and looked across the expanse of carpet that was his living room … then he belly crawled to the stairs and, not making a sound for fear of betraying his position, he moved slowly up the stairs to the room where he could sleep ... and there he did sleep, for he hadn't slept for many, many hours.

The woman lay on the wooden slats of the recliner, her eyes shaded against the sun, feeling the rays bake her body. Later that afternoon she would rise from the sun chair and dive into the pool, 'the Master' liked his dinner at 6.00 p.m., just as the sun was setting, he loved to eat alfresco, though he preferred simple, easy to prepare meals, and that suited her admirably. The mobile phone beside her on the tiled floor of the swimming pool surround rang with a tinny tone, she reached for it, feeling for it with her long fingers, without opening her eyes, and finding it, lifted its compact lightness to her ear, pressed receive and said, 'Hello...'
'Is Michael there?' The voice sounded familiar, she couldn't place it ... one of the Master's friends, his inner circle to which she was not privy. Her purpose in life was to set the villa off, be there to look attractive, to soften the house, to cook the meals and wash up afterwards and to go round the house once a day with the dustpan and brush ... and to satisfy his other needs ... but it was distinctly better than being an audio typist in Birkenhead, from which horror he had rescued her.
'He's in the study.'
'Can I talk to him?'
'He doesn't like being disturbed when he's working.'

'He'll be disturbed for this.'

'Who's calling?'

'Toby Etherington.'

'Yes ... Mr Etherington.' She sat up, turning as she did so. 'Of course,' that voice, she heard it so many times, silly of her not to place it. 'I'll go and get him.'

'Thank you.'

She stood, tall, bronzed, statuesque and utterly naked, and walked on raised heels, as if wearing a pair of invisible stilettos, to the villa. She entered the villa and shivered slightly at the coolness, walked through the kitchen, where soon she was to labour, and across the marble reception area to a wooden door, lightly varnished, which stood at the far end of the hallway. She halted outside the room and heard the busy, hollow-sounding pattering of a computer keyboard. She tapped on the door.

'What!' The reply was angry, short-tempered.

The woman pushed the door open. 'It's Toby Etherington,' she held up the mobile. 'I told him you didn't like being disturbed when you were working, but he said you'd be disturbed for this.' She approached him and handed him the phone, he took it with one hand and curled his other round her thigh, just below her buttocks, stroking her appreciatively. She remained there, it was not her place to pull herself away when he was enjoying her body.

'Toby!' Michael Filsell smiled down the phone. The woman watched and listened as she saw his face turn from a smile to a frown. His hand slipped from her thigh and he waved her imperiously away. She turned and left the room, closing the door behind her and returned to the pool, sweeping through the multi-coloured strands of the fly screen, out into the sun, to languish the afternoon away until it was time to prepare the meal. He was her sugar daddy, she was his sugar babe. He was older than her father and she wasn't privy to his inner world, the world of his friends or the glitter of his 'opening nights', but it was still an awful lot better than being in the typing pool of the shipping office, with the bitchiness, the rain from the grey sky. An awful lot better.

Later that day she rolled off the chair and dived into the pool, swam for a few minutes and then went into the house, and wearing one of his shirts, prepared a paella. That evening they sat together at the table, he at his 'the top end' and she 'at hers' the opposite, bottom end. She dared not speak, she dared not even make eye contact ... something was troubling him, that phone call from the politician, Toby Etherington, whom her sugar daddy in one of the rare moments when he spoke to her of his friends, had confidently described as 'a future prime minister' ... had troubled him. She kept her voice and movements to a minimum and stayed out of his way for the remainder of the evening.

Sydney Household left the house in Warkworth Terrace and walked past the police station, glancing up at the window of the CID room as he did so. He saw David Tracy and Penny Wiseman standing at the window, facing each other, evidently in intense conversation. He walked on, crossing East Road at the pelican crossing and on to Mill Road, glancing at the curved roof of the rebuilt swimming baths as he did so. He turned off Mill Road and walked down the rectangular shaped Collier Road, finding the house he was looking for just before he rejoined Mill Road. Number 42 Collier Road was, like the house he had just left, also a terrace, also of grey brick, but much, much smaller. The two houses were clearly of the same age but Warkworth Terrace was built for the professional middle-class man and his family, Collier Road and the houses thereon were built for the artisan and his. The door of number 42 was painted brown with white trim on the panel beadings. There was no doorbell, no relic of the nineteenth century in the form of a metal knocker, and so Household tapped on the door with the classic police officer's knock – tap, tap ... tap. Not particularly loudly, it was the spacing of the taps that transmitted the presence of authority on the threshold.

The door was opened slowly, almost curiously, by an Afro Caribbean woman who was clearly unimpressed by Household's knock or else unfamiliar with it. She was a short, overweight woman, dressed in a black gown over which was draped a highly coloured sarong. She had chunky but dull metal jewellery round her neck, bangles on her wrists and large wooden earrings. She looked at Household as if waiting for an explanation as to why her door had been knocked on.

'Michael Wales?' Household asked. 'I understand he lives here?'

'Mr Michael?' the woman said, sounding to

Household like 'Meester Mykal?'

'Yes,' Household smiled. 'Mister Michael.'

The woman turned and bellowed into the house, projecting her voice mainly upstairs, but only mainly, it seemed to Household. 'Meester Michael ... for you ... the doorway to the street.' And that done, and wanting no reply, the woman walked into the downstairs front room and closed the door behind her.

Household stood at the threshold. And waited. And waited. He was about to enter the property and call out Michael Wales's name when a man appeared at the head of the stairs, and crouched so as to be able to see who was at the doorway to the street. The two men looked at each other for a few seconds, before Household spoke. 'Mr Wales?'

'One of many, I dare say, squire, but the only one in this house. Who be you?'

'I be the police.'

'Be you now,' said with a smile, 'you don't have a uniform.'

'Only wear the uniform on special occasions, like when I want to terrify people, especially weak and innocent children into confessing to dreadful crimes they didn't commit.'

'Ah ... and I take it you don't want to terrify me?'

Household pursed his lips and shook his head. 'Nope. I seek information I think you may have.'

'Thought it must be something like that because my last knowingly committed felony was a number of years ago... rode my bike home while in a state of intoxication.'

'Could have been fatal.'

'Yes, I know, you don't have to tell me ... could have lost my balance, under the wheels of a lorry, could've been killed.'

'Yep ... just like Edward De Beer.'

Michael Wales relaxed, slumped against the wall. 'Eddie ... oh my ... I read the report in the paper, that's who you are calling about?'

'Yes. I gather you knew him.'

'Yes ... yes ... I knew Eddie ... course I knew Eddie. We just clicked, we understood each other, on one level anyway, in fact we used to say that if one of us had been female ...well. Kick the door shut behind you and come up.'

Household closed the door behind him, allowing it to catch on the barrel lock with a gentle 'click' and walked up the stairs which, by further contrast to the house on Warkworth Terrace, were narrow, steeper, darker, and the house altogether mustier smelling. On the landing he saw three doors, one of which was open. He walked to it and said, 'Hello?'

'Yes, come in,' Wales called from inside the room.

Household stepped across the threshold. He was met by a blaze of colour and visual stimulation. Not one part of the wall was without covering, from small postcards to larger posters. The bed, a double, was pushed against the wall, and under the window two chairs sat facing each other in front of the fireplace, as indeed had been the arrangement in the room once occupied by Edward De Beer at Warkworth Terrace, but here, again, the living conditions were cramped by comparison.

241

'Cup of tea?' Wales asked.

'No, thanks, I've just had lunch.'

'OK. Well, take a pew.'

Wales sat in one of the chairs, Household sat facing him. Wales was a slightly built man in his fifties, but he wore the clothes of an undergraduate; flip-flop sandals, denim jeans, a faded red T-shirt with the image of Che Guevara still visible, a trimmed beard that failed to properly hide a weak chin, and his hair, dark but greying, worn behind his head in a ponytail.

'How can I help you?'

Household relaxed. 'Well, as I said, it's about Edward De Beer, his family mentioned your name.'

'Did they? After all this time?' Wales seemed flushed with the compliment.

'Apparently Eddie mentioned you from time to time, you seemed to be the only friend he spoke about and his brother said he saw your name on posters ... as I see in the one on the wall there, "Fifth Fenland Poetry Festival, org. Mick Wales, 42 Collier Road", that has to be you, same name of this address. As you said, there must be many people named Michael Wales in the world, but only one at this address.'

'Yes, that's me.'

'Well, I typed in "Fenland Poetry Festival" into my search engine and lo' and behold.'

'You are a skilled and determined detective.'

'I also typed in your name and possible year of birth into our machine and got a result. Fined five pounds for possession of cannabis resin at Cambridge Magistrates' Court in 1975.

242

Occupation given as "poet".'

The open window allowed a breeze to waft the net curtain. Household breathed in the fresh air. Wales smiled and shrugged.

'I confess that was a little ... shall I say, optimistic of me. But "apprentice poet", "poet in the making", "poet [unpublished]", didn't seem quite right, so I just plumped for "poet".'

'I see.'

'Published now, though.'

'Good for you.'

'Mainstream publisher too ... well, one poem in an anthology of poems on the theme of "Summertime".'

'And when not writing poetry you are employed as?'

'A poet, man ... it's a full-time occupation ... it's more full-time than a full-time job, you never switch off, words just tumble in and out of my head ... but I am subsidised by the state.'

'The dole?'

'The dole.'

'And you have lived here in this room since 1975?'

'Yes ... longer. Took this room at the beginning of the second year at the Tech. Been here ever since, man ... hey it's cool ... I have few needs.'

Household thought that Michael Wales's life was not dissimilar to doing a life stretch in an open prison, but he didn't comment. 'Published much in that time?'

'An anthology of my work with the No Name Press, twenty-five poems.'

'The No Name Press?'

'A small outfit. Actually they went out of business, my book of poems was one of the last books they published. But the anthology I mentioned...'

'Summertime, theme of.'

'Yes. Ashton's published that.' Michael Wales beamed with pride. 'They won't publish anything ... if Ashton's will publish you, even if only as part of an anthology, you are a poet. And that is how Eddie and I got to know each other. We shared a love of poetry. It was about the only thing that Eddie and I had in common, he'd sit there, in that very chair, and read the poems he'd written. You see that was what we had in common, we would take each other's work seriously, we would analyse it, deconstruct it ... offer improvements ... we were the only people we knew who could do that without smirking or sniggering. I would read one of my poems to someone else and they'd smile ... you'd give it to them to read and watch their face while they read it and always, always, you'd see a smile, a snigger being suppressed ... but not with Eddie. I didn't do it with his work and he didn't do it with mine. In fact, the warmest and fondest memories of my student days are of me and Edward De Beer spending the evening in this room ... in the winter, that gas fire hissing away, the rain driving down out of a black sky hammering against the window ... and me and Eddie in here, talking poetry. Then at ten o'clock we'd pull on our army coats...'

'Army coats?'

'Early 1970s, the student's uniform was an ex-army greatcoat, bellbottomed jeans and desert boots. Hair long, of course. The hippie movement had lost its edge ... but it was still with us, hadn't yet been replaced by punk, it was still peace and love ... it was anti-Vietnam protests. In fact, the Vietnam War stopped the year I took this room. Anyway, after an evening talking about poetry, we'd go across to the Locomotive for a pint or two. It was pretty well original then, not the revamped pub it is now. Now it's still a pub, same name, same location, but a totally different animal. Then Eddie would go back to his room in the large house in Warkworth Terrace.'

'I was there just an hour ago.'

'Really?'

'Yes, really. I was in the room he rented thirty years ago, and now I am told I am sitting in the chair he sat in thirty years ago.'

'It seems like yesterday. You know if I met Eddie now, I think we could pick up the last conversation we had and just carry on.'

'So, tell me about him.'

Michael Wales relaxed back in his chair and glanced up at the ceiling. 'Well he was a mate of mine...'

'But?'

'But he was a queer bird. A very queer bird indeed. And I don't mean homosexual, in the early seventies the word "gay" hadn't established itself to mean what it means now. Eddie was queer in the real meaning of the word, unusual, difficult to understand ... always had the impression that there was a lot going on inside his head ... he was confused, I think.'

'Can you give an example, to tell me, saying

somebody was "confused" doesn't really conjure up any image.'

'Well ... alright ... when I came to the Tech, when I was a first year, I was chatting to a final year student in the degree students' common room ... it was just a portakabin with a TV and a few chairs and a bar football game. Anyway, this fella told me that there are girls who come to the Tech whom you never see except in lectures or tutorials, they come to the Tech to pull a university guy and all their socialising is done at the university bars, or they join university societies ... and it was quite true. I can think of one girl right now who did just that and got what she wanted, marriage to a university graduate, and that's just one I know because I had a couple of chats with her, but there were others. After three years I never knew their names, just saw them in lectures, never came to any of the parties, never went to the club.'

'The club?'

'The Tech had a drinking club, bar in the cellar, dance floor and TV room upstairs, on the street level, in King's Passage, right opposite King's College ... it was practically the only time any of us went across Parker's Piece, to go to the club. The premises are now a "play room" so called.'

'A play room?'

'Belongs to one of the university colleges who use it to stage amateur dramatics.'

'Ah ... play ... I see ... I thought a room for children.'

'Yes, that's not unintentional, I think, clever use of words. Then the Tech club moved to the

"Kite", behind the police station, and now the Tech has become APU it's got licensed premises on site ... but these girls I mention were never seen at the club and Edward De Beer was like that. Very unusual for a bloke. One or two blokes never socialised, they were reserved, bookish ... but Eddie didn't socialise because he was like those girls I mentioned, trying to ingratiate himself with the university types, for what purpose I don't know because he wouldn't have won acceptance. There was a massive barrier between the university and the Tech. Many people at the university just refused to acknowledge its existence. Many of us had experiences of chatting to other students on the train going to Cambridge for the start of a new term or at a party and the person you'd be talking to would say 'What college are you?' and you'd say the Tech and even after holding a conversation for a while, they'd just shut up and look out of the train window, or say, "Excuse me, I've just seen someone from my college" and walk away.'

'Complete snobbery.' Household began to warm to Michael Wales.

'Oh, total snobbery, and it extended outside the university as well. There was a spate of theft of books from the bookshop in Cambridge and they were quoted in the *Evening News* as saying they suspect a lot of thefts are down to the Tech students because "that college attracts a lower quality of student".'

'Oh dear...'

'They had a small apology printed on the front page of a later edition but the sentiment remained the same. I think people felt threatened by the Tech for some reason. For example, the Tech football team was truly excellent in the early 1970s and in order to get games they were allowed to play in the university knock-out cup, each college fielded a team, and the Tech was allowed to play even though it wouldn't be allowed to win the cup. Everybody expected it to be knocked out in the early stages.'

'And it wasn't?'

'Nope. Despite playing college teams which fielded footballing blues and despite some allegedly very biased refereeing it made it to the final and played Clare College. Clare won and the local press reported the game with the headline, "Clare Puts the Tech Firmly in its Place".'

'Blimey.'

'Well, you can cope with that if you are secure enough in yourself, you can even laugh at it, as many of us did, in fact. But occasionally it got a bit ugly.' Wales paused as if remembering something. 'Once, I visited a guy I met who was at Pembroke, he'd written this amazing poem. I wrote to him, telling him how impressed I was with it and explained that I too wrote poetry. He wrote back and invited me to come and see him in his "rooms" at the college to look at some more of his work and asked me to bring some of mine. So I went one winter's evening and sat in his room and had the same sort of chat I used to have with Edward De Beer. Anyway, I left and walked towards the exit and these guys stood there. I had the Tech written all over me and they stopped me from leaving. They had appointed themselves as sentries to the college. They wanted to know who I was, who I'd been visiting and one of them said, 'You're not at the Tech, are you?' So I kidded on I was visiting from Hull University. I said the guy I had been visiting and I were at school together ... but if I had said I was at the Tech they would have rolled me. On another occasion, I was walking into town and got surrounded by some university guys, again because I had "Tech" written all over me, they were about to roll me as well but I pointed out that I was on a public highway and they were contemplating a very serious crime, it would finish them before they had even started in life and so they let me walk. I mean, that was allegedly the cream of British youth from the top public schools ... plain street thugs. That was the attitude the university and its adherents had to the Tech, yet De Beer seemed to want to ingratiate himself with them.'

'Do you know why he did that?'

'I don't. He wasn't a snob ... he didn't seem to me to be holding himself aloof or thinking he was above the Tech in some way.'

'But he didn't socialise with his fellow students, with the one exception of yourself?'

'And the occasional beer in the Loco when the Tech darts team was playing – they had T-shirts printed, you know those nineteenth century American locomotives you see in Western films ... huge funnel and a cow catcher on the front?'

'Yes.'

'Well, the t-shirt had one of those, showing a train coming towards you on the front, and the caboose going away from you on the back ...

never knew who designed it. Anyway, occasionally Eddie would come and cheer on the Locomotive darts team when they were playing, and drank pints and then he was an all round good bloke ... but he hardly ever did that. He seemed to be pursuing a different agenda. Quite frankly, I don't think he ever got further down Mill Road than the Locomotive, which is just down the road from his house. He never got over the railway bridge and into Romsey Town.' Wales paused.

'You're thinking of something?'

'Yes.' Wales sat forward and rested his elbows on his knees. 'It's nothing concrete ... but it might just hint at the reason why he was orientated towards the university, despite the prejudice he would have encountered.'

'Well, float it ... see if it makes sense.'

'Cup of tea first.' Wales stood. 'Sure you don't want one?'

'Well ... yes, thank you ... I will.'

Michael Wales returned with two mugs of tea. The mug he drank from had 'Strychnine' emblazoned in gold on a black background. The mug Household was given to drink from had 'Arsenic' similarly emblazoned on it. Wales resumed his seat. 'Well ... this is a bit of a wild card ... many of us at the Tech reported that our parents told their friends and relatives that their son or daughter was "at Cambridge" and allowed said friends and relatives to assume the obvious ... and thus enjoyed the envy. My parents did it, which caused me amusement here, but when I was at home I lost no time in disabusing any relative or family friend of any notion that my

250

parents might have put into their head that I was at university here. And that was the attitude of everybody I spoke to, except Edward De Beer.'

'Interesting.'

'You think so?'

'Well, it might be.' Household sipped the tea. The mug was clean, the tea well made, and piping hot. 'Carry on...'

'Eddie told me his parents had also broadcast that he was "at Cambridge" but he didn't laugh it off, he was serious. He told me in the manner of confessing a problem ... today we would say disclosing.'

'Yes.'

'Well, that's it ... he felt it a real problem ... as though he had to go along with his parents' fantasy about being "at Cambridge". He felt he had to make it an actuality, out of a sense of loyalty, probably misplaced loyalty but possibly that was it ... I don't know.'

'It would help explain it. He must have been very confused.'

'Must have been ... I couldn't have done it. If that was what was going through his head, living a lie like that ... ugh.' Wales shuddered. 'Horrible ... that would push me over the edge ... you can see my life, no structure to it, no colleagues, living with a shifting bedsit-land population ... it's difficult for me to keep my feet on the ground sometimes.'

'I can imagine.'

'So I have to cling to what I know is real. I go into APU each day and read the *Guardian*. Nobody bothers me ... every college has its hangers

251

on, people who hang round because they like the college atmosphere ... reckon I've replaced the chicken.'

'The chicken?'

'The Tech chicken. In our era it was legendary. It was a chicken that lived under the huts near the East Road entrance to the college ... just kept itself alive somehow. Where it came from, and what happened to it, that's a mystery, but I'm like the chicken, hanging around the Tech, or APU, pecking a living.' Wales stood and lit a joss stick, the sweet smell of incense began to fill the room. 'It's a hangover. I no longer smoke dope but I like burning joss sticks.'

'Did Eddie ever talk to you about the people he lived with in Warkworth Terrace?'

'A little. He seemed to be pleased to be rubbing shoulders with them.'

'Remember any names?'

'Only one ... a bloke called Filsell.'

'Filsell?' Household reached for his notepad.

'Yes, Michael Filsell.' Wales spelled the surname for Household. 'Ring any bells? Remember Edward De Beer's love of the language and his attempts to use it creatively? Do the bells get louder?'

'The playwright?'

'Yes.'

'Well, well, well,' Household said.

'Cambridge,' Wales raised his eyebrows. 'The Tech produced a lot of middle ranking professionals, teachers in the main, but the university has produced high fliers. People who were at the university when I was at the Tech are now leading politicians, captains of industry, heads of university departments up and down the country, and overseas ... and even wealthy playwrights.'

'Wealthy?' Household queried.

'Wealthy enough by anyone's standards. He was profiled in a glossy magazine. I read the article while in the dentist's waiting room, markets his plays through the "Good Move Company" and lives in a villa on Malta.'

'I wonder,' Household put his hand in his jacket pocket. 'Can I show you this photograph, see if you recognise anyone?' He handed Michael Wales a copy of the photograph which had been given to him by Edward De Beer's elderly father.

'Good heavens,' Wales looked at the photograph. 'It's all coming back to me now ... there's Edward De Beer, as he was.'

'Do you recognise the other people in the photograph?'

'The tall bloke, I think that's Filsell.' Wales studied the photograph. 'In a word I don't recognise anybody else, they aren't anyone who was at the Tech with Eddie and me, that's for sure ... but the tall fella, he looks to me like a younger Michael Filsell. I only know Filsell by the photographs of him which are published from time to time. Are you familiar with him?'

'I am not.'

'I don't mean personally, but he's a bit of a self-publicist ... I mean his PR image.'

'I know what you mean, but no, I am not familiar with him.'

'Well...' Wales continued to study the photograph. 'If you entered "Michael Filsell" into your search engine and pressed "go" you'd have his image on your screen ... and quite a few to choose from. Compare what you see on your screen with the tall youth in this photograph and see what you think. But that's definitely Edward De Beer on the edge of the group ... the outsider ... but by his body language, he seems to want to be part of the group ... there's a need in that stance.' Wales handed the photograph back to Household.

'A need in that stance?' Household liked Wales' use of words and unashamedly echoed them as he looked again at the photograph. 'Yes, that's a good way of putting it. It tends to bear out what you said, about him wanting to be part of the university set, feeling the need to live his parents' lie.'

'I remember when he disappeared,' Wales drank his tea. 'He wasn't noticed missing for a while ... you'd go to the pub and if Eddie wasn't there it was nothing remarkable.'

'He didn't mix socially, anyway?'

'As I said, really only with me ... but he hadn't signed in for a few days and it was announced at the beginning of a lecture that Edward De Beer appeared to be missing and a murmur went round the room, as you'd expect ... if anybody knows anything at all of his whereabouts, would they notify the college authorities or the police. Then the bloke delivered the lecture, couldn't do anything else. It was the talk of the Batman café for the next few days and the club the next few evenings. Then he got mentioned in passing only when he came to someone's mind. The mystery deepened when it became clear he hadn't "dropped out", as was the expression. Then it became clear that he hadn't gone home or joined a commune in London, but that he had seemingly just vanished into thin air. I reckon today we'd be mooting the possibility that he'd been snatched by aliens ... but that was still an unknown concept in the 70s. That's what it was like though, a vanishing act. Sudden, swift, silent. Complete.'

Household thanked Michael Wales for his time and information, and Wales escorted Household to the front door of his house where he shook his hand with his right-hand and with his left made the hippie peace sign, warmly urged Household to 'keep it together, man' as he gently closed the door.

The woman smeared sun block on her body as she once again lay on the recliner, enjoying the warm southerly breeze which brought with it the mystical scent of Africa. The sun was still warm, but was sinking. She thought she had an hour's more bathing that day. She became aware of sound from within the villa ... 'the Master' was stirring ... a short siesta for him. That, she thought, was unusual, it only happened if he was troubled. The recent phone call really had seemed to trouble him, and she sensed something in the offing. She watched as he walked through the doorway, pushing the fly screen aside. A well-built man, always tall, he was strong and muscular and in better shape than many of his age and, she had found, much, much better in bed than many a younger man she had known. He just knew how to press all the right buttons. He was dressed in a blue shirt with a loud yellow pattern, pale blue shorts and sandals. He sat beside her on the neighbouring recliner, took the sun block from her and began to apply it to her body himself, gently, sensitively, causing her to moan appreciatively.

'We're going to have a couple of visitors,' he said as he worked the oil into her flesh.

'Oh, aye...' she said with her eyes closed. 'Who's that then?'

'A couple of friends of mine.'

'Toby Etherington?' she asked. 'Britain's future Prime Minister ... I'll be able to tell me dad I met a celebrity.'

'Yes,' Michael Filsell growled. 'He and another friend.'

'Another politician?' She spoke with an emphasised northern accent because she knew it annoyed him. It was, she had decided, the only way she could keep a little sense of "self" about her in a situation where her function was mainly decorative and entertaining and provision of meals. It was especially so since the promised "spending money" had not been forthcoming. After six weeks the "spending money", her "allowance", had yet to be given.

'Yes, you'll find out who it is anyway, so I'll tell you, it's William Aughty.'

'Name means nothing to me. When are they coming?'

'As soon as they can, they're trying to get a flight tomorrow, but this is the height of the tourist season, so I don't know. They'll phone me when they know, it might even be from the airport ... the airport here, I mean.'

'Must be important.'

'Well, it's something we have to talk about, so I want you to make up beds in the guest rooms and buy in more food, you'll be cooking for four for the next few days. And while they're here, I want you to cover yourself up.'

'Oh...'

'They won't be here very long ... a couple of days.'

'Michael...'

'Yes,' said testily.

'This may be a bad time, but there isn't a right time ... it's about my money ... my allowance.'

'You'll get it, my dear girl. I told you.'

'But when?'

'Soon ... as soon as I have signed the contract for the new play, then I'll get an advance. I explained to you before ... being a writer isn't like being employed ... it's not like having a salary, the money comes in fits and starts, and you're right, it isn't a good time.' Filsell stood. 'In fact it's a very bad time ... don't pester me about anything while my friends are here. Just make the meals, clear up after the meals and keep out of our way.'

'Seen and not heard?'

'That, my pretty Liverpool lass, would be ideal.'

'It's Birkenhead! I'm from Birkenhead,' she sniffed indignantly.

Michael Filsell walked away muttering that once you're north of Oxford you're in foreign parts anyway, loud enough for her to hear.

Sydney Household stood on the corner of Collier Road and Mill Road. He glanced at his watch. It was nearly three p.m. Michael Wales' information had been useful, but Household didn't think it merited an immediate return to the police station. The visit to the now elderly lady who still owned the guest house in Warkworth Terrace would have to be done the next day. Elderly people have to be called on at home at very civilised hours, especially if their co-operation is sought. Further, elderly people are wont to sleep in the afternoon and so he reasoned that visit would have to be done in the forenoon, anyway. He was standing where he was standing because of the De Beer inquiry and he thought of something that Edward De Beer's father had said, about how he appreciated the police contacting him, even after so many years and so he also thought of the missing persons file he had chanced upon in the void and for some reason had made a note of. He consulted his notebook ... Sara Bullwood, home address given as 37 Romsey Road, Romsey Town, Cambridge. He decided to call on the family.

He walked down Mill Road, narrow and barely able to cope with the volume of traffic it carried, across the railway bridge and the streets of small terraced housing that was Romsey Town. He turned left down Hemingford Road, after consulting his neat pocket-sized Cambridge street atlas, and right into Romsey Road. It was with no small trepidation that he knocked on the door of number 37.

It was opened timidly by a frail-looking lady who looked questioningly at Household. 'Yes?' she asked in a high-pitched voice.

'Police.' Household showed her his ID.

'About our Sara?'

'There is no new development but yes, really, this is just a courtesy call.'

'Oh, please come in, sir.'

'Mr Household will do, rather than, sir.' Household entered the cool, narrow hallway of the house. The woman shut the door and called out, 'Barry ... Barry, it's the police, about our Sara.'

'Sara!' The voice was urgent, hopeful. It came from the back room of the house.

'Through there, sir ... Mr Household.' The woman, Mrs Bullwood, presumed Household, indicated the room in which 'Barry' clearly sat.

Household entered the room. He found it cluttered, but also cosy, a very lived-in room, deep, comfortable armchairs, a mirror hanging on the wall over the fireplace; a table stood against the wall furthest from the door and was covered by a heavy rubber matting, atop which was a wooden bowl containing a heaped bounty of fruit. The window of the room looked out onto the narrow strip of garden which contained a small potting shed, and seemed, to Household, to have been divided between a small lawn and a larger vegetable garden. 'This really is nothing more than a courtesy call,' Household said softly. 'I have no news, either good or bad.'

'Please have a seat, Mr Household.' Barry Bullwood, Sara's father, had a pleasant sounding speaking voice, nearly region-less, thought Household as he sat in one of the armchairs, but he did detect a hint of Cambridge. 'The phrase "no news is good news" doesn't apply to Sara ... any news is good news and would be welcomed after all this time.'

'I can imagine, but really the reason I called was to let you know that while the police are not active in the case, that doesn't mean we have lost interest.'

'That's very kind of you.' Barry Bullwood, short, slender, a hooked nose, a man in his middle years, shirt sleeved, casual summer slacks, clearly was the head of this household. He spoke, his wife remained, it seemed to Household, timidly silent. 'Well, the police never did seem to be particularly active in "the case" as you put it.'

'I am sorry you had that impression.'

'Had? Still have. Came and took statements, took a photograph and that was it. It was up to me and Mrs Bullwood to search the recreation ground, and the common ... she used to play on Coldham's Common a lot ... we walked across it, her brother too, looking for her, calling her name. We went from house to house, we put up posters, we did all that ... the police...' Barry Bullwood waved his hand dismissively 'Our neighbours were more help than the police, searched their sheds and outhouses, spare rooms ... anywhere and everywhere that a ten year old little girl could fit into. That was twenty-three years ago this autumn. She'd be thirty-three years old now ... married, children...' He shook his head. 'All that was taken from her you see, it's not just the being alive that was taken, it was the life she could have had, the experience, the joy ... she never saw London. All she ever wanted to do was stand beneath the clock tower of the Houses of Parliament as Big Ben chimed. We promised we'd take her...'

Household remained silent. He could imagine the sense of loss. After a few seconds of silence, he asked what sort of girl she was.

'Well, she wouldn't go off with a stranger ... the police did ask us that. She was a bit quiet ... reserved, never many friends.'

'Just one really.' Mrs Bullwood spoke for the first time since Household had sat down. 'Henry.'

'Never quite took to him,' Barry Bullwood glanced at the hearth, 'strange boy.'

'Henry?' Household's ears pricked up at the name.

'Strange surname...'

Household thought, 'Perigo', for some reason he could not have explained. He remained silent.

'Sparrow.' Mrs Bullwood seemed pleased with herself, as if she'd answered a question correctly on a quiz show. 'I remember you said they had come like a Sparrow and left like one.'

'Yes ... they were only here for a couple of years, if that ... mother and son. She could never settle, that woman ... small woman, quick, hurried movements, very nervous. That poor son of hers ... born round here in Romsey Town, went to London ... it's all flooding back now ... went to Southampton, one relationship after another ... she told me when we had a street party for the Silver Jubilee, it was the only time I spoke to her yet we were practically next door neighbours. Came here because she picked up with a teacher at one of the village colleges so young Henry was dragged back to Cambridge, sheer coincidence they came back here ... that didn't last because she sold up and moved to Eastern Europe.'

'The East!' Household was genuinely shocked.

'Well, if not Russia, then one of those Eastern European countries ... that was cruel.'

'Cruel?'

'Yes.' Bullwood sat forward and rested his elbows on his knees. 'Some people, they just never think about what they do to their children in here,' he tapped the side of his head. 'That poor little lad, Henry, he'd been bounced from pillar to post as his mother tramped round England from one boyfriend to another, no stability, no roots ... that was bad enough, but to take him to a foreign country, and Eastern Europe at that, because she thought she'd found the love of her life ... that was really cruel.'

'Iran,' Mrs Bullwood said, 'or Iraq.'

'I thought it was Eastern Europe?'

'I thought Iraq or Iran. No ... Iran ... definitely Iran.'

'Whatever, but she took him away from what little he was used to and to God knows where, and I often wonder what became of him. But it was when they were living next door but one, it was then that Sara disappeared. Mrs Sparrow searched her house, let me search with her, because Sara and Henry used to knock about together ... looked in their garden ... never saw the pond.'

'The pond?'

'Sara had said Henry was digging a pond for fish, and she was helping him.'

Household, the police officer, said nothing, but a chill ran up his spine.

'Just a small garden,' Bullwood leaned back in his chair, 'same size as ours, only place to hide anybody in the garden was the shed. First place we looked, nothing in it, saw that in a glance. Mrs Sparrow was genuinely worried for Sara, I could see that, it was then we started to walk over Coldham's Common ... she must have run into the bogey man ... been grabbed.'

'Oh...' Mrs Bullwood whimpered.

'Sorry, love.'

'Was Henry the same age as Sara?'

'No, he was older, he was twelve and that's quite an age gap ... a twelve-year-old boy at the secondary school, playing with a ten-year-old girl at primary school, and he was a big lad for twelve, but all that moving about, he probably could only handle younger playmates. Sara didn't seem to have many friends ... we saw no harm in it.'

'Which was their house?' Household asked.

'Two doors that way.' Bullwood tossed a thumb towards the corner of Romsey Terrace. 'Beyond the alley.'

Household took his leave of the Bullwoods. He did so with a gnawing feeling in the pit of his stomach that Sara Bullwood's body would transpire to have lain very close to her parents' house these last twenty-three years. He turned left, towards Hemingford Road. He enjoyed Romsey Town, the neat, homely terraces, everything to the human scale, as pleasant a working-class area as could be had. He stopped at the entrance to the alley, typical as any alley in Romsey Town, dividing two houses, forcing a gap in the line of the terrace, driving from the road at an angle of 90 and joined a pathway which ran along the back of the gardens, parallel to the road. The pathway and the alley afforded each home a 'back door' to and from the street. Household walked up the alley, walking the length of the brickwork which was the side of the houses on either side of him and emerged into the sunlight with rear gardens beside and in front of him. He looked at the garden to his right. It was fenced in by chicken wire which had been stapled to a series of wooden posts about three feet high, he guessed, but which made for easy viewing of the garden. The garden which belonged to the house once owned by Mrs Sparrow, was not as neatly tended as Barry Bullwood's, with its careful division between lawn and vegetable patch, and a small shed for potting plants and for storing tools. The garden that Household now looked at was really an area of trampled soil. No attempt had been made to cultivate any part of it. That would make it easier for the police, he thought, much easier when they came to dig it up because it was here, in this garden, that lay the body, by then the skeletal remains, of Sara Bullwood. He was an old copper, and his waters told him that that was the case. Household returned to the road and knocked on the door of the house, the garden of which he believed to contain a dreadful secret.

The door was opened by an overweight woman

264

in a yellow t-shirt and denims. She was barefoot. She held a newborn child in her arms and wore a welcoming smile. 'Saw you round the back – volunteering to do a bit of gardening?' she asked in a solid Cambridge accent.

'Funny you should say that.' Household showed her his ID 'Police,' he said.

'Any trouble?' The woman displayed no trace of guilt.

'There's always trouble,' Household smiled. 'How long have you been in this house?'

'Us ... about ten years. Husband and four children ... that's why the garden's like it is, flattened by the children. My husband lets them have the run of it. That's what I thought you were thinking when I saw you looking at our garden, "nice plot of land going to waste", or something like that.'

'Well, it wasn't actually.'

'My husband says we'll let the boys trample it all they like, whether it's ball games or making roads for their toy cars, that's their bit of ground. When they grow out of that bit, then we'll start doing something with it. Give us something to do when they don't need us anymore.'

'Was it like that when you bought the house?'

'No ... it was a mess ... a bit overgrown in fact.'

'Did it have an area of stones, or concrete perhaps? Any sign of a hole?'

'There's a patch of concrete, yes ... why?' A note of alarm crept into the woman's voice. 'It's mostly covered with soil, but tends to surface from time to time ... then the boys cover it again.'

'How large is it?'

265

'About three feet long, two feet wide. Can I ask why?'

'Not at the moment ... I can't tell you. Would you show it to me?'

The woman turned and walked back through her house, asking Household to shut the door behind him and follow her. The house proved to be chaotic, things appeared to be thrown anywhere and left where they fell. The woman seemed to anticipate his reaction, because she said, 'Don't mind how we live ... it's just the way we are.'

'Fine,' Household said. 'Fine.' He noted the children's drawings pinned to the wall, the toys strewn liberally around. It was what he believed psychologists would call a 'child-centred home' and was a little too child-centred for his conservative tastes. But the kitchen, as he glanced in, seemed orderly and clean and spoke of some reassuring semblance of adult control.

They walked out into the garden, to a location against the wall which separated their garden from the neighbours'. Alley and chicken wire on one side, a wall, then an adjacent garden on the other. A wooden fence with a gate set halfway along it, was at the bottom of the garden. 'About here,' she tapped her naked heel on the sun-baked soil, 'just under the surface.'

'Do you mind?' Household took his penknife from his pocket, opened it and probed beneath the surface of the soil with the point of the blade. He came upon resistance about one inch below the surface. 'Ah, yes,' he probed about the area, 'seems to be lengthways parallel to the brick wall.'

'It is,' the woman hushed the child as it began

266

to cry, 'about two feet out from the wall.'

'Did the last owner of the house comment on it?' Household stood, folded his penknife and slipped it back into his jacket pocket.

'Only that it was there when he bought the house. He said that the person he bought it from told him it was a hole filled with rubble and concreted over for the sake of neatness.'

'I see. Do you know anything about the last owner but one?'

'No, only know about the last owner ... single man who went to live in the north. Got a better job up there, he told us. We don't know anything about the history of the house.'

'Which estate agent did you purchase it from?'

'We purchased it from the last owner, not the estate agent.' The woman smiled as she gently bounced the infant.

'Point to you.'

'He used Henry Morton. We saw the photograph in his window, me and my husband, we turned to each other and said, "That's the one". Walked in and expressed our interest. Survey was good, and we offered a good price. Then it was ours. Four children later, it's still ours.'

'Henry Morton? Don't know that estate agent.'

'On Mill Road, just this side of the railway bridge. Small agent, seems to specialise in Romsey Town properties ... or the bottom end of the market terraces ... mostly this side of the tracks, and definitely this side of Parker's Piece.'

Household warmed to her sense of humour. 'Your husband and other children are out of the house, clearly so?'

267

'Yes, he's taken them to watch the cricket match at Fenners. They'll be back soon.'

'He's not at work?'

'We're both teachers, primary ... schools are closed at the moment ... long, lovely summer hols. Why? Do you want to talk to him?'

'Not especially, but we may like to excavate the concrete, so we'll need both your permission and his.'

'I see ... there's more than rubble under the concrete? Is that what you're saying?' She brushed a fly from the child's face.

'Possibly. But don't be alarmed.'

'Well, you can't not be alarmed. But I'll try not to be.'

'I have to go to see the estate agents. I can get there before it shuts...' He glanced at his watch.

'Catch a bus from the top of the road, save a few minutes and in this heat too ... not the weather for a brisk walk.'

Household took the woman's advice and a single-decker took him two stops down Mill Road. He alighted at the last stop before the railway bridge. He looked around him for Henry Morton, estate agents, which seemed to be hidden in the plethora of small businesses, kebab shops, launderettes, bicycle shops, food shops, then he saw it, small frontage, white lettering on a blue background. His work that afternoon had taken a sharp turn, but the trail of Sara Bullwood had suddenly become warmer than the trail of Edward De Beer. There was nothing to connect the two disappearances, except that they had both disappeared about the same time, thirty

268

years ago. One had been found, and Household was grimly confident in himself that the second was going to be found quite shortly.

He crossed Mill Road and entered the premises of Henry Morton, Estate Agent.

'Help you, sir?' The slender middle-aged man shot to his feet as Household entered the building. Behind him on the wall were photographs of properties for sale.

'Hope so. Police.' Household flashed his ID.

'Police?'

'Making enquiries.'

'Oh?'

'About a property on Romsey Lane. You were agents for the sale of the property ten years ago.'

'We were?'

'You were.' Household told him the address.

Moments later, courtesy of efficient filing, Household and the agent sat opposite each other as the agent leafed through the papers in the file in respect of the property in question.

'We have acted for the sellers of this house on three occasions. The present owners, the Walkers, bought it from Mr Fordham I see here ... and we also acted for a Mrs Sparrow ... she sold it to Mr Fordham ... and we also acted for Mr and Mrs Blyth ... who sold it to Mrs Sparrow. Often happens, the same property comes back to the same agency time and again. We sell a lot of property in Romsey Town.'

'So I see. Where did Mrs Sparrow go after she quit the house in Romsey Road?'

'Abroad, it seems. We sold the house and the contents.'

269

'And the contents?'

'Yes, so it says. She left all her furniture, carpets, curtains, the lot ... she wasn't moving within Britain. She wasn't intending to come home by all accounts, otherwise all her furniture would have gone into storage, I would have thought.'

'I would have thought so too.'

'Only her solicitor can tell you where she went to. He'll have her forwarding address.'

'Who are?'

'Withern & Co.' He picked up his phone and handed it to Household. 'You might catch them before they draw stumps for the day'

He recited the number as Household dialled. Moments later Household replaced the receiver. 'Believed to have gone overseas. They handed her the proceeds of the sale in hard cash, she signed the receipt for it, and left their premises with a shopping bag full of money. They remember her well.'

'As they might,' the agent said, 'as they might. Why, is she in trouble?'

'Really don't know, yet.' Household stood. 'Let's just say she might have left something in her garden. Thank you for your time and assistance.'

The Panther saw the girl enter the house, turning a key, just one, a barrel lock. She was tall, black, sensuous. He continued walking but noted the number of the house as he passed by. An ordinary looking man, walking slowly, without evident purpose, an onlooker might describe him as 'strolling'. He walked past the Job Centre offices and on to Milton Road, which he crossed when the traffic allowed him to, and followed the road round the small island on which stood terraced houses, and rejoined Chesterton Road. He continued strolling until he neared the junction with Elizabeth Way, then crossed the road and walked back in the direction from which he had come, and half an hour later he again walked past the door of the house into which the black girl had entered. He glanced at the house, and saw her standing in the front room reading a letter as if having come home and picked up the day's mail. That the Panther found interesting: she was far too young to be the owner of the property. It wasn't let to lodgers, not a house like that, yet that day's mail was not picked up until late in the afternoon. It meant that the house had been unoccupied all day. The woman looked like a student ... the middle of summer, the long vacation ... home alone ... parents out at work, the front door could be burst open ... but not on this street. This would need a more subtle approach ... this gazelle in the grass would have to be pounced on during the day. Then killed. The last girl, the last gazelle in the grass had to die, she had seen his face. But killing felt good. He had forgotten just how good it felt. He had rediscovered his taste for it. He crossed the river by the footbridge and walked across Jesus Green towards Drummer Street, and a bus.

The night wrapped round them, hiding them from view, and so they felt it safe to walk slowly together, in step and arm in arm, making sedate progress through Chesterton Churchyard, on the path that was the shortcut between Elizabeth Way and Penny Wiseman's flat.

'One very felonious felon,' David Tracy grinned. 'Quite a few Piggots in East Anglia, as you know.'

'Oh I know, I know.' Penny Wiseman squeezed his arm with hers.

'Oh, but this Piggot, track for everything, burglary, receiving stolen goods, indecent exposure ... and he's only about three and a bit feet tall ... and the hovel he lives in ... ugh!'

'But the information he gave sounds promising.'

'Oh yes, I'm not looking a gift horse in the mouth, I'll take it to Dominic tomorrow ... a van that was like a police van he said and heavens, he sounds like a man who knows what a police van should look like.'

The woman strolled amid the bright lights of the 'Gut' in Valetta, amid the shops which stayed open late, catering for impulse-purchasing tourists. She wore a black cotton dress, bare legs finished in white sandals, carried a white bag and wore a silk scarf round her head. She had no allowance, that didn't look like it was ever going to materialise. She had long since learned to distrust Filsell, despite his charm, and the fact remained that none of his promises to her had been kept. His charm was a veneer, a sour and sarcastic personality lay beneath. And, she also thought, a ruthless personality as well. But as she had once heard, 'like finds like', and she could be ruthless too. The phone call had shaken him. He was a worried man. She had accumulated a little hard cash, change from the near-daily shopping trips she had been sent on which now hung heavy in her bag. She found the sort of shop she was looking for, one that sold electrical appliances, and entered it. A few minutes later she exited the shop, her handbag much lighter, having exchanged the bulk of the coins she had accumulated for a battery-powered pocketsize cassette player – with a microphone attachment, and a packet of blank tapes, the sort that play for 45 minutes each side.

She had been born between the 23rd October and the 21st November, she was a Scorpio. She was more than his mindless bit of decoration from the North Country in respect of whom promises of generous amounts of spending money do not have to be kept. She was not going to be promised much and in the event given nothing but an all expenses paid holiday in the sun and a lot of free time when not in the bedroom or the kitchen or driving the mini-moke along the dusty road between the villa and the little supermarket.

She smiled.

She was a Scorpio. She had a sting in her tail.

7

Nigel Atkins listened to Sydney Household's submission with furrowing forehead and narrowing eyes. When Household had finished, he asked, 'Remind me again how you happened to come across the file?'

'Quite by chance, as I said, sir ... when I was looking in the void for mis per files that might help us identify the skeleton which was discovered out by Bottisham. Fell into my hands. And after we had identified the body as that of Edward De Beer, the elderly Mr De Beer told me how much it meant that the police had come to see him in person about his missing son. So when I found myself within a few minutes of Sara Bullwood's home and having time to spare, I acted on a whim, really ... nothing more than that. Called on her parents, just a courtesy call, really, just to let them know that their daughter hasn't been forgotten.'

'Dangerous, Sydney ... could reawaken fresh hope.'

'Possibly, but I did make the point at the outset that I had no new information and then, as I said, I seemed to pick up the trail ... and we sit here.'

'And we sit here, as you say.' Nigel Atkins leaned back in his chair. 'Where would you like to go from here?'

'Only one place to go, sir, the concreted-over

section of ground in the household once occupied by a lady called Sparrow.'

'She married an Iranian and took her little boy with her?'

'Yes, sir, twelve years old.'

Atkins shook his head in disbelief. 'Uprooted from England to go and live in Iran at that age. How can his mother be so thoughtless? The culture shock, his school experience ... he'd be hated by the other children ... oh my...'

'Yes. I thought the same, sir, though I don't think he was uprooted, he seemed to have been bounced round England all his life as his mother moved from one boyfriend to the next ... but still it's a wrench ... just when he needs stability, he gets the most massive move yet.'

'No way of contacting her, I suppose?'

'Don't see how we can sir, even if she is still alive ... she and her son would have been there at the height of the Iran/Iraq war. So I think they are lost unto the wilderness.'

'Yes ...' Atkins paused. 'Horrible story, though. In fact I think it's going to upset me for some time to come, wondering what happened to that little boy.'

'Yes. It is distressing, but it still leaves the area of concrete to be explained.'

'Yes ... a bit embarrassing for us, if she is there in the garden of the neighbouring house for the last twenty something years.'

'It will be, but in fairness to the investigating officers, this was pre HOLMES and pre CATCHEM. If they had computers in those days and logged into either programme they would have been told to search all neighbouring houses and be suspicious of recently dug holes ... but in those days they confined themselves to making house to house enquiries and if the household said they had no information, they left it at that.'

'Yes. I dare say there is a place for these computers after all. So do you want the case marked as open to you?'

'Yes, please, sir. If there's nothing under the concrete, all I can do is return it to the void, and if she is there ... well, as I said ... lost unto the wilderness ... all I will be able to do is return Sara's body to her parents, let them put her to rest ... either way, not a lot of work.'

'How's the De Beer case progressing?'

'Well, positive ID of the skeleton, but the investigation is thinning out after all this time. The big one at the moment is the Panther investigation.'

'Yes, I know,' a look of worry crossed Atkins' face, 'that has to take all the resources. Perigo should have made more progress by now ... now that he's become a killer. The pressure's really on. Anyway, when do you want to dig up the concrete?'

'This afternoon, sir. I have to visit an elderly lady this morning.'

The Panther looked at the house from his vantage point by the bridge. He knew that time pressure was on him, now that the body had been found, laid out neatly on the verge, as neat as neat could be. He thought that he could do one of two things. He could act quickly, take another victim, give himself somebody else to look after, somebody else to keep for a while, or he could lie low, not take anybody else for a long time ... not for a year or more ... but he thought and thought, and pondered, and deep within himself he knew he couldn't stop, not for as long as year, not without at least one more victim, one more young lovely to look after. And then kill. He had decided on his course of action the previous night and had driven the van from where he had parked it, in out of the way Greville Road, to Milton Road where he left it overnight. He returned to the house in the morning, dressed neatly in a suit and white shirt and blue tie. He watched as the lady of the house, a tall, elegant black woman, left the house and crossed the road, turning in his direction.

She walked past him, not glancing at him for a single moment, and he in turn felt weak-kneed for he recognised her. He recognised her very well. He walked round Jesus Common; old men played bowls, a couple walked arm in arm on the path beside the river. This made a difference. It's true, he thought, how true, if you have nothing to do with the university then this part of the city of Cambridge can be a very small village. He pondered the idea of seeking another victim, but he had settled upon this plan, and the knowledge that he knew his victim, not at all closely, but knew of her, added to the sense of power he felt. It gave her something that none of the others had had, it gave her an identity, made her more real. That made her more attractive. More valuable somehow. He had a plan. The plan would either work or it wouldn't. He waited for an hour, he waited for a second hour, then walked to Milton Road to where he had parked the van.

'Yes, I remember the little technical college boy who disappeared.' Mrs Telford revealed herself to be frail, elderly, she sat in a cardigan despite the heat of what was widely regarded as a 'hot' summer, not a record breaker, the weatherman had said, but a hot one, 'with England and our region particularly edging near to drought conditions'. Beside her was a low table which contained an array of bottles of medicine and tablets. But the woman's mind, as her son had promised, was sharp as a tack, as sound as a pound. He thought that the Tech had been a college of 'Art and Technology', which isn't quite the same as a 'technical college', but he didn't comment. 'I let rooms to male students at the university, bed and full English breakfast. There was one room in the house which was too big for a single room but the university wouldn't allow their students to share rooms, each had to have his own room, so I used to let that room to two technical college boys ... the Tech didn't seem to bother about their students' accommodation. De Beer and another boy took it. The other boy quit after a bit so De Beer continued on by himself for an increased rent ... not the full rent for a double room. That would have been expensive for him, but he was staying, that was plain, no matter how much it cost him. See, sir, it's not just that the old boy stayed, paying an expensive rent and disappeared in the middle of it that makes me remember him ... it's his attitude.'

'Oh?'

'Well, the other little technical college boys I had in the room, they kept to themselves, shared the room, went out with their old mates from the technical college and came back and went to their room. Didn't talk to the others in the house except at breakfast.'

'But he was different?'

'Yes.' The elderly woman paused. 'You see, I was a long time in that house, the family flat was in the basement and I used to be sitting in front of the old TV and listen to them coming home ... big house, but I knew by which door had opened who had come in. The other technical college boys I had over the years, before De Beer and after De Beer, well they just used to go straight up to that room and shut the door behind them, but with De Beer I heard the university boys come in, they went to one room or another, then they would go to their own rooms and drink the coffee and smoke whatever it was they smoked ... and De Beer was with them. I heard him walk back to that big room he had to himself.'

'He mixed with them socially?'

'Yes. The only old technical college boy I had that did ... others didn't want to, or weren't allowed to, but with him, he was allowed to go out with them, not all the time.'

'How often? About?'

'Oh, now you're asking, it's going back a long time, thirty years. To think I used to be able to go all over that big house, upstairs, downstairs ...

279

now I can't hardly manage a single step, got to live in a bungalow now, but it suits this old girl ... paid for my family that old house did, paid for this old bungalow too, now it's paying for my son and his family ... but I own it.' She smiled at Household.

'How often?' Household pressed.

'Often ... oh, De Beer and the university lads, the mongrel with all the pedigrees ... not often, about once a week. They used to go into each other's rooms but they never went into his. He got to go into their rooms about once a week. But he picked up their ways in the few months he was with me ... the manner of walking, the manner of talking ... got quite pukka, but he was never the real thing ... saw his family when they came to pick up his things, ordinary folk, like me. His father was a railwayman from Norwich, same class as my family, simple folk really, but the way that old boy carried himself you'd think his old father was ... well, don't know who you'd think he was, but not a porter at Norwich Station or whatever he was, not that; that's for sure. Mind you, he gave me my money though, the last week's rent for his son ... can't complain there, I can't.'

'You seem to remember him disappearing?'

'Well, who wouldn't? So it was his old body that was found out by Bottisham ... well, I never. My son phoned me, said you'd be calling. See people disappear, you read about it, but I never knew anyone disappear on me ... only that old technical college boy ... De Beer.'

'Anything happen about the time he disappeared? Any arguments, anything of that nature?'

The elderly woman shook her head. 'Not that I remember, and nothing in my house anyway. I would have heard a row. Nothing at all.' The woman paused, Household thought she was remembering something. 'You know in that old house, I had eight students all told. When the other little technical college boy left I had seven, De Beer and six other university boys. De Beer used to mix with three of them ... the others, he had nothing to do with them, but he seemed to be well in with the other three, on a weekly basis ... not a daily basis.'

'I see.'

'Well, that old week that De Beer went missing, for a few days only, the three that De Beer didn't have nothing to do with, only those old boys came down for breakfast. De Beer and the others didn't. The others eventually started eating breakfast, but old De Beer never did. Funny that.'

'Isn't it?' Household said quietly.

'Possibly he was one of their friends then, I thought, possibly they were upset about him disappearing ... perhaps that was it?'

'Perhaps it was. You don't remember their names by any chance?'

'No,' she replied with a 'you've got to be joking' tone of voice, and Household conceded that it was a long shot. 'Never took any record of who lived in my old house. Never did. Maybe I should have kept a guest book ... those old boys go on to do something in life, could even have had a few future prime ministers in that house over the years ... never know. But no, I don't remember their names, no ...'

It had gone easier than he thought it would have, by far the trickiest 'lift' he had thus far undertaken, but it had all gone smoothly ... into the van so willingly, turned off into a suburban side street, eleven in the morning, bundled her into the rear of the vehicle. He had strength, he had skill, he had expertise ... she was his before she knew what was happening ... so trusting by nature, she probably didn't fully realise what was happening until it was too late. The drive out to the bungalow done without attracting attention, keeping up with the traffic flow, that's the main thing, just like any other van, except in the back of his, on the floor, trussed up, gagged, blindfolded, lay victim number six. His until he tires of her. He turned into the rough track that led to the bungalow and saw his old neighbour strolling towards him. The man's face lit up as he clearly recognised the van and stopped, anticipating a chat, but the Panther, knowing that whilst the gags may well prevent the wearer from speaking, they do not by any means prevent the wearer from making a very loud noise should they wish to do so, slowed the van, nodded to his neighbour, who was clearly disappointed that the expected chat was not forthcoming, and continued driving. Even to say 'hello', thought the Panther, was to alert his victim that someone was within easy earshot. So he said nothing, but nodded and smiled. He turned into the driveway of the bungalow, catching sight of his elderly shirt-sleeved neighbour, watching him go and wearing a perplexed expression as he did so. Clearly some explanation was needed or the old man would come calling, wondering if he had offended in some way. But seeing the ambling neighbour was useful, very useful. Knowing the man's likely movements, the Panther calculated that it gave him a time window of approximately twenty minutes to convey the girl from the van to the bungalow. Plenty of time. He got out, walked round to the rear of the van and opened the door. She was lying on her side, not making a sound, stiff with fear. The Panther walked down the driveway and looked up and down the lane, not a soul in sight and plenty of lush, rich summer foliage to conceal his activity. He returned to the van, leaned in and pulled the girl out and carried her, tied up, gagged and blindfolded, into the house through the kitchen area, and into what was to become the living room, now freshly painted following the departure of the last victim. He dropped the girl onto the floorboards, took the chain and padlocked it round her neck and ensured the other end was securely fastened to the wall.

'Listen, I know you can hear me.' He knelt close to her. 'So listen. You can make it hard on yourself or you can make it easy … it's up to you. I am happy either way.' He didn't touch the girl but he saw her fear and smelled it as well … it was true, he realised, it was true you can smell fear off a person, a smell similar to decaying leaves. Then he realised he had smelled it before … from himself, many years earlier. He knew what she was feeling. 'You have to stay here for a few days, you and I have to get to know each other … we have to get to like each other. You have to let me look after you ... and I will, you know ... I do ... I always take care of my girls, the last one, she saw me, she could recognise me, so I had to kill her, do you see? I had no alternative.' He allowed his voice to trail off as the girl trembled with terror. He sat back on the floor, realising that he had just made an error, yet another error, he was getting careless. This victim would have to be his last for a while, any hope of co-operation from this girl had gone. It went the moment he had told her he had had to kill his last victim because she had seen him, and what had he done that morning but knocked on her door? She had opened it with all the innocence of youth, whereupon they had looked each other in the face from just two feet distant ... she was quick on the uptake, quick to see the significance and her fear had turned instantly to terror. He had been careless and had let her know that, despite what he might say, he had no intention of letting her live. Now she knew that.

Careless. Careless. Careless.

Now he had a very, very dangerous victim. He felt the chain, tugged it against the bolt in the wall. It was secure. She wouldn't be able to break free. But she could make noise ... she could make a great deal of noise, not just shouting, through the gag, but if he released her wrists and feet she could throw things, stamp her feet, anything. He stood. This was difficult, the others had been given the promise of eventual freedom, and in all but one case he had kept that promise. Because of that promise they had been cooperative. This girl ... this girl presented a new challenge, how to keep her so he could look after her, because he wanted to look after her, wanted to feed her, and keep her and ensure she did not want ... that's all he wanted to do, like all the times he had wanted but couldn't have ... the dogs that were promised, the other pets, promised but never became real, just promises, promises, promises, promises... So he had learned to provide for himself, to obtain something to look after. 'I will feed you,' he said. 'I will keep you warm and dry, keep you from the cold. I can't let you go because you'll run away, then where will I be with no one to care for? I need someone to look after you see, somebody of my own. I must go outside now. Please don't make a sound, for your own sake. I will come back, clean you up, let you use the toilet if you need to use it. It's only a chemical toilet but the others managed with it, so you can, then I'll tuck you up for the night. I'll be back with breakfast tomorrow.' He stood and walked out of the bungalow into the heat and glare of the mid-afternoon sun. He walked slowly to the van and from the van to the lane and, as expected, his neighbour was returning home. The Panther waved and smiled and waited till his neighbour drew near to him, then said, 'Sorry I drove past you. In a bit of a hurry.'

'Oh,' the old man nodded. 'I thought I'd hurt your feelings. I was going to come knocking on your old door, glad I saw you.'

'Glad you did, too,' the Panther grinned warmly. 'Don't like fall-outs between neighbours ... or neighbours to be.'

'Aye. When will you be moving in?'

'Not long now ... end of the summer. I want to be in before the nights start drawing in.'

'Wouldn't mind looking round your bungalow once it's done, it would be interesting to see what you've done with it. I used to call in on girl Jane ... like going back in time going in that old bungalow.'

'When I've finished,' the Panther said, 'of course you can come round, see what I've done to the place, but you don't want to see it now, it's a mess ... paint everywhere, camping stove. Richard, believe me, you don't want to see it. Not now.'

'Well, I'd like to see it when it's finished.' The old man turned and walked towards his own cottage, down at the end of the unadopted road, where, the Panther knew, he'd remain for the rest of the day. He returned to the bungalow, to the room where the girl lay. He assisted her to use the chemical toilet, then chained her ankles close together, her hands behind her back, and once again tested the chain that attached her neck to the wall. He pondered removing the blindfold. The gag would have to remain in place come what may, but the blindfold served only to disable her, to keep information withheld from her, but she had already seen him, she knew what he looked like. The main reason for keeping the girl blindfolded had gone; in this case it didn't apply. But the blindfold did still force some disability upon her. She could hear, but she couldn't see and for that reason he left it in place. He pushed cotton wadding into her ears and slipped the ear defenders over her head. Sound was by that means not wholly cut out, but limited. He had tried the ear defenders and found that they let in sounds near at hand, especially if high-pitched, but more distant, low frequency sounds were eliminated. She would not be able to hear anybody passing in the lane and would not therefore, the Panther reasoned, cry out for help. He left the bungalow and drove the van into Cambridge and, leaving it parked once again on Thoday Street, took a bus into town, and a second bus out again.

The parents and their children remained in the house, hidden from view by the screen that had been erected in their garden. The officer holding the pneumatic drill looked at Household. Household nodded and the officer activated the drill and the metal bit, with ear-splitting noise, began to shatter the concrete. Moving from side to side, he systematically splintered it within a few minutes, helped by the fact that the layer of concrete proved itself to be no more than two inches thick at its deepest, and considerably thinner at its shallowest. Having been poured over a pile of rubble, it had an uneven underside. The concrete having been shattered, and the pneumatic drill dragged away, Household nodded to the sergeant, who said, 'Right, lads, one bit of concrete at a time', and two officers fell on their hands and knees and began to pick the concrete and rubble away, one piece at a time. After about four or five minutes, one of the constables kneeled up, raised his hand in the air and said, 'Sir!'

Household walked over to the hole. He saw a bone, a small bone, an arm bone, he thought,

287

child size, but human, definitely, horribly human. 'That's her,' he said. 'Carry on, please, carefully. You know the procedure.'

The constables continued to pick away carefully and one hour later the skeleton in a foetal position was fully revealed. A little hair remained on the scalp, upon which was a blue plastic hair clasp, All other clothing had deteriorated save for a pair of leather sandals which, while decayed, were still identifiable. Household stepped outside the screen and spoke to the Scenes of Crime Officer who stood, camera in hand, chatting to a white-shirted constable who had been stationed on the path to keep the garden clear of onlookers. 'You're needed,' he said.

Veronica Sleaford picked up the phone after letting it ring twice. She always let it ring, believing that a sudden snatching up of the phone before even the first ringtone had been completed was unnecessary, alarming and insensitive to the person who was making the call. She identified herself, listened, putting the report down as she did so. She scribbled an address on her notepad and said, 'I'll be there directly.' Rising from her desk, she told Harry Hewis that she was going out, that the police had found a skeleton. She turned away, black bag in hand as Hewis said, 'Very good, doctor.' Within thirty minutes of receiving the call, she was kneeling over the skeleton which had been found in the backyard of a small house in Romsey Town.

'Female child, I'd say,' she said, 'but the gender differences are not so marked at this stage of development. I'll be able to tell you once I get it back to the lab. But the hair clasp on the skull, the sandals ... the decayed textile material, looks to me to be more akin to a cotton frock or skirt, than to heavier material which would be boy's trousers.'

'Can I take the hair clasp?' Household asked, production bag in hand. 'It will help with the identification.'

'You can for me, Mr Household.' Dr Sleaford held the skull delicately with one hand and removed the clasp with the other and dropped it into the productions bag. 'Do you know who she might be?'

'Yes.' Household spoke softly. 'Yes, I think I do. I'd better wait until the bodybag has been removed. If it is who I think it is, she has been missing for thirty years and her parents live just two doors away.'

'Oh, my.' Veronica Sleaford stood and glanced at Household. They held eye contact for a few seconds and then Veronica Sleaford said, 'Oh my, oh my, oh my ...'

'Indeed,' Household grimaced. 'Her parents may recognise this, her mother particularly, but I'll wait until the body ... the skeleton, has been removed.'

'You can have that done now. I've seen the remains in situ, there's nothing here that can explain the cause of death.' She turned and glanced towards the house. 'And these people?'

'Both school teachers, co-operating fully ... doubtless unnerved, but only moved into the house comparatively recently. We'll take the body out via the path.'

'I should hope so!' Veronica Sleaford spoke sharply. 'Can't carry a bodybag through someone's house. I'll go to the path, supervise the conveyance into the mortuary van.' She turned and walked out of the screen, into the house, into the street, turned right and walked up the path. Household stung at her rebuke, said softly to himself, 'I never had any intention of carrying the body through the house'. He sighed, then added 'Women!'

The skeleton having been removed, the screen dismantled and removed, Mr and Mrs Walker and their wide-eyed children thanked for their co-operation, Household walked the short distance to the Bullwoods' house and tapped gently on the door.

'Is it her?' Barry Bullwood opened the door suddenly upon Household's knock. The police activity clearly had not gone unnoticed.

'May I come in?' Household asked.

Barry Bullwood stepped aside and Sydney Household entered the cool of the shade in the hallway. He walked into the parlour where he saw a tearful Mrs Bullwood sitting in an armchair clutching what appeared to be a saturated handkerchief.

'Well,' Household said, 'there's no easy way of saying this, so I'll just say it. We have recovered a skeleton from the rear garden of the house two doors down, that of Mr and Mrs Walker, the school teachers. The skeleton is that of a child, and the forensic pathologist thinks the skeleton is female. I wonder if I can show you this...' he held up the clasp in the production bag. 'I am sorry if this is upsetting.'

'Can I see?' Barry Bullwood took hold of the bag. 'Yes,' he said, 'that's Sara's. I bought it for her on holiday in Cromer, earlier in the summer she disappeared. Have a look, Molly.' Bullwood handed the clear plastic bag to his wife who clutched it and nodded tearfully. 'That's Sara's ... she loved it ... she loved the blue ... she said blue was going to be her colour. Can we keep this?'

'No, you can't. I'm sorry, I have to take it away with me. It will be returned to you in due course, but now it's evidence as to the identity of the child ... not by itself, of course, in itself it isn't sufficient.'

'How will you be sure it's Sara?' Mrs Bullwood sniffed, reluctantly handing the production bag back to Household.

'Perhaps by photographs... I'd rather not go into how.'

'I know how,' Barry Bullwood growled. 'I watch those crime documentaries on TV. I know how it's done.'

'Or by DNA.'

'I've got just the photograph you need. It shows her teeth that's what you want, isn't it? Full face, showing teeth?'

Household nodded. 'Yes,' he said. 'Yes, I am afraid it is.'

'Took it just a day or two before she went missing. What with all the worry, I forgot I'd put it in for developing, wasn't 'til a week or so later that I picked up the film. I'll go and get it for you.'

'Thanks. The thing now is for you to remember anything you can about the Sparrow family ... anything, anything at all.'

'Please sit down.' Barry Bullwood indicated a vacant chair. 'I'll get that photo. What do you remember, Molly?' Bullwood left the room and Household heard him running up the stairs and reflected upon his agility for one of his years.

'You know, I remember that Harry's face was badly scratched,' Molly Bullwood said as Household sat in the chair.

'Scratched?' He reached for his notebook and took a ballpoint from the inside pocket of his jacket.

'Yes ... really deep gouges. At the time I was so vexed about Sara that I didn't think anything of it but now, if he did kill her...'

'Do you remember how he said he'd gotten the scratches?'

'In a fight with another boy on the common, or on the recreation ground.'

'Now?'

'Well, now, I wonder ... boys don't scratch each other when they fight – girls do. That was our Sara fighting for her life as that boy was killing her ... I just know it was.'

Barry Bullwood came downstairs and handed Household a colour photograph of a smiling, freckle-faced, blonde-haired girl. 'That's the clasp in the photograph, the same clasp,' said Barry Bullwood. 'It isn't really clear, but it's the same one.'

'Seems so,' Household said, 'but as you say, it's not very clear.'

'But it's the eyes and teeth you want, isn't it?'

'Yes.' Household put the photograph into his jacket pocket. 'This will help us make a definite identification. One way or the other.'

'Oh, it'll be Sara...' Barry Bullwood sank rather than sat in his chair. 'To think she's been just a few feet away from us all this time, and to think she'd be lying there still if you hadn't called round yesterday out of courtesy and we hadn't remarked about the hole in the Sparrow's garden. If only we had thought about it at the time.'

'You shouldn't blame yourselves,' Household said, but he knew that the Bullwoods would probably blame themselves for the remainder of their days. 'You were too close then, too frightened, so much going on ... and the thing to remember is that you couldn't have saved her, anyway. It's not much by way of compensation I know but ... well ... it's something to think about.'

Molly Bullwood nodded and mouthed 'thank you'.

Household stood and left a card on the sideboard. 'If you think of anything else, please get in touch, my number's on the card.'

Household left the Bullwoods' home, walked to Mill Road and, as the day before, took a bus for two stops towards the city, and went into the premises of Henry Morton, estate agents.

'Twice in two days!' The estate agent smiled in recognition of Household.

'The file on the property owned by the Walkers'? Can you tell me again who bought the property from Mrs Sparrow?'

'Easily,' the estate agent stood, 'I'll get the file.'

He left the public area of the office and went into the rear of the building and returned moments later. 'Mr Fordham,' he said.

'Any forwarding address?'

'All contact via his solicitors. He engaged Stand & Jackson.' He picked up the phone and placed it nearer Household, facing him. 'Please feel free.'

Household picked up the phone, dialled the number of the solicitors just as he had dialled the number of another solicitors from the same phone just twenty-four hours previous. He asked for Mr Fordham's forwarding address and explained that he quite understood that the information couldn't be given out over the phone and asked that the information be relayed to Parkside Police Station and left for his attention. The polite and efficient woman at Stand & Jackson promised to attend to his request directly.

David Tracy and Penny Wiseman sat in front of Dominic Perigo's desk.

'So that's useful information,' Perigo said. 'You did well.'

'Well, it's a description, sir,' Tracy said. 'And the person who gave the information has been in and out of gaol so often he ought to know what a police van is. So I think we are looking for a black Ford Transit, a large but limited number, and the description of the culprit as being tall, strong and slender ... clearly a man in good shape. It's a real breakthrough, sir.'

'It is,' Perigo smiled. 'We'll publicise that.'

'There's more.' Penny Wiseman sat forward eagerly.

'There is?'

'Yes, sir ... you were sick yesterday.'

'Yes?'

'So Mr Household attended the post-mortem on Joyce Dance for the police.'

'Yes?'

'It may be that Joyce took her own life ... punctured her own arteries rather than let the Panther take her life.'

'Yes?'

'But she gave us something.'

Tracy and Wiseman saw Perigo's forehead furrow, his eyes seemed to harden. 'Left us something?'

'Akin to a present ... there were flecks of paint in her mouth.'

'Paint!'

'Yes, sir. The pathologist didn't recognise them, neither did Mr Household, but they were sent off to the lab with a request for priority processing ... got the results this morning, paint ... flecks of paint. So it adds to the description ... not only do we have a description, not only do we know what type of vehicle he uses, but we also know that he keeps his victims where painting, or paint stripping, or something like that, is going on, such as a garage where cars are being repainted.'

'Won't be that,' Tracy said, 'cars are spray-painted ... flecks suggest paint being brushed on or taken off something, but Penny is right sir, it adds to the description.'

'It's a real breakthrough.'

'You're right. Can one of you notify the press office, ask them to release a statement giving that description?'

'I'll do that,' Tracy said, equally eagerly. 'Tell you, this is it, boss ... it's all downhill from now on.'

'Hope you are right ... you'd better ask Traffic to stop and search all black Transits they see.'

'Will do, boss.' Penny Wiseman clenched her fist. 'David's right ... we're on our way now. We are really on our way.'

'Yes,' Perigo smiled.

Tracy thought he detected something forced about Perigo's smile, as though the man's mind was elsewhere. 'We believe we should ask for the Panther to be profiled, sir. We believe we need a psychological profile.'

'We?'

'Penny and I.'

'Oh ... you do ... well ... perhaps you'd better see to it. Who will you contact?'

'The Department of Psychology at the University.' Tracy's voice trailed off. 'Sir ... I'm sorry, but are you alright?'

'Yes.' Perigo seemed startled. 'Yes, I'm fine. Why?'

'I'm sorry, sir, you don't seem to be yourself. I know you were ill yesterday ... it's as though you are not firing on all twelve cylinders.'

'I would say the same, sir. If you are not well, you should go home. You really shouldn't be in if you are not one hundred percent. We can take care of things ... we have Mr Household and the Chief Inspector ... and the Panther normally takes his victims months apart.'

'What! Yes, he does ... months apart ... months apart. Well, since you are so astute,' Perigo forced a smile. 'I confess I probably shouldn't have come in ... seems something I can't shake, better go and see my G.P. See if he can tell me what's wrong. So, the Traffic police to be told to keep an eye out for a black Transit ... stop and search every one.'

'Yes, sir.'

'Press release ... you'll have time to get that out for the final edition of the *Evening News*.' Perigo glanced around him. 'What was the other thing?'

'The profile, sir.'

'Yes, can you do that, David?'

'Certainly, sir. I'll phone the Department of Psychology, see where I get. If they can't help me they will doubtless know a man who can.'

'Doubtless.' Perigo smiled as he stood. 'Well, I think you're right ... I feel ... well ... some bed rest I think.'

Tracy and Wiseman also stood. 'Leave it with us, boss. Will you be able to get home alright?' Tracy spoke. 'We can arrange a lift for you.'

'I'll be alright!' Perigo snapped at Tracy. He paused, then added, 'Sorry. Thanks, I'll be able to get home. Thanks ... thanks.'

'Another long day for you, Inspector.' Veronica Sleaford adjusted the stainless steel anglepoise arm above the highly polished metal table on which the skeleton lay.

'A day in the life...' Household smiled in response, watching from the corner of the room as Sleaford stood to one side, allowing Harry

Hewis to photograph the skeleton from all angles. Hewis made sure he took a frontal photograph of the skull, as Household had requested. The photographs taken, Harry Hewis retreated to the far side of the instrument trolley and placed the camera on the top of the shelf which ran along the rear wall of the pathology laboratory. Beneath the shelf was a battery of drawers, containing Household knew not what.

'Well,' Veronica Sleaford looked at the skeleton, 'the deceased is fully skeletonised and is of indeterminate sex.' She turned to Household. 'I am sorry, but I am unable to say whether this is a male or female skeleton. At this stage of development it is really impossible to say.'

'I see.'

'The teeth seem to be fairly well advanced in terms of their growth with relatively small canines ... that suggests a female, but only suggests it. So I think the superimposition of the photograph you said you have of her, the one taken just before she died, onto the photograph of her skull, once Harry has had the film developed ... that will be the best means of identification in this case. Now, as to the cause of death ... well, that is going to be difficult too, there is no apparent injury to the skeleton. No fracture of any bone for example, the skull is perfectly intact – the plates of the skull incidentally show fusing consistent with the deceased being about ten years of age when she died – but no injuries. So whatever did kill this little girl – because intuitively I think this is a female skeleton – whatever killed her did not damage the skeleton.'

'Strangulation?'

'Yes, as an example. Why do you say that?' Dr Sleaford glanced at Household, and once again they held eye contact.

'Well, the little boy she was known to associate with was seen to have a badly scratched face at the time of Sara Bullwood's disappearance. Said he'd been in a scrap with another lad but Sara's mother pointed out that boys don't fight by scratching.'

'But a girl being strangled by him ... she would put up that sort of fight, is that what you are saying?'

'That's what Mrs Bullwood implied and I would be inclined to agree with her.'

'I would too.' Dr Sleaford pondered the skeleton. 'Would you like me to trawl for poisons? That could have killed her without damaging the bones, but only traces of the heavy poisons will be left by now, arsenic, strychnine ... but what child can, could, get hold of substances like that?'

'Well, for the sake of completion,' Household said, 'even if it is only to rule it out.'

'Very well, I dare say you are right, I am getting lazy as I get older. I can send the scalp hair to Warboys and a sample of bone ... any toxin will be contained in the long bones.' She paused. 'So that's as far as I can take this p.m. Not very satisfactory. All I can do is tell you that the level of development of this skeleton is consistent with that of a ten year old child of good health. I can't determine sex or cause of death. Actual time of death is more easily determined by the artefacts found with the skeleton ... the hair clasp, the remains of her clothing. They seem to point to late twentieth century.'

'Oh, I know ... in my waters ... I know it will be Sara Bullwood. If it isn't ... oh, my, that doesn't bear thinking about but it will be, I am certain.'

Sydney Household drove from Addenbrookes Hospital back to Parkside Police Station. He checked his pigeonhole immediately after signing in and found a message waiting for him from Stand & Jackson's, solicitors. It gave the last known address of Mr Fordham. If the gentleman was still alive, he lived conveniently close, at Great Shelford. Household clutched the piece of paper and walked up the stairs to the CID room. He was not surprised to see that Penny Wiseman and David Tracy were out of the office, but he was surprised to see that Dominic Perigo's desk was unoccupied. He gave it little thought, however, and sat at his own desk. He added the last known address of Tom Fordham to the growing file on the disappearance of Sara Bullwood, then a detailed report about the discovery of the skeleton, Mrs Bullwood's remarks about scratches on the face of Harry Sparrow, and the outcome of the post-mortem. He replaced the file in the grey Home Office issue filing cabinet and, with great reluctance and a heavy heart, walked from his desk, beginning the journey home to Bedford, to an icy cold reception from his wife, the stony, stressed silence at dinner, and his inevitable solitary walk into Bedford to seek solace and succour in a quiet pub. As he drove across the flatlands, he found his thoughts turning to Veronica Sleaford, the eye contact they had had, the learned knowledge she possessed, her manner which he found warm and charming. As he drove further away from Cambridge, he sensed that his car seemed to be dragging an anchor behind it, and he found he had to force his right foot to keep the accelerator depressed.

The woman fast forwarded the tape until it was nearing its end, then switched it to record. When the tape reached its end, the machine sent the 'record' and 'play' buttons into the 'off' position with a loud click. Too loud to be disguised. She realised she had to be very careful if she was going to do it. If it was heard, the tape found ... she didn't know what Filsell would do, but she wouldn't put actual violence beyond him – he had a vicious streak. She had never seen him commit an act of physical violence, but she had seen the look of anger which flashed across his eyes from time to time. She had seen the jovial man turn sour and foul-mouthed in an instant, she had known his emotional violence, his psychological cruelty, the promised generous allowance which had never been forthcoming being one such instance. And because of that, because she had come to know the man who had 'known' her in the biblical sense these last few weeks, she found him to be what he appeared, rich, still good looking for his middle years, but spiteful and mean and violent. She doubted that he would murder her, not intentionally anyway, but to be left stranded, penniless on the island, badly bruised about the face and ribs was, she believed, a real possibility. She glanced out across the ocean ... so blue ... then she walked back into the villa, enjoying the cool of the marble floor on the soles of her feet, and stood in the open doorway, looking out beyond the pool to where the 'Master' and his friends sat in white plastic chairs, round a white plastic table, in hushed and intense conversation. They glanced at her as she stood in the doorway, then forgot her. She, being reminded of her place, retreated into the villa. She clearly was not, at that moment, required to be 'decorative'.

Dinner that evening was taken in a silence which the woman found difficult to describe. The men here, she thought, Cambridge University educated, and one a playwright, the others senior politicians, they would be able to describe the silence, but she had only a clutch of 'O' levels, snatched via an exam in her final year of school and which surprised no one more than herself when she obtained passes in half a dozen subjects. She just didn't have the words to describe it. It wasn't a highly stressed silence, a silence caused by waiting for something to happen, a silence which would end with a fight or with somebody screaming at someone else. It was, she thought, more of a silence which follows something which had happened, the silence of a family which had suffered a bereavement, when for the first time there is a vacant chair. It was, she thought, that sort of silence. It was not a perfect silence, it was punctuated by a little conversation, a remark, an answer, then more silence save for the occasional sound, as knife met fork or as either met porcelain. It was clear

302

that had she not been there, the three men, two future prime ministers and the internationally famous playwright would be continuing the intense conversation they had been engaged in when they sat at the far end of the pool, well out of her hearing.

Something's up, she thought, then thought in Birkenhead vernacular 'summat's up'. The two men had arrived that morning, they must have got a very early flight from London to arrive at Malta before lunch. Filsell had driven to Luqa airport to meet them, taking the Mercedes which he only permitted to be used on very special occasions. They returned to the villa and Filsell had perfunctorily introduced them to her as Toby Etherington and William Aughty 'friends of mine'. The two guests had the same self-confident bearing as Filsell, the same very English 'pukka' attitude. Both were tall, and she resisted the sudden impulse to curtsey or bow, but the class distinction was there, and all four knew it. The two men looked at her, giving her a brief nod, then they had turned to Filsell and raised their eyebrows and smiled and nodded vigorously. It was an appraising of her, a 'she'll do' message to Filsell, but as to her personality, they clearly had no interest in that small item. They had dropped their bags imperiously in the hallway of the villa and she had been asked by Filsell in an equally imperious manner, so imperious that it was a thinly disguised order, to take 'our guests' bags up to their rooms. That she had done, one at a time, being unable to manage both at once, and finding the sarong she was wearing upon Filsell's instructions unbearably constricting after the freedom of a swimsuit or nakedness. Filsell and the two guests meanwhile had lost no time in commencing their jaw. By the time she had struggled up the stairs with the second suitcase, the three men had sat round the table at the far end of the pool and had commenced what was clearly an intense conversation and one to which she was obviously not going to be privy. She was only to be allowed in their company at meal times, that, she felt, was obvious, and the conversation would be very limited and very superficial. That, she realised, was also obvious.

After dinner the men retired to the balcony to enjoy the evening, and the view of the lights of Valetta in the middle distance. She meanwhile had washed up after the meal and cleaned the kitchen as was her expected duty. She walked to the balcony and heard the men talking and then, realising she was approaching, Filsell had said 'Quiet!' and the conversation ceased.

'Can I get you anything?' she asked, and found herself emphasising her Birkenhead accent, enjoying the inverted snobbery for she wasn't going to change herself for these three toffs. She saw Filsell glare up at her for using her accent and was pleased she had annoyed him.

'Gentlemen?' Filsell turned to Aughty and Etherington.

'Something to drink?'

'Nothing for me,' Aughty said. 'Nothing alcoholic anyway we'd better keep clear heads.'

'How about coffee?' Filsell suggested.

'Just the thing,' Etherington said.

'Three coffees, then,' Filsell addressed the woman, and after a deliberate and noticeable pause said, 'please.'

'The name,' she thought as she turned, 'is Margaret. Just in case you had forgotten, Margaret Neston, and I live at 23 Prescott Street, Birkenhead', parroting the phrase in her head just as her parents had taught her to parrot when she was very, very small, in case she got lost. Then she added, still silently 'and I'm going to nail you, Filsell'. The trick she believed, the trick lay in pretending not to be interested, the trick lay in letting the three toffs believe that a lassie from Lancashire can't eavesdrop, won't notice anything and that people in the North of England really do have black pudding for brains. She went to the kitchen and poured water into the kettle and switched it on. Then she went to the master bedroom where she had concealed the tape recorder among her clothes in her drawers. She returned to the kitchen, made coffee in a pot, and with a rapidly beating heart and a cold sweat breaking out, she switched the cassette player onto 'record' and hid it beneath a thin layer of paper napkins. She carried the coffee, plus three cups, milk and sugar, on a tray to the balcony. It was a risk. It was one major risk, but if she wanted something to hold over him, if she wanted something to say 'I won't be lied to ... you promised an allowance and I should have had an allowance', then the risk should be taken. She placed the tray on the table next to Filsell and asked if she should pour.

'No, just leave it,' was Filsell's curt and cutting reply.

'OK.' Margaret Neston turned on her heels and walked away and sat in the lounge, noting the time. It was a forty-five minute tape she had put in the machine. She would have to go back before the forty-five minutes was up and decided to give herself what she had once heard an American describe as a 'fudge factor' of ten minutes. She curled up on the settee in the lounge, browsing through her back copies of *Cosmopolitan* nervously glancing at the clock, trying to calm her nerves. After thirty-five minutes, she walked back to the balcony and once again she heard Filsell say, 'Quiet' as she approached.

'More coffee, gents?' she asked, glancing at the tray. The napkins hadn't been disturbed.

'No,' Filsell snapped, 'but take these cups away.'

Margaret Neston silently collected the cups and the coffee pot and placed them on the tray, and with a sense of relief, carried it back to the kitchen. She had gambled that the men wouldn't make use of the napkins, that one of those very proper gentlemen with polished manners wouldn't spill his coffee and reach for a napkin to wipe up the mess and it was a gamble that had paid off. All that remained was to see what, if anything, she had recorded in the randomly selected thirty-five minutes. She bore in mind that after the very intense session by the pool that afternoon, all the men's conversation might well be out of them. She would listen and find out. Having cleared the coffee pot and cups away because 'Master' Filsell likes things 'just so', Margaret Neston crept to the front of the house and opened the door and sat on the porch. It was a dark Mediterranean night, few lights were to be seen from that vantage point, and the air was filled with the sound of chirruping crickets. She rewound the tape and listened with growing horror, and growing fascination.

Her departure from the balcony had been followed by a period of silence broken only by Filsell saying, 'How do you like your coffee?' and both Etherington and Aughty saying, 'Just milk, please'. Either they were waiting until she was well out of the way or they had, as feared, exhausted all conversation. It seemed to her that the latter was the case when a jet airliner roared overhead and when the noise of the plane had abated Filsell said, 'You get used to the aircraft, and I actually enjoy watching them.' This comment was followed by another pause which lasted for a matter of about thirty seconds until Aughty asked, 'How long have you had the girl?'

Margaret Neston felt stung, as if an arrow had pierced her heart. That she might hear herself talked about had not occurred to her, yet it was so obvious. She reproached herself for not preparing herself for the discomfort of that possibility. She had heard it said once that if you overhear yourself being talked about, you will hear something you don't want to hear. So she was 'the girl'. She braced herself because she knew worse was to come.

'Few weeks ... since I've been here. She responded to the ad I put in the café on the harbour front: "English writer, own villa, seeks Girl Friday". I put the same ad in the café each time I come here ... always get bites, pick the one I want.

They're all the same, secretaries who can't sit down because it makes their brains sore.'

That comment was greeted with smug laughter.

'They don't want to return home to dull jobs... I enable them to extend their holiday. In her case she'd have to go back to living in her parents' council flat in Liverpool...'

'Birkenhead,' Margaret Neston snorted indignantly.

'...and whatever dull little job she had to go back to. Here she does a little work on the word processor, but mainly she's a bedroom and kitchen worker.'

Again there was a ripple of laughter.

'What's she like?' Aughty asked.

'Well ... passable ... you sampled her cooking ... in bed she's about the same, passable ... nice body but doesn't really know how to use it, sort of lets me get on with it rather than offers anything herself.'

'Frigid?'

'Not frigid ... sort of five out of ten "must try harder". Why, are you interested?'

'Could be.'

'Well, it's up to her, but if you put in a bid, I won't object.'

'Thanks,' Aughty said.

'You too, Toby.'

'Thanks,' Etherington replied.

Margaret Neston's eyes flooded with tears, then anger welled up in her. She continued to listen.

There was then a longer period of silence. Then

she struck gold. She listened with rapt attention.

Filsell: 'So what are we going to do?'

Aughty: 'Nothing ... I told you. We don't know what to do, so do nothing.'

Etherington: 'William's right ... a lot of people in our position came unstuck because they drew attention to themselves.'

Aughty: 'Confess we were lucky to get away with it for so long, in fact there are times when I forget we did it.'

Filsell: 'We! We did nothing ... you did it.'

Aughty: 'We all buried the body.'

Filsell: 'Careful what you say! I told you ... there's another set of ears in this house, if it should come to it, Liverpool Lucy could disappear as well ... but it would be better not to let her hear anything in the first place.'

Aughty: 'You'd do that?'

Filsell: 'Of course. I'm fifty years old ... look at my lifestyle. There's not a lot I wouldn't do to avoid a long prison sentence.'

Etherington: 'Nigel's right, William ... look at you and me ... we'll win the next election, that means you and I are in the Cabinet. Want to swap that for a cell in Parkhurst?'

There was another brief period of silence.

Aughty: 'What a mess. How would you get rid of the girl anyway?'

Filsell: 'Salt the bath water, hold her head under until she drowns ... feed her into the Med at some isolated cove ... accidental death by drowning. Believe me, the Maltese Police couldn't investigate a drinking session in a brewery.'

Etherington: 'And all this because of De Beer. What did you let him come along for anyway? He was just a pushy social climbing tit from the Tech who didn't know which side of Reality Checkpoint he belonged to.'

Filsell: 'I liked him. We "met" you know, we "clicked", briefly but we "clicked". We were both interested in writing. We both wanted to be writers ... I even visited him in his bedsit once or twice.'

Margaret Neston let the tape play until the point that she heard Filsell tell her to take the coffee pot and cups away and then she switched it off. She felt numb. She doubted she could stand. She had been right ... something was up, but more, much more than she could have imagined. And her own life was now on the line. That she had not anticipated. She was treading water, she was well out of her depth, and despite the close heat

310

of the evening she felt cold.

Very cold indeed.

Richard Wynne could not avoid the dread possibility. He sat in front of his old television, an old black and white set. The TV had worked well for forty years, he saw no reason to replace it, he just had to renew a valve every so often, of which he had a plentiful supply. Hearing of the phasing out of valves in favour of transistors, he had bought up all the old valves he could, ensuring he had sufficient to 'see me out' as he would say. He enjoyed living alone, keeping himself to himself, not involving himself with anything, but he did sit down each evening and watch the news, national and then local. The description of the Panther that had been issued by the police was broadcast, a tall, slender, fit man with a black van and there on the screen was a photograph of the type of van the Cambridgeshire Police believed the Panther was using. The bulletin added 'the Panther is believed to have some access to paint ... is a decorator perhaps...' then the news item finished and was followed by an item about the current hot spell, reporting that after a winter of floods 'our region is now threatened with drought'. But Richard Wynne –who when he was a young man had got aboard one of the last departures from Dunkirk and five years later had stepped aboard French soil again on D+2, and whose proud boast was that he had never knowingly shot an enemy soldier, who was now racked with arthritis and bronchitis, who could just about manage to walk to the shop once a day

– was suddenly chilled. He was chilled because the description of the Panther fitted exactly that of his new neighbour, the man renovating the bungalow which he passed twice a day on his way to and from the shop. The athleticism, the van, its type and colour, and what does renovating a bungalow involve but painting?

He wondered what, if anything, he should do. In the army it would be easy ... the sergeant, or the duty officer ... but now ... the man seemed so pleasant, always ready for a chat but he'd never let him inside the bungalow ... always promised to but never did, as if he didn't want him in the bungalow because those girls had been kept in there. He stood. He didn't want to offend his new neighbour, but he knew he must report his suspicions. He would have to walk past the bungalow to get to the phone in the village. If the van wasn't there, he would look at the bungalow, closely.

He walked out of his cottage, relishing the warmth of the evening, just the weather for short sleeves and a stroll ... he might even have a pint at the Man at Arms after he had phoned the police ... a rare luxury for him these days but he would want something to calm his nerves. He approached the bungalow and saw, with no small amount of relief, that the black van wasn't there. He walked up to the building. He tried to peer in but the shutters up against the windows prevented him from doing so. He walked to the front door, tried it and found it locked. He walked round the rear of the building, to the overgrown garden. He saw that the windows there were

312

similarly shuttered. There was nothing for it, he thought, nothing to do but phone the police ... report suspicions as we are always told to. He turned. His heart missed a beat. His neighbour was standing there, holding a crossbow in his hands, a large, powerful-looking crossbow.

'So it is you?' Richard Wynne said. He was surprised to find he wasn't afraid, because he knew that the younger, fitter man with the powerful weapon in his hands was going to kill him, and for him, elderly, hardly able to walk, hidden from view, there was no escape.

'Yes,' the man said. 'I thought you'd come when you saw the television or heard the radio ... you see I want someone ... something to look after ... things I was going to look after were always taken away, or I was taken away from them.'

'I'm sorry...'

'I never meant to hurt them ... just look after them for a while, but the last one, she saw me... You realise if they catch me they are going to lock me up for the rest of my life? Me. I once walked across a mountain range to get from one country to another, and the freedom to return to England, with an army chasing me ... can you imagine what a cell would do to me?'

'You should have bought yourself a dog if you wanted something to care for.'

'Wouldn't have been the same ... you see they had to be snatched away from what they were familiar with to learn that they were totally dependent on me ... as she will learn.'

'She?'

The Panther nodded towards the bungalow.

313

'There's another one inside. Brought her here this morning. She might not even be noticed missing yet.'

Richard Wynne glanced at the bungalow. Then back to his new neighbour, the Panther, the man who was soon to kill him. He often wondered how he would die, and this, he thought, this was not a bad way to go ... he was in his eighties ... it would be quick ... he was in the right ... and he would die doing something as he had always believed a man should, not a lingering death ... no statement there. 'What are you going to do with my body?'

'Hide it for a few days ... let the blood settle and solidify, cut it up ... burn it ... bury the bones here in the garden.'

Richard Wynne looked at his last resting place. 'Over in the corner by the tree ... that would be good.'

'I'll see what I can do for you.'

'Where's the van, by the way? I wouldn't have come near the bungalow if I had seen the van.'

'It's in Cambridge, parked up a side street. I'll set fire to it tonight, the police are bound to find it and open it up ... even if they did, they couldn't trace it back to me, but I'll torch it anyway. So where do you want it? How do you want it ... front or back?'

'Front...' Richard Wynne pulled himself up to attention as best he could, 'but I'll shut my eyes, if you don't mind.'

Veronica Sleaford sat alone in her house. As the night had drawn in and darkness had fallen she had not switched the light on. She sat still in the darkness. She had returned home, leaving Addenbrookes shortly after performing the post-mortem of the possibly female skeleton and had come back to an empty house. There was nothing unusual in that, she reasoned, nothing at all, in fact it was often the case that Sojourner had walked into Cambridge or had gone to visit a friend. What was a little unusual was that she hadn't returned by supper time, nor had she phoned to say she was going to be late. Veronica Sleaford ate slowly that evening, picking away at her food, fighting a gnawing feeling that all was not well. She couldn't finish her meal and placed it in the oven, she could re-heat it when Sojourner came home, panting her apology, upon which Veronica Sleaford was sure that, despite her anger, she would recover her appetite. By mid-night, Sojourner had not returned. Leaving a note on the kitchen table, Veronica Sleaford walked to Parkside Police Station. At the enquiry desk she said, 'I'd like to report my daughter as missing.'

'Yes, madam,' the constable reached for the missing persons pad, 'name and age, please.'

Veronica Sleaford proceeded to answer all questions asked, then added, 'I am especially worried, you see, the person they call the Panther...'

She walked home slowly. She reached her house to find it still empty, no message on the answer machine. By then it was in the early hours of the morning and she knew, she just knew, that some ill had befallen her daughter. She phoned her ex-husband in London, and his protestations about

315

being called 'in the middle of the night' evaporated when he heard the reason for the call. They talked as two intelligent and learned persons can talk and it was agreed that he could do nothing if he came to Cambridge, but agreed to come 'at the drop of a hat' should he be needed. And she in turn, to inform him of any development.

She showered, succumbing to a need to cleanse herself of something, of some evil, that she could not see or feel, that she could not identify yet which had somehow contaminated her being. She crept from the bathroom to the bedroom and lay under a single sheet, her mind whirled as dread possibilities occurred to her and sleep avoided her.

8

The house owned by Michael Filsell stood square, solid and ivy-covered, set back from the main road that snaked across flatlands into the village of Swaftham Prior. Household drove up the gravel driveway of the house and halted his car in front of the house. He left his car and walked up to the front door. A circular metal ring seemed to invite him to pull it. He did so and heard bells jangle from deep within the house. Household looked about him whilst he waited for the door to be answered. The grey stonework above the door had the date 1740 carved into it and Household pondered that just five years later there had occurred the bloody Jacobite rebellion in Scotland, and the house was already nearly two hundred years old when Hitler's forces devastated Warsaw. The lawn at the front of the house was closely cut, the mower having been moved in opposite directions as it crossed the lawn, producing strips of grass which alternated from dark green to light green to dark green to light green. The house was of sufficient distance from the road that the noise pollution from passing traffic seemed to Household to be minimal. There was birdsong, blue sky. It felt to be isolated in the country, yet the village of Swaffham Prior was only half a mile distant.

The door was opened by a woman in a maid's uniform. She was in her twenties, and seemed to Household to be 'bonny'. It was the one word which occurred to him, she was 'bonny', dark hair above a well balanced, very feminine face, a warm smile, doe eyed ... bonny of appearance and he was sure that she would reveal herself to be bonny of personality as well.

'Yes?' she asked with a soft but full voice. 'Can I help you?'

'Police.' Household showed her his ID. 'I'd like to talk to Mr Filsell, please.'

'He's out of the country. Could Mrs Filsell be of use?'

'Possibly she could ... if I could have a minute of her time.'

'If you would care to step into the hallway, sir, I'll tell her you are here ... it's Mr...?'

'Household. Detective Inspector Household.'

'I won't be a moment, sir.' The maid turned,

and on shoes with rubber soles, which made hardly a sound as they crossed the tiled floor of the entrance hall, left Household standing in the cool and the shade, looking at a room with panelled walls, a wide, dark wood staircase in front of him, rooms to his right, a corridor which seemed to lead to a door to the rear of the property, and a corridor to his right, down which the bonny maid had silently walked. With impressive rapidity she returned and asked Household to accompany her as she ascended the staircase which angled round the sides of the hall until it reached the first floor. On the first floor landing the maid turned to her left and stepped in front of a door. She knocked twice on the door and waited. Then a female voice said, 'Come in.' The maid opened the door and said, 'Detective Inspector Household, ma'am.' She stepped to one side and Household entered the room.

'Some tea, please, Polly.' The woman, clearly Mrs Filsell, was of angular facial appearance, handsome, Household thought, in a feminine way, natural looking blonde hair tumbled onto her shoulders. She was as old as he had expected her to be, late forties, early fifties. She was slender of figure and wore a cream cheesecloth blouse and an ankle length blue skirt, wooden and leather sandals encased her feet. She was also in a wheelchair. She turned the wheels so that she faced Household. 'Detective Inspector,' she smiled. 'How may I help you?' She sat by the window at the far end of the room.

'Well,' Household walked towards her as Polly exited.

'Please ... if you'd sit in that chair there.' She pointed to a chair close to where Household stood. 'It doesn't matter that we have to raise our voices to speak to each other, it's a price I am prepared to pay, and a price I ask you to accept. Don't think of it as a personal slight, all my visitors are treated in the same manner. Doubtless dear Polly will explain as she shows you out. She must do so I know, because if anybody re-visits me they gladly accept the invitation to sit in that chair and do so without question or any expression of puzzlement.'

Household sat. A fireplace stood to his left, the floor space between him and Mrs Filsell was interrupted by a solid table of polished mahogany. Bookshelves full of books interspersed with objects of personal interest and framed photographs lined the wall opposite the fireplace. The room smelled heavily of polish and air freshener.

'I do hope there is no trouble, Inspector?' Mrs Filsell had a pleasant sounding, very cultured voice.

'I can't say really, Mrs Filsell. But I think your husband can help me with my inquiries.'

'Me? Not us?' she smiled. 'I understood the police sought help with "their" enquiries? And I note you are alone ... whenever I have been visited before I have always been visited by two officers, one who asked the questions, the other who didn't take his eyes off me for a second, looking for some telltale give-away sign ... not that I have been often visited in that manner.'

'I'm sure, but this is an old case, we are trying to tidy it up and they gave it to me, we are quite stretched at the minute.'

'The so called "Panther" case,' she nodded. 'Yes, horrible for those poor girls ... and one girl was murdered ... poor thing, so young.'

'Yes.' Household raised an eyebrow. 'All the others were abducted and released. She was the only one to be murdered.'

'And you are sure it's the same man that abducted the other four girls?'

'I am not involved with that inquiry but I believe the officers are working on the assumption that it's the same man, the method of abduction appears similar. The young women who were released all tell of being bundled into a van ... and we know that serial criminals escalate, move from assaults to serious assault, to murder...'

'I see. So you have been given this old case because of your experience? You seem to be about my age, the age when police officers retire.'

'Yes, I think I am being allowed to soft pedal towards my pension. I am being kept busy and out of harm's way.'

'You do yourself an injustice.'

There was a gentle tap on the door.

'Ah ... Polly ... come in.'

The door opened and Polly entered balancing a tray of tea on one hand, which she carried to the table and placed it thereon.

'How do you like your tea, Inspector?'

'Just milk, please.' Household took the photograph of the young Edward De Beer out of his jacket pocket.

'I wonder if I could show you this photograph, Mrs Filsell. I don't know whether you knew your husband at Cambridge?'

'I did. That's where we met. Polly, would you mind...?'

Polly took the print from Household's hand and politely and diplomatically did not look at it, but walked across the room and handed it to Mrs Filsell, who squealed with delight upon recognising it.

'Well ... I never ...'

Polly handed Mrs Filsell a cup of tea, and another cup to Household who smiled his thanks.

'So you recognise the photograph?'

'Yes, that's Michael when he was an undergraduate ... such a good looking young man. That photograph was taken when we went out to Grantchester Meadows and built a bonfire on a whim. Wherever did you obtain it?' She looked almost lovingly at the photograph and ran her fingertips over it with a clear demonstration of affection. 'Well really ... yes ... I recall it now, that day.'

'Do you know the people in the photograph?'

'Well, there's Michael...'

'Which is he?'

'The tall, thin one ... the other two near him are Toby Etherington and William Aughty. The blonde girl is me,' she paused, 'me in an earlier life ... before my accident, and the other girl ...what was her name? She was with William at the time, briefly so, they didn't become an item like me and Michael. Oh ... what was her name? Welsh ... Gaynor, yes, that was it, Gaynor Evans, couldn't get more Welsh than that. The photograph must have been taken by Toby's girlfriend,

Dorothy ... Dorothy Farmer. She was at New Hall, I was at Girton and the other man, the small man, he was at the Tech ... a hanger-on, really. I can't remember his name, he attached himself to Michael. The boys were all living in a house in Cambridge, near the police station, down a side street and we decided to go for a walk and that boy from the Tech was with Michael, they talked about writing, you see. Even back then Nigel knew he wanted to write ... and he has done ... plays, mainly, *The Secret Life of Julian Julian* is still on at the West End, after all these years. He's written novels and short stories, but mainly plays. That boy from the Tech ... he had a room in that house and he seemed to want to latch onto the university set as much as he could.'

'You didn't approve of him?'

'None of us did ... except Michael, and Michael was the leader of the group, so the Tech student was tolerated ... but you see it shows in this photograph how much on the outside he was.'

'Yes, I noticed that. You didn't like him?'

'I didn't dislike him. I suppose I'm just a dreadful snob but it's not really about that. I think he came from a working-class background and worked hard to assume a middle-class attitude and mannerisms but I, and I think the others in that group, would have felt the same if he had been from our background ... you see, he just was not at the university and that was it. But he pretended to be. He was happy for people who didn't know us to see him with us and think he was a university student, when in fact he was a hanger-on from the Tech. When he was with us we were colluding with his lie ... but he said nice things about Michael's work ... that encouraged Michael and so occasionally he would be allowed to follow on, to "tag" as we used to say at school. At the school I went to a girl wasn't allowed to walk about by herself, if she had no one to walk with she had to wait until two girls were going where she wanted to go and "tag" behind them, if they let her of course.'

'Of course.'

'So in that same way, every so often, that boy would be allowed to "tag" behind us. Michael accepted him, but William and Toby never did. He irritated them, particularly William ... his needy clinging really seemed to get to William. Didn't know what happened to him. Left his room in the house, didn't enquire after him. No reason why I should.' She continued to gaze at the photograph.

'No reason at all.' Household took out his notebook. 'Your husband is overseas, I believe ... Polly said so?'

'Yes ... he's in Malta.' She beamed with pride. 'Whenever the muse is upon him he goes to Malta ... we have a villa which overlooks the harbour. Like all artists, he needs space.'

'He's alone?'

'Of course ... he can cook simple meals ... what is that phrase? Survival cooking. He can grill a chop, boil vegetables and pour sauce over it all. He'll be producing another play ... this house and the villa, all paid for by the Good Move Company.'

'The Good Move Company?'

'My husband's company. The company's

products are Michael's plays, novels and short stories. His accountant told him that because of his success, financially speaking that is, he'd pay less tax if he formed himself into a company rather than continue to pay personal income tax ... he suggested that it would be a "good move" if he was to do that. So the Good Move Company was formed.'

'I see. Now do you know what happened to the other two men in the photograph?'

'Yes! Don't you?' she smiled another proud smile. 'William Aughty is Member for Newmarket and Ely and Toby Etherington is Member for Bishops' Stortford North. The country is "on loan" to the other side at the moment but we'll romp home at the next election ... and both Toby and William are tipped for Cabinet office ... they are both in the Shadow Cabinet now. The present lot have to ask the Queen to dissolve Parliament before the end of November this year – about three more months, then we'll have the country back again. Michael will come home long before then to help with the election ... he's a name, you see, and his canvassing helps. He'll be particularly active in Bishops' Stortford, Newmarket and Ely because of his lifelong friendship with William and Toby.'

'Well, thank you, Mrs Filsell, that's been very useful.' Household stood.

'Wait, please.' Mrs Filsell reached for a phone that had remained hidden from Household's view. She picked it up and dialled a single number. 'Polly, the Detective Inspector is leaving now, could you please come up?'

Polly returned to the room within a matter of minutes, so few minutes that Household was surprised at the speed of her response, yet she showed no sign at all of having hurried.

'If you'd give this photograph back to the Inspector, please, Polly?'

Mrs Filsell held up the photograph, Polly walked across the carpet, skirted round the table, collected the photograph and returned it to Household. Household thanked Mrs Filsell for her time and information and followed Polly out of the room.

'Don't take it personally,' Polly said softly as they neared the bottom of the stairs and were safely out of earshot.

'Take what personally?'

'That she didn't let you get too close to her. She broke her spine some years ago in a riding accident and she has no control of her bladder. It's easier for men who have had such an accident because they can drain their urine into a catheter, and so long as they empty the bag before it overflows there isn't a smell, so she told me when I started work here, but women have to drain into pads and no matter how often they change the pads there is a constant smell of urine about them.'

'I see. I noticed the air was heavy with air freshener and furniture polish.'

'That's to help suppress the smell.'

'Does she live upstairs?'

'Yes, that's where the bathroom and bedrooms are. There's a lift she can use to get downstairs should she choose to use it, to get out into the garden, for instance, but she seems to prefer to stay upstairs.'

'How does she fill in her time?'

'Reading ... reading ... reading. Books, newspapers, especially politics ... you might have guessed she is mad keen on politics.'

'Yes ... Mr Etherington and Mr Aughty.' Household stopped as they reached the front door. 'How long have you been employed here?'

'About three years now ... time to move on.'

'You feel like that?' Household smiled.

'Well, I never meet anybody ... and my biological clock is beginning to tick.'

'So you know Mr Filsell?'

'A little ... he spends a lot of his time away, mostly at the villa in Malta. They said they'd take me there when they go ... but "they" don't seem to go any more, only Mr Michael. Mrs Charlotte stays here with me and Cook and the gardener.'

Household nodded. 'Yes, I can see why you might want to move on ... tranquil as the house and grounds are.'

It was a modern building at the university, concrete and glass, with a wide patio area, a pool and a modest fountain, enough to break up the harshness. The room in which they sat was neat and functional, everything ordered, and the man too, young, possibly early thirties, neatly dressed, more like an insurance salesman than a psychologist. Though neither of them expressed it, both Wiseman and Tracy felt a pang of disappointment that when they kept their appointment with Dr Lecky it was not with a wild eccentric, but with a man who seemed devoid of imagination, nor was his study in this world famous, illustrious university in a medieval court with ivy clad walls, but in a modern building that could have been anywhere in the developed world.

'The Panther.' Dr Lecky looked at the notes he'd made. 'You understand that this is probing?'

'Yes, sir.' David Tracy sitting in front of Dr Lecky, replied for both of them but Penny Wiseman sitting beside him also said, 'Yes, sir.'

'Well, the most striking thing that can be drawn from the information you have sent to me is his desire to care for somebody. Utterly twisted from our perspective but from his it would make sense ... he may not see that what he is doing is wrong, though he would also know he will be in trouble for doing it. He may see it as ethically defensible, although a criminal act ... ethics and criminal legislation more or less coincide, but the match isn't perfect. As you know, some things are not against the law but are morally reprehensible ... equally, things are ethically defensible but yet are unlawful.' Lecky saw a look of puzzlement cross the faces of Tracy and Wiseman. He paused and then explained himself. 'Well, take cannabis for instance, unlawful to smoke it ... but suppose you are not a youngster smoking it for a stimulant, to be rebellious or to be accepted by your peers, but are an elderly person taking it in tea because it is a powerful painkiller with no side effects and helps arthritis sufferers get through the day. Is it then unethical? I put it to you that it is not unethical if used for the latter purpose, and I get annoyed, muchly so, when I read about elderly people who hobble into magistrates' courts on two aluminium sticks and are fined a few pounds for possession of a controlled substance, when the only reason they have been in possession of the drug in the first place is to help ease dreadful pain. I have to own that I believe that neither the police officer who made the arrest, nor the magistrate can have any idea just how painful arthritis can be. I mention that as an example of how someone can believe they are right, but accept that the law thinks otherwise. And that, I believe, is the Panther.' Lecky paused. He glanced out of his window across the expanse of concrete which seemed to bake under the relentless sun and from which a heat haze rose. 'Wish it would rain,' he said. 'My garden is surviving on recycled bath water ... plants don't like detergent but it's better than nothing. Oh ... sorry, I digress. I think the Panther is a man who has a strong need to care, but who for some reason cannot attract a partner. There are two basic reasons why somebody cannot attract a partner – if they want a partner, because some people, like me, choose to live alone. The first is that the person is of unfortunate appearance ... he or she is not, visually speaking, an attractive person ... the second is that their psyche is so damaged that they cannot sustain relationships. Now I understand that the Panther is believed to have been seen?'

'Yes, sir,' David Tracy answered. He was a little stung by Dr Lecky's accusation of insensitive policing, knowing that more often than not a blind eye is turned when appropriate.

'He seems to be fit ... athletic ... strong ... is the

witness credible?'

'I think so, sir. I took that statement in fact. That witness is a poacher ... a career petty criminal, but eyes like a hawk ...'

'I see ... attuned to night vision as poachers reputedly are. So not a man of unfortunate appearance ... not grossly obese, for example, nor an undersized weakling.'

'No, sir. Seems not.'

'So we are probably looking for a man whose challenge is psychological, not physical, a man with dreadful emotional scars ... can't sustain a relationship but has a need to care for someone, so he abducts someone, cares for her for a few weeks then releases her?'

'That has been the pattern, yes, sir.'

'Until a couple of days ago, when he murdered for the first time?'

'Yes, sir.' David Tracy glanced to his left and watched a slender young woman carrying a shoulder bag saunter through the heat haze. Penny Wiseman, following his glance, cleared her throat in disapproval, then they smiled at each other, all unseen by Dr Lecky.

'Two possible explanations ... that he is escalating and will kill again, or his victim, the murder victim, knew something that could identify him.'

'None of the others saw his face, sir,' Penny Wiseman said. 'We think that perhaps Joyce Dance did.'

'Perhaps. But it means he's ruthless. A man who wants to possess something so he can look after it, yet is also ruthless enough to kill what he possesses should said possession be in a position to threaten him.' Dr Lecky stroked his chin. 'A badly disrupted childhood, as if he had been separated from something he had to care for ... being forced to abandon a dog he had loved, for example, or been told he could have something as a pet and then not given it and that promise repeatedly made and repeatedly broken. That sort of experience could explain this behaviour. He'd be distant in himself, a difficult person to reach. I think we are looking at someone who lives alone rather than with an elderly relative or even a pet, because that may have been sufficient to answer his need to care. He has a source of income ... he can run a motor vehicle, that vehicle that was burnt out in Romsey Town last night?'

'Possibly the one he used, sir,' Tracy said. 'We asked the media to broadcast the information about the Panther having access to a black Ford Transit type of vehicle and shortly after that, when night had fallen, a black Ford Transit was set on fire in Romsey Town. It's at the forensic science laboratory now, sir but I saw it ... we saw it this morning, it's a burned out shell. The number plates belong to a black Transit owned by a courier firm, so if he was stopped and checked the vehicle wouldn't be registered as having been stolen.'

'Clever.'

'Yes, neat,' Tracy smiled in agreement, 'easiest thing in the world to copy down the number plate of a similar vehicle and have number plates made up to fix onto your vehicle. But when we checked the chassis number, we found that the van had been stolen in Chelmsford some time ago, but not before the first abduction. So he may have stolen other vehicles and kept them until their road tax disc was about to expire.'

'So a man who knows how the police work?'

'Well, yes, but no more than the average informed citizen, sir, nothing that speaks of inside knowledge.'

'Alright ... if you are happy with that.' Again Lecky paused and so like an insurance salesman did he seem that Tracy half expected him to say 'We do have this package, sir, which would suit your needs admirably' but instead he said, 'Now, tell me about this latest abduction.'

'Ah ... close to home, sir.'

'Really, I hope not the daughter of a police officer?'

'The daughter of the forensic pathologist, sir, so we know the lady.'

'I see ... close to home as you say. So tell me what you know about that abduction.'

'Believed to have happened yesterday morning, sir. Morning because when Dr Sleaford returned home the breakfast things remained unwashed on the kitchen table, and had the young woman eaten lunch then the breakfast things would, at the very least, have been transferred to the dishwasher. And we know that the young woman ate sensibly ... didn't miss meals to stay slim, for example.'

'That's a reasonable deduction. So what in turn do you deduce from that, about the Panther, if it is the Panther?'

'Don't know what to deduce about it, sir ... if it is the Panther, as you say.'

'Well, it means that he has a job which enables him to be out and about at the time of day when most folk are at work.'

'Yes...'

'So his job takes him out and about, such as a delivery driver, or he works shifts, allowing him free time during the normal working day ... but that's really for the police to deduce, I am encroaching on your territory a little bit. From a psychological perspective, I would say that if this is a "Panther" abduction, then he is getting dangerous. You see, in all known serial crimes against the person, serial rapes, serial murders ... the perpetrator tends to escalate in terms of his or her savagery, and also in terms of the frequency of attack. The last victim was murdered, that is an escalation for whatever reason, but an escalation nonetheless, and this abduction follows so closely upon the last that it is also an escalation. So if it is the Panther, and I would say it is, same M.O., same area of the country ... this man is highly localised as serial criminals go, then he has become very dangerous indeed. I envy you not ... in the past all other serial killer investigations have had the pressure to find their man or woman before the next victim is taken. Here the next victim has already been taken and you have to get to her while she's still alive.' Lecky leaned back in his chair, behind him was a poster of Venice. It was clearly the only decoration allowed in the room. 'Have you pondered about the nature of the place he keeps his victims?'

'The victims who were released all speak of a lock-up of some sort, in the country ... just country sounds ... no nearby road, railway, nothing of that sort.'

'Just owls hooting at night, that sort of thing?'

'Yes, sir.'

'You've searched for it?'

'Yes, sir. Mr Perigo, who is leading this inquiry, divided the area round Cambridge into segments, vectoring from the city and the inquiry team took a segment each. Even Mr Perigo took one because we were so thinly stretched. All farms have been visited and asked to check their out-buildings, all houses that stand in their own grounds have been visited ... all derelict buildings and sheds have been checked.'

'How far out did you go?'

'About ten miles, and that stretched us to the limit.'

'I bet it did ... beyond that the search area becomes so large as to be meaningless and I don't think it has to be larger. Our boy is a home boy, his M.O. speaks of that. He doesn't like to wander. I would add that to his profile.' Lecky tapped his pen on his desk top. 'It may well be that an influential phase of his life was one of sudden and unexpected moves, geographically speaking, uprooted then planted somewhere else, then uprooted again probably over great distances. It's filled him with a morbid dread of travelling. So that's it ... oh, and he'll be white ... by ethnicity, northern European or Caucasian, if you like, because all serial killers are. There is only one known black serial killer and he was convicted on evidence so shaky that it makes painful reading ... so he'll be white European. So ... shall we recap?'

'Yes, please, sir.' Tracy held his pen poised above his notebook.

'Male ... which you know.' Dr Lecky closed his eyes and clasped his hands behind his head. 'Lives alone, thirty to forty ... mobile, which you know, probably lives alone, has relationship difficulties ... is hard to "reach", very remote ... traumatised childhood, probably moved a great deal ... not at all settled in his early life, now very local to Cambridge, possibly has a knowledge of police procedure but, as you say, nothing more than the average television watcher would also know. In good physical shape by all accounts. He'll be somebody's neighbour. He'll live in an ordinary house in an ordinary street ... and if you broadcast that description it will probably, hopefully, prompt someone to pick up the phone.'

'Hope it does.' Tracy stood, Wiseman did likewise. 'Thank you. Appreciated.'

From Mrs Filsell's house in Swaffham Prior, Household drove the six miles to Great Wilbraham to the address of Tom Fordham, as had been provided for him by the solicitors who acted for him in the sale of his house in Romsey Road. He revealed himself to be short but well built, with a ready smile.

'I've been expecting you.' Fordham stood in the doorway for a second before stepping to one side, a very English gesture, thought Household, letting him know that he was entering the house

334

on the owner's terms. 'Do come in.'

Fordham directed Household to the living room of his bungalow and asked him to take a seat. Household did so and declined the offer of a cup of tea. Fordham sat opposite Household in an old and very comfortable looking armchair.

'You have been expecting the police?' Household asked.

'Well, yes ... article in the *Cambridge Evening News* and a courtesy call from my solicitors advising me that the police sought my present or last known address in respect of a serious crime.'

'Yes, the little girl whose body was found in the garden of a house you once bought.'

'Yes...' Fordham's voice trailed away as Household read the room, solid furniture, which seemed to be older than Fordham, as if he had inherited it from his parent's house and had chosen to continue to use it out of economic necessity or respect and fond memory. Its age gave the room a comfortable 'lived in' homely feel in Household's view, as did the books which lined the bookshelves, text books in the main, it seemed. The window looked out onto a narrow garden, a wooden fence and fields beyond. A low flying black jet aeroplane moved slowly through the sky, so slowly that Household barely believed it could remain airborne. Beyond it the sky was blue and cloudless.

Fordham continued, 'To think that the body had lain there all the while we were in the house. Rather put me off my evening meal when I realised that. We were in the house for five years, until my marriage went pear shaped. Bloody, bitterly contested divorce ... she got the children and I picked up the solicitor's bill.'

'We believe the girl was murdered prior to your purchasing the house.'

Fordham smiled. 'Well, that's a relief.'

'Yes...' Household returned the smile, 'so we are keen to find the owner, a Mrs Sparrow ... we can't locate them so anyone who knew them in any capacity is the next best thing for us.'

'Us? And you are visiting alone. I always thought the police visited in pairs.'

'I have just had this conversation with the last house I visited.' Household proceeded to give Tom Fordham the explanation he had earlier given to Charlotte Filsell.

'Retirement is very nice really – I went early. The trick is to keep yourself occupied. I'm working on textbooks. This is a very pleasant set-up, it's modest, but the mortgage is paid off ... virtually. What I pay each month is less than students pay for a single room ... potter about in the morning, doing the housework, watching anything I taped from the previous night's television, work in the afternoon, wander into the village for a pint in the early evening.'

'Very nice.' It did indeed sound very nice. 'But to matters in hand, matters of a more serious nature.'

'Of course ... well I put two and two together and turned my thoughts to those days, trying to remember anything I could about the weird Mrs Sparrow and her luckless son.'

'Luckless?'

'Growing up with a mother like that. Poor

lad...' Fordham paused, 'well those days, early 1970s ... thirty plus years ago. I remember Don Maclean's "American Pie" was the song that shaped those days, and a song about crossing the desert on a horse with no name which the Tech students used to change to crossing the desert on a horse with no legs.'

'You taught at the Tech?'

'Yes. Geography. The Tech had a very strong Geography department, London University external degrees and CNAA degrees. Now though, AFU as it is, has only a small Geography department. It was all different then, the cars of the time were Ford Capris and Morris Marinas, students dressed like hippies – long hair, flared trousers – and met in the heady Daffodil Café on East Road or their club in King's Passage. Going to "the club" was the only time they went across Parker's Piece. By and large they kept themselves in Romsey Town. Except when they occupied Owlescroft. That was fun.'

'Owlescroft?'

'Well, in those days the Tech students had an accommodation problem and they discovered that a large purpose-built nurses' accommodation block was lying empty so they occupied it and forced a good settlement ... they won legitimate use of half of it. Made quite a difference. Those that obtained a room there considered themselves fortunate. A bit of a trek from the Tech but lovely rooms, warm, dry, good dining and washing facilities. Better than a damp bedsit.'

'Mrs Sparrow...' Household brought the wandering mind of Tom Fordham back into focus.

'Yes ... sorry ... well, as you know, we bought the property on Romsey Terrace from Mrs Sparrow and well suited to her name was she, small, nervous, flighty sort of person, moved around the house in short, rapid bursts, and had a mind which kept going off at tangents. I swear, if she was a car driver she'd be making right turns without signalling.'

Household smiled. He enjoyed Tom Fordham's sense of humour.

'She had a boy ... a son ... and she had allowed him to dig a hole in the garden. He intended to line it with concrete and put fish in it, a bit too near the house for my liking, almost right against the wall, would have caused rising damp. But then she had taken up with an Iranian and was going to live in Iran and told her son to fill in the hole because he couldn't keep fish after all and he was beside himself ... floods of tears. We visited them to view the house ... she'd just told him he wasn't going to keep fish after all ... mind you, I don't know what sort of fish he could have kept ... pond life, yes, if he built ramps for them to get in and out of the pond and ledges in the pond ... and introduced plants ... he could have kept frogs and newts, but he wasn't going to have anything. Poor little lad ... Barbara ... my ex ... she didn't want to buy the house, she said it was an unhappy family and that they would leave an unhappy presence behind them. She might indeed have been right because our marriage seemed to go wrong when we entered that house. Without anything to set us off, it seemed, we were at each other from day one ... as though something had come between us.'

'So, by the time you moved in the hole had been filled in?'

'Yes, and concreted over. We put topsoil over it and allowed it to grass over.'

'Did you see Mrs Sparrow again?'

'No ... the house was empty for a few weeks before we moved in and when we did move in, all the talk among the neighbours was of the little girl who had disappeared from two doors down.' Fordham shifted his position in the armchair. 'The Sparrow family contaminated our life in that house, it wasn't the stressful presence that my wife feared so much as both of us fretting about the little boy. I mean, being taken to Iran at the age of 12 after living all his life in England, he'd be massively traumatised by the culture shock ... unable to speak the language ... victimised at school ... and then the Iran/Iraq war started soon after that, so he'd be conscripted. We both fretted about him, people in the pub, the Empress on St Philips Road, folk there used to mention him from time to time ... "young Harry Sparrow"; "poor mite"; "wonder about him from time to time". But we, me and Barbara, wondered about him all the time. We were living in what had been his home ... we had that immediacy ... but I think he returned, you know.'

'You do?' Household became alert.

'Yes, I read a report in the *Guardian*. Probably carried in other papers as well, but I have been a *Guardian* reader all my life. It was the story of a man who had deserted the Iranian army, putting his life at risk by doing so, and had escaped capture as he crossed the mountains into Turkey ... living off the land, real survival stuff. He had made it to Ankara and walked to the British Embassy there ... told them he was British by birth and they got him home. A bit of adventure, but I thought that it must be Harry Sparrow because the article said he'd been taken to Iran by his mother when he was twelve, about ten years earlier. How many twelve year old British boys were taken to Iran in the early 1970s?'

'Not many' Household had to concede that point.

'About one, I'd say. So he came back, good for him, I'd say.'

'That's very interesting,' Household spoke quietly, 'very interesting indeed.'

'Well, the article will be there to read. If the *Guardian* reported it, I am sure *The Times* did as well, and the library in Cambridge keeps *The Times* on microfiche ... be a bit painstaking, but it's worth the trawl if you want to find him. I think the article said he went to live with relatives.'

'Do you remember where?'

'In the East Anglia area, I think, but can't remember exactly.'

'Well,' Household stood, 'that has been a great help, thank you.'

'Only too pleased to help,' Fordham also stood, 'breaks up the monotony of the day.'

'I thought you enjoyed your retirement?'

'Oh, I do, better than working, but the days do tend to run into each other, so an interruption to the routine is always welcome, so long as it's positive and constructive.' Fordham led House-

340

hold to the front door of his bungalow and opened it for him and Household, with another word of thanks, took his leave.

Margaret Neston carried out the tray of chilled lemonade to the three men who sat by the pool. Again the conversation halted as she approached and placed the tray on the table. She also noticed that the two guests, Aughty and Etherington, avoided eye contact, only Filsell glanced at her for a split second and sneered a cursory 'thank you'. She turned on her heels and walked back to the villa. She sat at the kitchen table, enjoying the cool interior of the building.

Critical. Things were critical. Filsell was right, it's the easiest thing in the world to make someone disappear in the Mediterranean countries. Compared to the United Kingdom the Mediterranean basin is lawless, young white women disappear each year ... just don't return home from their package holiday. The issue is hidden because there is no overview ... they come from different countries and visit different countries, the police forces don't talk to each other, even if they were interested who would connect a Dutch girl who goes missing in Majorca with a Swedish girl who goes missing on Crete? They may not even be connected, except in that they are victims of the same crime ... abduction, rape, murder ... and the stories of white slavers with fast boats, with Africa one night's journey distant ... they are too strong, too numerous to be far-flung, excited, scaremongering fantasy. You hear such tales if you stay on in the Mediterranean after your package tour... Even if Filsell and his two pale-skinned friends from England were not a part of that activity, he was still right, she could disappear very easily or, as Filsell had suggested, her body be found floating in the sea. It would be death by misadventure, her body flown home to be met by her grieving parents at John Lennon International airport. She had to be careful ... very careful indeed. Yet her curiosity was roused ... she had listened to the tape three times, four times. 'We all hid the body' - that was the crucial line, spoken by William Aughty, in response to Filsell saying 'We? You did it'. So Aughty had done something, some time ago, and what could they have done but murder someone, if they talked about burying a body?

Should she keep her distance?

Should she try to find out more?

She stood, walked to the sideboard on which stood a bowl of fruit, took an apple and peeled it, more for want of something to do than for any other reason. She ate the apple slowly, slicing off a piece with a sharp knife.

In the event, the decision was made for her. She became aware of someone approaching the kitchen. She turned. Toby Etherington entered the kitchen. She smiled, 'Hello, sir.'

'Sir?' Toby Etherington returned the smile, 'You can call me Toby.'

'Toby,' she repeated.

'Do you mind if I join you?'

'No.' She sliced off a piece of the apple. 'Have some apple. Very sweet.'

'Thanks.' Etherington reached out and took a

piece from the knife blade. He sat down. 'Aren't you having a siesta?'

'No, "the Master" doesn't allow it.'

'The Master? Is that what you call Michael?'

'Yes ... but not to his face.' She looked at the man, tall, middle-aged, silver hair, confident, in reasonable shape ... in better shape than her father and probably older, but then unlike her father he didn't spend his days slinging dustbins for the council in all weathers six days a week. And here he was ... accepting Michael Filsell's offer to "put in a bid" for her lovely young body, even if she only pulled five out of ten in bed.

'And he forbids you to take a siesta? Forbids?'

'Yes.' She held eye contact and offered him another slice of apple. 'He takes one himself but doesn't allow me to take one ... not a proper one anyway ... he's a bit two-faced like that, a bit of a control freak. He can't do much about me falling asleep on the recliner by the pool, but going to bed in the afternoon is not on for little me.'

'Otherwise?'

'Otherwise His Nibs gets angry ... he might kick me out.'

'Where would you go?'

'Where could I go? I have no money ... he wouldn't even drive me to the airport. I could get home by some means but my return airfare is conditional upon me leaving the villa on good terms with the Master, so I don't annoy him. If he says no siesta for me, then it's no siesta.'

'Seems unfair.'

Margaret Neston shrugged her shoulders. 'Well, it's a pleasant life – better than typing in

343

the shipping office – and he's an Englishman, wouldn't want to be mistress to a Maltese or a Spaniard, no matter how wealthy.'

Toby Etherington smiled. She smiled back and thought, Oh yes, please, Mr Etherington, please put in a bid as you say, because you don't know what I know and you might tell me more ... and should my tape recorder be running, then who knows what little indiscretions may be captured on tape?

'Well, in a sense I agree with Michael ... I think siestas are lazy and not for the English, but unlike Michael I am not a hypocrite about the matter ... Michael and William are going to take a nap now. I, on the other hand, don't wish to sleep away the day. Michael said I may have use of the moke ... I have never been to Malta before, I thought I might take a drive, I wonder if you'd care to join me?'

'Love to,' Margaret Neston smiled. 'I know just the place to go. And you don't have to worry ... I'm on the pill.' And she loved the look of surprise, of total disarmament that was his expression, and which was rapidly followed by a look of joy. 'Let me get my bag.' She stood.

'Of course,' Toby Etherington spluttered, barely able to contain his excitement. 'I'll meet you outside the front door in a few minutes.'

'You'll need your trunks, we're going for a swim,' she smiled. 'If you wear them, of course ... me, I choose not to ... it's really isolated. No one is ever there. Trust me.'

'Oh I do.' He stood. 'I do, I do, I do.'

344

The Panther crept back into the bungalow. He went into the room where the girl was chained to the wall. She heard him enter because she stiffened with fear, the ear defenders clearly did not isolate that sound from the wearer. But the blindfold prevented any vision. He strode over to the girl and took the ear defenders off her head. 'That's done,' he said, 'that's old Richard buried where he wanted to be buried. Not intact, of course ... had to remove the head. He can be identified from his teeth.'

Sojourner Sleaford whimpered.

'Had to let the blood solidify before the body could be chopped up. All the clothing had to be burnt. No one suspects a fire in the grounds of a building being renovated. Then the body is hacked up ... left with a pile of bones ... they got put into a hole in the ground, two feet long, one foot wide, one foot deep.' He turned on the Calor gas stove and lit the gas with a match. 'Doesn't look like a grave ... I'll plant something over it, perhaps put some rocks there ... some heavy rocks, because the bones might be attractive to a fox ... but the head will have to go ... it's already chained to an air brick ... you know what an air brick is? Like an ordinary house brick except it has holes in it, designed to allow air to circulate between the cavity walls of houses ... could have been made for the likes of me, wanting to dispose of some old boy's head. I'll drop it off Elizabeth Way Bridge tonight, in a plastic bag ... when it's dark of course, no one to see me, no traffic on the river at night ... no legitimate traffic anyway ... and if I hear the bag splash into the water, then that's old Richard gone forever. He lived alone, be a while before he's noticed missing ... silly old fool ... just had to nosey around. You see I had to do what I did, you understand that, don't you? He would have spoiled everything ... and you are going to be the last one, the police are getting a bit close, you see ... have to let things quieten down ... things will move on. I know how the police work, there's just never enough hours in the day for them, never enough officers. Right now they're hunting for me ... hunting for you as well ... hunting for both of us ... but we have fled like two young lovers, just you and me. You mustn't be afraid, I am here to look after you ... that's my job you see, keep you warm ... well in this weather that's not a problem, but fed ... keep you fed. I'm making a meal soon ... we'll eat it together ... won't be much but it will be wholesome. I see you have found the toilet ... it's in your interest to use it. I can't properly clean you if you soil yourself, I don't have the facilities ... there's no running water in the bungalow. I carry all water in in huge plastic jerry cans. I'll keep you for a week or two ... then what? I can't tell you ... you see, you saw me ... the last one saw me too.'

'I won't tell anybody.'

'Oh, but you will ... you see they will make you, they will tell you that if you don't help them then I can carry on capturing young women ... and would you like that on your conscience? They will say things like that to you ... they will make you feel so bad about yourself that you'll tell them what they want to know because you want to feel good about yourself. We all like feeling good about ourselves and you are no different ... so you'll tell them about me ... and help them compose an e-fit. But you have a few days, a few weeks yet. We'll get to know each other and I can care for you ... see that you never go hungry, always have enough to drink ... and if you are still here in the autumn, I will make sure you are warm and dry. You'll be here for me to come home to and you will depend on me for food ... and I won't let you down ... mine to care for. I won't violate you, I promise ... I never have done that and I never will – that has to be given voluntarily. Once, in a foreign country, I saw rape take place on a large scale ... I was even made to take part in it ... you don't get much choice about it if a gun is pointed at your head but I didn't like doing it. Do you believe me when I say that? That was not caring ... that revolted me. I feel that I did it for no reason, because they shot them all afterwards ... all the women they had raped, they shot them ... but I won't do that. I won't rape you, my job is to care for you. And I will. Tonight we will eat rabbit stew. I will go out hunting ... I will bring in food for us ... I will get and skin the rabbit ... boil the meat and make a pie ... man the hunter ... man the provider.'

The Panther strode forwards with two long, effortless strides, the strides of a man with strength in his loins, and gently hooked a finger under the blindfold and took it off the head of Sojourner Sleaford. She blinked and squeezed her eyes against the sudden rush of sunlight. 'There really is no need for me to keep you blindfolded

... the early ones, I kept them blindfolded so I could let them go. I cared enough to let them go, and I could let them go because they hadn't seen me ... but I have to leave the gag on, I don't want you to scream. It's fairly remote here but there is a minor road about one field's width away ... a few hundred feet ... a scream could carry that far so the gag stays in. It's just me caring for you ... you see that, don't you? I am just looking after you, just sit at peace now until I return.'

He walked out of the room. Sojourner watched as he picked up the ferocious, powerful-looking crossbow from where it lay in the other room, put a quiver full of bolts round his neck, and reached for the door handle. He turned and smiled warmly as he opened the door ... in other circumstances it would be a warm smile, a smile of fondness, of approval and she realised he probably was sincere in his own insane way. He shut the door behind him. She sat against the wall, in the shade; through the window she saw lush green foliage and a blue sky, the things that she had always taken for granted had been taken from her. She examined the chain round her ankle, not so tight that it bit into her skin, but tight enough to prevent her removing it ... it was lightweight chain, chrome ... but strong ... very strong, held only by a padlock, a small brass padlock, also very strong ... and the other end of the chain fastened to an eye bolt which was fixed to the skirting board. Her wrists were chained together behind her back, thus preventing her from undoing the gag. She felt empty in the pit of her stomach. It was not possible ... it was not fair ... she should not be here, not in the room ... in this ramshackle house ... but he had killed and could kill again. She was just seventeen years old, but she realised, intuitively, that her survival depended upon passivity, upon her co-operation. This man, the Panther, wanted to care for her ... very well, she thought, very well, he can care for me. I will show my appreciation. Each day I can stay alive is a day nearer rescue.

Margaret Neston drove to a small cove she knew, near Golden Bay. She parked the mini-moke off the road. She took hold of Etherington's hand and, carrying a shoulder bag and a large, brightly coloured beach towel, guided him down the rocky pathway to where the warm waters of the Mediterranean lapped against the sand. The cove itself, he saw, consisted of a small beach. Toby Etherington thought it would accommodate just three medium-sized family saloon cars parked side by side. Rocks at either side of the beach about ten feet above the water, which stretched about twenty feet out into the Mediterranean, formed a small swimming area. He was thrilled at her taking his hand and was further thrilled when he saw the small beach.

'It's not well known,' she smiled at him, and laid her hand gently on his chest. 'There's a kind of unwritten rule...' she began to unbutton his shirt and sensed him arouse with excitement. 'If a car is parked where I parked the moke it means the beach is occupied.' She spread the beach towel on the sand. 'All you have to worry about is passing boats.'

'Really?' He undid the knot of the sarong and let it fall to the sand.

'Yes, really.' She did not object as the hand caressed her breast. 'We won't be disturbed and there's no one about ... good job, really, I can be a bit of a screamer ... if you are good enough...'

'I think I can come up with the goods.' He picked her up and carried her to the middle of the beach and laid her down, carefully, gently.

'Don't you want to swim first?' She held her arms round his neck, allowing her eyes to dilate as they gazed into his.

'No,' he skilfully removed her bikini top, 'I don't want to swim at all.'

Later he lay on his back, a towel over his middle. Margaret Neston lay naked on her side, her left arm across his chest, the fingers of her right hand caressing his hair.

'Nobody's ever made love to me like that.' She kissed him. 'Thank you.'

He smiled. His left hand found her small bottom and he allowed it to rest there. 'You are right,' he said, 'you are a screamer.'

'Only if it's done right.' She reached out, behind his head, and pulled her shoulder bag towards her. She fumbled in the bag, found the cassette player and pulled it to the opening of the bag, ready to be switched on. She took a bottle of sunflower oil out from the bag, poured a generous amount on his chest and began to spread it with her fingertips. 'And you did it right ... so masterful, but so gentle ... a younger man wouldn't have made love like that ... banging away until he came and if I feel any pleasure

350

that's incidental, but mature men give pleasure before they take theirs ... give me a mature man any day ... and a successful man. Are you really going to be a cabinet minister?'

'Probably.' He tapped her bottom, encompassing the whole of the right cheek in his meaty paw-like hand. 'I'll get re-elected, I have a safe seat ... reasonably safe ... healthy majority at the last election, and if the party wins ... well, I am in the Shadow Cabinet. Nothing is certain until the party leader chooses his Cabinet but...' he nodded. 'It's more than on the cards.'

'Michael says you and the other gentleman, William, are future prime ministers.' She massaged oil into his groin and enjoyed his low groan of pleasure. 'It's just sunflower oil,' she said. 'Michael says it's as good a sun block as any expensive lotion.'

'Feels very pleasant, whatever it is ... don't know about being the PM ... too much responsibility. I'd make a good minister, though.'

She massaged the oil into his legs and then told him to turn over. He did so, slowly but willingly. She poured oil onto his back. 'Oh, I scratched you, I'm sorry ... it's a good job you were lying on the towel, don't want to get sand into those cuts. I've got some antiseptic cream...' She foraged in her bag, and ensured the tape recorder was close to the top of Toby Etherington's head. She mustn't push ... she knew she mustn't be pushy. She took the cream and smeared it over the abrasion her nails had caused on his back and returned the tube to the bag. 'It's quite nice having you in the villa.'

'You like the company?' Toby Etherington rolled back over to face her.

'Yes ... didn't think I would but...' she shrugged her shoulders. 'It was getting dull ... just me and him.'

'Well, we won't be here much longer.'

'Oh?' She teased his nipple with her teeth as she deftly pressed the 'record' button of the tape recorder. 'I thought you were here for a holiday?'

'Oh, I wish...' He squeezed her buttocks, closing his eyes against the glare of the sun. 'This cove is quite a little sun trap.'

'For about an hour in the afternoon ... about this time, the sun shines directly down between the rocks, it gets a bit shadier after that.'

'You've been here before, that's plain.'

'Just by myself though ... I heard about the cove at a party I went to with Michael, then a group of us came here. Now I come by myself when His Nibs is having his afternoon nap.'

'You don't like Michael very much, do you?'

'Nope.'

'I thought you gave yourself a little easily.'

Margaret Neston pulled herself away from him. 'Don't know how I should take that.'

Toby Etherington leaned up and rested on his elbow. 'Don't be offended, it wasn't meant that way.'

She allowed him continued eye contact. 'Well he doesn't own me ... he treats me like a skivvy and he hasn't kept his promise about an allowance. He said he'd let me have some spending money but in fact I'm more like a slave. I work, I get fed, but can't escape ... and he's not very good either. You know … in bed…'

'Funny you should say that.' Toby Etherington smiled and lay back down, face up, eyes closed.

'Why?'

'Nothing…'

'Did he say that about me! Well…'

'He's a friend of mine … thirty years we have known each other, so I won't say anything that betrays him but let's just say I was pleasantly surprised by you.'

'So he did say something.' She fell silent and lowered her head onto his chest. Then she asked, 'Are you married?'

'Yes. Two children, one grandchild.'

'Nice…'

'I think so.'

'Michael hasn't any children, has he?'

'No. His wife … she can't.'

'I see.'

'She had an accident…'

'He never speaks about her. Reckon that's my job as well, to set the place off.'

There was a lull in the conversation, a sudden warm zephyr gusted into the cove like the blast from a suddenly opened oven. Then it faded.

'What was that?'

'From Africa,' she said, 'from the desert. I don't know how it works but little pockets of air seem to cross over the surface of the Med … Michael says they come from the Sahara desert. It's not that uncommon.'

'Fascinating. So, shall we do this again?'

'If you like, but not at the villa … if Michael doesn't want me, I have a room of my own but it wouldn't seem right in Michael's villa, and I am not quiet.'

He held her to him. 'I like you for saying that ... that speaks of integrity but I meant here, just here ... tomorrow.'

'So you'll be here tomorrow?'

'Yes ... we have a little difficulty to clear up, a ghost from our past has crept up and tapped us on the shoulder and said "hello ... remember me?"'

'Oh ... what's that?'

'Can't tell you ... won't tell you and you must never ask.'

'OK, sorry don't want to be nosey.'

'For your own sake, Margaret.'

'That's the first time you've said my name ... but OK.'

'You're a sweet girl. It could be dangerous for you if you knew too much.'

'OK.'

'It's just that William ... he can be impulsive. He's calmer now, but thirty years ago he was a bit wild and did something really stupid, and I mean really stupid. Michael and I did something really stupid as well. Helped him cover it up ... what he'd done and if we had just come clean at the time, Michael and I wouldn't have been in any bother and William could have plea-bargained something ... but we didn't, we just dug ourselves in deeper. For thirty years, the ghost slept but now, with the three of us at our apogee...'

'Apogee?'

'Highest point ... or furthest point. Well, Michael's at his apogee, he can only fade from where he is now ... internationally known play-wright, dripping with money ... bet you haven't seen his house in Cambridge, have you?'

'Nope ... he keeps me well separate. I am well tucked away from all that.'

'Well, take it from me ... Georgian manor house...'

'Georgian?'

'It's over two hundred years old, anyway, and in grounds which are more extensive than some parks in northern towns.'

'As big as Princess Park in Liverpool?'

'Never been to Liverpool ... but big. Liverpool's your home town, isn't it?'

'Birkenhead. Michael says it's the same, but it's not.'

'Anyway, Michael can't go much further ... William and I, if or when we win the election in the autumn – it has to be called soon – we'll likely get Cabinet posts. Like I said, that will be our apogee, and all that, all three of us, could be destroyed if it comes out and what "it" is you must not ask.'

'OK.'

'I mean it.'

'OK. OK.'

He relaxed. 'So long as you understand.' He paused, then asked, 'So you are not happy here?'

'Nope. It was exciting at first, but it gets samey ... each day seems the same, and like I said, he's got me in a state where I am dependent on him ... he could throw me into the street anytime.'

'Well ... he's a friend of mine, but all is fair in this business...'

'Love and war.' She kissed him. 'But yes, I will.'

'Will what?' He opened his eyes and looked into hers.

'I'll be your mistress if you take me back to England.'

He smiled and nodded. 'You are no northern numpty, are you? Your ability to anticipate ... it's ... well, very impressive.'

'Let's just say I want it as much as you. I won't worry about "the Master", there's plenty of girls who'll want to take my place – his villa, or back to the typing pool? No contest.'

'OK.' He leaned forward, took her in his arms and kissed her. 'I've got a flat you can have, but you'll have to be discreet.'

'I will, I promise ... a Cabinet minister ... powerful men are so attractive.'

'Power is a great aphrodisiac.'

'Is it?'

'It's a quote. Henry Kissinger said it.'

'Who's he?'

'Before your time. What's the water like?'

'Like a warm bath, but we've just put sun block on...'

'Well,' he rolled to one side, crouched and stood, 'can't come all the way to Malta without a dip in the sea, sun block or no sun block. Join me?'

'Of course.' She watched as he walked on tiptoe across the hot sand and when she judged him to be safely out of earshot, she cleared her throat, just to be doubly safe, and switched off the tape recorder. She in turn stood, and followed him to the sea.

It was a dangerous game. She knew it was perilous. Having information about someone is having power, yet having information is also very risky. People have been silenced because of the information they held. It was a double-edged sword and she thrilled to the menace and the hazard.

The room had become dark without Sydney Household noticing. He had returned home to an unusually silent house and to a note left for him on the kitchen table. He had read the note, and numb with shock, had walked to the living room and had sunk into an armchair and remained sitting as dusk fell. He came out of shock to realise he had been sitting in darkness.

The shock had then given way to a sense of pressure and stress sliding off his shoulders, a weight being lifted from him. He then found he relished the tranquility of the house and the notion of being alone appealed to him. The note, from his wife, said that she and the children had gone to her mother's. It said 'sorry, but it's for the best'. The move made sense, they couldn't have carried on much longer, he knew that ... something had to give way and it was something he had been anticipating. But it was shocking when it did come. Nonetheless, that was the surprise, that her departure could still be shocking despite the fact that it had been in the air for a long while. Going to her mother's made sense ... her mother was elderly but had a large house, roomy enough to swallow his wife and the children. The children were old enough to cope with and understand the separation, and going in midsummer was the least disruptive time in respect of their education. He stood and switched on the light. Yes ... yes ... it all made very good sense indeed.

9

William Aughty's house was quite modest in comparison with Michael Filsell's impressive property. The Aughty residence stood on the eastern edge of Newmarket and revealed itself to be a substantial 1930s detached house with a front garden of approximately the dimensions of a tennis court, and a rear garden, so far as Household could tell when he glanced down the side of the property, of about the same area. He went to the front door and rang the bell. The door was opened by a small, brown-haired woman of trim figure, and a healthy complexion, who looked to be in her mid-forties. 'Yes?' She looked alarmed.

'Police.' Household showed her his ID 'Detective Inspector Household. The Constituency Offices in the town gave me your address but only after I showed my identification.'

'I see ... how can I help you?'

'Is Mr Aughty in?'

'No, he's abroad. I'm Gabrielle Aughty, his wife.'

'Abroad?'

'Yes. Malta.'

'Malta?' Household couldn't contain his surprise.

'Yes, he's visiting an old friend, Michael Filsell, the playwright. They were at Cambridge together.'

'So I understand. I wonder if I could ask you a few questions?'

'If you like ... you'd better come in.'

The interior of the Aughty house met Household's expectation, conservative tastes in furniture as well as hangings. Solid, comfortable furniture, deep pile carpets. He glanced out of the window of the rear room of the house into which he had been invited and saw that the rear garden was indeed about the size of a tennis court, bounded by shrubs and with a wooden shed in the bottom right-hand corner. The skyline was broken up with the roofs of nearby properties. He sat, as invited, while a flying insect travelled noiselessly across the room and landed on the window pane. Both he and Mrs Aughty watched it pass.

'A crane fly,' Mrs Aughty smiled apologetically, 'the house was full of them a few days ago. I don't know where they come from. They don't make any sound as they fly but are very docile, not like bluebottles. It was embarrassing, or it would have been had I had visitors, that window there was black with them one morning. I came down and opened this door and thought I'd left the curtain closed. They were so numerous that they darkened the room ... I screamed ... I'd never seen anything like it. William came bounding downstairs ... he must have thought I was being attacked, but he knew what to do, he got our vacuum cleaner – it's one of those with a sort of hosepipe, rather than the upright ones on wheels

– and just sucked them off the window. All done and dusted in about fifteen minutes ... that's one of the survivors. I've learned to catch them with an old coffee jar now. What happens then depends on how I'm feeling,' she smiled. 'If I'm in a really foul, vindictive mood and feel that my house has been invaded, I squirt fly spray into the jar. If I am filled with munificence, I take the jar outside and let the creature go free.'

'I see.' Household settled into the armchair. He heard the rattling of cutlery in the kitchen.

'That's Mrs Lismore ... our daily.'

'Ah ... well, your husband is in Malta, visiting Michael Filsell?'

'Yes ... why?'

'Was it a long-planned visit?'

'No ... heavens,' Mrs Aughty sat forward and clasped her hands together on her knees, smiling an eager-to-please smile. 'No, it was just the opposite. William was at the House ... Parliament is in recess for the summer, of course, but there's still work to be done.'

'I can imagine.'

'Well, he came home and asked me to pack a bag for him for a few days, he said he and Toby Etherington were going to Malta.'

'Toby Etherington?'

'Yes, he's the MP for Bishops' Stortford North. William, Toby and Michael all knew each other at Cambridge and have kept in close touch ... soldiers three.'

'Really,' Household smiled. 'Did Mr Aughty say why he was going to Malta at such short notice?'

'No,' Mrs Aughty shook her head slowly. 'No, he didn't.'

'What was his manner like?'

'His manner?'

'Well, was he happy to be going?'

'No, in fact he was quite agitated. Look, I hope my husband is not in any trouble. I don't want to say anything that might compromise him.'

'I'm sure there's nothing to worry about.' Household dipped his hand into his jacket pocket. 'I'd like to show you this photograph, Mrs Aughty.' He stood and walked across the floor to where Gabrielle Aughty sat, and handed her the photograph.

'Oh, that's William ... and there are Michael and Toby. Well I never, this must have been before I met him. I didn't meet William until after he graduated, but of course I recognise him, and his friends, and that girl there. Oh, that's Michael's wife ... they were only married a few years before her horse threw her, poor girl ... but he stayed with her.'

'Do you recognise anyone else in the photograph?'

'I don't ... just the three boys and Charlotte.' She extended her arm and once again Household crossed the room, this time to retrieve the photograph.

'When do you expect your husband to return?'

'When I see him, is the answer to that question. Inspector look, you are sure he's not in any trouble?'

'No, Mrs Aughty, I am not sure, quite frankly ... I am not sure at all.'

'Well, in that case I would like you to leave my house. I fear I may be compromising my husband and family if I continue to talk to you.'

'Family?' Household stood.

'My family.' Gabrielle Aughty pointed to two framed photographs on the mantelpiece showing students in graduation dress and holding their scrolls, a male and a female. 'Our son and daughter, both doing their pupilage with Barristers Chambers.'

'On their way to the bar?'

'Yes, and to great things beyond that. I am a proud and a fulfilled woman, Inspector ... a husband who is very likely to become a Cabinet Minister in the next Parliament, two children who are very likely to become barristers. We have a position to maintain, a reputation to uphold.' Gabrielle Aughty no longer had an eager-to-please manner, she had become angry, defensive, protective.

'Well, when your husband returns, please ask him to contact me.' Household handed Gabrielle Aughty his calling card.

'Detective Inspector Household,' she read. 'Cambridge police?'

'Yes.'

'What on earth has happened in Cambridge that the police would want to interview William about? He hasn't been in Cambridge for years. He dislikes going back, wants to preserve the memory of the city as it was in his student days.'

'If you could ask him to contact me.'

'I will, don't worry,' she placed his card on the mantelpiece, 'I want this to be cleared up as soon as possible. This way, please ... I'll show you out.'

'I was getting worried,' Sojourner Sleaford said. She looked into his eyes. They were icy, cold and tunnel like, but she allowed hers to 'smile' at him. 'I was getting hungry. Can I have some food, please?'

'Of course,' he spoke softly. 'Just let me unpack.'

'Unpack?'

'Just bought a few things ... some tins ... can't rely on rabbit or hare.'

'If you say so.' She adjusted her position on the floorboards.

'Did you sleep alright?'

'I got an hour or two.'

'You'll get used to the floor. When the weather gets colder you can use the sleeping bag.'

She caught her breath. 'When the weather gets colder'. She repeated the words to herself. So he really wasn't planning on killing her just yet. She had to build up a relationship with him, had to keep humouring him.

'How old are you, girl?' He stood in the next room.

'Seventeen.'

'Just seventeen...'

She heard him scrape the contents of a can into a saucepan and switch on the Calor stove.

'Yes ... just seventeen.'

'Just,' he repeated. 'You know a lot had happened to me by the time I was seventeen ... really quite a lot.'

'Oh? What?' She raised her voice, allowing it to

carry to the next room.

'Just a lot ... don't ask questions, you're here to be looked after ... remember that.'

'Sorry.'

'You like me looking after you?'

'Yes.'

'Really? I don't just want you to say that now, girl ... only say what you mean.'

'I mean it ... it makes me feel secure. I don't like it when you're not here.'

He spoke no further until he brought her meal of baked beans on a slice of toast and she intuitively knew she had said the right thing. She had told him what he wanted to hear. She would tell him more of the same, but must remember not to ask questions. She knew she had to keep her head, keep him well humoured, keep herself alive. Each day is a day nearer rescue, because by now they will be looking for her, and by now her poor mother will be beside herself with despair, but for both of them, her and her mother, she had to keep up the game.

Household drove to Bishops' Stortford. He found Toby Etherington's home quite easily, having been given excellent directions from the Constituency Offices in the town. Household was surprised at the Etherington house. He had expected, as with Filsell's home and Aughty's house, a building of character. Instead what met him was a white bungalow, glaringly white in the day's fierce sun, low and squat. Even for a bungalow it was low and squat and with a flat roof which a builder had once told him 'never work because they shrink'. He left his car at the kerb and crunched his way up the gravel drive to the front door as dogs barked from within the building, clearly responding to the sound of his footfall. Gravel *and* dogs. Sydney Household, the long serving police officer knew that this property was unlikely to be burgled. The door opened before he reached it. A tall, angry looking woman stood in the doorway, holding two Alsatians both straining at the leash. She wore a white dress, as white as her house.

'I'm not going to talk to you!' she shouted over the dogs barking.

'No?' Household stood on the path.

'No! Gabrielle Aughty phoned me. She said you might be coming. She phoned Charlotte Filsell and Charlotte said you visited her yesterday ... you have a photograph of our husbands when they were students and you want information about them.'

'Just a few questions.'

'No, I won't say anything that might compromise my husband. Gabrielle's upset that she let you in her house and advised me not to do the same ... and I won't. She's a sensible woman. I always take her advice. She's phoned her husband, he knows you were asking questions...' She slammed the door shut.

Sydney Household turned and smiled as he walked back to his car. That, he thought, that should set the cat amongst the pigeons very nicely indeed. If the three men shown in the photograph with Edward De Beer should suddenly want to confer very shortly after his body is found, and are prepared to travel many hundreds of miles to do so, then they have something to fear, something to hide. His old 'copper's waters' told him so.

Margaret Neston considered the three men. There was Filsell – 'the Master', who she felt regarded her as a possession and a lower quality of human life because she came from the north of England. There was Toby Etherington – warmer than Filsell, who promised her an escape from the island. The previous evening, the evening of the afternoon they had spent at the cove, they had talked together, whilst Filsell and Aughty sat drinking in the lounge. They had met by the pool and sat on the poolside letting their feet hang in the water. He told her how he'd do it … buy her a ticket whilst he was here … she could even fly back with them if a seat was available … would it take her long to pack? No, just a few minutes. She had no possessions at the villa, just her passport and the clothes she stood up in. Excellent, he had said. He would fix her up in his flat in London … it isn't a penthouse, but somewhere safe. She'd 'entertain' him about three nights a week, the rest of the time was hers to do what she wanted … but no drugs and no other men. And she had said 'lovely … lovely … lovely'. They separated after a brief kiss, he to join his friends, she to an early bed. The third man, William Aughty, had done something stupid about thirty years ago. It must have been when they were students, or just after, couldn't have been before, because they met at Cambridge, and he had implicated the other two in whatever it was he had done. He was small, at least smaller than Filsell and Etherington, impeccably dressed and manicured with cold, piercing eyes ... he would glance at her once each time she entered the room and pointedly turn away from her. His attitude towards her was, she felt, the same as Filsell's – she was a nobody from the north, a Liverpool Lucy. Except it was even worse. He showed no interest in her at all. The message she received from him was that she did not exist, he did not recognise her existence. William Aughty, Aughty the Naughty, William the Bad. She felt he was more dangerous than the other two put together and she also knew that, despite the offer made by Toby Etherington, warm Toby Etherington, her life was still in danger – the salted bath, her body slipped into the Mediterranean one night – if they thought she represented a danger. If the truth of her death was to be known, she had to smuggle the tape out of Malta somehow. The only thing she could think of was to post it home to Birkenhead with a note saying whose voices were on the tape and to take it to the police if something happened to her.

Then, at lunchtime, the phone rang. Filsell, in his usual way, had looked at her and tossed his head in an upward direction, a clear 'go and answer it' instruction. She had stood, mid meal, and answered it, then returned and had announced, 'It's Mrs Aughty for Mr Aughty'. Aughty had folded his napkin, threw it down beside his plate and walked past her without looking at her. She had sat down and resumed her meal. Moments later Aughty had returned and said, 'We can't not do anything now ... they've been to our homes.' Margaret Neston kept her head down but felt Filsell and Etherington look at her, and then at him, as if to say, 'You shouldn't have said that in her presence, William'.

'Let's go outside,' Filsell had said, and he and Toby Etherington and William Aughty went to the far end of the pool and sat round the white plastic table, talking in earnest. She had finished her meal with a growing feeling of fear. She then stood and walked to the rear door of the villa where she could be clearly seen by the three men, but cautiously kept herself out of earshot. She considered them, Filsell, Etherington and Aughty, and she knew then that they intended to murder her. The danger came from Filsell and Aughty – particularly Aughty. Etherington, she thought, would be too soft-hearted to go through with it, but the other two... She knew she had to get out of the villa. Then the three men looked at her and Filsell called her to come to them, just like the bigger boys did on the estate when she was small, really friendly ... come here we've got something to show you, you can take it home to your mum ... and when she ran to see she was shown a paper bag full of dog faeces which was then rubbed into her face and hair and down her back and up her skirt ... show that to your mum. She didn't know whether to go to them or to run. To go would be to walk into a trap, make it easier for them, to run would be to advertise that she knew more than she ought. She chose to run.

Sydney Household returned to Cambridge and

added his recording to the De Beer file, to the effect that Michael Filsell, playwright, William Aughty, MP, and Toby Etherington, MP, were, he believed, implicated in the murder of Edward De Beer, that presently they were overseas, apparently together in Filsell's villa, and would be interviewed immediately upon their return. He noted that Dominic Perigo still seemed to be unwell; it wasn't his empty desk so much as his very full in-tray. Wiseman and Tracy too were both out and that did not surprise him; the Panther enquiry, he realised, must be running them ragged and now it was very close to home. It had been with a sickening feeling that he had learned of the identity of his latest assumed victim. He completed his recording, signed out 'to Public Library, not coming back today' and strolled out of the police station, jacket under his arm, and across Parker's Piece to the library in Lion Yard, in the centre of the city

In the reading room he leafed through copies of *The Times* of the early 1980s. He found it more quickly and more easily than he thought he would. There it was, the astounding story of Harry Sparrow, twenty years old, who had been taken to Iran by his mother when he was twelve, who had been conscripted into the Iranian army and had fought against Iraq. He had deserted when his unit was at a rest station at the south west of the Caspian Sea. He had lived off the land as he made his way westwards. The journey to the border alone, read the article, was nearly three hundred miles and took him six weeks. Then, once over the border, he had another six hundred mile journey to Ankara and the British Embassy, which he did without money. The journey over mountainous terrain was completed largely at night. During the day when it was warmer he slept, because he had thought to sleep at night in that cold would be fatal. He travelled entirely on foot whilst still in Iran. Once in Turkey, he hitched rides whenever he could, and even jumped a goods train trundling in a westerly direction. He arrived at the British Embassy in Ankara in an emaciated, semi-lucid state and had to work hard to convince an uninterested official of his story. He was eventually fed and allowed to wash and given a plane ticket home on the next British Airways flight to the UK. That, read the article, was the offhand way the British Consular Service treat their own when their own come to grief in foreign lands. The British Consular Service had refused to comment on the case. Household consulted an atlas. The journey did indeed look remote, mountainous and perilous. Household formed the opinion that the article hid as much as it told. How a man 'lives off the land' during a nine hundred mile journey wasn't explained ... it would certainly involve more than eating berries and milking goats. What did he steal to survive? What did he kill? Whom did he kill? And nine hundred miles... Household looked for a territory familiar to him so that he could perhaps visualise the journey better. He found that London to Warsaw approximated nine hundred miles, as did Madrid to Munich but that was a ballpoint pen laid across a map in the comfort of a public library on a warm summer's afternoon. Harry Sparrow's nine hundred miles had been across mountains in cold weather. Just what a nightmarish, emotionally scarring journey that must have been, Household dared not imagine. The article concluded that Harry Sparrow intended to live with relatives in Norwich to rest for a while and consider his future.

'Norwich again,' Household smiled, 'well, I never.' He sat back in the chair and assumed a more serious attitude. He didn't at all mind returning home to Bedford and to an empty house ... in fact he quite relished the prospect of the journey and the tranquillity that lay at the end of it. What he did ponder was whether or not to make a visit to a certain house before returning home. The visit might not be considered to be within professional guidelines ... he might be prying ... but the urge was to visit. He decided to go with his urge.

The Panther took Sojourner Sleaford's hand as he sat down next to her. She found his touch oddly gentle and affectionate. 'It's so nice having someone to look after,' he said. 'It's really all I ever wanted, and I do like looking after you because you appreciate it ... you appreciate me. I like that ... people need to be appreciated.'

'You've never had anybody?' Sojourner Sleaford smiled as she held eye contact with him. Then she averted her gaze. She didn't want to transmit the wrong message, but he did not seem to be interested in her sexually ... so far.

'No ... not anything ... pets were promised when I was a kid but I never got anything ... and later I saw men doing things to provide for their own and I never had anyone to provide for ... so I grabbed a girl off the street ... looked after her for a few days, but she was really unsettled so I let her go ... the next four were too ... they just didn't appreciate being cared for, didn't know what I did for them, just how patient you've got to be to hunt a hare or a rabbit. I could buy meat in the supermarket, but that wouldn't be the same ... that's not providing. The last one ... the one before you, I had to kill her. I haven't killed for a long time ... I forgot how good it felt.'

'Why did you kill her?'

'I told you ... she saw me.'

'So you are going to kill me too?'

'I have to. I won't like killing you because you appreciate me but I have to. You see, I don't think this is wrong, but they do out there ... they think this is wrong. I will spend the rest of my days in gaol if they capture me ... and you know something?'

'What?' She tried to sound interested, she hoped her fear didn't reveal itself in her voice.

'It's not being locked up I mind, it's the fact I'll be dependent. I love being independent, surviving ... animals survive ... I want to be able to survive and to care for someone, this suits me ... I can take game from the woods, I can bring it here and cook it for both of us. I feel alive doing this ... I wouldn't feel alive in prison.' He stood and reached for the gag and the blindfold. 'I have to go now. I'll be back tomorrow.'

Sydney Household pressed the doorbell. It was

opened quickly by Veronica Sleaford. 'Sydney!'

'I felt I had to call, I don't know why ... as soon as I heard about Sojourner. I am so sorry.'

'No ... please come in.' She turned and led Household into her house. He shut the door behind him and as soon as the door closed with a satisfying 'clunk', Veronica Sleaford turned, threw herself at Household, put her arms round his neck, buried her head in his chest and burst into uncontrollable weeping which lasted, and lasted. He held her close to him, as he felt his shirt begin to stick to his chest, saturated by her tears. Eventually she pulled herself away and said, 'Sorry ... sorry...'

'No need to apologise.' Household let her slip from his arms.

'It's the need for someone personal ... the police are very kind ... I have a liaison officer, a WPC Wiseman.'

'Penny ... yes, I know her, she's a good officer.'

'Yes ... a good woman as well, very sensitive. I like her. But the police can only offer so much on an emotional level ... that special person isn't there.'

'Your ex-husband?'

'He's very detached, emotionally speaking. He said he'll come to Cambridge "if something happens" by which I suppose he means if her body is found ... besides which, he may be Sojourner's father, but we don't really connect. Look, it's silly standing here in the hall, come through to the kitchen, I'll percolate some coffee ... I want something to do.'

'My grandfather was one of the first immigrants from Jamaica,' she said as she sipped her coffee. 'Not exactly the "Empire Windrush", not the very first boatload of us, but one of the first ... went to live in the shelter in Brixton.'

'The shelter?' Sydney Household let his coffee cool, resting it on a coaster on the surface of the table. It was not the time nor the place to comment but he couldn't prevent himself being taken by the balanced beauty of her face ... her poise, her dignity in the face of adversity with the awfulness of the possible outcome. She seemed to need to talk, so he listened as she continued.

'A huge air raid shelter in Brixton, in the park. It was built in the Second World War and could accommodate two thousand people. The first wave of the West Indian immigrants, in the late 1940s occupied it – squatted in it – and from there they moved out to flats in the Brixton area, and from there to home ownership. It's why there's still a huge black population in Brixton.'

'I never knew that.'

'Yes ... well, my father, lovely man, grew up with prejudice but he said that there is a confusion about prejudice, he said that what people think of as racial prejudice is in fact a cultural prejudice. He believed that black people would gain more acceptance if they adopted English ways, became "more English than the English", that's what he used to say. Our surname, Sleaford – I reassumed my maiden name when I got divorced and Sojourner calls herself Sleaford by choice. The name on her birth certificate is "White", but as she says "White is such a naff name" and how can she be proud of being black with a surname like

White? She's probably sensible, because her father told me he was ridiculed at school – a black boy called White. His nickname "Whitey" was always said with the irony emphasised. Sleaford was doubtless the name of a slave owner and upon emancipation, his slaves took his surname for their family name, as was the practice.'

'Didn't know that either.'

'Quite true...' she forced a smile. 'So if you ever come across a black man called Household, you can claim your inheritance. You see, as a black woman I can make that joke. You couldn't say that.'

'Not without getting into serious trouble, I couldn't.' Household returned the smile.

'Anyway, Daddy then discovered that our surname was also the name of a town in Lincolnshire.'

'That's correct, small market town, on the river Witham, south of Lincoln. I think it's in Kesteven ... the Lincolnshire "parcels" are Kesteven, Lindsay and Holland ... I am sure Sleaford's in Kesteven.'

'Whatever ... but when Daddy found out that Sleaford was also an English place name, he said we could use it with pride, that it helped our family become English. He was very strict about table manners and politeness – always saying "please" and "thank you" and holding doors open for ladies in the case of my two brothers. A lot of West Indians will say he sold out ... they with their dreadlocks and devotion to Haile Selassie and addiction to "ganja" ... but that was daddy's philosophy and he was able to get a job in a bank. Good for the National Westminster, I say, it was courageous of them to hire him. He never got as far in the bank as he believed he would have done if he was white, but he said that that's what he expected. The next generation of black people will go further – my two brothers are now with the bank and already more senior than my father's position when he retired.'

'Good for them.'

'So Daddy's strategy worked ... had my brothers become Rastafarians, which they could so easily have done – there was a lot of pressure from their peers to do that – they would have become known to the police by now.'

'Unfortunately, that's probably true.'

'But I wanted my daughter to acknowledge her heritage, which is why I called her Sojourner.'

'I have never come across the name.'

'It's the name of a black woman, she was a slave in the antebellum south who escaped to the north and became a campaigner for complete emancipation. Sojourner Truth being her full name.'

'Complete emancipation?'

'Well, in the northern states black people might have been "free" but they couldn't vote. Even in the early twentieth century in New York City the buses were segregated, whites at the front, blacks at the rear. She campaigned against that. It's a good name to carry. A name to live up to.'

Drinking their second cup of coffee, and after a period of silence Veronica Sleaford said, 'She is a lovely young woman ... very sensible.'

'I am sure she is doing everything right.'

'You know, it's the little things I appreciate ... she speaks perfect English without any of the affectations of youth ... never used the "Australian inflection" for example.'

'What's that?'

'Oh, you'll have heard of it ... saying a sentence then pausing before the last word and pronouncing it with an emphasis which seems to suggest surprise or exaggeration or something unusual, as in ... "and we did the journey by ... bus",' she said, placing a higher pitch on the word 'bus'. 'You see, as if the journey in question should have been done by some other means.'

'Oh, yes ... didn't know what it was called. This conversation has been a real education.'

'Been? Are you going? Is your wife expecting you?'

'No ... we've separated.'

'Oh, I am sorry ... that was insensitive of me.'

'I'm not,' Household smiled. 'It's been on the cards for a long time and I can't describe the beauty of the peace of the house now she's gone and taken the children with her. My two are about Sojourner's age, old enough to cope and understand.'

'I felt a sense of freedom when I separated, as I told you, so I know what you mean. Do you think you'll get back together?'

'Not if I can help it.' His eyes met hers. They held eye contact ... then he broke it. 'I had better be going.'

'Oh ... please stay a little longer, I appreciate the company at a time like this.'

10

For the second time that week Sydney Household drove to Norwich. He had remained with Veronica Sleaford until about nine p.m. the previous evening, providing company, talking, listening, and as the evening had worn on they had become very relaxed in each other's presence. He drove home to his lovely empty house in Bedford, and throughout the drive and the remainder of the evening until sleep took him, Veronica Sleaford filled his thoughts. The following morning he drove back to Cambridge, signed in, and then signed out 'to Norwich Police'. He parked his car in the multi-storey in the town centre and, wearing a panama hat and holding his jacket over his arm, walked to the cottages by the railway line, to the house of Thomas De Beer.

'There is little news, really,' Household said as he sat in the armchair, having been invited into the small cottage. 'We have learned something of Edward's life as a student, and are waiting to interview three people when they return from abroad ... they're in Malta at the moment.'

'Who are they?'

'I can't tell you their names, of course – they may not be implicated in Edward's murder – but we do want to question them. They clearly knew him about the time he was killed. He didn't seem to mix with his peers at Cambridge Tech but tended to associate with the university students as much as he could, they seemed to be more his friends than anyone at the Tech, with one exception, that exception being Michael Wales. But if anything develops, we'll let you know, of course,' Household stood.

'It's good of you to drive out all this way to see me, sir. I appreciate it.'

Household smiled as Mr De Beer also stood and reached for the front door handle. It seemed to him to be churlish to tell the elderly gentleman that he was in the area anyway on another matter. He walked away from the cottage in the knowledge that the old man felt given to, cared for. It would make his day go easier although the wound of the loss of his son had been re-opened.

Household walked to the police station on Castle Meadow, which stood opposite a building which caught his attention, an old psychiatric hospital built in the pre-Victorian days when 'lunatic asylums' were pushed to the very edges of the town. It was presently empty, about to be re-developed, but nonetheless served as a reminder that the current social policy of 'care in the community' wasn't particularly original. At the inquiry desk he identified himself. He was quickly and politely ushered within and introduced to the duty officer. Over tea, Household explained the purpose of his visit.

'Sparrow ... Sparrow...' Detective Sergeant Walls reclined in his chair, 'and he trekked from Iraq or Iran to Turkey? Yes, I remember that now. He came to this area, had relatives here.' Walls was a large man, heavily-jowled, bald head, nearing retirement age ... no further promotion for DS Walls, thought Household, but a Detective Sergeant's pension is sufficient to provide a very comfortable retirement. 'You know, I think we knew him. I was still in uniform then ... tell you who would know.' He reached for the telephone which stood on his desk and Household watched as he jabbed a four figure internal number with a thick, fleshy finger. 'Yes ... it's DS Walls, is Sergeant Palfreman in the building? He is? Could you ask him to come to my office ... thanks.' He replaced the phone with surprising gentleness for a large man. 'Palfreman will tell you everything you want to know ... amazing man, he has one of those magpie-like minds. He can hoard details ... unconnected details. He never got beyond Sergeant because he can't focus his mind sufficiently to pass the Inspector exam and board, though he applied. Me, I never even applied, I am happy at this level ... not long to go now, just a few years.'

'Same here,' Household smiled. 'Gone quickly.'

'Too quickly, I still remember my first day on the beat, I was so self-conscious I felt I was naked.'

'We all did,' Household replied. 'No copper ever forgets his first day out in public in uniform ... nor his first single-handed arrest.'

There was a tap on Wall's door.

'Ah, Tom,' Walls beamed. 'Please come in.'

A tall, uniformed sergeant entered the office.

'Tom,' Walls indicated towards Household, 'DI Household from Cambridge. Tom Palfreman.'

Household stood and he and Palfreman shook hands.

'Take a pew, Tom.'

Palfreman sat in the empty chair adjacent to Household.

'Tom, we want to pick your brains.'

'OK, if I can help.' Palfreman spoke with a soft and distinct Norfolk accent. Household noticed a prominent scar running down the left side of his face, a 'service wound', he thought, and which served as a reminder that Norwich, despite its pleasantness, has, like every city, a dark underside.

'Go back twenty years, Tom. First space shuttle flight...'

'OK, just before the miner's strike ... yes, I'm there ... I was a constable.'

'Alright ... now the name, Harry Sparrow.'

'Ah...' Palfreman put his hand up to his mouth, then lowered it again. 'Young man ... wasn't he the one who had escaped from the Iraq or Iranian army ... did this amazing trek over Turkey ... nearly a thousand miles?'

'Yes.' Walls smiled at Household. 'I told you Tom would come up with the goods.'

'What do you remember about him, Tom?' Household asked.

'Not a lot, but what I remember, I remember clearly. He came to our attention a few times ... drunk and disorderly ... hardly surprising after what he had been through. He wasn't prosecuted ... never did any damage. The Inspector we had at the time said we wouldn't prosecute considering his history ... heavens, taken to Iran, I think it was Iran, when he was about twelve ... just an ordinary English lad, taken to Iran because his

381

screwball mother had taken up with an Iranian ... by fifteen he was in the army fighting Iraq.'

'Fifteen?' Household gasped.

'So he told me. Then risking death for deserting the army when he was about twenty-two in order to get back to England ... and that amazing journey over mountains in winter weather ... he was a bit of a local hero. We could all understand why he got drunk. So the Inspector said no prosecution, but still a warning ... unofficial ... he'd done so well to get here, we didn't want to give him a criminal record as soon as he got here.'

'Understandably. Where did he live?'

'With his uncle ... maternal uncle ... now what was his name? Lived out towards The Broads ... unusual name ... and we know the uncle, he's as dotty as Harry's mother apparently was ... odd name, what is it? ... what is it? Yoward ... that's it ... Meltham Yoward ... Meltham being his Christian name.'

Walls beamed. 'Ever met a man with a mind like that before, Mr Household? The amazing Mr Memory.'

'Confess I haven't.' Household looked approvingly at Palfreman.

'Hasn't got me anywhere,' Palfreman shrugged, 'still a sergeant.'

'Is Meltham Yoward still with us?' Household asked.

'As far as I know. He has track for petty offences but nothing recently ... he was younger than Harry Sparrow's mother, in fact I think he was nearer Harry's age than Harry's mother's age ... he was in his thirties when Harry moved in with him.'

'So now he'll be a comfortable mid fifties.'

'Does he live far from here?'

'Small village called Upton ... less than a half hour's drive. I could take you now, if I could be spared.' Palfreman appealed to Walls.

Walls opened both palms, 'Please escort Mr Household.'

Palfreman stood. 'Willingly ... won't need my jacket, day like this.'

Penny Wiseman and David Tracy stood on Parker's Piece, hidden from the view of anyone in the police station by a parked double-decker bus. Tracy had asked Wiseman if he could talk to her. He said for some reason he couldn't put his finger on he'd feel happier talking outside the building. They left, having signed out for '30 minutes' ... but it won't take that long, Tracy had said. They crossed Park Side, walked across the pavement and stepped onto the grass and walked until they were behind the double-decker. Tracy then told a paling Penny Wiseman what he wanted to tell her.

'I feel sick,' Wiseman said. 'But you're right, it makes sense.'

'I'm not over the moon about it either. If I'm wrong I'll have a lot of apologising to do, but I'm not prepared to ignore a suspicion like this.'

'No, you're right,' she looked him in the eye. 'We can't ignore it ... and I mean 'we'. I'll go with you. If you're right, you can have the credit, if you're wrong, I'll share the flak with you.'

He reached out and held her forearm and

squeezed it.

Meltham Yoward's house in Upton revealed itself to be a low roofed bungalow, made to appear lower because it had clearly been built in a natural hollow in the ground. So low in fact that when Household and Palfreman got out of the car and walked along the pavement to the gate, they looked down upon the faded and decaying thatch roof of the property and Household, with his recent experience in the forefront of his mind, thought 'flood'. 'Not a good bet in a flood,' he said.

'No bet at all, I'd say,' Palfreman also glanced at the property, 'but strangely the Broads have not flooded like the Fens. So far this area has escaped ... so far. I made sure I bought on high ground, I am well away from the Wensum where I live.'

'I live in Bedford,' Household replied, as they reached the gates. 'No bad news there.'

The two police officers walked side by side down the steeply sloping drive of the property, and to the front door. The faded paintwork on the door told Household that it was south facing. Palfreman knocked loudly.

'What do you want?' The question was growled from within the cottage.

'Police,' Palfreman said loudly enough to be heard inside. He turned to Household. 'That's Meltham. Quite a character.'

'I know, I saw you coming ... what do you want?' came the voice from within.

'Some information, Meltham, please. This is Mr Household from Cambridge. He wants to ask

384

you a few questions.'

'What about?'

'Your nephew.'

'Which one?'

'Harry. Harry Sparrow.'

'You're not after me?' There was a note of surprise, of hope, in the voice.

'No. Promise.'

The door creaked open. Meltham Yoward stood in the doorway, stout, portly, unshaven, a ruddy cider-drinker's face. Household found it hard to age him. He looked to be a lot older than his reported fifty plus years. 'Aye?' he eyed Household curiously.

'It's about your cousin, Harry Sparrow.'

'Boy Harry, aye ... my sister's son. He came back from that place ... more than she did.'

'Really?'

'Aye. Her letters stopped arriving a long while back.'

'Do you know where Harry is now?'

'No. He stayed with me for a few months, just calming down after his trip ... took him some old time but eventually he stopped getting drunk every night. Then said he was sorting out, "No offence, Meltham," he said, "but I'm turning my back on the Sparrows and the Yowards ... I'm going to change my name and disappear".'

'He changed his name?'

'Yes. Proper like ... deed poll ... he's a clever old boy, did it proper. He hated his mother ... can't say I blame him, what she put him through.'

'Do you know what he changed his name to?'

'Yes, he told me ... he said he wanted a bit of

class to get along so he became Dominic. Dominic Perigo.'

Household took an involuntary step backwards as if he had been kicked in the stomach. He reached for his mobile. He dialled a number as he walked away from the cottage back towards the road.

11

'Why did you run?' Filsell spoke quietly. 'We wouldn't have been suspicious if you hadn't run.'

Margaret Neston sat in the chair. She had long since given up struggling against her bonds, a silk scarf round her ankles and wrists. Filsell had kindly explained to her that they had used silk because it doesn't leave any bruises. 'Couldn't pass your death off as an accidental drowning with rope burns on your body,' he had said. That had been the previous evening. They had kept her alive on William Aughty's insistence, not out of clemency, but because he wanted to know exactly what she knew. They had searched her room, examined her possessions as she sat there, knowing that she would never see home again. And now this morning they had it, they had found the tape recorder in Filsell's room.

'I thought you were going to kill me,' she said lamely.

'We will now ... but when we called you we only wanted a pot of tea.'

Margaret Neston felt sick. She looked appealingly towards Toby Etherington, who just the day before had promised classically to 'take her away from all this'. He shrugged his shoulders in an 'I can't help you' gesture.

Filsell turned to Etherington. 'How much salt do I put in the bath?'

'Three percent of the total volume of water.'

'How do I measure that?'

'I don't know ... but three percent is the salinity of seawater. Guess it.'

'I don't think I've got any salt in the house.' Filsell sounded to Margaret Neston to be close to panic.

Etherington put his hand to his forehead. 'Brilliant. Now we've got to go shopping...'

'Well, we can't do it until this evening anyway, we need the cover of darkness ... plenty of time.'

Margaret Neston watched as the ice cold William Aughty, from whom she realised she could expect no mercy, but who had remained strangely quiet all yesterday, throughout the night and all that morning, slowly stood and calmly announced that he was going for a dip in the pool. She gasped ... at a time like this ... it may not be his life about to end, but still, at a time like this, he could be so detached as to find 'a dip in the pool' appealing. She sank back in her chair; all hope had faded.

David Tracy gave one final loud knock on Dominic Perigo's front door, then stood to one side and turned to the massively built constable behind him. 'Put it in, please.' The constable stepped forward and kicked the door open with disarming ease.

David Tracy had always found going into people's houses a depressing experience ... no matter what, how, whom, they appeared to be, it is in their houses that their vulnerability is exposed, and Perigo's house was no exception. It was in fact an exaggeration, an emphasising of that experience. For here were the home circumstances of the man who was their superior officer, the man they had been calling 'sir'. The police officers, CID and uniformed, toured the house in subdued silence. The kitchen was neat, basic, functional and kept clean. The main room of the house had blue wall to wall carpeting and nothing else. No furniture, no wall decoration, nothing, just the carpet. Upstairs there wasn't even a carpet. Just bare floorboards. Perigo clearly slept in the back bedroom in a sleeping bag on the floor. The clothes he wore were in neat piles on the floor at the foot of the sleeping bag as if awaiting inspection, military style. The room smelled musty, as if the windows were rarely, if ever, opened.

Tracy and Wiseman looked at each other.

'The vector he searched,' Tracy said, 'it was out beyond Milton ... out by Landbeach and Waterbeach, that way. That's where he is.'

'All units?' Wiseman reached for her radio.

'Yes, request that ... check all buildings, especially ones with a red Vauxhall parked nearby, that's the car he drives, a red Vauxhall. We'd better get out there ourselves. We'll leave one officer here ... this is now a crime scene.'

Margaret Neston sat alone in the room. Filsell had acquired a packet of salt, then he had produced a bottle of gin and he and Etherington and Aughty had gone outside by the pool to share it. She sat, resigned to her fate, yet noticing how things seemed more real, colours louder, brighter somehow. Then William Aughty walked into the room and sat opposite her, looking at her with his piercing blue eyes.

'You're not drinking with your mates?' she asked with unconcealed defiance.

'One of us has to stay sober to drive the car and I don't need a drink to kill someone. I wasn't drunk the last time, I don't need to be this time.'

'The last time? You know I never did find out what you did. I know you murdered someone but I don't know the details.'

'Need to know?'

'No, but it would help me understand why I'm going to die, aged twenty-three ... never been in love and the only place I've been outside Birkenhead and John Lennon International airport is Malta. Not much of a life. But I was pretty.'

'Still are.'

'Only for a bit longer.'

'You're quite brave.' He raised an eyebrow. 'Other women I know would be in a real state in your place.'

'Well, I'm not the other women you know.'

Aughty smiled. 'Well, I killed someone. We three ... I and those two outside were at Cambridge together, the university. In the house we lived in –

opposite to the police station by some irony – was a little guy, a short fella who was at the Tech, another college in the town. He was a hanger-on, wanted to be part of the university set. He latched on to Filsell ... they both wanted to be writers. One afternoon Toby and I, we were in Toby's room, and we decided to get out into the country, just to get out of Cambridge for a few hours. We knocked on Filsell's door to invite him ... he was sitting with "that tit from the Tech" as I think I described him when you were taping our conversation.'

'Yes...'

'Well, they were talking about writing, showing each other the stuff they'd written, and Filsell invited said "tit from the Tech" to come – didn't ask us if we minded him coming along, but Filsell's selfish like that. So we went out, drove out in Etherington's car – we were not allowed to bring cars to the university, nowhere to put them, but he kept his in a side street in Romsey Town where the Tech is. Anyway, we drove out and started walking in green fields and all the while that little guy from the Tech just wouldn't stop talking ... pushy little twerp ... and not saying anything interesting ... even Filsell was getting irritated. We walked over a meadow and there was a branch on the ground, I just picked it up and brought it down on his head and said, "Shut up!" Did the trick more than I meant it to. Anyway, we hid the body in the ditch by the hedgerow. Next day we went out with spades and buried it in the middle of the meadow. It stayed buried for thirty years – very obliging of him, I must say. It worked its way to the surface and was found a few days ago and the police have linked us to him – don't know how. Anyway, they've been to our homes.'

'Thanks ... so now I know.'

'Why did you tape our conversation?'

'Curiosity ... my dad always said that it killed the cat, and perhaps he was right. I knew something was up and I wanted to know what, then I listened to the part where you said you'd kill me, so then I needed some explanation if I disappeared. I was going to post the tape home with a note – bit of a drama queen ... "if something happens to me, take this tape to the police", that sort of note.'

'What are you wearing under that sarong?'

She thought it a strange question, but answered, 'A bathing suit ... one piece.'

'OK.' He knelt down and untied the scarf round her ankles, then the scarf which held her wrists behind her back. 'Go and pack a few things, enough to get you home – and don't forget your passport.'

She looked at him questioningly.

'Go on!'

She needed no second bidding. Moments later she returned to the living room carrying a change of clothes and her passport in a shoulder bag. Aughty stood there twirling the keys to the minimoke in his fingers.

'Shall we go?'

She nodded her head vigorously.

'Don't worry about Filsell and Etherington, they've demolished nearly a full bottle between them.'

He drove her out to St Paul's Bay and stopped the vehicle and stared out over the Mediterranean. He turned to her. 'Hope you don't mind, but I won't be seeing many sea views or breathing sea air once I have turned myself in.'

'Is that what you are going to do?'

'Yes. After I have dropped you at Luqa, bought you a flight back to the UK and given you enough readies to get home to Birkenhead.'

'You're going to do that for me?'

Aughty nodded. 'Killing that guy has been on my conscience for the last thirty years. Even though at times I actually forgot I did it, the memory always returned and in the last ten years or so, it's remained constant. One more murder...' He shook his head. 'I wouldn't be able to cope ... the Party has a strong anti-crime ticket, "Get heavy with heavies" ... you might have seen the poster. How can I be an MP for the Party with two murders under my belt, to say nothing of how it will eat away at my conscience?'

'What will happen?'

'I'll be going down for a stretch ... can't hope for an open prison with middle-class fraudsters, not for murder. How long for? I might be able to plea bargain something, but I'll serve time ... how long doesn't really matter, the issue is that I am finished as a politician. So's Etherington ... and us just a few weeks away from Cabinet office. I don't know about Filsell, the notoriety might even enhance his success.'

'Are you really going to buy me a plane ticket home?'

'Yes.'

'You won't be playing some cruel trick?'

'No,' he smiled, 'I promise. I want to do at least one good thing to compensate.'

'I am prepared to tell them what you did for me ... that will help you.'

'No.' He squeezed her hand. 'Let's keep that our secret, it would be impossible to prove anyway.'

'If that's what you want.'

'That's what I want.'

'I'll write to you.'

'I'd like that. I'll reply to every letter.'

'Not many sea views in prison, not much sea air to breathe, as you say ... not much else either.'

'I can cope with that ... Mrs Aughty and I haven't communicated in that way for some time.'

'Well, I know a place we could go, it's on the other side of the island from here ... if you don't mind going where Toby Etherington has already been ... in more ways than one.'

'You'd give yourself?'

'Yes,' she squeezed his hand, 'I'd like to. Really, I would. We'll have to manage without a beach towel ... and you've no idea where those grains of sand can get.'

'We'll manage.' He smiled as he started the engine. 'We'll manage admirably. I'll see to it, especially because it will probably be the last time for me. I will probably come out of prison at some point, but at my age, I doubt that I will come out to any kind of sex life.'

Sydney Household drove from Norwich back to Cambridge on the A10. The radio bulletin had confirmed his fears, that all units were now searching for Dominic Perigo. His eye was caught by a car travelling in the opposite direction ... a red Vauxhall, the type of car Perigo drove ... it passed in a flash ... he couldn't be sure whether Perigo was at the wheel or not. Too much uncertainty to phone in with the possible sighting, but he turned his car round at the first opportunity and increased his speed. He caught up with the red Vauxhall but remained two vehicles behind it. He watched as the car slowed and turned left down a narrow lane. Household slowed, giving the Vauxhall time to get a safe distance down the lane, then he too turned into the lane. The lane drove straight across the landscape as did many roads in this part of England, but was flanked by woodland to either side. He proceeded cautiously. A road sign indicated he was approaching a village, Cookham, and through the trees to his right he noticed the roof of a house, a bungalow he thought. Instinct, or a taste for thoroughness, urged him not to proceed into Cookham until he had investigated. He turned into the road on which stood the bungalow and saw it to be unadopted and pitted with holes. He drove slowly until he saw the red Vauxhall parked in the driveway of the bungalow, which itself was in a semi-derelict state, boarded up windows but with signs of recent renovation work having been done. He felt unwell and said to himself 'flecks of paint'. He opened the car door and stepped out into the heat of the sun. He didn't close the car door, wishing to avoid announcing his presence. He reached into his jacket pocket for his mobile, then released it again. He feared being seen as alarmist ... so far it was just a red Vauxhall, thousands like them, and a house being renovated, thousands like them as well.

Household walked slowly up the driveway of the bungalow, making as little sound as he could. He walked round the side of the bungalow to the door. He saw it was open. He crept inside. He noticed movement in the room beyond the room he stood in. 'Hello,' he called softly, 'Police.'

A muffled cry came from within the further room.

Household stepped forward and in the gloom of the room saw Sojourner Sleaford, fastened with a chain, a gag in her mouth, fear in her eyes. Household stepped forward as she let out a cry which seemed higher pitched than the first sound he heard her make. He took the gag from her mouth.

'OK, I'll have you out of here...'

'He's behind you!' she spluttered, 'behind you.'

Household turned. Perigo stood in the doorway, holding a loaded crossbow levelled at Household's chest.

'Can't let you do that, Sydney. Can't let you take her anywhere. I saw it was you on the A10, saw you in my rear view even though you kept a few cars behind. Your surveillance technique is a bit rusty. So does this mean I've been rumbled, or are you acting alone?'

'Yes, Dominic,' Household remained calm. 'Atkins knows. He knows everything. It's over. You used to be Harry Sparrow ... and you killed Sara Bullwood and buried her in the garden of your mother's house in Romsey Terrace.'

'I was going to keep fish ... then she told me to fill it up again ... just wanted something to look after, you see, Sydney ... and that girl there, she likes me looking after her, she said so. You've ruined it.'

'It's over, Dominic. Tracy and Wiseman and a team of officers, they've been to your house, you can't go back there. You can't go into the station again ... unless it's to give yourself up. Why did you kill Sara Bullwood?'

Perigo shrugged. 'She was there. After my mum told me to fill the hole up and have it filled and concreted over by the time she came back from town Sara was there ... I was angry and I didn't want to go to Iran.'

'Your mother shouldn't have done that to you, Dominic. That was bad.'

'Well, she didn't last long. He butchered her one night ... but by then I was in the army. I've done a lot of killing, Sydney, a lot.'

'No need to do any more, Dominic.'

'Oh, but I like it,' Perigo smiled. His finger curled round the trigger of the crossbow. 'Each time I take a life I feel stronger ... the person's strength becomes mine.' He stepped inside. 'I don't want to shoot you in front of the girl, Dominic. Come outside. I'll put you where I put Richard.'

'Richard?'

'The old boy who lived in the next cottage. He got curious.'

'It's futile, Dominic.'

'It's not. They still don't know where I am.

396

They don't know about this bungalow ... I can live for weeks ... we can live off the land – rabbits, hares – can't we, my pet?'

'You're ill, Dominic. They won't send you to prison.'

'Secure psychiatric facility ... it's a different name for the same animal.'

'No, it's not.' The voice came from behind Perigo.

Perigo spun round. Household breathed a sigh of relief. Tracy stood in the doorway. Two constables stood behind him.

'Searching this area,' Tracy spoke to Household, 'saw his car and yours.'

Household nodded.

'It's finished, sir,' Tracy appealed to Perigo. 'You've only one bolt in that thing, there are four of us. But Mr Household's right ... a hospital isn't a prison.'

It happened quickly. Perigo turned the crossbow against himself, as if wanting to shoot himself in the mouth. Tracy and Household sprang forwards. Tracy held the weapon vertical, Household pulled the trigger and the bolt thudded into the ceiling, went through the plaster and was later found embedded in one of the rafters.

Perigo sank backwards. He was held by Household and Tracy.

'I crossed the mountains, once,' Perigo said, as one of the constables stepped forwards and slipped handcuffs onto him.

'I know you did, Dominic.' Household allowed the constable to take Perigo's arm.

'You have no idea what I did to survive ... I

mean, no idea...'

'I can probably guess, Dominic.'

'Can you? Have you ever eaten human flesh? Raw? Because you were too hungry even to cook it?'

'Just go with the constable, Dominic.' Household looked at Tracy. 'Help me with Sojourner.'

One week later the weather broke and rain, lots and lots of lovely, clean, life-giving rain, fell on Cambridge and the Fens. It brought an end to the heatwave and the feared drought was avoided. Sojourner Sleaford looked out of her bedroom window at the rain as it fell vertically. She eagerly anticipated the end of the shower because she had recently discovered the joy of walking in summer foliage which had been freshened by rain. Two people were dancing on the small concrete octagon near the bowling green on Jesus Green, dancing a waltz in the rain, She gasped ... they weren't students ... one, one was her mother and the other the officer who had come into the bungalow alone, who had stood unflinchingly as the Panther held a crossbow aimed at his chest. They were dancing ... dancing as if nobody was watching.

The publishers hope that this book has given you enjoyable reading. Large Print Books are especially designed to be as easy to see and hold as possible. If you wish a complete list of our books please ask at your local library or write directly to:

Magna Large Print Books
Magna House, Long Preston,
Skipton, North Yorkshire.
BD23 4ND

This Large Print Book for the partially sighted, who cannot read normal print, is published under the auspices of

THE ULVERSCROFT FOUNDATION